# Merely This

## and nothing more

WRITERPUNK PRESS

Published in the USA by Writerpunk Press
Design, layout and cover by Lia Rees

Fonts used: CALENDAS PLUS by Atipo
Kingthings Trypewriter by Kevin King
Cardo by David Perry
Angst Dingbats – ✺✾❀◉⊕ – by Angst

ISBN: 978-1530999187

Art on facing page: "Quoth the Raven, 404" by Mario Cordova

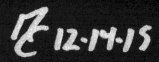

*This book is dedicated to the reviewers — whether they review on Amazon, Goodreads, book blogs, or all of the above. Speaking from the perspective of a bunch of indie and small press authors, there is possibly no better thanks from a reader than a review.*

*To all who take that extra minute or two, we give you our sincere thanks.*

*This one's for you.*

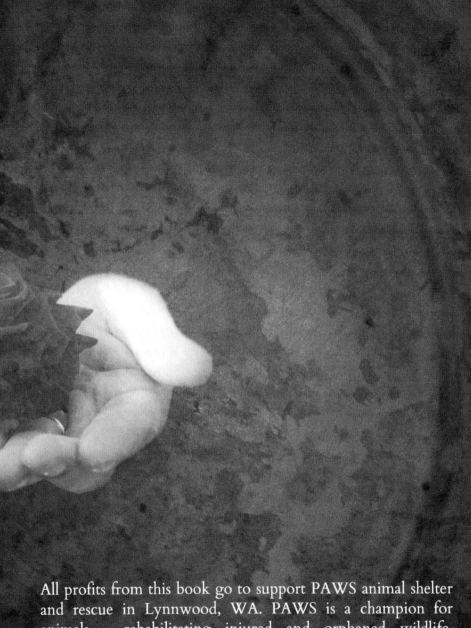

# CONTENTS

# INTRODUCTION

## Why Poe?

I WANT YOU to try something. Go find someone and say the name Edgar Allan Poe. Make note of their reaction and come report back. I'll wait here.

Did they recite the opening lines of "The Raven"? Confess how much "The Cask of Amontillado" creeped them out? Roll their eyes and recount the horrors of English class and their teacher's unnatural love for the sensory imagery in "The Fall of the House of Usher"? I'll bet that anybody you try this on will give you an immediate reaction.

Love him or hate him, everyone knows who Poe is.

His stories have stood the test of time because readers fall in love with the haunting but beautiful language of his tales, poetry, and plays. Writers look to his stories as a master class in creating mood and tension. Reading and analyzing "The Tell-Tale Heart" is still a rite of passage for high schoolers. And the sheer number of adaptations and recordings of his works alone is a testament to his cultural influence. Small wonder that nearly two hundred years after his death, we continue to read and study Poe. But why punk his stories?

Punk fiction is more than it first appears to be. Dieselpunk is not all leather bomber jackets and loud engines. Gears, goggles, and corsets are the surface of steampunk. And, yeah, cyberpunk is gonna have chips and mirrorshades, but look a little closer.

Punk fiction throws light into dark corners of the mind and heart. It explores the lives of misfits, criminals, outcasts, detectives, scientists, and loners. Through the characters we glimpse into the depths of madness, rage, and obsession. And that's not all. The scope of punk fiction is not limited to darkness and despair. There is humor and love and light and humanity in all its rawness.

But you know who did all of that first, right?

Choosing Poe as the inspiration for this anthology was easy because his stories are widely known and loved by readers and writers alike. The subject matter is timeless and adapts to other settings easily. And we just couldn't resist playing in his sandbox.

J Sarchet

# PREFACE

## How We Got Here

IT'S HARD TO BELIEVE that Writerpunk Press has only been around for two years. In that time, we've grown closer as a community. Together we've accomplished some amazing things: several high schools have copies of *Sound & Fury* in their classrooms or libraries, and it is required reading at one university's Shakespeare course.

We started our adventure with an idle chat in the Writerpunk Facebook group. One member, Esaias, mentioned something about writing a punk version of a Shakespeare play—and the game was afoot. Others chimed in and staked a claim to which tragedy or comedy they would like to punk, and before we knew it we were at work on our first anthology! Beyond the excitement of seeing the Bard's plays in alternate settings and with punk elements, we realized that the project would give all of us—writers, editors, artists—a chance to practice our respective crafts. None of us could have predicted what a successful project it would be.

*Sound & Fury: Shakespeare Goes Punk* contained five stories, and was put together by a handful of people who all wore many hats. It was well received and quickly sold enough to allow us to make a donation to PAWS. We were ecstatic, but that was only the beginning. We learned a lot in that process and set about putting those hard-earned lessons to use immediately. Our next publication, *Once More Unto the Breach: Shakespeare Goes Punk 2* was well underway. More submissions meant more behind the scenes folks were needed. A full team of editors and proofreaders made our second anthology a reality.

We upped our marketing game, too. An online release party with over twenty-five artists and authors, giveaways, and contests helped our second release make a splash. We refined the process yet again and saw an incredible number of stories submitted to *Poe Goes Punk*—so much so that our Head Editor keeps a color-coded spreadsheet with over fifty columns to keep track of all of the stories and people involved. Also, for the first time, advance reader copies were made available to bring in reviews prior to release day.

We are quite proud of the progress we've made since our early days, and look forward to bringing more punked tales to our readers. None of our accomplishments would have been possible without the support of our fans. For that, we offer our sincerest thanks.

J Sarchet

# PEOPLE TO BLAME, PART 1

## The Writers

On the title page of each story you'll find the author's name, accompanied by their biography and a note of which Poe work they have punked.

# PEOPLE TO BLAME, PART 2
## Editorial and Design

RACHEL A. BRUNE served five years as a military journalist with the U.S. Army, including two tours in Iraq, and a brief stint as a columnist for her hometown newspaper. After commissioning as a military police officer, she continued to write and published articles for a number of military and civilian news publications, as well as short fiction stories and two novels. She blogs her adventures, writing and otherwise, at: http://www.infamous-scribbler.com.

AMBER MICHELLE COOK is the Director of National Novel Editing Month (http://nanoedmo.com), which she's also participated in (and 'won') for the last eight years, and been involved in long-term critique groups for well over a decade. She's working on The Writer's Guide to Editing Resources (and no one has yet found a typo in any of her self-published novels). Find her website at: http://ambermichellecook.weebly.com.

T.J. FORD is just a girl who can't say no, which is how she found herself agreeing to be Assistant Editrix of the Poe Goes Punk anthology. A crack copy editor and lover of both steampunk and Poe, she's found it rather a fun project on which to work. In between rescuing dangling participles and saving serial commas, T.J. is a mind-body therapist with bicoastal practices in New York City and in Portland, Oregon, where she lives with her food-scientist husband and a taxidermied steampunk rabbit named Lady Lucretia.

CAROL GYZANDER is the Editor of this book, responsible for overseeing the many small editing and proofreading projects—as well as being one of the writers ("The Clockwork Raven"). Her only regret is that she doesn't live at Hogwarts, because then her color-coded spreadsheets would move and fill themselves in. See what else Carol is working on at www.CarolGyzanderAuthor.com.

ANDREA HINTZ loves helping other authors put their best words forward…and she also loves an excuse to break out her red pen and mark up those words. In the interest of helping, of course. She blogs as the Inspector at www.themanuscriptdetective.com, where she investigates sci-fi & fantasy books from her lofty perch aboard Airship Ampersand.

H. JAMES LOPEZ was born on a Navy ship in the Caribbean Sea outside of Barranquilla. He is a construct of too much sun, too much alcohol and not nearly enough time on land. Since 2009 he has been writing fiction in all forms that come to mind.

https://www.facebook.com/profile.php?id=100008073497597
http://www.amazon.com/H.-James-Lopez/e/B00TR962IE

KATHERINE PERKINS lives with her husband and cat. She is a collaborator of Jeffrey Cook and co-author of the Fair Folk Chronicles.

LIA REES, the designer of this book, likes melancholy music, evocative language, wild places and unpretentious people. It has to be admitted she is easily bored. She's dabbled in jewellery making, crochet, music, T-shirt design, and lately book formatting and videos for authors and others. Her main business is Free Your Words (www.freeyourwords.com), and she is writing a book about her ten-year battle with the beast of chronic illness. Interact with her on Facebook; she won't bite.

www.facebook.com/LiaWayward

KEN RODRIGUEZ is a transplant from other worlds. In his first life, he danced ballet professionally for seven years. He decided to retrain and become an English teacher instead of going the dance studio route. He thought that it would lead to another career in the arts...little did he know that it was also a career in babysitting. (He has been known to have a sarcastic sense of humor at times, and in the appropriate company.) Ken is now retired from that noble profession and lives and plays in Tempe, AZ, with his wife and dog in their empty nest. He's also very excited to be on the editing team, and looks forward to causing more mayhem from the comfort of his recliner, conveniently situated next to a desktop computer.

J. SARCHET has been writing all her life. In fact, she often remarks that she likes words more than most people (present company excluded, naturally). The first story she ever wrote was scribbled in a small spiral notepad and stashed behind her family's piano for safekeeping. Though she has seen the most success as a poet, she has a speculative fiction novel in the works. When it is completed, J won't be hiding it behind a piano, but rather shouting the news from the rooftops.

RIE SHERIDAN ROSE had her first novel published in 2000. Her short stories appear in numerous anthologies, including *Nightmare Stalkers and Dream Walkers* Vols. 1 and 2, *Come to My Window, Shifters, The Grotesquerie*, and *In the Bloodstream* as well as Yard Dog Press' *A Bubba In Time Saves None*. Mocha Memoirs has "Drink My Soul...Please," and "Bloody Rain" as e-downloads, and as part of the collection RieTales. Online, she has appeared in *Cease, Cows, Lorelei Signal*, and *Four Star Stories*. She is also the author of seven novels, five poetry chapbooks, and lyrics for songs on several of Marc Gunn's CDs. She edited the Steampunk Airship Pirates anthology *Avast, Ye Airships!* for Mocha Memoirs. You can find out more about her work on her website, www.riewriter.com or follow her Facebook. She tweets as @RieSheridanRose.

DAVID STEGORA is elusive and reclusive; one thing we know for sure—he is the editor of *Dark Futures* magazine. Find out for yourself at www.facebook.com/DarkFuturesFiction and:
www.darkfuturesfiction.net.

JANICE STUCKI is a writer and playwright. She contributed *The Tragedy of Livingston*, her nanopunk tale inspired by Shakespeare's *Coriolanus*, to the previous anthology and now offers her editorial support to this Poe-inspired collection. Janice lives in the midst of hard-core suburbia in northern New Jersey with her family and their stubbornly adorable mixed-breed rescue hound, Mellow. They have recently added a foster cat to their household, a former stray now named Ziggy, who had been living underneath a holly bush in their front yard (Mellow insists this arrangement is temporary).

MARY ZEMINA is a recent graduate of the Professional Writing Program at Champlain College. She loves reading anything that can be classified as fantastical, and hopes to be an author of YA fiction someday. You can follow her reviews on Goodreads at:
https://www.goodreads.com/user/show/9547248-mary-zemina.

Words have no power
TO IMPRESS THE MIND
without the exquisite
HORROR of their REALITY

*A nanopunk story inspired by "The Fall of the House of Usher"*

Jenny Blenk is a Pacific Northwest native who is currently earning a Master's Degree from Portland State University. Her focus is in English Literature with a certificate in Comics Studies. She loves reading, writing, hiking, and most things goth or punk. Currently she lives in Portland, OR, with a typewriter, three houseplants, and a rabbit.

JENNY BLENK

import Fall
Fall.system("HouseofUsher")

The bitter autumn wind gusted hard enough to rock the entire two-man cruiser as it sped along just above the winding gravel path. Shitty stabilizers. They'd need recalibration for sure once I returned to the City. If they didn't fall off first, that is.

I wasn't thrilled to be out flying through the smog-shrouded ruins of a former upper-class neighborhood an hour outside of the City. The shadows of abandoned mansions and statuary, along with unkempt hedges and briar roses, sulked in the gloom just outside the cruiser's xenon beams. But there are just some requests that you can't easily reject. The reasons vary but remain. While I was visiting an old friend in my official capacity as a nanotech systems expert, this wasn't exactly company business. I counted myself fortunate that the Company had agreed to lend me a cruiser at all for this house call, bad stabilizers or not.

Apparently, like me, not even the Company thought it wise to hinder a request from the Usher family. In truth I'd been beyond surprised to receive Roderick Usher's comm. Initially I hadn't even recognized him when his face had appeared in the corner of my vision some three days ago. His recorded message there explained that his elderly parents, after an extended time under the care of his sister Madeline, had recently passed away. Roderick and Madeline were as yet unsure about whether they wanted to retain ownership of their historic family home or invite the Company to make an offer on it. In any case, the property would need some extensive updates to its nanosystems to maintain basic functions and structural integrity. Would I, as a favor to the family, be willing to stop in for a weekend to see what I could do to update the programs and maybe inject a new infusion of nanites into the system? After all, he reminded me, nobody else knew the house and its tech quite like I did.

It was true. As an orphan of the Borough Plagues years ago, I was taken in by the philanthropic Ushers at the age of six. To earn my keep and build a future for myself in the City, I was apprenticed to Barnes, the Ushers' in-house technical specialist. Everything about the house of Usher, from the hardwiring of the original climate-control computers to the model number of the nanites that cleaned the air in the third-floor intake vents, was embedded in my brain as surely as the digital skull plate that monitored my own nanites' functions. I owed my life and the foundations of my entire career to the Ushers. A weekend trip out of the City was a small price to pay in return.

As I navigated the winding gravel road, swimming through the swirling gray smog that enveloped nearly everything below the City on the hill, I chewed absently at the end of one of my dreads. It hadn't just been simple obligation that made me pack up my toolkit and head out of the City; it had been something in Roderick's face, a discomfort palpable even over the comm. I called up the message with a thought and replayed it, mutely, in my left eye as I continued to navigate the circuitous gravel drive. Since childhood, he and Madeline both, twins, had shared the same narrow features graced with thin lips and elegant, aquiline noses. Deeply embedded between high cheek bones, Roderick's luminous blue-gray eyes regarded me evenly as his mouth moved, silent, hinging a delicate jaw set with picket fences of straight, white teeth. He was alien somehow, but still undeniably beautiful even in the way his ashy blond hair curled around the red-and-green data readouts of his skull plate.

The drive rounded a tepid pool of greenish water, which sent the odd bubble of gas spiraling up from its murky depths. On the other side of it emerged the outline of the Usher family home, flanked by leafless trees in neat ranks. The house's stern marble facade stared coldly down the front drive. Three stories of eyeless windows gaped out at the empty, enshrouded landscape of former opulence. I parked the cruiser with a sigh of its air cushioning at the foot of the wide stone stairs that cascaded down from the dark main entrance to pool on the drive.

Dismissing the now repeating image of Roderick, I swung my door up and hefted my tool kit over my shoulder. As I took in the cold, crushed stone of the drive, the gray face of the house in the miasma of the smog, an involuntary shiver danced down my spine. Unease coiled up in my stomach. The place felt cold in a way that couldn't be alleviated physiologically, even by my nanites, no matter how they adjusted my internal temperature. I could hear their click and whir behind my eyes as they sought a solution to my discomfort, to no avail.

As I mounted the steps, I could see thin fingers of stringy lichen stretched across the square corners of the entryway, beckoning me up towards the dark maw of a heavy woodSim door. My thin boots made no sound against the stone, and the opaqueness of the fog encircled me as though I were the last person on earth. I resisted the urge to duck and slouch as I approached the doorway. Time had not improved the effects that this intrinsically sinister edifice had on my subconscious. An iris scanner whirred to life as I approached the door, but I ignored it and waited instead. My iris patterns wouldn't be in the house's system anymore anyway, but staff should have been notified by the security system that someone had arrived. The urge to put my back to the solid woodSim and warily watch the fog was almost unbearable, as a dark sense of unease itched between my shoulder blades.

With a mechanical click, the door slid backward and then to the left, revealing Roderick Usher. I blinked in surprise but managed to school my expression to neutrality before I could embarrass either one of us. His face now was even thinner than it had been on the comm, the bones of his skull protruding from tight, waxy skin. His eyes still shone bright as he gave me a small smile of welcome, but their light held more of a feverish quality than any actual warmth.

"It's wonderful to see you," he greeted me softly as he pulled me into a hug that threatened to impale me on his angular frame. His cream-colored linen suit felt soft against my scar-riddled palms, and he smelled of cedar and electricity. But he also trembled under my tentative touch. Something was definitely not right, with Roderick or with the house. I casually angled my head so that I could scan the readout on his skull plate. At first glance at least, his nanites and their programs seemed to be running normally. Whatever was ailing Roderick, it wasn't a system error. Perhaps it was merely fatigue.

I was escorted into a formal parlor paneled in the same dark woodSim as the door. The light dimmed and fluxed as I settled myself on the arm of an antique sofa and looked around at the faded opulence of a long-dead way of life. Roderick watched me, his eyes considering, from an armchair across a dusty coffee table. The decay of the place was palpable in the stale air and the lackluster gleam of the lights overhead. I rearranged my tech kit in my lap, feeling awkward and out of place. I itched to put this place to rights, but remained fearful of being impolite to this family who had given me everything when I needed it most.

Finally Roderick broke the silence. "Purple, mm?" he observed, gesturing at the nest of dreads piled on top of my head. "It's nice on you." His calm, resonant voice and soft smile struck at odds with the crumbling walls around us, the threat of mildew in the corners, and the thin coating of dust on nearly everything in the shadows. And yet he seemed so at ease, so comfortable with the slow death of his home.

"Thanks," I mumbled. "I was sorry to hear about your parents' passing." The sentiment sounded hollow, forced even to my own ears. But what else was there to say?

Roderick leaned forward, his elbows on his knees, and shrugged. "They were slipping away for a long time. Madeline is the one who really took care of them over the past few years. I'm afraid that's part of why we let the house go, being busy with the distraction of looking after other matters."

"Of course," I replied. "It does look as though some major updates are necessary, in the nanites themselves as well as in their software and in that of the house, to even keep this place standing. Provided that it's still running on the same operating system that it always used, I should be able to load a new infusion of nanites with all the relevant updates and just inject them right into one of the nanite hubs in the house. We'll reboot the system without even shutting down the old nanites, and the new information should be uploaded through the new ones sharing the information. Any nanites that are too old to be compatible with the updates will be recycled by the new machines."

Roderick took in all of this with an amused half-smile propped on his lips. I paused, suddenly self-conscious of my expertise despite the fact that it was precisely this that had brought me here. "Do you still run the same security system in the house?" I asked, too loudly, to cover up my unease.

"I imagine so," replied Roderick.

"Good. I'll need to know that as part of the nanite updates." There was another awkward lull in the conversation. "Is Madeline still here as well?" I tried desperately. "Surely she hasn't left again already?"

"She hasn't," Roderick confirmed, although I noted the undertone of hesitancy in his voice. I subtly tuned my hearing in closer on the sound of his words. "She's somewhere around here. Since our parents passed, she's seemed to wander a lot, as though she's somehow lost. I don't know if she quite knows what she's doing here anymore, after having cared for our parents for so long. I'm afraid she lost everything else that gave her purpose." A very slight tremor rippled his voice, nearly inaudible even with my nanite-augmented hearing.

I considered this for a moment. "Well," I ventured, "why don't you allow me to fix up the house systems before anything else, and once the place is back up and running within normal parameters, Madeline may perk up again. It's something we can do to be proactive, at least." And to get me out of this awkward conversation, I added silently.

Roderick showed me to the operations room down in the basement, its lights surging and dimming on and off in neat rows along the wall of the computer banks secreted away there. The soft hum of electricity was marred by the odd hiccough, marked by blanks and fragments in the readouts that cycled through on the single large display monitor.

A heap of metal shavings in one corner caught my eye, under a small open shaft: nanites, defunct, cleaned out of the system by their fellows and deposited here as waste. I zoomed my vision in on the bottom of the pile and ran a calculation from the moisture content in the air, the known makeup of the nanite model used in the house, and the amount of rust buildup on the discarded metal. The approximate resulting time frame made me inhale sharply. Ten years. This place hadn't been cleaned out or seriously updated in a decade? That couldn't be right. But if it was even close to the truth, this would prove to be more than a quick job; it would require some diagnostics before I could even know whether the house's delicate system of atmospheric controls, self-maintenance and even security, all run by nanites, could withstand such a complete system overhaul.

Behind me, Roderick watched with an odd sort of detached intensity while I fired up my diagnostic tablet and plugged it into the ports of the main interface computer. Sure enough, Shield, the security system that had been in place since I lived here, was still running steadfastly. I couldn't help but smile slightly as I observed this. Shield was what we in the tech industry referred to as an "oldie but goodie," performing its same basic task endlessly. It would be the simplest possible program to incorporate into the diagnostic scan so that neither one interfered with the other.

The entire room looked as though it hadn't been touched since Barnes the tech specialist died two years after I'd moved to the city. It felt as though I'd walked into a technological tomb, or some long-forgotten space capsule left to drift beyond the reach of human knowledge.

"I thought," mused Roderick as he watched me attach the last cable, "that professionals such as yourself were outfitted with an adaptable direct link for projects like this?"

"It's true," I admitted as I fired up the diagnostics. I tapped on one of the ports in my skull plate with a thin finger to show him. "But direct links are only safe for systems that we know are fully standardized and updated. Quick dives like that work for minor troubleshooting, but you need years of immersion training before a person can do longer, more intensive dives without getting lost or shorting out the whole system." The diagnostics began running, and I stifled a groan as I looked at the time estimate blinking on my screen. The Ushers' house was running so far behind that it would take an hour to even figure out what parts of the system were salvageable. "It's complex," I continued, "trying to keep your own program to yourself when you're swimming in someone else's. Problems happen when things get mixed up. I honestly think that even if I were prepared to do a real dive here, your house wouldn't know what to make of my updated programming. The whole place might just fall apart on top of us."

We left the tablet running alone in its crypt, and Roderick gave me an extended tour of the old house. Much was exactly the way I remembered it. He then showed me into the library before going to the kitchen to prepare us some tea. The dull, tired light produced by the house's poorly maintained generators shone gamely on, turning the deep leatherSim armchairs into hulking shadow monsters against the shelves full of discs. Thick carpet cushioned my steps as I browsed through them, not looking for anything in particular but enjoying the experience nonetheless.

When the library door opened again a few moments later, I turned, expecting Roderick with tea. But instead his twin met me with startled eyes. "Oh," Madeline said. "I do apologize. I wasn't aware that you'd arrived. What day is it?" Her voice was breathy and lyrical as always, a reflection of her brother's tones just as her features mirrored his. But her voice, like Roderick's, had an undercurrent of wrongness to it. Where her brother's had been hesitant and tremulous, Madeline sounded stilted and almost mechanical. She bit off her consonants with such precision that I feared she might lose a piece of her tongue.

"Aah, it's good that I thought to bring an extra cup," Roderick said mildly as he entered the library behind his sister. "Do you think you might manage some tea with us?"

Madeline nodded and brushed her ash-blond hair behind one ear with a trembling finger. As she reclined on a leatherSim couch, her diaphanous dress billowed around her, exposing more than masking her thin frame with its delicate layers of satiny material.

"How long were you here taking care of your parents?" I asked once Roderick had served the tea and both of them had asked after my life in the City.

Madeline's bone china teacup rattled ever so slightly as she replaced in on its saucer. "I'd say it's been close to six years now," she replied in the same stilted tones as before. Roderick stared uncomfortably at the teacup in his hands. "Mother degraded naturally over time, and Father, being the romantic that he always was, decided one day to sync their program so that neither one of them would have to suffer a day without the other." She smiled wistfully at the memory, but even her facial muscles looked brittle.

The romantic anecdote wasn't what really caught my attention though. "You've been here, in this house, for six years?" I clarified, to which both Madeline and Roderick nodded, somewhat bewildered by the sudden intensity of my tone. "The house hasn't updated in even longer than that. Are you certain that your software has been getting the updates it needs in that time period?"

Madeline looked uncertainly at me. "Well I received the internal notifications that my programs had updates available, and I used the house portal for that the same way I did before I moved back here to take care of things." A small crease formed between her perfect brows as she

8

regarded me. "I feel fine," she said as she looked to her brother. "But I'm not, am I?"

"I'm sure that if you've missed a few updates it won't be anything serious to get it taken care of," Roderick reassured her while looking at me. "I thought it was maybe losing Mother and Father that made you begin to drift, but perhaps it would be good to run some diagnostics on you, too?"

I nodded emphatically at this. More and more, I was becoming concerned by what I saw of the state of things in this house as well as its occupants. I felt out of date if my program needed more than five updates at any given time, and as part of my job working for the Company I received a new infusion of nanites every two years. With our technology so deeply ingrained within us, so completely integrated with our natural systems, was it even possible for someone to go six years without a proper update?

I knew I would have crashed for certain. The very thought had me rubbing at my skull plate for reassurance as I walked briskly down the familiar dark hallway, with its moldering carpet runner, toward the basement to retrieve my diagnostic tablet. No house with properly updated nanotech would have ever been in such a state. I swallowed down a mouthful of panic. This "small favor" was turning out to be much more involved than anyone had anticipated.

"About fragging time," I muttered to myself as I looked over the tablet. It had just finished compiling the extent of damage to the house's nanosystems caused by the lack of updates and general neglect. It was extensive, to say the least. After detaching the rope of cables from its port in the wall, I made my way back towards the library with the tablet, scrolling through it as I walked. With so few working nanites left in the system, it was something of a wonder that the place had managed to run itself this efficiently. Less than a third of the normal full complement of the tiny bots patrolled the house now. And with so few, it appeared that the house's very structural integrity was on the brink of collapse. This was exactly what I had feared.

The other disturbing thing that I noted amid the clutter of defunct programs was that the house's programs themselves seemed to have been patched up and rewritten from other sources. This was certainly not standard, or even safe. Some of it was downright unrecognizable. Perhaps it was the work of an amateur, trying to do the family a favor. Or maybe Barnes had lost his touch toward the end of his life. Either way, it would all be wiped away when the new updates were launched into the system. The house could continue operating at optimal parameters, with a new host of nanites to carry out the programs' instructions.

Upon reaching the library, I found Madeline resting comfortably, Roderick brushing the hair away from her forehead with one slender finger. "You might feel a bit of a buzz when I hook you up," I warned her as I took out different cables from my kit. "Maybe a little static too. I'm reconfiguring the diagnostics to run for biological tech now, so it won't think you're a house." I smiled weakly at my sad little joke, but neither Madeline nor Roderick responded. "What this is going to do," I continued, "is essentially run through all your basic, everyday programs to see what, if anything, isn't operating optimally. It'll flag those programs, and I can tell whether they just need an update, or if there aren't enough nanites in your system to carry out all of their parameters, or if it's something else. Those are the two biggest sources of glitches, though, and they're both easily fixed." I smiled in what I hoped was a reassuring way as I bent over Madeline and plugged my cable into the jack in her skull plate.

"Should we run diagnostics for you, too?" I asked Roderick, raising an eyebrow.

"No," he murmured, "I was in the City and updated just last week."

"Okay then," I responded. Then, "Here we go," as I tapped the screen to run the diagnostic program. Madeline's eyes widened slightly, their pupils dilating as the tablet's program began to shuffle through the software that ran her daily life. On her skull plate, data blinked placidly, green and red, reflecting nothing of her anomalous behavior.

"This shouldn't take long at all," I told Roderick as he hovered. "And right now there are some other things of which you should be aware."

When he heard how questionable the state of the house had become, Roderick's first concern was for us and our safety. I assured him that once I could program the nanites to work with Shield and load them with new updates for the house, they should be able to repair everything in next to no time.

Madeline stirred only once or twice during the diagnostics, her pallid face composed and her wide eyes staring at the ceiling. But suddenly her back arched against the leatherSim, her limbs rigid, and she let loose a horrible choking cry. Roderick leapt to his feet from a nearby chair and fluttered helplessly above me as I scrolled through the information compiling on the tablet. My stomach sank.

The diagnostic program had hit a wall, a gibberish of nonsensical and fragmented code that it was unable to sort through or make sense of. In its attempts to probe around this software snarl, the program was interfering with and shorting out the rest of Madeline's functions. As she twitched and writhed in spasms on the couch, I tried furiously to stop the program's explorations, typing any command I could think of to stop the reaction. Above me, Roderick screamed something about how I was killing her. Finally I gave up and pulled the cable directly out of Madeline's skull plate, but she continued to choke and twitch.

"What did you do to her?" Roderick demanded, leaning over his sister protectively. Her seizures had abated, but her wide eyes reflected the dim library light with a glassy vacancy. My tablet ran through its data placidly, compiling what information it had been able to access. How could I have foreseen this?

"Something went wrong," I said, then kicked myself for stating the obvious. Roderick's glare could have melted aluminum alloy. I took a deep breath before attempting to elaborate. "Because her nanotech is so out of date, not just the software but the nanites themselves, they've had to repair themselves with whatever they can piece together. This created a strange, inelegant patchwork of code in her system that works for her, but that my tablet couldn't read. It tried to find a way around the problem and in doing so it, ah, may have shorted her out." I spoke the last words quickly as I needed to get busy and try to rectify the situation, but even then I couldn't beat the immediate surge of rage from Roderick.

"You shorted her out?" he yelled in my face. "My sister is dead? Is that what you're trying to tell me?" Spittle flew from his gnashing teeth, flecking the screen of my tablet. "She's dead?"

"No," I reassured him quickly, struggling to keep my own voice down at normal levels. "No, she isn't dead. But she needs to be rebooted, with the proper software this time and some new nanites to carry out the programs. I'll have to bring her back to the City for that. I can do basically the same thing that I'm doing for the house, updating the whole system at the same time by loading the nanites with up-to-date programs that she's missing and injecting them into her system."

Minute beads of sweat formed on my upper lip. I could feel this whole situation rapidly swimming out of control, with the house on the brink of collapse from neglect, one Usher sibling vacant on the couch in front of me, and the other angry enough to rip out my larynx with his teeth. "Let me just complete the procedure for the house, so that it's still standing when we return, and then we can get Madeline to the City for treatment. A few extra minutes here isn't going to do her any harm at all." It took effort to keep the quaver of uncertainty out of my voice. I was the expert, the one who was supposed to be in control. So why did I feel so helpless?

"Why can't you just use the tech you brought for the house to reboot Madeline instead?" Roderick demanded, brushing a stray strand of hair away from his sister's forehead.

"These nanites aren't biologically compatible," I said. "They were designed to work within inanimate systems, not in a human being where—"

"Then hurry up and do whatever the hell it is you have to do to keep this place running, so we can leave and get her to the City," Roderick cut me off with a snarl.

I swallowed my pride with the lump of anxiety in my throat and opened a panel in the dark woodSim wall of the library. Tubes, wires and hubs criss-crossed within. So old was the setup, I doubt I would have been able to find what I sought had I not already been familiar with the old house and its systems. I found the Plexiglas tube, set with dim lines of blue lights, and followed it to the hub that transmitted information and directions to the nanites still in the system. With a sigh of relief, I found an input port there on the hub. I could inject the nanites here and know that they would reach the entire system shortly.

Retrieving my kit, I hooked up my tablet to a large glass vial full of nanites. They floated around inside like a milky metal ocean, reminiscent of the glass thermometers of the old days with their silvery mercury cores. The tablet plugged neatly into a port built into the vial's stopper. I only needed to upload the data for program updates into the first few layers of nanites in the vial, and the little hive-minded machines would share the data amongst themselves within minutes. With such an enormous quantity of data that needed to be integrated into the old house, though, the transmission to the nanites seemed to take forever. My eyes roved nervously over the tablet's screen. So close.... I could almost feel Roderick breathing down the back of my neck, his wild eyes regarding the back of my head as I worked. All I wanted to do was finish stabilizing this place so that I—we—could all get the hell out of here and I would never have to return to the house of Usher.

The process took approximately fifteen minutes, millions of nanites being imbued with the information and instructions that would save the house. When all the nanites were ready, I carefully walked the vial to the wall hub and, working to steady my trembling hands, I plugged it into the vacant port on the hub. Slowly, so slowly, the cloudy suspension of nanites in the vial cleared as the tiny machines traveled through the port and into the house's system.

The whole room went immediately dark. My already tight stomach plummeted. What the hell was happening now? I had made certain that everything was compatible, that Shield would let the updates through. Had the house's antique system been overloaded simply by the presence of so many new nanites at once? It just wasn't possible. I wanted to put my head through the woodSim. Fighting back tears of fury and frustration, I hooked my errant dreads back behind my ears and searched in my kit for a glow rod.

As soon as I cracked it, the room became suffused with a soft green glow. My nanites adjusted my ocular function to maximize what illumination there was. The faint noise of air filters upstairs wound down into silence. Roderick stared around us at the suddenly deadened house.

Then in the darkness, Madeline sat bolt upright on the couch. Roderick leapt backwards into an ottoman as his sister gasped and shuddered, curling into a protective little ball with her knees tucked up to her chin. I scrambled over to her as Roderick disentangled himself from the furniture. Madeline clutched at my hand, her eyes wide and terrified, as I gently checked her skull plate. To my bewilderment, not only did her programs appear to have been rebooted, but updated as well.

Madeline continued to gasp and squeeze my hand as I stared dumbfounded at her readout.

"Madeline!" Roderick cried as he clutched his sister to him in the dimness. Swathed in the translucent layers of Madeline's dress, they both looked like corpses. I shuddered and pushed away the thought. "What did you do?" Roderick asked, tears gleaming in his too-bright eyes.

"I don't know," I admitted, completely at a loss. It was as if I had shot the nanites into the woman instead of the house, so sudden and opposite had their reactions been. But that was impossible. I had physically loaded the nanites into the house. And even if I hadn't, as I explained to Roderick before, the nanites I had with me were only designed to interact with nonbiological systems. "She's somehow rebooted, but I don't know even if it'll last. I can't—"

An agonized moan that rumbled up from the very foundations of the house interrupted my wondering aloud. It reverberated through the woodSim walls, through the soles of my feet in their thin rubber boots and caused my teeth to hum uncomfortably in my skull.

"The house…" murmured Roderick.

A resounding crack made all three of us start. It was followed closely by a rising rumbling. If the nanites meant to repair the house and its systems obviously hadn't done their job, then the entire place might be coming down on top of us. "Grab her!" I yelled to Roderick over the rising tide of noise. My nanites did what they could to buffer my hearing, but even then, the sounds of grinding and cracking in the walls around me fast became deafening. I swept up my tablet and the rest of my tech kit in an untidy armload and rushed for the front door. Roderick, with Madeline cradled against his chest, followed closely.

I vaulted down the wide steps to skid to a stop in the gravel near my cruiser, turning back to watch Roderick make a slightly slower exit. Behind him, a plume of smoke and dust jetted out of the open door panel to dissipate into the fog surrounding us.

We stared, motionless, together on the front drive as with another series of crashes and groans, the entire house collapsed in on itself. Support beams twisted, woodSim and plastic shattered, and stone dust from the cracking marble facade rained down. I coughed and shielded my eyes, watching the formerly glorious house fall. In a matter of

14

moments, it was nothing more than a pile of rubble.

Roderick, bewildered, turned to look askance at me. The fog settled around the domestic ruin of their lives, smoothing the edges of the old house, blurring the sharp angles of the wreckage. In the silence that followed, I shook my head and turned toward my cruiser. It had been left miraculously untouched by the flying bits of debris, as had we. The shining white gravel crunched under my boots. "Where are you going?" Roderick called softly behind me.

"Same place as before," I replied with a sigh. "The City. Get in. We'll have to squeeze Madeline into the back. Also," I added as an afterthought, "you should know that the stabilizers are shit."

***

The Company was more than happy to furnish the remaining members of the Usher family with the facilities to run full diagnostics on both of them. Roderick's results proved to be completely normal, as he had said, and recent updates kept his system humming along smoothly.

Madeline, on the other hand, proved to be more of a puzzle. After a shot of sedative to keep from inducing another episode like the previously one, she lay placidly on the comfortable medical bed of the plush, snow-white diagnostic chamber. I plugged her into a bank of sleek white computers that were cold to the touch. Almost immediately, readouts sprang up on the wall of laser screens, scrolling through her programs and monitoring how they ran in real-time, spreading her bodily and mental functions on the wall of screens in front of me.

But as I scrolled through the readout, my brow furrowed more and more deeply. None of this made sense. Intermixed with the code that defined her basic bodily functions, her heart rate and respiration and even internal temperature, were pieces of programs that I had uploaded into the nanites for the house before it collapsed. Her breathing was monitored by the same program that would normally ensure the quality of the air passing through the ducts of a building. The medical program that directed her nanites to repair any scrapes or ills was the same that would repair similar damage to a structure.

I marveled at the impossibility of it, scrolling by on the screens,

15

completely unaware of its own significance. "This can't be," I whispered, twisting one of my dreads around a finger. But the truth played out in dancing streams of code right in front of my eyes. Considering how long she'd gone without having new nanites injected into her system, she was running remarkably smoothly. It was due to this impossible combination that I watched operating, working steadily away.

"You said you got your updates through the main computer at the house," I addressed Madeline in her half-conscious state. "Which jack did you use to do that, do you remember?"

"Yes," she replied dreamily. "It was the big jack, the one in the middle."

I exhaled shakily. "You mean the same one where the man put the nanites, when we were little and Barnes updated the systems?"

"Yes," Madeline said again with a sigh.

A shudder ran its fingers down my back and into the plush upholstery of the shapely chair in which I sat. "You can't be fragging serious," I breathed.

"What?" asked Roderick from his seat by the soft white bed on which his sister reclined.

I rested my head in my hands. "Do you remember what I told you about jacking directly into another system? How difficult it is to maintain your separation from all the programs around you?" Roderick nodded and I ran a hand through my dreads. "Your sister's been jacking directly into your house system, thinking that she's been downloading her updates. None of her programs were impacted by updates; she wasn't getting any. It was because she and the house were comingling data that she managed to stay running. Her nanites picked up on the programming there. Maybe it was because they were both so outdated. Madeline's nanites adopted sections of the programs that they found in the house systems to keep themselves running. To keep her running. That's why it's all tangled up inside her tech, all intertwined."

"I thought you said that was impossible," Roderick said.

"It is," I said, my eyes glued to the monitors. "And yet here it is in front of us. But what I can't figure out, is how when I injected the updated nanites directly into the house, she was somehow the one who rebooted. There was no connection there; it should have been impossible."

16

"It was the house," Madeline spoke up dreamily from the bed.

"What did you say?" I asked, incredulous, turning to look at her prone form.

"The house," she repeated. "We were both dying. The house gave it to me. And now through me, the house lives on."

*A steampunk story inspired by "The Mystery of Marie Roget"*

Rachel A. Brune served five years as a military journalist with the U.S. Army, including two tours in Iraq, and a brief stint as a columnist for her hometown newspaper. After commissioning as a military police officer, she continued to write and published articles for a number of military and civilian news publications, as well as short fiction stories and two novels. She blogs her adventures, writing and otherwise, at http://www.infamous-scribbler.com.

RACHEL A. BRUNE

# THE CASE OF THE
# LONESOME CIGAR GIRL
# IN THE SIXPENNY
# TEMPLE

"Olimpias Gestalt schwebte vor ihm her in den Lüften und trat aus dem Gebüsch, und guckte ihn an mit großen strahlenden Augen, aus dem hellen Bach."

*"Olympia's figure hovered before him in the air, and rose to meet him out of the bushes, and gazed at him with her big, bright eyes, from out the clear, blue stream."*

(E.T.A. Hoffmann, *Der Sandmann*)

The pre-War façade of the Tower Infirmary loomed through the mist, the nooks and crannies of the small plaster friezes lost against the squat, brick structure that hunkered, glowering, against the evening. The dirty yellow glow of the hospital's bustle and fray shone out many of the windows, each keeping close their inner tales of tragedy and miracle. The building had sustained minimal damage during the War, thanks to the city's policy of neutrality—shying away from attacking those who nurtured life instead of taking it—yet the scars remained for those who knew her lines and history.

The weather was unseasonably warm for December, even in this city that lay close by the line of the Tropics. Sergeant Thomas Woodson, lowly officer of the police force of the Free City of New Orleans, sweated under the heavy wool of his old Army greatcoat and steeled himself for the ordeal ahead. As one of the city's finest, and a former member of the Union Descent Troop Corps, Woodson had faced dangers and horrors that haunted his infrequent dreams. And yet—he would rather grasp the descent line, swing out into the great void, and drop from the dubious safety of the great airships, than drag his steps into the hospital. Grasping the bottle of fine Kentucky bourbon carefully concealed in the voluminous folds of his greatcoat, Woodson drew a deep breath and forced his feet up the steps of the Infirmary.

***

The object of his trepidation sat restlessly on the edge of a narrow bed in the charity wing of the Infirmary, an open space reserved for those patients whose status teetered somewhere between impecunious and barely solvent. A scant two years ago, the City found the means and wherewithal to renovate one of the Infirmary wings with the latest improvements in copper-plated piping, hydraulics, and steam-powered heat and sanitation. That wing was on the other side of the building from the charity dorms.

Detective Mignon Boudreaux found the beds not only narrow, but too short besides. The night nurse made her last rounds half an hour ago, shivering against the cold, and Boudreaux was supposed to take the little white pill and go back to sleep. The pain came again, and she palmed the pill, wincing against the sharp fire that lanced her side. Every night since waking up in the dorm with a cleaned and bandaged furrow left by a small-caliber round, she had waged a short debate against dulling the pain or the rest of her senses. The past three nights the pain had won, but now she found herself reluctant to spend any more time outside of her head.

A disturbance came from the front of the room and she turned, careful not to twist her torso against the firmly-wrapped bandages. In the open doorway to the dormitory, a white-uniformed orderly attempted to stop Sergeant Woodson in his forward path.

"Excuse me! Excuse me, sir!" The orderly grasped Woodson's greatcoat, pulling futilely against the tall man's forward motion. "You cannot go in there."

Woodson paused. "And what is the reason for that, and who upon your honor intends to stop me?"

The orderly stammered. "It's—it's for ladies. That area is for the ladies." He looked Woodson up and down. "And you're—you're—"

Woodson stared the man down. As the orderly broke under his gaze, he slowly dug in the interior pockets of his coat and fished out the badge of his office. He extended it to the man. "Any further objections?"

"No, no sir," the orderly answered. "I—go in, sir."

Boudreaux grinned widely as Woodson approached, his presence causing a stir in the occupied beds, his tall, confident stride out of place in this place of female recovery.

"That's adding insult to injury, *frère*." She leaned back against the wall, one knee folded under her, her left foot resting on the floor. Awkward as it was, it was the most comfortable position she was able to find.

"If I called him a pompous gas-sack what couldn't find his tail with a map and a glass, *that* would be an insult." Woodson remained as deadpan as ever he was. "As for injury, how's that channel that flash toff carved out in you?"

The dry tone masked Woodson's concern well. At Boudreaux's grimace, the news he carried faded on his lips. The wound had taken its toll on his partner, her normally lean frame even more gaunt, the shadows under her eyes more pronounced. Lying there in her hospital pajamas, removed from the familiar trappings of her office, she exuded a fragility that belied what Woodson knew to be an inner hardness, undimmed by mortal concerns such as pain and high-caliber rounds from flash gentlemen. Still, it was hard to see her that way.

"Out with it." Boudreaux adjusted her position on the bed, trying to get the flimsy metal headboard out from where it wedged in her spine. "What's got your face all in a crease?"

"Came from the station," Woodson grunted. He pulled up a chair and shrugged off his greatcoat, tossing it over the back. He sat down at the foot of her bed. "Commissioner's blowing a mighty noise about what there's going to be an investigation and great clanging of alarums regarding the death of the most respectable Judge Allan Johnson."

"That *bâtard* shot me first!" Even as Boudreaux protested, she knew the falsity of her surprise. The bloody gully along her side was just another memento to add to the badge of service on her cheek and the faint line on her hand from her Descent Troop Corps days. And the city, and her own fellow officers, would have preferred that the latest token would have taken her life rather than consign her to this ward, the embarrassing reminder of her transgressions against good taste.

"Well, that was your own damn fault, getting shot by such a high society gentleman, and a judge besides," Woodson returned. "Anyway, I didn't come to talk about our imminent unemployment. I brought this."

He tossed her a small object, immediately regretting his choice when she stretched to catch it and pain flashed across her face.

Boudreaux straightened up. "My lucky charm." She held in her hand the rope-and-dagger badge first pinned on her the day she graduated Descent Trooper training. It had indeed served as her lucky charm, worn pinned to the underside of the lapel of her jacket now that the War had ceased and she pursued a less respectable office. Woodson had taken it into his safekeeping as they took her from his arms on the hospital steps.

"And something to warm you right from the inside." Woodson reached into his jacket and pulled out the bottle of bourbon. "And also—"

"*Dobre vecher, rebyata!*" The short, burly Russian figure of Lieutenant Mikhail Feryusovitch, known as Misha to his friends, barreled right past the figure of the orderly, whose attempt to stop the forward momentum of the soldier was more half-hearted than not.

"*Merde.*" Boudreaux sank down in the bed as Misha stomped his heavy tread toward them. "How did he find us?"

"It's pretty common knowledge," Woodson said. "The yellows couldn't quit slinging the hash, even rechewed and slightly stale."

"Hello and good evening, I brought these for you." Even here in the infirmary, Misha wore his large, multi-barreled rifle slung across his back. In one hand he carried a bouquet of lilies, and in the other a rolled up copy of the *Free City Times*, a notoriously yellow publication of ill repute. He pulled to a halt next to Boudreaux's bed and thrust these objects forward. "You look like *sri*. You almost one of those bodies like down in the basement."

Boudreaux and Woodson had taken the young Russian on a visit to the morgue in the Case of the Clockwork Dragon. It had evidently made quite the macabre impression.

"*Merci.*" Boudreaux shivered slightly taking the lilies, and not from the damp cold that the small fire at the end of the dorm failed to alleviate. She was of course much too polite to say, but lilies chilled her to the bone, a pale flower most associated in her mind with the flat shroud of monochrome death.

She reached for the paper, wondering why the lieutenant had

chosen such a gift for a sickbed offering.

"There is an article about you on page three." Misha beamed. "It's very good. Good drawing."

Boudreaux affixed him with the gaze that had soiled the pants of more than one junior officer. Being Russian and immune to steely gazes, Misha spotted the bourbon. Eyes alight, he pulled up a chair and reached for the bottle.

"Ah! I have heard of Kentucky bourbon! I've never tried it."

"Help yourself." Woodson shook his head. He glanced over to Boudreaux, but she ignored the Russian's poaching of the booze. Her attention was captured, rather, by the story on the first page, above the fold.

"They found her?" asked Woodson.

"Found who?" Misha asked curiously.

Woodson stilled his face. "Mellie Rogers."

"Ah, I have read this story." Misha took a slug from the bottle, offering it to Woodson, who took it from him, wiped the mouth, and drank a long swallow.

"Who?" Boudreaux frowned, confused, at the thick columns of small print, crammed together around the line engraving that claimed pride of place on the front page.

"Went missing a few days ago," Woodson explained, a strange note of bitterness underlying his matter-of-fact tone. "Washed up on shore yesterday."

Indeed, the article proclaimed the sensational news that the body of a young woman, Mellie Rogers, was discovered by the perambulations of a group of afternoon pleasure seekers. The death of another young woman of dark skin wouldn't normally be worth mentioning, let alone be afforded such privileged space in the yellows, except for the extreme circumstance of her sad and lonesome end.

"Did you know her?" Boudreaux searched her partner's face for explanation.

"Her mother came by the station a few days ago." Woodson kept his face as still as possible. "She left the station…unsatisfied by the great, important men what afford citizens the shelter of the law."

Boudreaux bent her head to the page. Some engraver had captured

24

the dramatic, pithy moment, the mother's arm stretched out thin and entreating before the stern gazes of the men of the gentry and the law. Boudreaux and Woodson knew better the state of those whom the great river coughed up, releasing its treasures reluctantly—the bloated, twisted remains of the tide.

Young Mellie Rogers had been a beautiful young woman, most recently in the employ of J.A. Anderson & Sons, Ltd., purveyors of fine tobacco—specifically at the *Confreres Blanc*, a very quiet, very flash club for gentlemen of a certain set. In its dark wood rooms, amid its paneled halls, she was the sole feminine presence, tolerated for the novelty and the convenience of the fine West Indies tobacco.

As it turned out, *Mademoiselle* Rogers had been missing for three days. She had taken leave of her mother on a rainy afternoon Saturday last, making her weekly trip across the Border into Jefferson Parish to visit her maternal relations. She had assured her parent that she would return by dusk, as her beau had planned to call. And yet, as she walked away, her mother was seized by a great well of emotion and called out, "I fear that I shall never see you again…."

When she didn't return that night, her mother and her beau traveled on foot from the Night Ward to the main police station to report her absence, only to be turned away, the answer written on the face of the desk sergeant who took in their dark skin and the worn, shiny patches on knees and elbows.

The news account continued in its quite vivid description of the cigar girl's body—the strip of fabric tied around her hands, the second strip tied and knotted around her neck. By the mottled flesh, the yellows came to the conclusion that she was drowned three days ago, by some gang of villains, who restrained her in such vulgar fashion. More than one innuendo against her virtue by nature of her profession made it into the heavy rows of gray. The end of the article devolved into a highly eloquent reproach of those who would employ pretty, impressionable young women of a certain sort in a position where they could so easily be…exploited.

"They think it was one of the gangs?" Boudreaux's voice broke the silence. She extended her hand for the bottle, taking her first draught of the evening. It took a nice edge off the chill.

"That's the public consensus," Woodson answered.

"In congruence, I assume, with the judgment of the most honorable Commissioner?" Boudreaux raised an eyebrow, and swallowed another mouthful from the bottle.

Woodson grunted. Misha looked back and forth, his youthful face open with questions.

Boudreaux folded the paper and put it to the side. "What did you come here to ask me?"

Woodson gazed at her, face immobile. "Whatever do you mean, Captain?"

"I mean to quit beating around the cogs," Boudreaux said. "And quit calling me Captain. That was long enough ago. And besides, you only use it when you want something. So what is it?"

"This case is going to be closed in the way what most quickly throws a veil of silence over the whole distasteful affair." Woodson reached for the bottle. "I want your help to find the truth."

Misha snatched the bottle on its transit between the two and took a quick drink. "I will help, of course."

Boudreaux regarded her partner with a raised eyebrow. "Commissioner won't like it."

"The Commissioner can hang for what he won't know," Woodson growled. "But you and I both know it wasn't no gang what put Mellie Rogers into the river."

"And?"

Woodson's face grew even more still. "And I want you to help me find who did this to my cousin's girl. My mother's sister's boy sits in a cell as we speak, and you and I both know that it won't make any difference in the investigation whether he swings."

"Ah." Boudreaux quietly folded the paper and placed it to the side. It was more common an occurrence than not that the police of the city would lay hands on the most convenient villain, especially if his skin was a little darker than society cared for. "You know of course I will, *frère*." She took the bottle, which had once again made its way into Misha's hands. "And we get caught by the Commissioner, we can be hung for meddling interlopers together."

Outside in the square, the bells of the small hospital chapel tolled to mark the hour, the previous day merging into the next.

"Come tomorrow," Boudreaux said. "Both of you. Meet me in the day room, and bring what you can find from the yellows and the sergeant's desk." She lifted the bottle in salute. "And for God's sake, steer clear of any of the official investigating parties—and especially the Commissioner."

***

The next day brought an explosion of theorizing and moralizing, flowering in the hot morass of public outcry against violence done against pretty dark-skinned girls in the employ of white gentlemen. Most of the hue and cry was fashioned against the gang of blackguards and villains, who were assumed to have taken advantage and then cruelly discarded her into the river's murk.

Boudreaux sat in the gloom of the infirmary's day room, squinting to read the print in the flickering artificial lights, lit against the morning downpour. Woodson sat silently across from her, legs crossed, watching the raindrops as they struck the glass panes of the windows, drizzling down in rivulets. Misha was to meet them later, after Boudreaux had time to glean what could be found in their flimsy pages.

"They've spoken with her family already?" Boudreaux's voice broke through her sergeant's reverie.

"They came by yesterday evening," Woodson said. He nodded at the thick paper folder she held in her lap, a folder that included all the notes his photographic memory had assembled and copied from his private walk through the actual investigators' work. "What do you think?"

"They seem pretty certain they've found the truth of the matter, and in only one revolution of a clockwork hand."

Woodson nodded. "Ayuh. And all the good folk of the City in agreement."

"I must ask you a question that…might cause you some discomfit, frère."

Her partner stood, turning slightly away. The set of his shoulders betrayed the tension held therein. "Ask what you will."

Boudreaux cast about for the right phrasing. She was much better at teasing out the details of observation with the fiddly gears and cogs of the apparatus of her own invention. But here there were no hidden fibers to pluck, no ridges and valleys of prints coaxed from their latency by the silver brush. Once more, she cursed the ill luck that confined her to the walls of the infirmary, and the secondhand gathering of knowledge.

"Your cousin's girl ...she had been previously...had perhaps accompanied a gentleman?"

"Ayuh." The bitter note returned to Woodson's voice. "She did at one time see much of a certain Naviation Officer and gentleman, although I use that word in the loosest sense." He cleared his throat. "It did not take the yellows long to strip that sweet piece of flesh from her bones."

"Ah." Boudreaux nodded, the weight of any further conversation resting unsaid in the air between them. She thought of her old Naviation goggles, now sitting useless by her bedside. She shut the folder. "There is nothing more to be found here." She gritted her teeth against another twinge of pain from her side. "All these learned opinions—they've solved it, within the narrow boundaries of their understanding." She closed her eyes, rubbing the bridge of her nose. "They don't know how to find what they're not looking for. That's where you'll find our answers."

"And where do we start looking for what for we're not looking?"

Boudreaux narrowed her eyes suspiciously at his phrasing. "You do that on purpose, *n'est-ce pas?*"

"Do what?" Woodson asked.

"Take your Yankee ass down the Quarter." Boudreaux ignored his protested innocence. "Talk to this *Monsieur* Anderson. Breach the gears of this *Confreres Blanc*, and see what stones can be kicked."

Woodson touched his forehead in the briefest hint of salute. "Aye, Captain."

Boudreaux glared. "Go place your hands on that infernal Imperialist and take him with you." She straightened, and winced. "Someone needs to watch your back while I'm confined here."

\*\*\*

Jonathon Anderson sold fine tobacco products under the name J.A. Anderson & Sons, Ltd. His shop was small, nestled on a quietly upscale street that saw enough foot traffic from the passersby to turn a modest profit. This state of affairs was barely tolerable for the owner and proprietor, who incurred risk with every submersible packed to the brim with fine West Indies leaf that slipped by the Confederate taxmongers. Still, the shop itself boasted a fairly extensive selection of loose and rolled cigars, which Lieutenant Feryusovitch ostensibly sought to peruse, while keeping a sharp look out the front plate glass window.

Sergeant Woodson nodded over his notebook as Mr. Anderson explained that the late Mellie Rogers had worked for him as a cigar girl at the *Confreres Flash*. She was one of a platoon of young, pretty *grisettes* dispatched to various centers of entertainment around the city—the younger and prettier, and more exotic, the better. Mellie Rogers was a stunning beauty, and Anderson swung a deal and installed her at the upscale club for gentlemen, where she returned his investment into much more than a simple, modest profit.

Anderson's face darkened as he related the struggle to place her at the club, what with her skin dark as café au lait. Misha frowned at Woodson.

"What this mean, her skin was too dark?" The Russian still hadn't quite caught on to the local cultural peccadillos. "This the Neutral City, *pravda?*"

"Well, yes, Lieutenant," Anderson answered. "But still, there are some things that, well…" He trailed off. "But then she went and disappeared for that week, and it took everything I could not to—well, I don't wish to speak ill of the dead. But she listened to sweet words from a certain gentleman who seduced her away from her post. I told everyone she had gone home to help with a family matter, and made discreet inquiries."

"Were any of your inquiries returned?" Woodson made a note in his minute, precise hand.

"No." Anderson shook his head. "There were some rumors, and some old women wrote long letters to the editor about the dangers of my girls selling the Devil's weed to gentlemen in intimate circumstances." He snorted. "But hell, boy, that's why it made me so much money."

Sergeant Woodson raised an eyebrow at the slur, but didn't pursue it. "Had you seen anyone sniffing around lately? Did she mention anyone at the club? Anything like that?"

Anderson shook his head. "Nothing more than rumors."

"Ah…Sergeant Woodson, there appear to be two *militseeya* heading our way." Misha coughed and nodded out the window.

"Thank you, Mr. Anderson." Woodson snapped his notebook shut. "We appreciate your cooperation."

"What? That's it?" Anderson frowned in confusion at the abrupt farewell.

Misha and Woodson made it out the door and half a block down the street, far enough away that they hoped the two men wearing sidearms and carrying the badge of the Free City Police did not catch a glimpse of them before turning into the cigar shop.

***

The night gathered close, drawing its dark green cloak around the hurrying footsteps of the passersby huddled deep in their intentional solitary tracks. Out on the streets, the fetid humors clamored around the amber streams from the intermittent gaslights. They stood as reclining sentries, plaintive guards against the evening, casting small rings of light that glowed briefly in the fog but did little to illumine a traveler's paths.

Sergeant Woodson told Feryusovitch to wait outside on the street, as much to keep an eye on anyone who might be following them, as to not make it obvious that he was investigating the matter of the lonesome, murdered cigar girl. A more prescient supervisor than the Commissioner might have studied the signs, and put together the presence of Woodson's cousin in the small precinct cell with the tenacious nature of the two detectives least likely to accept any official conclusions. However, the Commissioner was a politician and relied on others for his prescience, and so Woodson's presence requesting just a short visit with the prisoner went unnoticed and unremarked upon.

They had briefly considered making a frontal assault at the *Confreres Flash*, but turned their tracks. Sergeant Woodson would not be allowed in the front door, and had no intention of sneaking in the back. And Lieutenant Feryusovitch still didn't understand what a 'No Weapons, No Entrance' policy meant. Thus, they found themselves somewhere it would raise no questions to be found.

***

The basement of the precinct was all that was left of the original structure, obliterated in one of the vast, undiscerning night assaults of the Southern Artillery Air Corps. Later in the war, once the airships and ground crews of the Union Descent Troops had re-secured that part of the city, the remains of the structure were quickly cleared and used to hold the unfortunate members of the Confederate militia, both proven and suspected. Echoes whispered through the building of what happened before the final Neutral order was restored. As Woodson walked through the halls, the dreary stones sweating with condensation, he tipped his hat to any *haints* that might dog his footsteps.

"Who's there?" The voice, strained around the edges, queried from the small, barred window.

"It's me, cuz." Woodson was tall enough to have to stoop to peer into the room. His cousin, a tall, black man by the name of Saint-Eustis Jones, sat on a solitary bench, still in the grease-flecked clothes from his labors at the Steamworks on the edge of town. "Came to see what you did this time."

"It's all right, boss, I got a friend on the po-lice force." The thick drawl stood in sharp contrast to Woodson's Yankee twang. The two men may have been able to pass for brothers in the similarity of their physiognomies, but Woodson felt every day the sharp delineation between his New Orleans-native kin and his New York City roots.

"My partner and I got an eye on your case." Woodson folded his arms and leaned against the door, slouching to see through the window. "We've torn up the city once or twice—we'll find out the truth of what is what."

"What's what is that they ain't gonna try too hard when they already locked up one ni—"

"Say it and I will tell your momma, and you will never get the taste of soap out your mouth." Woodson would never get used to the slang that co-opted a word he had spent his whole Northern life decrying.

"Can't hide from the truth, *frere*." Jones shifted on his seat. "So what you come down here for anyway? Social call?"

"My partner and I took your case."

31

"For real?"

"As real as can be." Woodson scratched the back of his neck. "Only we're taking it on the sly, like, and not in any interpretation what might be termed 'official.'"

Jones laughed shortly. "You know, they catch you, you gonna be sitting right here on this bench next to me."

"I'll take that chance." Woodson turned his mind away from the fact that his cousin was correct, and moved instead to what Boudreaux would be likely to ask him when he got back to the Infirmary. "So tell me—how did Mellie get on? How'd you get caught up?"

"The night she went missing, we had a date—were gonna meet up at her Mama's place and go out someplace nice." Jones crossed his arms and leaned back against the wall. "My foreman asked me to stay an hour later, some kind of glitch gumming up these new gears we have on the sluices up north the Quarter. Took me two hours, and by that time I wasn't nowhere near ready to take my girl out. So I thought I'd swing by, let her know I got stuck, and see what she wanted to do. But when I got to the house, her Mama was pacing the floor cuz Mellie hadn't never come back from visiting her Auntie out across the border."

"Her Mama lives in the Night Ward?"

"Yeah, little house right nestled up to the border trench. She got family that never came to the City, and now they can't get in real easy. Rationing's gotten pretty hard, so Mellie heads over there once or twice a month with some kind of special treat and all the latest gossip." He stopped, catching himself. "Headed over there, I guess. Don't know who'll go now. Her Mama too old to get around easy, and waiting all that time to cross is too much."

Woodson stood in silence for a minute. Down the hall, two uniformed officers came around the corner. They were unarmed, the usual protocol in the cells, and sauntered slowly, giving each individual room a desultory look before returning to their conversation. As they passed him, Woodson casually unfolded his arms and placed his left hand on his hip, pushing back his greatcoat just enough to reveal his badge. The officers nodded and continued on their way. He waited until their footsteps faded around the next corner.

"Had she talked about anyone what couldn't leave her alone when she was busking Mr. Anderson's leaf?" Woodson asked. "Maybe someone what couldn't stop trying to call on her, maybe without benefit of chaperone or good taste?"

"She always had some gentlemen who sniffed around." Jones waited a beat, enough that Woodson was about to ask another question, but then continued. "There was one gentlemen."

"At the club?" Woodson prompted.

"Seems like it." Jones paused, thinking. "She told me he always bought the finest North Indies leaf, loose-rolled. She started carrying it special for him—he paid top dollar and left a tip besides, which always helped especially with her Mama's condition. And he looked awful fine in his Naviator's uniform—a captain, she said."

Woodson raised his eyes at that. The Naviation Corps was small, and had been disbanded after the war. While some, including Boudreaux, retained some of the trappings of their time in service, it was rare that one would continue to dress in the uniform. In the Free City of New Orleans, at least, it was considered to be of the lowest poor taste.

"Did he ever say anything? Do anything?"

"She told me he liked to watch her as he smoked." Jones coughed, the hacking a result of the damp in the deep basement. "Just stared all the time. A week or so, he brought her a ribbon, asked her to wear it to tie up her twists."

"Did she?"

"Not my girl." Jones wiped his mouth. "She would flirt for a tip, but she was always my girl. She'd never wear another beau's token."

Woodson thought about Mellie's prior unexpected, unexplained absence, but took the path of discretion. "He ever do anything else?"

"Couple days ago, she told me he followed her home. Right up to the border of the Night Ward."

There was something in Jones' voice that Woodson couldn't rightly discern.

"He just followed her?"

"Yes. Then stopped at the border to the Ward and watched her walk home."

This time the feeling that his cousin was hiding something hit Woodson with the icy cold fingers of doubt. "You telling me everything, cuz?"

"I'm telling you everything I'm going to tell you, cuz." Inside the cell, Saint-Eustis Jones swung his feet up on the bench and laid back, forearm over his eyes. "You such a hot shot police officer, you let me know what you find."

Woodson straightened and turned to go, but Jones' voice stopped him from leaving.

"You tell me if you find her ring, cuz. That was Grandmama's ring, and I'd like Auntie to get it back."

***

Sergeant Woodson and Lieutenant Feryusovitch arrived at the Infirmary late next morning to find Detective Boudreaux pacing back and forth in the dayroom, muttering to herself.

"Misha, how about you go…stand someplace." Woodson waved in the general direction of the hallway. "Trust me, friend, when I tell you on my vow as an Eastern Brother, you do not want to go in there."

Misha took one look in the room, shrugged, and stepped aside. "*Da*, Sergeant."

Woodson took a deep breath. Boudreaux wasn't the pacing type—she was more apt to a slow burn and sudden violent action. Something was not right. On the other hand, if she had reached the burning stage, it was best to proceed with caution.

"Keep that up and you'll bust through all your stitches and leave me with a great bloody mess what I'll have to explain to the Commissioner, and he already wants to toss us to the river hounds."

Boudreaux turned at Woodson's voice and snarled. "The Commissioner is a great heap of bloody piles *sur le cul d'un chien*. He can *fous le camps et morte. Merde de poutain*." She finished by clearing her throat and spitting on the floor.

"Am I to understand from that mess of French profanity that you have had the pleasure of an encounter with our brass-plated gentleman of the law?"

Boudreaux cursed again, but with less vehemence than before. She abruptly stopped pacing and dropped into the nearest chair, one hand at her side. "He came by this morning."

"The Commissioner? Here?"

"Yes, right here in this room." Boudreaux grimaced against the pain that returned once she stopped moving.

"What did he have to say to you?" Woodson didn't think he wanted to know the answer.

"Remember how I told you and that Imperialist to navigate below the sonar?" Boudreaux fixed him with a glare.

"Yes."

"You didn't."

Woodson frowned. "We were discreet."

"You were spotted at the cigar-makers," Boudreaux told him. "And apparently someone mentioned your presence at your cousin's cell door."

"Shit." Woodson closed his eyes. "Shit."

"Exactly." Boudreaux gritted her teeth against the dull pain in her side. It improved every day, but the ache lingered, an unwanted visitor. "Which means you have to get moving right away."

"Where are we going in such great haste?"

"Morning papers were full of the news that they found the lot up near Esplanade where the unfortunate Miss Rogers met her end."

"The lot? Esplanade Ridge?" Woodson frowned even more deeply. "She was found by the river's edge."

"Very true." Boudreaux raised an eyebrow. "And yet, her earthly possessions and the very over-garments she wore are described in this morning's yellows down to the last detail. Children of the neighborhood chanced upon them when they went to play."

"Well, that makes no earthly sense." Woodson rubbed his forehead. "If she was murdered in a lot all the way up there and then dragged to the shore, someone would surely have seen them."

"It's a very convenient explanation, even if it leaves more questions than it explains away," Boudreaux said. "As the papers tell it, the children go often to that lot to play. The appearance of those items and possessions after two full days of inquiry into her death tells us that we should trust not in the official statements of the police." She looked as if she wanted to spit again.

"Shit." Woodson wondered if it would be worth it to go out to the scene, picked over as it had to be by first the police, then the yellows.

Still, Detective Boudreaux had her tool bag of various instruments of detection—most of her own design—that had ofttimes before revealed what remained hidden to others' eyes. Still, the danger was in being found at the scene, and the notoriety of the location guaranteed that particular turn of events.

"Exactly." Boudreaux sat forward in her chair. "So I need you and Misha to head out, before anyone else thinks of it."

"Where, exactly, are we heading, Detective?"

"Follow me here, Sergeant." Boudreaux rested her elbows on her knees and steepled her fingers. "The yellows make a great deal of mention of the late Miss Rogers' articles of clothing, and some few particular possessions. A parasol. A book, its pages wet and ruined by the dew."

"Yes?"

"These are small, cheap things of little value."

"Ah—but if she had something of value on her— Damn. My Grandmama's ring."

"Indeed, Sergeant."

Woodson nodded. "We'll wander up that area a bit, this afternoon. A stroll among the secondhand shops might be an excellent way to get some fresh air and acquaint our Russian friend with some of the local flavor."

Boudreaux smiled for the first time, a wolf-like grimace more unsettling than not. "Happy hunting."

\*\*\*

The proprietress of The Lucky Duck, a shop of secondhand curiosities and curios, squinted suspiciously at Woodson and Feryusovitch when they crossed the threshold. The tall, black man and the short, pugnacious man in a Russian uniform with his weapon slung over his back was a pairing of note, but Woodson was used to the attention and Misha was oblivious in the face of the treasures contained in the many shelves and glass cases.

"Can I help you fine gentlemen?" The proprietress smoothed an imaginary wrinkle in her impeccably starched shirtfront, and patted a hair back into place in her bouffant.

36

"Yes, madam, we are in search of a ring."

"Any particular type?" She stilled her eyebrow; these foreigners sometimes had strange ways. And anyone with a Yankee accent that strong just *had* to be a foreigner.

"Thin gold band, small ruby in a plain setting." Woodson smiled, all teeth and open friendliness. "My old Auntie lost her ring, and I hoped to perhaps find one similar to it. For a sentimental gift, you understand."

"Ah! Yes. Of course." The proprietress nodded in understanding. "Wait right here, I think I have just the thing."

She bustled into the back, her high-topped boots click-clacking on the parquet floor.

"Look at this, *bratuschka*."

Woodson turned. Misha stood near a cabinet of random items that didn't appear to fall into any particular category. He held up a small folding fan, spread out to show the red, white, and blue banner of the Union flag, and the phrase "New York City, 1869." The year the peace was signed in that Northern city. The ruins of the former Union capital were deemed still too far in disarray to properly host all the dignitaries present at the historic decision which divided the continent into opposing geographies, with only the Free City of New Orleans to stand as lone buffer between.

"You looking for a souvenir, brother?" Woodson asked.

"Look at handle." Misha folded the fan and showed him the handle. "That is her initials, *pravda*? That is your "M" and then an "R", I think?"

Woodson reached over and took the fan. The Russian was correct. The footsteps of the proprietress warned them of her approach, and he hastily placed the fan on the table, stepping in front of it to conceal his interest.

"I found a few pieces in the back," the proprietress told them. "One or two of them might suit." She placed a small, black velvet-lined tray in front of the gentlemen. "Please, take your time."

Woodson bent to the tray. There were six rings nestled into fabric. Two of them he ruled out immediately—one of the rings sported a silver band, and the other had a tiger's eye in place of a ruby. The other four rings were gold with rubies, although two had small decorations in the settings, a leaf in one, and intertwined hands in the other. Woodson picked up one of the remaining two rings, examining and weighing it. The proprietress kept a respectful distance but a close eye on the Sergeant.

There was one detail Woodson had neglected to mention, a marker that would inform him if they found the prize they sought. He replaced the ring he held, and picked up the last one. He turned it over to look at the back of the setting and there, engraved in minute script, he saw the "A" and the "J," the initials that identified the ring as belonging to Annabella Jones.

"That is a very nice piece, brought in just the other day by a fellow who claimed he hated to part with it but couldn't bear to be around it anymore." The proprietress leaned just a tad closer, scenting a possible sale.

"That sounds like a tale," Woodson said, leaving the question in the air.

"Well, I'm not one to pry," the proprietress said, "but he had the face of a man who…well, I don't want to speculate or pass on rumors. But his eyes were those of a man who knew a deep loss."

"What kind of man was he?" At her raised eyebrow, Woodson hastened to add: "I just want to know if there might be any of that loss clinging to his piece. I don't want to bring it into my Auntie's house with no sadness about it."

"Oh, well, he was a very thin man, and very tall—even taller than you." She thought for a moment. "Had a little bit of a beard, but the pox got him and weren't no more than a few wisps on his chin. Wore a black suit. Top hat." She shrugged. "That's about it. I told him we charged a twenty percent commission on any sales, and he signed a standard agreement and that was it."

Woodson waited.

"There was one other thing." The proprietress filled the silence, as the Sergeant knew she would. "He was a gentleman of prodigious strength. His path was blocked by a barrel full of cast-iron steamworks parts, and he lifted it right out of his way and set it down there." She gestured to indicate the barrel. It was, indeed, full to the brim with heavy, metal items.

"Ah, very interesting." Woodson pretended to think. "How much are you looking for, for this piece?"

"Not less than one hundred and twenty."

Woodson frowned and the haggling commenced. "The sentimental value will be attached later. For now, this is a thin band with a small stone and no ornamentation. I offer sixty-five."

The proprietress feigned shock and glared. "Yes, but this is a piece of fine craftsmanship and a story that will add to its value. I could not accept any less than one hundred ten."

The Sergeant shrugged. "Eighty-five, or as much as I love my Auntie, I might just have to get her a card of sympathy."

"Well, a fine nephew you are, haggling over your Auntie's happiness," the proprietress scolded. "No less than ninety-five."

"Hm." Woodson made a show of mulling over the offer. "Ninety-five." He shook his head. "Were you to rob me, Madam, you would wound me less. Still, perhaps this poor man will find some solace with his twenty percent commission." He held out his hand. "Sold."

The proprietress ignored his hand and picked up the ring. "Very excellent selection, sir. I will wrap it for your Aunt."

Money exchanged hands—although the proprietress was very careful to ensure that those hands didn't actually touch, social propriety and all—and Woodson left the establishment with his Grandmama's ring in his pocket, securely wrapped in a light green paper parcel, tied with string and ribbon. The proprietress had included a small lagniappe, a lace handkerchief with a solitary rose hand-embroidered on the corner—her way of acknowledging her satisfaction with the sale.

★★★

Early afternoon drew on, casting Woodson and Feryusovitch's shadows longer and longer across the cobblestones. The sun's presence after three straight days of rain and mist brought out the bustling masses, reveling in the warm beams. Even the women's dresses looked brighter under its rays; the folds of the men's frock coats appeared slightly less dreary.

"It is your cousin's ring?" Misha asked, breaking Woodson out of his reverie.

"Ayuh. It is the very same." He patted his pocket, feeling for the package. "It will be a small matter of comfort to the family."

"What will you tell Detective Boudreaux?" Misha swung his arms as he walked, gazing down the street, taking in the sights.

"That we found the ring. A description of the man who brought it in. Perhaps she will have an idea of how to navigate around these streams of air."

"*Da*. She is very good at her job."

Woodson couldn't think of a reply worth making the effort and instead subsided into silence.

Feryusovitch admired the bustle of the street, and the many colorful stalls set up to entice a weary or hungry passerby—or perhaps one in search of a trinket for his sweetheart. He thought about asking Woodson for permission to stop at one of the stalls, but sensed the Sergeant would not be receptive to that suggestion.

From the rooftops down the street, Misha caught a familiar glint. The flash of light was so casually unexpected, his reflexes stuttered before catching.

"Sergeant, get down!"

The Russian pulled Woodson to the side, diving behind the flimsy concealment of a flower cart.

The round ricocheted off the pavement, deflecting off the stone and lodging in the bottom of the wooden cart.

Woodson tried to struggle up, but Feryusovitch pushed him down. "Stay there, *tovarisch*. A man shooting from that range will have more than one bullet."

The loud crack of the bullet striking and deflecting had gone almost unnoticed in the din of the street.

Woodson felt his pocket again. The package was still there, intact. "We can't set up camp on this sidewalk, brother." He stood up, his legs shaky. "Perhaps it was a mistake, or someone shooting for fun."

"That was no mistake, my friend, and I don't believe someone would shoot that precisely for…what you call it…fun." Misha straightened up as well, taking care to place himself behind the flowers that overflowed the cart. The cart owner gave him and Woodson funny looks, but then went back to ignoring anyone who wasn't buying flowers.

"Let us take perhaps another route back to the infirmary?" Feryusovitch had his weapon before him, holding the giant, many-barreled rifle effortlessly as he scanned the rooftops, seeking a target. But there were no more glints in high places. "Perhaps in visiting that shop, we venture too close to the truth, my brother."

***

With the fall of the evening, the fog had rolled back in over the city, obscuring the scutterings in corners and the shadowy figures that reveled in the night. At the Tower Infirmary, the gas lamps beat back the darkness, the flickering amber glow illuminating the hallways and windows against the night.

Detective Boudreaux was calmer than earlier than in the day, although it was a calm belied by the tension of forced immobility. When she saw Woodson and Feryusovitch push their way past the hapless orderly, she jumped to her feet, only belatedly remembering why it was a bad idea to do so.

"You found something, I can see it." She steadied herself on the back of the dayroom chair. "Something more than we expected."

"Some infernal bastard took a pot shot at us as we left one of the shops," Woodson replied. "Misha—sorry, Lieutenant Feryusovitch—here pushed me out of the way."

"I suspected something like that might happen." She nodded at the Russian. "Good thing you were there."

Misha blushed and looked down at the floor.

"Sit, sit. Standing hurts and I don't want to look up at you." Boudreaux lowered herself back down and waited until Woodson and Feryusovitch pulled up two chairs to face her. "Tell me what you have."

Woodson closed his eyes, and Boudreaux knew from past experience he was calling up that marvelous memory of his, seeing the images and words in front of his eyes, as if he were just now witnessing them.

"We know that Mellie Rogers worked at the *Confreres Flash*, selling Jonathon Anderson's 'imported' tobacco," Woodson began. As he spoke, he leaned forward, elbows resting on his knees, hands loosely clasped. "Except for that week she was missing, she sold cigars there every day except Saturday, when she would normally cross the border to visit kin out in Jefferson Parish, past the Neutral Line."

"And it was a Saturday she disappeared." Boudreaux leaned back in her chair.

"Ayuh." Woodson continued. "Saint-Eustis Jones was late to pick her up that night, and when she never showed up, he and Miss Rogers' mother went to the police station to make a complaint."

"Where they were turned away."

Woodson narrowed his eyes. "Yes, where they were turned away. Would you perhaps like to take over the narrative of my tale, *Madame le Detective?*"

"Keep telling it, Yank."

"Thank you." Woodson started again. "She had many admirers, as girls in her position are likely to do, but one in particular, a Naviation Officer, showed a specific, pointed interest." He ran the events of the day over in his mind. "My cousin tells me that the man even followed her home this past week. And then, three days ago, Miss Rogers is discovered on the shore. Yesterday, her things are discovered in a vacant lot a long walk from the river. And her ring is discovered in a second hand store, at which point someone, who most certainly was watching us tread closer and closer, attempts to permanently dissuade us from following her path."

The three sat in silence while they mulled the facts over. Finally, Boudreaux spoke. "What would you surmise happened to Miss Rogers, Sergeant Woodson?"

"I believe she was set upon, most likely by one individual, such as a Naviation Officer who became obsessed." Woodson thought of his cousin's description. "He followed her, gathering his courage until one night he followed her all the way into the Ward, found her alone in her journeys, and forced himself on her. He discarded the body with haste to ward off discovery, but couldn't help himself. He kept her things, and then when he feared discovery and notoriety, cast them off, too."

"And the ring?"

"Perhaps greed overcame his fear."

Boudreaux nodded, thinking. Finally, she spoke. "How did the ring get to the pawn shop? Surely our officer, fearing discovery, would not have brought it himself."

"Perhaps he had an accomplice?" Misha ventured. "Or maybe some person found it?"

"Did the shop owner provide you a description of the gentleman who placed the ring with them for sale?"

"Taller than me," Woodson said. "Pox-scarred face, wispy beard. Stronger than an ox. Top hat, faded."

The light cleared in Boudreaux's eyes. "Ah."

"Ah?" Woodson asked. "What does that mean?"

"It means that your cousin's fiancée was a guest at the Sixpenny Temple."

Woodson recoiled. "How do you mean? How could you know? That..." He subsided.

Misha spoke, confused. "What is this—Sixpenny Temple?"

"It's a place for women who...find themselves in a certain way," Boudreaux explained delicately. "Its location is well-hidden, away from the vultures of polite society. You can find it if you need it though—every woman in the city knows the doorman at the Sixpenny Temple."

"The man...with the ring?" Misha guessed.

"Yes."

Woodson dropped his head into his hands.

Boudreaux spoke softly and slowly, choosing her words carefully. "A woman who finds herself in this way, without benefit of marriage, or at the mercy of a man who forces himself upon her—" Here she nodded to Woodson. "She may have no choice but to seek the Temple. And yet sometimes...complications occur. And then that situation must also be dealt with."

"My cousin's girl was not that sort." Woodson looked up. He patted his pocket again, feeling for the package within. "She wouldn't have just...he wouldn't..."

"There are only two people who know how it came to be," Boudreaux said. "And one of them is beyond confession."

"But, we have solved the murder," Feryusovitch broke in. "We can arrest the Temple man."

"And well we should." Woodson stood.

"Sergeant."

At Bourdreaux's admonition, Woodson sat back down.

"Leave her to rest, Sergeant." Boudreaux rubbed her eyes. "That doorman didn't kill her. The man who sent her to the Temple did." She sighed. "I will be leaving here tomorrow. It's time for us to get back to work."

"And the Commissioner?"

"The hell with the Commissioner." Boudreaux covered a yawn. "We tell him—reinstate us and have no more talk of letting us go, or we will tip the yellows and they'll swarm all over the club, the secondhand shop, and the police force like hungry bears over wild honey. And elections are coming, besides."

"So now, we play politics as well?"

"I prefer to think of it as keeping ourselves employed." Boudreaux closed her eyes. "Let us return to our place of employment tomorrow. There are many others out there who await our particular talents."

## CODA

### Special to the New Orleans Messenger

### EXTRA, EXTRA: DEATHBED CONFESSION REVEALS TRUTH BEHIND CIGAR GIRL SCANDAL

The stunning admission of a well-known and upstanding boarding house proprietress, Mrs. Susannah Chivers, has cast new light on the series of sad events chronicled in this paper a mere six months ago.

Mrs. Chivers, long suffering from a mysterious, fatal malady, made call upon this newspaper, claiming she had something to confess before God and the people of the Free City of New Orleans.

Upon questioning, she admitted she had "treated" Mellie Rogers, who had been a guest in her unofficial infirmary, known in local parlance as the Sixpenny Temple. Under her ministrations, Miss Rogers had suffered a complication and the loss of her life due to her grievous wounds.

This admission brings a final conclusion to this sad tale, which saw the only suspect arrested, her fiancé Saint-Eustis Jones, hang himself in his cell while under suspicion of murder. With his death, the Commissioner of Police closed the chapter to the story of the Beautiful Cigar Girl, which must now be once again opened.

The sad events of Miss Rogers' death demonstrate the need for a reformed police force, one which approaches the investigation and prosecution of crime with a more systematic and scientific method of policing.

As of press time, the Commissioner returned no comment.

*A futurepunk story inspired by "Mellonta Tauta"*

DeClerck, AR. Author. Mother. Wife. Reading ninja. Food assassin. All-around goofball. Self-proclaimed nerd.

AR was born and raised in Western North Carolina amidst grand mountains and gorgeous scenery. She now lives along the mighty Mississippi in Illinois with her husband, two daughters, two dogs, and a cat.

AR is a dialysis technician, and spends her days helping people with kidney disease lead productive, healthier lives.

Blog/Website:
<u>www.amyreadsandwrites.blogspot.com</u>

AR DECLERCK

# Things Of The Future

# A MOST CURIOUS LETTER

July 3161
New London
Empire of His Royal Majesty Emperor Haruto James Johanssen III

I rose from my chair at the sound of the postman. He handed me my delivery with a creaky bow before scuttling off to the next door, his wheels clattering against the brickwork. I frowned down at the message cube in my hand. It was rather odd to see an older model such as this, and especially at half past thirteen on a quiet Shineday.

"Who was it, darling?"

Islevetta, my wife, bustled about me in the parlor, straightening the pillows and shooing Percival, the cat, from the settee. Her byzatium hair waved lazily about her head, and she occasionally pushed the living strands aside as she worked. Against her navy skin it was quite the contrast, and still a striking figure she cut as she smiled at me, bathed in the red light of the youthful second sun.

"A most curious letter." I held up the cube. "I quite think the old man is up to his tricks again."

Islevetta's smile grew with her mirth as she took the cube from my hand to hold it up to the light. Lunarian eyesight was twenty times my own, and she handed it back to me with a nod. "'Tis your brother, indeed."

I bussed her cheek, the smell of her an aphrodisiac to me still, after many years of pleasant marriage. "Though why he sends me this old thing I cannot imagine."

Vetta's hand was soft on mine as she moved away to collect our afternoon tea from the table. She knew how I worry for my brother in

48

his travels, and she was ever my voice of reason. "At least he is well. I'll leave you to it, but dinner is at nineteen."

I nodded absently as she closed the door, my eyes locked on the cube. What manner of adventure had my brother come upon now?

I poured myself a snifter of strong scytch and placed the cube on the table before me. "Play message."

After a hesitant moment the cube flickered and a trembling image of my brother appeared before me. He was windblown, his cheeks pink and his smile wide. He clapped and laughed, making me smile in return.

"Ah, Vanguard, I am glad this message has reached you. I am many miles over the Atalantiac Sea as we speak, and I know it has been many rotations since we've spoken. Please, give dear Vetta my best." He rubbed a hand over his long beard and his merry eyes grew serious. "I have much to tell you, brother, and my time is short. Know this, we are halfway to our destination, having crossed the edge of Kanadaw. Soon we will reach the site of the Emperor's new Pleasure Garden, but I must share with you what I have discovered for I know this is of interest to you."

I leaned back in my chair, the seat adjusting to my weight and height smoothly. I shifted as the pillows plumped and my back received the exact amount of support the chair calculated me to need. Was I wrong to worry that I seemed to need more support as the years wore on?

I turned my attention back to my brother as he removed a long narrow item from his pocket. I gasped when I realized he held something very rare indeed. An item only referred to in obscure cristal texts. *Paypier.*

"I know you will recognize the significance of what I hold." Carefully, he unfurled the ancient artifact. The last shred of fabled paypier to be discovered had been a decade ago, the delicate stuff crumbling to dust when touched. That my brother held an entire long sheet, and one that appeared to be intact, was a miracle indeed.

"It is not the paypier itself that holds me fascinated," my brother continued. He turned the paper around to show me markings upon it, "but what this paypier says." He leaned closer to me, his smile wide beneath his beard. "A journeyman's letter."

I swallowed the last of the hot fire of my scytch and put the glass on the table, paying no mind as it scuttled off toward the kitchen to be washed and dried. I leaned forward toward the image of the paypier in my brother's hand. My lips were dry, my heart a strong tattoo in my chest as he stared hard at the artifact.

"Well?" I demanded, impatient. "What does it say?"

The grafik of my brother wavered, as if in his humor, and he cleared his throat. "Very well, I can feel your impatience from here. A most intriguing story, brother. Listen carefully, for this is the tale of a wanderer from the early days of the Alpha Lyrae."

I could not contain my gasp. The appearance of the second sun in the sky had happened a thousand years ago. No one knew why, or where it had come from, but something in this letter might give us insight into life on this planet before its appearance. Our scholars were rife with dissension in their hushed library arguments, some decrying our ancestors as warmongers and near-destroyers of our world with their greed and their science. Others said the rains wiped clean our world by sheer cosmic accident when the Lyrae ripped its way into our skies. We cared for our world, loved it as fierce, protective custodians of its great gifts. Were we once so careless that we had nearly brought our own destruction? I gripped the arms of the chair tight as my brother began to read, anxious to know these ancient truths.

\*\*\*

April 1, 2058
The Grand Balloon Skylark

Below us is the vast ocean that never ceases. I write to you from my perch high upon the pinnacle of our great transport. I find myself wondering why we cannot go faster, as other balloons pass us by at more than one hundred and fifty miles per hour and we move at less than one hundred. The captain says that we must conserve, but I find that what was once the peace of the blue waters below is nothing more than a sinister and lonely wasteland to me now.

I cannot say that I am not intrigued by the idea that nothing exists below us. I have seen ships on the waters, their propellers churning as they move. I might have worried that they will someday run out of fuel, but the captain assures me they, too, have perfected the drying and burning of the great *gutta pucka* fungi that provides fuel for us all. One bit of the pungent plant that grows upon the top of the sea can keep us running for days. The boats are far more crowded than our own vessel, the throngs of poor and unwashed below me eliciting my pity and some admitted relief that they are below and I am up here.

The question we all ask ourselves remains unsaid. Will we find land again? We have traveled much, from the only bit of soil that remained untouched after the great cataclysm, searching for some bit of terra firma that may exist across this ocean. None of us recall the days of walking upon the land, and I myself was born upon a ship much like the one I sit upon now. What would it be like to feel real dyrt between my toes, as my grandfather used to expound upon to us on hot nights. Even when we started out, the captain tells me, there was only that small island of sand remaining upon which to build our vessels for this trek.

How much time has passed since humanity left that sand dune in ships and boats? There is no real guess. Days grow longer now, and the dual orbs in the sky keep it light for twenty seven of our hours. The captain has a theory about this, as well, and he says that the rotation of the planet has slowed thanks to the appearance of the Alpha Lyrae in the sky. It is why the days stretch on to forever, and we age much more slowly than our parents and grandparents. Wiggins, the captain, has even suggested that we are as near to immortal now as our species will ever be.

I look, now, to the Alpha Lyrae. The cause of all this tremulous questioning of our fates. It is only a sliver of light upon the sky, the edge of something sharp and slick piercing the blue of the horizon. The tales of old say that it was us who moved, bringing our planet into its orbit. It smashed the Lunaria, an asteroid that used to circle the planet, and took its place in our sky. Pundit, the old astrologist aboard, spends hours staring at the light from our second sun. When asked about it, he has only to say that we have long believed our planet and our sun orbited something massive at the center of our galaxy, but we could never see it. Now we are set in a binary revolution with the Lyrae, trapped within its gravity, never to escape.

As I stare at the light of our apocalyptic visitor I recall the other tales of old. Once, we lived upon the ground, with only a bit of water surrounding us. We did not fly for long periods; we did not sail far. Then the Lyrae appeared and the sea rose up, smashing to pieces all of what we had built and leaving us only the ships that could survive and the few balloons in the air. How our species survived I do not know, but by the temerity and hard-headed refusal to die by our ancestors.

And so we live upon the sea, old friend, trapped and forever searching for land.

***

April 2, 2058
The Grand Balloon Skylark

Today was momentous. The whip of the wind smashed a man overboard, and he fell to the waters below. I watched as he waved and cried out for retrieval, but the rules are clear. His lifejacket and pale face were only dim pinpoints as we continued on. Is it not tremendous how the fate of the one has been overtaken by the survival of *mankind?* I cannot help but to wonder if such relentless pursuit of survival is what dooms us all, in the end. Is not one man's life as precious as that of the whole of our species? The captain says nay, despite my clever and witty debate.

Pundit and I sat in the afternoon at the helm with his macro-lens, watching the play of the planets in the sky. The Neptunian moons were of some interest, as the Lunarians built a temple at the Daphnis. Our astrological amusements were great as we watched the tribes going about their routines on what appeared to be solid ground. How strange to watch them through Pundit's lens and to know that they did not seem aware of our existence at all. Was it simply that the strange Lunarians, with their magnificently colored hair and skin, did not know we existed, or that they did not deign to care? Their exploits entertained us far into the waning of the day as the ship plowed forever onward.

I dared to ask Pundit of our ancestors. This is a subject he can speak on for days if I should let him. My mind has wandered to the last days of their great civilization upon the land. The rains came, we learned from our schoolmasters, driving us to the air and to ships to survive. It was the Alpha Lyrae's appearance that changed the weather. A cosmic disaster humanity could not have predicted. Pundit's ideas are more radical, though I have heard others express the same opinions. Humans were greedy. We chased power and did not care for the land upon which we lived. The universe, Pundit assures me, exacts its revenge on those who do not treasure its gifts.

Did we bring this cataclysm on ourselves? Pundit's answer is, "Likely". He tells me that the same science that built our ships built weapons of war so deadly they could tear the world apart. Perhaps, he speculated to me once, those land-bound ancestors had brought the Alpha Lyrae to the skies with their science.

When Pundit had gone to bed I stood on the deck and looked out across the water, shimmering with the light from the Lyrae. I let my hands go tight on railing as I worried over the future of our people. Perhaps we are up here because we did not appreciate the land beneath our feet. Are we here because we deserve to be here? We must cherish land, if we find it. We must never give the universe any reason to take it from us again.

***

April 3, 2058<br>The Grand Balloon Skylark

Something invigorating is happening. Pundit has spoken with a friend from a ship ahead of us. Something has been sighted, and perhaps it is land. I cannot bring myself to become excited at this early juncture, as the possibility sets my blood afire. Pundit has explained that an ancient learned man by the name of Aries Tottle once said that the world existed on a ream of straight lines. Lines, he insisted, that seems to curve but never did. By following a line one could always surely find his way. It was by Tottle's principle that the ships have been mapping their journey all these years. And now, by land, it is hoped that our homeland is within sight!

I stood at the ship's railing and looked out over the waters below us. The smoke of the ships below us rises this high, and it stings my eyes, but I looked anyway. I stared hard for some sight of this miracle of dyrt that might exist. Pundit joined me for a bit, telling me more of Aries Tottle and his followers who knew much about science and little about the true ways of the universe. Tottle, he laughed as he pointed to the Lyrae, had no idea that giant bugger was waiting to draw us in and try to drown us all, did he?

When Pundit left I kept my eyes to the horizon. The Atalantiac stretched on forever, but I rubbed my tired eyes as the wink of something in the distance made me blink. I squinted hard as a sound I had never heard roared from the ship. I looked down, the sound came from the boats below us, too. Soon the deck was filled with people, pressing against me to look at what had caused the captain to sound the alarm. All around the word was whispered but no one dared give hope to it. *Is it land?*

I pushed my way to the captain and he stared down at me from his wizened eyes in his young man's face. He was twice my age or more, but we could have been brothers in appearance. Without asking he knew my question, and because I was known to be a thinking man, somewhat of a scholar, he nodded once in answer. Something had been discovered by the ships and boats ahead of us.

\*\*\*

## April 4, 2058
## The Grand Balloon Skylark

The wait has become excruciating. Even Pundit cannot soothe the ache that lies within me to set foot on this newly discovered land. Even the word is beyond my comprehension. What will dyrt feel like? Smell like? Look like?

The first men to step upon the land have been sending frequent word. All is well. All appears safe. There are no words to describe what they see. I can barely write these words upon this paper without the shaking of my hand and the turning of my stomach. Excitement boils within me. We have removed our weapons from the hold. Weapons! Guns, as old as the Builders. Older than my grandfather and his before him. They are heavy and cold in my hand, powered by black powder and round metal balls that are said to fly through a man as if he were air. Nothing is certain, the captain has warned. All who travel ashore must be prepared.

I shiver with excitement as I write this. My family has long since died, and I am all that's left of us to see this place we have searched for. The captain has assured me that I may be in the first group to touch the land, as I will catalogue and detail our travels. I pack my bag full of paper and quill, the ink of the slithering sea witches carefully packed in cloths. I cannot waste nary a drop if I am to write of all I see.

Already we are being told that the land is newly risen from the water, perhaps a hundred years or less. Young, but it gives us hope that more of what lies beneath the water will surface. We will vie for space upon the land until there is enough of it for us all.

I am careful to keep these thoughts to myself. The boats carry as much disease and depravity as one could imagine, and they are not filled with kindly nor upstanding peoples. I do not know how we will handle what we find, but there will be blood, that much is certain. I know the captain has these same thoughts, as I catch his eyes upon me from time to time with his deep, worried frown etched across his mouth. He turns from me, but not before our eyes have met and our understandings are acknowledged.

I curse the slowing of time more now that I have something to anticipate. When the first curve of the dyrt appears to my eyes it is sure I will weep with joy and relief. A brand new start for us all, and the human race will once again touch their toes to the land.

***

April 7, 2058<br>The Grand Balloon Skylark—and Land!

I must write of this, the moment mine eyes have laid upon the land. It is green. A contrast to the blue of the water, it rises tall from the swell of the surf to a point against the sky. There are waving timbers jutting from its surface, and they, too, are covered in green. Nothing I have ever seen can liken to this sight. I do not know these things that I see, but my soul knows them. Some part of me that is primordial and as old as this planet knows what I see.

Trees, Pundit has informed me as we draw closer. The timbers are trees, and upon them lay lyefs. Plants, he assures me, of the variety that grows upon the land instead of on the water. He showed me his old book, translated from the ancient Innglitch that shows drawings of the plants. There are more, he promised as he tucks it into my bag with a pat, and I must draw and catalogue them all. We would need our ancestors to show us which of these plants are harmful and which are helpful.

I prepare to leave the ship for the first time since I was birthed upon it. I scribble this as the captain dashes about checking each man's gear and provisions. My gun is heavy and awkward as I try to juggle it with my pen. Now comes the moment and I stand tall next to Pundit and cannot explain the shaking fire that burns my heels and demands that I push ahead to the sight that lies before us.

Pundit has assured me that the ancient people of this part of the world were Ammercians, and they spoke the Innglitch that we find in many of our old texts. Their heroes, John the smith, Zachary the tailor, and Christfern Columbo, once felt the same trepidation we felt as they stepped upon their land for the first time. It is astounding to believe that history is repeated such as this, with man in search of land and freedoms for all of time.

My boots sink low into the ground below my feet. My knees buckle, unused to the feel of anything but sturdy deck beneath my heels. This ground is soft, reaching up to wrap around my boots in welcome. The captain wedges me upright and even he is smiling at the sights and smells of this thing that holds us. Land. I test the texture of the dyrt with my hands, and feel it grainy and somewhat moist. It smells much like the *gutta puka*. I touch a tree as we pass it, other plants clinging to our pants as if to hold us. Holding us with such gentle love, it seems.

The land welcomes us as well. The tree is rough, the outer edges spiny but running with a fine, clear offal. I touch that, too, and it is sticky. I am pulled along as Pundit and the captain keep my wandering eyes filled with sights of brightly colored balls at the end of some of the plants, and others with long fingers that wind around other plants and trees. I stumble as we come to water, running in a stream across the land. The captain kneels next to it and touches it, pulling back to tell us it's cold. Despite our warnings he dares to sip at it, and does not spit it out as one might the briny waters of the sea. We spend hours of time to remove the brine, but the captain has announced that this water lacks the brine all together. Enthused, we all try it, and I cannot put into words on this paper the crisp, invigorating taste of this water.

We walk the path the others have opened for us through the plants, and at last we come to a vast plain of waving plants. Not trees, but shorter, gently swaying in the breeze. Others from the ships before us are here, and they greet us warmly. The captain and Pundit wander off to speak to the others and I stand alone, amazed at the glory that lies before me. Surely nothing so precious has ever existed before.

***

April 8, 2058
On Land

*Plants*
Green, some tall, some short. Odors pleasant to pungent. Colored bells and tubules offer what seems to be procreating organs. Pundit assures me these are called flywers. Thrive near water and sunlight. Have prepared several from the ancient book re: edibles. No one has sickened.

*Dyrt*
Dry to moist, wetter if the land is opened up. Range of colors, dark to light. Pleasant smell. Plants grow from the ground with a system of long fingers that dig into the dirt and allow the upper parts to stand upright on the land.

*Water*
No brine. Rises from a protuberance in the ground and is cold and clear. We have deemed this "fresh" water, per Pundit's assurances that the ancient Ammercians called it this as well.

***

Have noticed some large protrusions from the land—Pundit tells me this is stone. Innglitch translation suggests the material from which the interior of the planet is made. Once, stone was removed from the dyrt by ancient Ammercians to build shelters. Some of the stone structures appear large; Pundit says they may be "churches." Ancient Ammercians built temples to worship gods called "Wealth" and "Fashion," if Pundit's books are to be believed. I spend hours examining the old structures as more ships and boats begin to arrive. For now, there is enough room here for everyone. How long that can last, I do not know.

I do know that we have begun to draw on our innovation and skill to create from the things the land has given us. Trees come down with tools and can be hewn into rough buildings to shelter us from the wind and rain. The weather here is temperate and so far we have been lucky to escape the storms that can whip the oceans into a frenzy. We have Pundit's books to give us ideas, and already small grouping of these shelters have arisen on the plain. Pundit calls this a "village."

More and more I am drawn to wander farther and farther from the camp. We have become aware of other living things here, small creatures covered in long hair with snouts and small black eyes. Pundit has taught us how to trap them and cook the meat, which is different than the sea witch and other ocean creatures we have always eaten. Sometimes it turns my stomach but my mouth waters at the thought of it all the same.

I am happier alone, looking for signs of the ancient Ammercians and drawing and cataloguing the things that live with us on land. I have come across many items that confuse and astound me. Pundit tries to tell me about them, if he can, but there are always more questions than answers. Will there come a time, I wonder, when this life is forgotten and we are nothing more than a question unanswered?

***

April 29, 2058
On Land

It has been some time since I have written to you. I do not know where you are, or how long it will be before you arrive. Many things have changed for us here on land.

More and more boats have arrived, bringing sickness to the village. Many died, and we quarantined the others to their ship. When they tried to escape they were killed. I do not know if this was right, but the captain assures me there was no other option. If they returned to the land, we would have all died. Now the boaters remain apart from the shippers, choosing to build their own village over a tall rise. We do not see them, and they do not venture to us. I have met one or two on my travels, but we avoid each other and do not speak. It is wrong, I think, to separate oneself from one's people, but I am only one man and the politics of this place interest me little. I have enlisted several of the men to help me dig beneath the land around the Ammercian ruins. This is allowed because I have discovered many artifacts that have aided us. One, a text chronicling Ammercian *meddicane,* has allowed a few of the women to begin treating the illnesses that arise. There are fewer deaths now, and less worry for the children.

Oh, to have been born on land! Imagine never knowing the deck beneath your feet or the sight of nothing but ocean before you. Several ships have continued past us, choosing to continue living the life they know rather than chancing the unknown here. Whether they are wise, or foolish, I cannot say.

Choose carefully, my friend, and if I see you again I shall be happy. If I do not, I will wish you much luck on your journey.

***

May 4, 2058
On Land

*Sunrise*
Today I have discovered something amazing! Our dig around the Ammercian ruins has uncovered a stone plateau, nearly three feet high and six feet across, inset with a plaque written in Innglitch. Today we will finally uncover the plaque and see the words written upon it by men who lived on this very land long before the Alpha Lyrae appeared. Momentous, my friend! And yet, I fear no one here will care much for what I find. Ammercian culture has aided us, and yet some of the things I

have found have made them seem foolish to us. Paintings of women in ridiculous clothes, with holes in their ears and noses and much skin showing makes many in the village wonder how much of Ammercian culture we should adopt. They are not wrong, I think, but this tableau is important; I feel it.

In the distant sea something has begun to rise. We see it from the peaks here, and as the days pass it lifts farther from the water. Long spikes of stone, and something Pundit calls *meetil,* adorn the massive visage of a woman rising from the ocean. Much of her nose is broken away, but her thorny crown and one massive eye are visible now over the break of the water. Who is this, I wonder? A god, worshipped by the Ammercians? An idol of Fashion, or Wealth? Pundit says these Ammercians governed themselves, the absurdity! Could this be the true leader of the Ammercians in all her glory?

Come quickly, friend. I would share this with you. I would share with you the discoveries I cannot share with the others. A book, filled with pictures of horror I cannot describe. Children, men and women, burned with fyre. It makes my gorge rise to see it but it is our history as much as the tales of glory.

Should I share these things with the others? Prove to old Pundit that his ideas of our past are true? Oh, friend, how I need your steady wit with me now! What should I do with these terrible things I have found? They could save us from the same fate, or incite us to strive for the same goals. We are doing so well. We are caring for our land. Disagreements are settled without violence, and seldom do we find ourselves without peace. For now, I leave things as they are and keep these discoveries to myself.

Hurry, friend. There is more to learn, I know.

***

May 12, 2058
On Land

*Discovery*
The time has come and past, my friend, and still you are not here. I fear you have been lost to the sea. Still, I must tell you what I have found. The

plaque, old friend, THE PLAQUE!

I pulled back the last of the dyrt from the stone and looked upon the words. Innglitch, which I have become adept at translating, was clear upon it. This is our history, you see, for all its absurdities.

So now I will tell you what was inscribed there.

# A CORNERSTONE TO THE MONUMENT FOR GENERAL GEORGE WASHINGTON

**Was laid with appropriate ceremonies on this day the 10<sup>th</sup> of October, 1847 the anniversary of the surrender of lord Cornwallis to general Washington at Yorktown AD 1781 under the auspices of the Washington Association of the city of New York.**

Some things have been made clear to me by this, I must admit. The visage rising from the waters must indeed be this General Washington, for who else could attain such glory? The glowering woman with the crown of spikes had managed to smite the dastardly Lord Cornwallis and gain the adoration of all the Ammercian peoples. This glorious monument had been erected to commemorate her glory in battle in some ancient city called New York.

The shippers around me burst into cheers when I told them the tale, and already stories of the mighty General Washington are circulating. I have little doubt that female children will carry the name George for generations. It is even a good bet that the next village will be called New York.

Now I stand alone and look out over the water at the figure of this Ammercian hero rising from her watery grave. Is this the legacy we have been meant to find? That always humanity will rise? I hope, dear friend, that this is truth. I have decided to keep my other findings to myself. Pictures of war. Of horror and terrible deeds. I have discovered that our ancestors warred often and brutally, and that they may have brought the Alpha Lyrae to us by way of some awful device that ripped a hole in the sky and brought the rain, just as Pundit had speculated. Rains that wiped away their civilization and opened the way for our own. Can we do better? We must! Should I tell these tales, I still wonder? Will that help us, or hurt us? If we know, we can avoid the mistakes of our forefathers, but we can also be tempted to follow in their footsteps. I struggle with this knowledge, but see the happiness around me and cannot squelch that. I cannot.

I have made up my mind, friend, and it was a difficult choice. My findings go with me to my grave. I tell only tales of the wonders of our predecessors, and not their evil deeds. Not their greed, or pursuit of greatness. Not the tools of their downfalls. I cannot tell of their disrespect for the land, a gift squandered and eventually lost. I must shape history now. I must make us great again. I cannot fail.

Now I must end this tale, and hope that we can see one another in the beyond. I shall throw this paper into the sea, bottled for you to find on some eternal shore. Keep my secrets, friend, and I will wish you well.

Farewell, my friend.

E.A.P.

***

## THE FUTURE OF ALL THINGS PAST

### July 3161
### New London
### Empire of His Royal Majesty Emperor Haruto James Johanssen III

I confess that I did not immediately speak when my brother finished reading the journeyman's letter. I sat silently in my chair and looked up at the twin orbs of both our sun and Alpha Lyrae. I pondered much of what the man in the letter had said, until my brother's shimmering grafik drew my attention again.

"Continue."

My brother rolled the paypier carefully and tucked it inside his pocket.

"Unbelievable."

His smile grew. "I thought the same."

"It seems impossible that the place he speaks of is the world we know." I rubbed my hand over my face, the glimpse into the past leaving me shaking. "So much has happened."

"But it must be," my brother insisted. His eyebrows drew close as he frowned at me. "Look out your own window to see the evidence of his truth before your very eyes."

I turned as he suggested, to look upon the fully erected statue standing in the waters at the edge of the city. She was tall, her arm aloft as if in victory. Her crown of spikes was broken as was her nose, but she was regal and most assuredly ancient.

"And does not New York still thrive, just beyond the borders of New London?" he continued on. "These are not coincidences, brother. This man was one of the first to step foot on the land of our sister city." The spires of New York were visible across the harbor.

"Amazing." I glanced up at Islavetta as she swept into the room to pick up a napping Percival, her wild hair dancing again. I imagine staring at the Lunarians from afar, never to know their beauty or grace! The thought saddened me.

"And so now we know the way the world was, just after the Alpha Lyrae." My brother folded his arms and we smiled at one another. What he carried could change the way we saw the history of our people; it could answer those scholarly questions so heavily debated today. We were survivors, and it was all chronicled by a man who saw the world as a place of beauty and hope.

"What will you find, brother?" I asked as Vetta left, smiling at me as she did. I turned back to my brother's grafik, my heart thundering at what he might discover. So much like the mysterious author of the journeyman's letter, he was traveling to an unknown land in search of answers.

"Much like our journeyman, I am excited to set my feet upon a new world."

I smiled at my brother. "Thank you for sharing this with me."

"What should I do with the paypier, Vanguard?"

"What you have most likely already done." I answered, and he chuckled at me, his grafik programmed with enough of his personality to understand my sarcasm.

"Are you angry, brother?"

"No. It is good to know it myself."

He showed me the bottle, and I watched him cork it and toss it over the railing to the Atalantiac Sea below the ship.

"I will throw this paypier into the ocean," he said.

"And hope it finds your hand on some eternal shore." I finished.

When the grafik went silent and the cube's light grew dim I picked it up. What remained of EAP's letter was encoded in this cube. Now I knew why my brother had chosen such an old model. With just the squeeze of my hand I could crush it. My brother was much like the journeyman. He cherished the land and the people who lived on it. He would never want to jeopardize our world with ideas that had destroyed the worlds of the past. But, he had left the decision to me, in the end. I could share what I had learned, or let it go like my brother and the journeyman had done.

I glanced up when Vetta popped her head into the room. "Nineteen, darling. Shineday dinner doesn't wait."

"Darling Vetta, come here, will you?"

She moved with such grace, and it stirred me, still. I pulled her into my lap, and let her hair coil lovingly around my arms.

"Is something wrong, darling of mine?" She looked at me with worry, for normally my heart was light and full of fun.

"I am troubled."

"The present from your brother?" she guessed.

"Indeed. It has me perplexed as to what I must do."

"Tell me."

So I recounted the story of our lost wanderer, trapped high above a flooded landscape. I told her of his joy and hope when they discovered land, most probably the land that lay just across the bay from New London. Our sister city had most likely been the first land these people had ever seen. I told her of my worries, that this story might shine darkly on the people who had come before us. Already the idea that they had been punished for evil deeds stood heavy in the minds of our peers—the world wiped clean because they could not keep it, and care for it. If I showed this cube to our leaders, would they use its knowledge to lead us again into those dark days?

When I was done with my story I stared broodingly into the fire until Vetta's hand turned my face to hers.

"The way seems clear to me, husband."

"Does it?" I shook my head. "I wish it was clear to me."

"Those who came before, he discovered that they brought their own destruction through war and violence?"

I nodded.

"And we have escaped those terrible ways, have we not?"

"We have." Our world was full of peace, full of light and wonder and hope. I could not bear to see it soiled by the truth of our past. We did not war. We did not strive for dominance above others. Our joy lay in beauty and knowledge, not the quest for power. Would this story change all that?

"The man who wrote this understood that the future is mutable. He knew that by destroying his discoveries he could make his people into better custodians of the earth they loved and nearly lost forever." Vetta pressed a kiss to my forehead. "Do not let his sacrifice be in vain, darling."

"What did he sacrifice?"

"He could be a renowned scholar; remembered even now for his discoveries. Instead he is a forgotten voice. He gave up his chance to be honored by the generations he molded, so that you could escape the darkness of your ancestry."

Her words pierced me. A man with knowledge that could change his world for the worse, but it could make him a god among men for its finding. I related to the author of the lost paypier. I held in my hands the same discoveries that he had so willingly let go of, for the good of his world.

Vetta stood and smiled down at me, her wild hair waving. "Come to dinner now."

"Are you so sure what I will do?" But I was smiling back at her.

"You are the man I have always loved. A good man, much like your weary traveler." She tapped the cube in my hand and walked away, the cat following behind.

I looked down at the cube and rubbed the metal with my thumb. So much power in history. Destructive power. It was hurtful to know that we had fallen so far that only a great catastrophe could bring us up again. I never wanted to see humanity fall so low again.

The cube became dust in my hand with one gentle squeeze. I tossed the remnants of the cube into the fire and stood, my heart lighter. This world was a good place, and I hoped that EAP and his friend stood together on that eternal shore when his bottle finally made its way home.

*A steampunk story inspired by "The Masque of the Red Death"*

Jeffrey Cook is an author living in Maple Valley, WA. He has published 10 books, covering everything from the *Dawn of Steam* regency steampunk series to the YA Fantasy Fair Folk Chronicles, along with some sci-fi, urban fantasy, and a nonfiction book about working conventions (just for variety). He works with an author's collective of sci-fi/fantasy writers based in Western Washington. Details on his books, and others, can be found at www.clockworkdragon.net

JEFFREY COOK

# RED SKY AT
# MORNING

T he Red Sleep began in the cities, spreading through the crowded populations rapidly. The plague set in with a shortness of breath and a feeling very much like water in the lungs. All color would drain from the victim's facial features soon after, and a terrible ache would set in, making the slightest movement—even blinking—painful. The plague earned its name from the victims' faces; slack and limp, despite their best efforts to remain alert. Their eyes would droop and lose focus, and, though the ache would not ease, the same sort of weakness would spread through all the muscles, until the victim first could not stand, then could not move to lift their arms. Long before death set in, the terrible burning pains through the body and the struggle to breathe would keep the victim awake and aware of every agonizing second; the body would be as if asleep, the mind trapped. At long last, the victim would either—all too rarely—awaken, pained, but moving and immune, or—far more commonly—blood would seep from their nose, the corners of their mouth, their ears, their tear ducts, and they would expire.

The plague was so contagious—and so inevitably struck those who tried to aid the victims, whatever precautions they took—that soon the stricken were left to their own devices, to find what comfort they could, and to live or die on their own merits.

At first, the crowded conditions of the city were blamed. The people did all they could. Buildings were scoured clean. The bodies of the dead were burned, as were all of their clothes, and then anything they might have come into contact with. Buildings were quarantined, and then destroyed. A bounty was put on rats, for they had been blamed for previous plagues, and thousands were killed. And still the plague swept on.

***

Through it all, Prince William insisted the plague had to end soon, and they would find either cause or cure and be done with it. In the meanwhile, he tried to keep spirits high with regular revels, filling the cities and townships with music. Many of the wealthy, who could keep some distance from most of the infected, attended these parties—though always wearing masks and gloves as a precaution. The common folk found little joy in it, commenting only that the Prince's festive music had become like a funeral dirge that no one could escape at any hour.

As the plague spread, William's words became more and more hollow, but he would hear nothing of ending his celebrations. Instead, determined to maintain the revelry and escape the Red Sleep, he decided to rise above it. He commissioned a new airship, trimmed in much gold and platinum, bedecked in silk, satin, and velvet throughout all the rooms. The crowning achievement, however, was the priceless stained glass windows.

Each one was but one color, but a dozen different hues of that color. A dozen shades of blue for the first, purple for the second, then green, orange, white, and yellow. When the light filtered through the panes—especially at sunrise and sunset, when the sun was lowest—and hit the glass just so, odd reflections of light hit the ship's deck, blending and shifting and dancing, depending on the ship's movement and the angle of the sun. The last window, however, was taken from a shop where the glassmaker had taken sick. It had been finished well beforehand, and was scoured clean, but the red glass still had to be delivered and installed by the ship's engineers. In the process, coal dust stained the panes in odd streaks and splotches, marking the red with black that would not come away, no matter what effort was made to clean them. Despite this, the Prince would not hear of leaving it off, and thus leaving an open spot where natural light might ruin the effect of the reflections from the glass panes upon the main deck.

He spared no expense in making sure all those allowed aboard showed not the slightest sign of the plague. His wealthy friends were simple enough, but he also made sure the ship had chefs and servers, jugglers and acrobats, and most particularly musicians. Furthering the precautions, he insisted that each and every man and woman who came aboard was outfitted with clean clothes, a full mask, and long gloves. No skin was to touch skin, and all that anyone saw of each other's faces were the eyes. There were no restrictions beyond this, and while the servants wore plain white or black masks, the wealthy guests wore all manner of carnival finery, and masks to match. There were porcelain masks with flowers, tear drops, butterflies, or other colorful decoration. There were long-nosed, macabre masks with overlarge grins painted on. There were demons, dragons, and mimicries of ancient kings and heroes. There were no two alike.

The ship rose high into the skies, and from so near the clouds it was impossible to tell the effect the plague was having on the land. The Red Sleep was soon all but forgotten, as the airship drifted where the winds would take it, using the engines only when necessary to stay in sight of land. The ship would land only rarely to resupply; occasionally dropping into range to fish, or to find those farm villages farthest from the cities and the centers of the plague, making sure there was no sign of it before exorbitant sums were paid for the finest bread and wine and meat. At all other times, the land and its cares were far away, and no man of noble blood set foot upon the earth.

Differing groups of musicians took turns, making sure there was music at all hours, should anyone wish to dance, or simply have the ill memories of the lands they'd left behind swept away. It was only when the bands needed to change, and twice otherwise, that the music stopped. No matter how the Prince paid them, the sailors and crew of the ship insisted that at the moment of sunset and again at sunrise, they needed to look beyond the glass in the direction of the sun. This small necessity came with a proverb, which the Prince shrugged off, but the crew put great stock in.

"Red sky by night, sailor's delight. Red sky by morning, sailor, take warning."

As best anyone could tell, it had to do with the expectations of the weather. Regardless, morning after morning, with the crew doing their best to stay well away from growing storms, and drift with the gentlest winds, the calls about the sunrise put the sailors at ease. While, night after night, the sun in the distance was red—as red as the plague they'd left behind.

Four months passed without a sign of trouble. The noblemen and women, hidden behind their masks, gloves, and fancy clothes, danced, and as the ship moved, and the sun with it, the lights danced with them—red in the earliest or latest parts of the day, depending on the ship's facing, and then each of the other shades of the stained glass, sometimes only blue, or only green, or one of the others when the sun hit just so, and sometimes the lights danced and mixed amidst the revelers, moving as if in time to the music.

The call went up one morning, "Red sky by morning." The crew begged the Prince to go below decks, to send the dancers and musicians and all of the crowd to quarters, that they might take down the glass, extend the sails, and try to run as far and as fast as the engines might take them.

The Prince would hear none of it, chastising the frightened sailors, insisting that he trusted in their skill, and the sheer size of his airship, and the good fortune they'd enjoyed so far. Instead, as he'd done before when the news seemed worst, the Prince tried to dispel it with the greatest of his parties yet. The entertainers were all called at once, that no part of the deck would be without spectacle, and he called all of his friends to come and enjoy the day. He had the cooks and servers prepare a feast, holding nothing back. Wine flowed freely, and the Prince looked upon all he had wrought, and was pleased.

A shift in the wind moved the ship about, and the blues and whites of the reflections abruptly shifted. The sun struck the uneven red pane, disappearing where the streaks of coal dust marked it, and uneven shadows played amidst the dozen shades of red that danced over the revelers as midday neared.

A singular figure that none could recall joined the dance. The figure was slender, wearing trousers, polished shoes, and a shirt of black. The jacket and top hat, however, were of the richest red crushed velvet, soft to the touch. The mask was the simplest of all the revelers, plain white porcelain, but wherever the figure moved, the light through the red window always caught it, dancing red lights shifting across the reflective surface.

None recognized him, but such was the revelry and macabre spectacle that he barely drew attention at first. He moved with a grace to shame

73

the most professional of dancers, making long strides while barely seeming to step, almost gliding across the deck of the ship.

He offered his black-gloved hand to a young woman, taking a turn with her about the floor. And then he moved to the next partner, at first surprising a young gentleman in a demon mask, but offering the dance with such smooth suddenness that soon he, too, took a short turn—the nobleman hand-in-hand with the figure in the red velvet jacket. Again and again, a touch of the hand, a bow to a new partner with perfect grace and politeness, and then a single turn.

And after each dance, as the figure in red and black moved to the next partner, and the next, each of his partners found themselves wearied, as if they'd danced the day away. They moved to the wings to sit and catch their breath. Their eyes grew tired under the masks, and their bodies slumped, as with exhaustion.

Though normally forbidden to join the revels unless asked, beyond doing their jobs, the commoners and hirelings were not left without their turn in the great party. The figure danced with them all, and treated them the same. Highborn noble or poor juggler, each received a graceful, mannerly bow and an offered hand, and none could refuse him. Even the musicians, one by one, received their turn about the dance floor, hand-in-hand with the figure in the porcelain mask and crushed red velvet.

The long shadows from the coal streaks and the dancing red lights hid the dancers and obscured the floor. Wits dulled by wine and feasting the day away, the Prince only took notice once numbers grew truly thin. It took some time after that to find the cause, with the figure continuing to spin and turn about the floor. And, though by now, many could see how several people rested quietly in the wings, watching only, so bewitching were the stranger's grace and perfect manners that none could leave the floor—or refuse him the dance.

The Prince struggled to rise, his half-drunk footsteps carrying him slowly. With even the sailors invited to dance, the ship rocked with the growing breeze, making footing more difficult. The figure did not heed William's shouts or demands that he identify himself. He simply danced on, closer and closer to the Prince.

They stood only a few feet apart, and all else was still, save the breeze, and with it, the rocking ship. The Prince demanded once more that the figure identify himself. The stranger tipped his head, as if questioning. As he did, the Prince looked aside, one way, then the other, anywhere but at the man in front of him. And everywhere he looked, he saw the same thing: guest after guest, crewman after crewman, all of their faces hidden away—tired eyes open but unmoving. And from the corner of each eye, streams of red ran down the masks in tears of blood.

The Prince turned back, recognizing the man at last, without a word spoken. And, when the figure, with perfect grace, bowed, and extended his hand, the Prince took it, and his turn about the floor with Death.

***

"And that is why," said the fisherman to his son, gesturing towards the sunset, "even though the plague has long passed, we still heed the warning. Most days, we take the boats out. But however rich or poor the fisherman or promised catch, if the sun rises red, not a boat leaves the docks. And if you look into the coming storm clouds on those ill-fated days, you can still see the ghost ship, drifting with the wind."

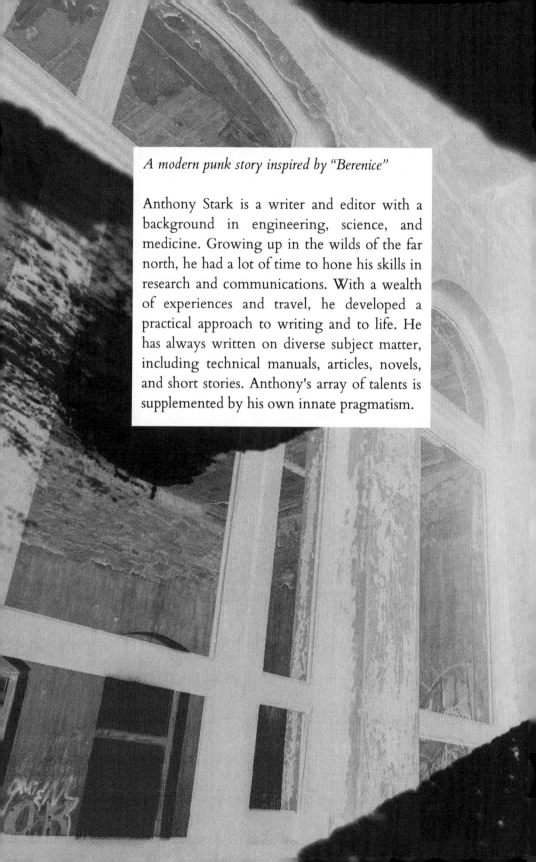

*A modern punk story inspired by "Berenice"*

Anthony Stark is a writer and editor with a background in engineering, science, and medicine. Growing up in the wilds of the far north, he had a lot of time to hone his skills in research and communications. With a wealth of experiences and travel, he developed a practical approach to writing and to life. He has always written on diverse subject matter, including technical manuals, articles, novels, and short stories. Anthony's array of talents is supplemented by his own innate pragmatism.

ANTHONY STARK

# THIRTY-TWO WAYS TO DE-OBJECTIFY YOUR LOVER

W̲e were sitting at a cramped table at the back of the cafe, watching a wannabe poet slam out a reading of something he said he was improvising, but sounded like something from Edgar Allan Poe. Beside me, my emaciated cousin Belinda shook her bare head emphatically at each emphasis. This was all so trite.

"Misery IS *Manifold!* The WRETCHEDNESS of earth is *Multi-FORM...*", he cried, trying his best to sound like grainy filmstrips of Leonard Cohen and Allen Ginsberg. I rolled my eyes theatrically and turned to Belinda to commiserate. She made a rude motion with her hand to indicate what she thought of the poet. She smiled a perfect smile at me as she did, two rows of elitist teeth shining in the dim light.

Belinda was no real relation to me; we were step-cousins, nothing more. But my father and my step-uncle had both bought a large oil pipeline company together when we were just toddlers, so we grew up together. Playdates here, vacations to Disneyland there. Belinda was the only girl I knew who understood from our earliest days the horrible, devastating desolation that came with all the fine vacations and latest gadgets our dads bought for us. She understood just how meaningless they were, even as her mother put Belinda's long, flowing blonde hair into ringlets for school each morning.

My cousin Belinda wasn't about the ringlets, nor was she about the Lincoln Navigator in which we were driven to private school. No, Belinda was into the hard, gory, *real* parts of life. She was reading the sort of thing this guy was belting out to atonal saxophone noise when she was eight. She was the first girl in our school to get a nose ring.

She was also the first girl to get a tattoo—it read in Arabic, "My friends told me that if I had visited my friend's grave, my sorrow would for a while be relieved." It was awesome, all the squiggles and diacritical marks nested in on each other. I traced my fingers over her forearm where the letters were indelibly marked. Her mother had cried at the permanent defacement of her daughter's lily-white skin. Her father had threatened to get it removed with laser surgery.

"Whatever," Belinda had said, tossing her long blonde hair out of her eyes. "I'll just get another one there again."

So the tattoo had stayed and been joined by many more in the succeeding decade; but the hair had left her head. Just recently, too. I had come back from my political science class at the University of Washington, my head reeling with thoughts of just how *foul* our parents were for helping out the global, blood-soaked Imperialist, Military-Industrialized Oil Cartel. I was bursting with things to tell Belinda. For that's what we had always done—helped each other to make us more real in the world, less cardboard cut-out Kens and Barbies.

My topics for discussions of mutual loathing died on my lips as I saw my cousin. She had the afternoon off from class and had used it to make the ultimate statement against 'femininity as product,' or that's what she explained her wild self-mutilation had been. I stared at her, my intellectual equal, the lofty, nonpartisan love of my life—she had shaved off all of her hair.

Chopped it off, to be exact. Hacked at it with the straight razor I had insisted on using, even though I wound up with a series of tiny, stinging cuts on my jaw and neck every time I used it. Having one was a man's statement that he was above the Madison Avenue scams of buying disposable razors and shaving creams. It was stylish to have one, stylish to use one... stylish to cut oneself with it in polite, horizontal welts on one's forearms to release the pain of being born so hideously, unalterably privileged. The straight razor was never something I thought Belinda would have used on herself, not on her hair.

There was a pile of golden curls in the bathroom, still floating idly to the floor from the vanity and the bathtub ledge. In front of that cascade of curls stood my Belinda with a bloody scalp, tufts of hair maybe an inch long sporadically interspersed with scalp shaved to the skin... and in some places, beyond.

"No one's ever going to mistake me for a plastic-fantastic goody two-shoes again," she said with satisfaction. She slicked the blood off the razor on the thigh of her ripped, skinny jeans and snapped the blade shut.

Belinda pressed the closed razor into my palm as she breezed past me into the kitchen.

"Gawd, I could use a drink," she yawned as she walked down the unpainted hallway.

At once I was crimson with shame. I had reacted to her bold statement in the most heinously masculine, controlling way possible. I had dropped my jaw in shock; I had been appalled to see her take her hair from me. Hair that, as I could plainly see now, I was enjoying like it was a possession. I was horrified that she had removed it, but why? It was her hair, wasn't it?

I repeated that over and over to myself as I threw up in the toilet, kneeling amongst Belinda's discarded locks. I was sick with myself for treating her like an object, for admiring things on her that just happened to be beautiful. She couldn't help that; it wasn't her fault. I was a pig.

Belinda interrupted my self-chastisement by calling my name. At once I came out of my disgusted reverie; she sounded concerned.

"Egg," she whispered. "I think there's something wrong with me."

I looked up, wiping my mouth with some toilet paper and flushing the toilet as I did. My face wore one of shock once again, but this time it was concern for my cousin. Her head was still bleeding where she had cut it. Blood had pooled around her collar, and her face was ashen white.

"It won't stop bleeding," she murmured, and collapsed into my arms. It would have been a perfect scene of gothic romance to have savored if I hadn't been so worried about her.

I called an ambulance. They bandaged Belinda's head and took her to the hospital; I rode along, answering questions. Belinda had not yet regained consciousness; she lay like a china doll in the stretcher.

The damn ambulance attendants were so bourgeois, they kept asking questions about Belinda's mental health. Was she on any medication, had she gone off any medication? Was she currently in psychiatric care? Had she taken any drugs today, was she a user? Come on, now, we won't report her, we just want to know... was she a drug user?

Filthy establishment freaks. I gave them a piece of my mind while we sped to the hospital, all about how a woman had a right to do to with her body whatever she wanted, and they were pigs to label her as a criminal or as "mentally unstable" just because she did. Typical.

The attendants were glad to hand Belinda and me over to the ER doctor; I was more glad to be rid of them and their suspicious questions. The ER doctor had none of those—he just ordered a tox screen and complete blood workup. I was about to lay into him about the same labelling when he cut the bandages off of Belinda's head.

The blood was unclotted. It still came oozing out in a steady, relentless stream.

"We're gonna need two units of O neg here!" the doctor cried. I fell back into the chair, queasy beyond belief at the sight of my beloved's lifeblood oozing out of her, unable to stop. The last thing I saw before I lost consciousness was them threading a small tube into the vein on Belinda's hand.

***

What can I say about those days in the hospital that came next? I got permission to take a leave of absence from school to tend to my cousin and got her a leave as well. Our parents showed up in their Polo shirts and their Donna Karan suits and cooed over Belinda and cried over her bald scalp and demanded in loud voices to know what was wrong with her. In a few days the results came back: multiple myeloma.

"What is it?" I asked, bewildered. "Some sort of cancer?"

Beside me, my stepmother pounded her clutched fist into her chest and started to cry. My step-uncle took off his glasses and rubbed his hand over his face.

"She's so young, so young!" my stepmother cried. "Our father, and our uncle both died of it, but they were old!"

The oncologist nodded in sympathy. "There is certainly a genetic component of the disease, and you're right, it usually does affect older people. But sometimes... well, sometimes it strikes people in their prime. With an aggressive course of chemotherapy and radiation treatments—"

Belinda sat up in bed. "No," she declared. Around her, the family started into an uproar. From my seat in the corner of the room, I caught Belinda's eye. We exchanged a look reserved for kindred, enlightened sprits amongst a mass of the ignorant plebes. I smiled, so proud of her for her integrity.

"All these therapies are taking medical care away from people who could really use it," Belinda told them, her face pale and resolute. "There's so much money that goes into researching and treating these 'rich people' diseases, and no money goes into health care and research for problems that affect the poor or the disadvantaged." She lay back on the pillows. "I'm not contributing to that imbalance of medical care."

"Damnit, Belinda!" her father, cried. "They've already poured the money into these treatments—you might as well get them!"

"Your dad's right," the oncologist told her. I looked over at him with disgust as he was pimping out his expensive medical advice to her. "These treatments are designed just for this cancer, Belinda... if you don't take them, they only go to someone else who has it, too."

"Then give it to someone with this multiple thingy who's poor," she said, closing her eyes and ending the discussion on the subject.

"This condition is far advanced, Belinda. If you don't get treatment," the oncologist warned, "your life expectancy is only about a month. Maybe less."

Our dramatic family cried and lamented loudly as the doctor took one last, significant look at my cousin and left. Belinda kept strong, though, even as her body faded; she took no treatment from people who needed it most but spent her last days enjoying the best of life with me.

So it was that we wound up in that crowded cafe, listening to the crappy oration of that wannabe poet. Belinda didn't have long left; she was nothing but skin and bones. She was bruising more and more, unable to keep down anything but weak tea and broth, the occasional lentils. Her scalp had healed, somewhat.

I had become enamored of the beauty of Belinda's bald, savaged head. She was absolutely correct—without her hair, the true attractiveness of her as a being was made apparent. I marvelled at her, her strength, her beautiful smile.

Her smile had always been lovely; her parents had made sure of that. Belinda had thousands of dollars in orthodontics when we first met each other; she wore headgear and braces the first couple of years we went to middle school. All that waste of money had left Belinda with an amazing dentition, however. Without her hair to distract from it and render it more "cookie cutter," I began to realize that

Belinda had an actually *perfect* smile. With actually *perfect teeth.*

They were white, they were perfectly spaced. They were clean and well-formed. A perfect example of the upper middle-class income that had made them. I found myself staring at her teeth poking out like ivory tombstones from her soft lips as she spoke. I was in love with them—in lust with them—and then, it occurred to me as we sat in that cafe, the truth. I was *objectifying them.*

I was objectifying Belinda. Again. As she died. I took one more look at her teeth, so white, so *strong*, so perfect, then excused myself hastily. I pushed through the crowd of standing hipsters watching the poetry slam, trying to get to the washroom.

I barely made it into the men's room before the bile hit my own teeth. I vomited into the sink, disgusted with myself again for having fallen so short of Belinda and her message. I splashed some water on my face and blotted it off with a paper towel, careful not to wipe off any of the eyeliner I had on.

Behind my closed eyelids, Belinda's beautiful teeth, upper and lower, swam before my mind's eye. Exclaiming in frustration and despair, I threw the towel away from me and went back to apologize to Belinda.

The scene that greeted me when I re-emerged into the club was transformed. The lights were on high and the poetry slam had stopped. A red and white pulsing light was streaking the walls and ceiling, from the parked ambulance outside as I shortly saw. There was a crowd of people standing in a ring around a table near the back—the table where I had left Belinda.

I pushed my way through them all, more harshly than before, until I reached the center. Two more ambulance attendants were trying to resuscitate my beloved step-cousin. They had cut open her Ramones t-shirt and were performing CPR on her emaciated breastbone. Two pads were stuck to her chest, connected up to a machine.

"She just collapsed," somebody said to somebody else.

"Probably an OD," someone else said.

"She's not a drug addict!" I cried in fury. "She's got cancer! Multiple myeloma!" I turned and cast a withering glare at the speaker, who looked down and away and melted back into the crowd.

The ambulance attendant pumping my beloved's chest looked up.

"Do you know if she's in treatment? Who's her doctor?"

I knelt down beside her where she lay. "No, she didn't want treatment. Doctor Stein," I added.

The other attendant, who was manning a bag attached to a mask fitted to Belinda's mouth, looked up at a fireman. "You want to take over here? I'll go call Stein, see if she's got a DNR."

I watched as the two emergency responders exchanged places. They did it smoothly, barely missing a squeeze on the bag. Even through the thick plastic of the mask, I could see Belinda's perfect, glistening teeth—the only thing that despoiled this act of selfless giving that she was displaying. She looked a perfect ascetic, devoted to the essence of intellectualism—except for those teeth. They made her look like a cheerleader, like a child's Barbie who had been sheared by a thoughtless pair of safety scissors and dressed in second-hand doll clothes. Those teeth were a travesty.

The next day and night were horrible. The ambulance attendants had been instructed to try to get her to the hospital where Dr. Stein would be waiting. They stopped every five minutes along the I-5, shocking my beloved, but to no avail. She still valiantly refused to live any longer a decadent life of privilege. I was crying, but with pride. The only marring of this uplifting finale to Belinda's brave life was that set of orthodonticized teeth. I watched them through the mask, hating what my step-parents had done to her.

Dr. Stein called her death when she arrived at the hospital. It had been forty-five minutes of constant CPR with not so much as a pulse. He filed the DNR Belinda had signed along with her death certificate. Belinda was taken first to the hospital morgue, then to a fancy funeral home at the behest of her parents.

I went with them at their request to make the funeral arrangements. Her mother had brought a *Big Brown Bag* from Macy's that she gave to the undertaker between sobs. In it was a set of pastel makeup that Belinda hadn't used since she was fourteen, a dress her mother bought her for Christmas but which made her look like a Jehovah's Witness, and worst of all, a long, blonde wig.

I balled my fists up with rage but said nothing. They had so the wrong idea about who Belinda was, who *my* Belinda was. They had marred her in life with those teeth, and they wanted her marred for all eternity as she rotted in the ground with these materialist trappings.

I wasn't going to let that happen.

It was easy to look over the shoulder of one of the receptionists to get the code for the alarm system; easier still to steal a spare set of keys for the funeral home. There was absolutely no way I was going to let Belinda go to the great beyond scarred with thirty-two permanent reminders of just how wasteful she had been forced to be. I bet that the undertakers would have a hard time making her look like a cheerleader without all those artificially perfected, beautiful teeth—even with her mother's chosen accoutrements.

I returned late that night, the night before the viewing, armed with a pair of vice grips. I would liberate Belinda in a way that she would have appreciated, had she lived. Because of her illness, we never got a chance to discuss that particular objectification that had been inflicted upon her, but I knew that she would approve. The cancer cut her down before she had a chance to make herself more Real, less perfect like her parents wanted.

I was terrified that the alarm code might not work when I entered it, that maybe it would somehow *know* that I didn't work there. I stood in the hallway in the dark, panting in fear, wondering if someone was going to show up. After ten minutes of limbo, I realized that I was safe. I was in. It worked.

Shaking, I crept downstairs to the room where Belinda lay. I risked turning on the light, even though there were two small, frosted windows that rested slightly lower than street level. I needed light to give Belinda this last freedom from objectification; it was a risk I was willing to take. It was easy to find the drawer that had her in it; I pulled out the gurney and removed the sheet.

There she was, my beloved step-cousin. So vibrant with her intellectual acuity, so strong of conviction, so wonderful with her insights into the many sources of materialist slavery. I stroked her cold forehead, where before I would have brushed away her hair. Nodding to her, I opened her mouth. Her jaw clicked stiffly and was hard to open, like forcing a rusty hinge.

I started to cry. The sensation of her rigid, lifeless muscles resisting me as I opened her mouth brought it all home. Belinda was dead. I took out the pliers.

A voice said in my mind, *Are you really going to do this?*

"Of course I am," I answered, determined. "For Belinda."

Then I began to Grip.

And Twist.

And Pull.

And again. And again. And twenty-nine more times. I set the teeth, perfect, beautifully kept by our family's illicit oil dollars, on a paper towel I laid on Belinda's chest. In the end, the pliers were greasy with blood and ichor, my hands were aching, but Belinda was free. Free of her orthodontic labels. Free of her dental chains. A spirit, devoid of any objectifying beauty. She was ghastly, her frozen mouth wide open, her gums raw maws of indented holes. She was finally truly beautiful, not as Madison Avenue wanted her to be, but as she wanted to be.

I shoved the pliers and the teeth into my duffel bag. I pushed Belinda back in the drawer and shut the door, then ran up the steps and out of the building. I told myself that I was going to look online for some charitable organization that needed teeth—maybe they could put them in some poor homeless person. Or maybe they could make a medicine for people out of it, a tonic. I was sure there was something I could do with them in Belinda's name. I'd give all the teeth to them... except, maybe one. As a reminder. Of the dangers of materialism.

I fell asleep with the teeth beside me, my laptop on my thighs, in the crappy apartment Belinda and I had once shared. When I awoke, there were two metro police officers standing over me. One of them had just finished taking a flash photo of me, sitting on my own bed.

"How dare you?!" I gasped, shocked at the audacious intrusion of my right to privacy. "What are you doing in my room?"

"Edward "Egg" Eeyce," the pig with the camera phone said, "you're under arrest for breaking and entering the Porter Funeral Home."

Chills ran down my spine. I made a motion to grab Belinda's teeth, but the other cop took them from me. He slapped one end of a pair of handcuffs on my outstretched wrist.

"... and for the aggravated assault of Belinda Beren-Eeyce," the other cop finished. I was being manhandled into the other cuff, but I managed to whip my head to face him.

"What are you talking about, pig?" I asked, laughing. "Desecration of a corpse, maybe—"

"The funeral parlor owner dropped by just after your little stunt," the cop told me. "He got a call from the alarm company about an unusual entry at the facility. It's a good thing he did, too, otherwise Ms. Beren-Eeyce might have choked to death on her own blood."

"What?" I cried. The bile was rising again. "How—"

"It seems the young lady was merely in a deep catatonia," the one copper said as he ushered me roughly out of the apartment. "Your violent attack on her got her blood flowing as a result of the illness she was suffering from, which got her heart pumping, which woke her up from her coma."

"Congratulations, you sonofabitch," the other cop growled as he tossed me into the back of their car. "Your sick stunt just saved Belinda's life."

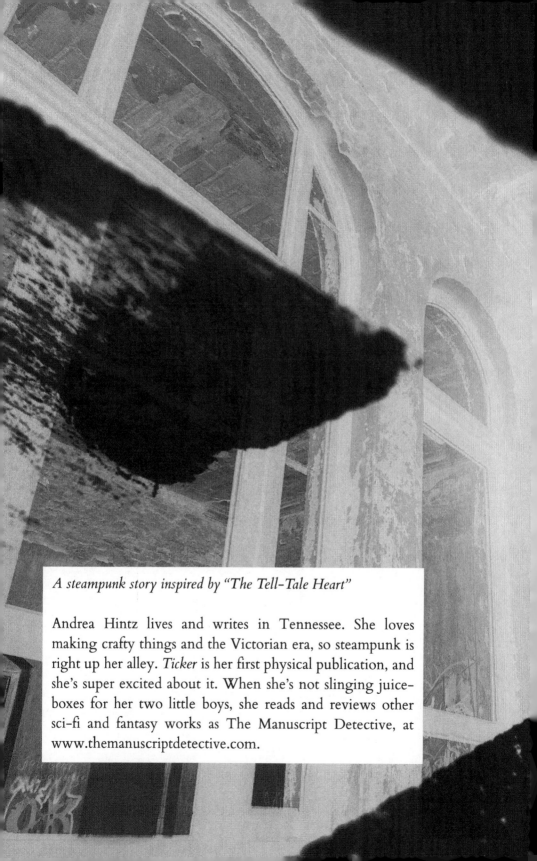

*A steampunk story inspired by "The Tell-Tale Heart"*

Andrea Hintz lives and writes in Tennessee. She loves making crafty things and the Victorian era, so steampunk is right up her alley. *Ticker* is her first physical publication, and she's super excited about it. When she's not slinging juice-boxes for her two little boys, she reads and reviews other sci-fi and fantasy works as The Manuscript Detective, at www.themanuscriptdetective.com.

ANDREA HINTZ

TICKER

My housekeeper claims that I haven't been the same since my apprentice Joseph died, that I am not quite right in the head. The poor lad. He was such an earnest soul, a real go-getter. Always willing to go the extra mile. I loved him as though he was one of my own dear, departed sons. Such a waste, those poor boys. Their lives cut short, all of them, and for naught. If only I could have done more, but alas, I could not. Perhaps my dear Mrs. Pittipat is correct, that so much death in such a short amount of time would addle any sane man's brain. I fear, though, that Mrs. Pittipat is only half right, and I am still very much in my right mind.

Joseph resided in my attic at night, and could be found at the table for tea with Mrs. Pittipat promptly at 2 o'clock in the afternoon, though where he went on his own time is beyond me. Often he returned with scraps and bits of metal about his person, claiming to have found them in a deserted alley. I've made it a point to note, of course, that I will not tolerate thievery in my household. Joseph said he came across his spare parts honestly, but one never knows, and it is best to get ahead of any negative situations. Joseph was a lovely soul, though a poor one, but he never accepted his station in life. I suspected he was stealing from other shops and put an end to it.

I have a new assistant now, Edward. He is a quick boy, minds the tools well. He has a lovely eye for the work. I never have to tell him twice, that one. Eddie, as that is what I call him, takes as much joy in the manufacturing of mechanicals as I must have, once upon a time, before all this recent unpleasantness. His attention to detail rivals that of some of our local masters, and very soon he will have soaked up all the knowledge I have at my disposal. I suppose I will lose this one as well, though happily to a better life instead of rotting away—quite literally—like poor Joseph. Terrible how that worked out, really. Though only time will tell, I'm sure.

On days on which we work together, and I provide instruction to

Eddie on the finer points of a particular mechanical creation, the time passes quickly and with a wonderful sense of camaraderie. My below-stairs provides ample room to work without our having to be in each other's way. The tools are spread around a large table, and often there are automata in various states of repair lying upon it. I specialize, you see, in the creation and repair of mechanicals, those of most use to my neighbors and friends certainly occupying the largest portion of my time. I have begun to give some effort to the creation of a more humanoid machine, privately, of course, though my recent attempts have not met with much promise. The human heart is a tricky, fickle thing to replicate in brass and steel, and indeed, quite a nuisance to test! Perhaps another opportunity will arise and I will rectify my earlier mistakes.

The work room maintains a low thrumming sound at all times—a dub DUB dub DUB dub DUB—due to the eclectic mix of electrical and mechanical equipment lining the walls, in boxes, on shelves, and hanging on hooks. A fair amount of those hanging specimens are repaired automata, though not one resembles a person in any way other than its capacity to walk upright! No proper limbs with which to gesture lovingly, no face with which to return a smile, nothing remotely designed to suggest anything other than function. Such love and effort into these machines! If only it could be returned to me, if only they could notice, just a bit, my sincere and undying adulation! Form and function, united into one perfect being! Alas, I fear that the time of such a noble beast is far from my own; perhaps young Eddie will be the one, eh?

I have neglected to mention one niggling fact about my Eddie. It has begun to weigh on my mind just a bit, you see. He has the most delightfully dedicated personality that I really should overlook it, but, alas, I cannot.

It is his eyes. His eyes are of two distinctly different colors. This slight imperfection did not bother me previously, when he was merely an associate of my beloved Joseph's. Now that we work in such close proximity, so near, every day, it pains me, I am ashamed to admit. I am haunted by that blue eye. The brown eye is fitting; his hair and skin are shades of brown, and the eye is a derivation of the two. But the blue eye—the blue is an abomination! Right in the middle of the tranquility of his features swims this azure orb, completely out of character with the rest of his face.

Oh, I *must* have it out. Eddie dear, I must, and you will not miss it, young man! No, no, no! I shall fix you a new one, Eddie dear, a glorious new eye! It will be a wonder, a marvel, a splendid contraption of the tiniest gears and finest lenses; you will never miss this blue devilry, my dear lad. I promise you that!

*What was that?* Is it you, my dearest boy? Are you here already, at the below-stairs door, now? Quickly, quickly! I am hardly prepared, Eddie; I wanted to be better prepared! Oh, dear Eddie, there you are, upon the stair. I hear you talking with Mrs. Pittipat, she asks will you want tea now? Perhaps I will take tea myself, dear lad, but after, after!

Oh, here is my special aether mixture—careful not to spill now, it wouldn't do to be sloppy; Eddie does detest a sloppy workbench. Sloppy will not do, not do…to the shadows, I must not let Eddie see me. Surprise! Oh, quietly, I must hush now. It must be a surprise, he mustn't see me, I cannot alarm him. Dear, sweet Eddie! I do not wish to harm you, but the eye, that terrible eye has vexed me long enough.

The door creaks open, and the hinges are so loud, I must get dear Eddie to oil them after, after. The door scrapes across the threshold and here is Eddie, clip-clopping down the stairs. Steady, steady! Wait until he passes by, there! Quickly, oh, Eddie, do not struggle! Please breathe, Eddie, into the cloth, yes, that's it, it's only me, my dear lad. Ah, the eye is closed. A momentary reprieve, it seems, as I haul him to the bench.

Delightful! My darling boy, we shall have you fixed up in no time at all. *Ooof!* Onto the table, that's a good lad. You have been eating more than your share of Mrs. Pittipat's biscuits! They are delicious biscuits, I do agree, whole-heartedly. Yes! Oh, here we are, adjust your feet just so, precisely! What a wonderful patient you are, Eddie dear. Simply wonderful.

Now, we must work quickly, lad. My aether concoction is much better than Eades' and a serious improvement on Bruckenridge's formula, but it is still experimental. I am still working out the proper chemical ratios, you know.

Yes, we must work quickly, Eddie, or else… well, we shall just have to be swift. I do apologize in advance; this will be a fearful pain. Just allow me to place the tip of my scalpel here, beneath the brow. Ah, Eddie, the first slice is always the sweetest, is it not? We'll peel back the skin, there's a good lad, minimal bleeding, excellent. I will remove the excess tissue here, and dearest Eddie, I am almost to it. The orb is almost within my grasp, such a slippery rascal. One last snip of the optical nerve, and it is done. Oh, joyous moment, I have long awaited you… *Wickedness, be gone from my sight!*

Lay quietly, dear Eddie, and rest a bit. Do stop that dripping from the socket, there's a good lad. I will return momentarily to implant the apparatus and stitch you up. My dear boy, you'll be good as new. Indeed better, certainly! Certainly better.

Now for the offending eye, shall I just dispose of it? No, no, something more for such a fiendish thing. Perhaps incineration? It might give a most satisfying *pop* before turning to ash, but, no. Not quite right. Shall I simply crush the thing beneath my heel? Hmm, tempting, so tempting. Oh! I have it. I have decided! Eddie, my dear lad, Eddie? For your eye, Eddie, do you want to hear it?

Oh, you cannot yet hear, of course. Hmm, I should fix that. Time is wasting, ever wasting, Eddie. Do you hear? Time is wasting! We must bring you back! Eddie? Eddie, you must be in there listening. Let me put this up for now. The vile thing is put away, dear lad, to be disposed of later, together, we can do it together, shall we? Would you like that, Eddie?

Dearest boy, what's this? You are covered in blood, and your shoulder is chilled! Eddie, we must wake you up. Quickly, quickly! The mixture was over-strong, so it would seem, oh, too much for dear Eddie, too much!

Oh, no, no, no! Not my Eddie! The mixture was too strong, Eddie, what shall I do? I told you to breathe, and you did, and then you did not. I did not say to stop, Eddie! *Breathe*! Never mind the eye, that blasted globe, I will put it back, just breathe, Eddie. No, of course it must stay out. Eddie, my dear Eddie, I will replace it, please, if you will only breathe.

Ah! You cannot. I see. I see, oh, Eddie! I see now, how foolish! How silly of me, oh, Eddie, I am so terribly sorry.

It is the heart; it has stopped. I see that now, oh, how utterly witless of me. I did not account for the blood loss. The eye, that blasted eye! Eddie, the eye is the root of it all, dear boy, blame that eye. If not for that blue ball of unholy blasphemy, we would *never* be in this predicament! My dear one, not for a moment did I think your heart would falter. I would have simply left you awake for the procedure…not ideal for you, of course, but I digress.

Your heart, dearest Eddie, has ceased working. It was too much, too much, I say! Too much aether mixture, too much blood loss, too much. Oh, Eddie, it was all just too much for us, was it not? Sad, so sad, and I thought you might surpass me, might be the one, but no—another lad lost. My dearest Eddie is gone, Joseph is gone, all my boys gone, all gone…

All gone. The heart has stopped, stopped, all gone, the heart, it was too much, Eddie. Oh, Eddie, you would have surpassed us all. You would have surpassed us all. You had the heart of a true master. I mean to say, you do! You do, and you will! Eddie, my dear, dear boy. It *will* be you, dearest. I will help, Eddie. I can do it now, I have had a thought, dear, sweet lad! I know, a thought! I must get started. Yes, Eddie, another surgery! Another, and another, and another, as many as it takes, Eddie. We will do it together, as we should, yes? You and I, we will be working side by side again soon enough, dear lad. Now, to prepare.

Eddie, I must think for a moment, and you must rest. Ah, well, just lay quietly then, no spiriting about. Ha-ha! Oh, how horrid of me, I *do* beg your pardon, Eddie. Something in the air, perhaps the aether, hmm? Now, on to the heart, remember, lad, the heart? Yours, sadly, is no longer viable, I do take all the blame, though you should recall the eye is what started it all, really.…

Yes, well, this heart, the artificial heart, it is a marvel, certainly, if a bit cumbersome. Though I believe I've a solution for that. Eddie, we will simply shrink it down to a manageable size, thus allowing it to actually fit into the chest cavity! Yes, it needs to fit into the proper place, Eddie, of course it does! You simply cannot be seen wandering around with tubes and pipes coming out of your chest, it isn't done. What would the neighbors think? Now, if I convert the pressurized valves to a smaller dimension—using smaller tubes, of course—then the pump can push the blood through at higher rate of pressure. Yes, Eddie, I do believe it can be done!

I'll just make a cut here, and here, through the layers of skin, muscle, and sinew. Eddie, poor Eddie, this is quite a mess we've made! Never mind that, this mechanical heart is a vast improvement over the one currently occupying your chest, I can promise you that! I just need to pop open the ribs and stretch them, yes, stretch them Eddie, wide enough, just until they crack.

Here we are, the unlucky heart, poor Eddie's dead ticker. Ha! Ticker, yes, dearest Eddie, indeed, do you hear it, lad? *Da-dum, da-dum, da-dum,* like a precisely wound clock, my boy! No, no, no, that is the new one, not the old, of course. I must dispose of it, the sad old heart, and clean up the blood, dear Eddie, the blood! Now here is the old, on the table, wait, what is that sound? *Da-dum, da-dum, da-dum,* Eddie? I hear something, but it cannot be…this heart, here, upon the table, Eddie, your heart, Eddie, your heart! Do you hear it? No, not the heart, it is a foot. Ha-ha! A foot, dear Eddie, and not even yours, your feet are still upon the table. It is a foot upon the stair.

Who is there? A sheet, a cover for your modesty, dearest Eddie. A visitor. We have a visitor, Eddie, look, the constable is here! Oh, if only you could see his face, he is simply astounded at your procedure Eddie, perhaps he'll put in a good word for us at the College, hmm?

Mrs. Pittipat is rather taken aback herself; what was that? I hear it, there! There it is again! *Da-dum, da-dum, da-dum.* He can hear it Eddie, the constable, I know he can hear it! Mrs. Pittipat too! *Da-dum, da-dum, da-dum.*

The heart, Eddie, *your* heart! They hear it! Eddie, it works! The ticker works!

*A cyberpunk story inspired by "The Facts in the Case of M. Valdemar"*

David Stegora is elusive and reclusive; one thing we know for sure is that he's the editor of *Dark Futures* magazine. Find out for yourself at www.facebook.com/DarkFuturesFiction and www.darkfuturesfiction.net.

DAVID STEGORA

# An Account of the Final Session of M. Valdemar

O f course I shouldn't be surprised the final surrogate session of M. Valdemar has caused a stir. We knew it would, which is why the decision had been made to keep it a secret, at least until we could further investigate the matter. I also shouldn't be surprised, despite my own best efforts, that a version of the account did reach the public and proceeded to spread like a wildfire. I'm told it has been trending on every network for more than a day now.

This is why I, Dr. Benjamin White, must now gather and record the facts of the session, both for the public record and for the CitySec investigators who are sure to appear at my door quite soon. These facts are as follows:

My greatest interest, and the sole focus of my research since my graduation from the Academy, has been the creation of true cybernetic surrogates. Not merely mentally controlled machines, but lifelike androids operated by a system which connects to the brain of the user and allows them to control, see, and even feel (with proper safeguards, of course) everything their surrogate does. It would effectively allow them to step into another life. It could make a daredevil of the timid or even a marathon runner of the handicapped. And I have had much success in this endeavor. I would even go so far as to say that I have a fully functional prototype of the system and need only fix some fine details in the interface and programming before it is ready for general use.

In the final stages of testing, an admittedly morbid thought came to me. Of the many scenarios we simulated, including how the brain would respond should the surrogate be destroyed while connected to the system, there had been one significant omission. We had yet to test what would happen if the subject were to die while mentally connected to their surrogate.

It remained to be seen how, in such a situation, the surrogate would respond and if there were a possibility for the consciousness of the subject to persist within the system for any amount of time as their body shut down. While brains had been mapped and digitally recreated in the past, this held the potential for something else entirely. Morbid though this idea was, it gripped me in a powerful way, and it was decided that the experiment must be performed.

Now, I could not simply connect just any subject to the system and murder them, for clear reasons both legal and moral. Instead, I set about seeking someone who could help perform this experiment. Before long, I thought of one M. Ernest Valdemar, an author of some note whom I had met little more than a year before. M. Valdemar, who resided in the western section and had for a few years, was known for his sickly appearance and nervous nature. He had been a test subject for me on a few previous occasions and had been of some small value in that role. I had always attributed the difficulties of his sessions to the failing state of his health, which he revealed to me was due to his being stricken with tuberculosis.

The poor fellow was born during the space of time when the American Reformation War was at its worst and vaccines which were standard before the conflict and have become so again were not available to be administered to every child. Our science is able to treat this illness to a certain extent, though this strain remains incurable. It has, however, been studied to a degree that a physician is able to determine with a startling degree of accuracy when the illness will at last take the life of the sufferer. This fact made Valdemar the perfect individual to aid me in one final experiment.

As M. Valdemar had no living relatives who would interfere, I approached him soon after to ask if he would help me with this. While I was not surprised by his agreement, the enthusiasm he showed for it seemed uncharacteristic. Perhaps the idea that some good may come of his passing brought a degree of light to his dark situation. Once his consent had been acquired and all the proper forms filled out, it was agreed that he would contact me some 24 hours before the time his medical practitioner determined would be his end.

Seven months passed before I spoke with M. Valdemar again, and that next communication was him informing me his time would soon be at an end. He had set the proper affairs in motion for his estate, and I sent a cross-city taxi to fetch him.

Half an hour more passed and the dying man was at my lab and wheeled in on a chair. While I had not seen him in some time, it was troubling to see the difference such a short time had made in him. His skin and eyes were dulled. He was so emaciated that his cheek bones seemed to have cut through his face, and some dried blood could be seen over them. When I checked his pulse, it took me nearly a minute to find it at all. Yet, in spite of all this, he seemed as mentally aware and sharp as ever.

Doctors Damien and Freitag were in attendance, and it is from them that I got a summary of M. Valdemar's condition. I was told that his left lung had been in a semi-osseous or cartilaginous state for more than a year and was utterly useless. Similarly, the upper portion of his right lung was partially ossified, the lower portion was covered in weeping tubercles, and much of it had adhered itself to the interior of M. Valdemar's rib cage at some point during the past month. Both physicians were of the opinion that their patient would die by midnight the following day.

As the doctors delivered M. Valdemar, they bid him what they intended to be a final goodbye. They had planned to not see him again should their prognosis prove accurate. However, I asked them and was able to convince them to return and check in upon him at one o'clock the following afternoon.

When they were gone, I spoke with M. Valdemar candidly and at some length about his approaching death and the experiment I proposed. He assured me that he was still completely willing and even anxious to begin. Two of my assistants were in attendance, though I did not feel comfortable beginning such a delicate thing without a medical observer of more skill than myself. We decided, therefore, to postpone the experiment until the next morning when a friend of mine, a man by the name of Theodore Leonard, who is a medical student at the Academy, could be in attendance. While I would have preferred to wait for the return of the accredited doctors, no offense intended to Mr. Leonard, the grimness of M. Valdemar's condition convinced me to begin early.

When Mr. Leonard arrived the next morning, he agreed to not only observe, but also to record, with an audio recording device, all that was to happen. What follows is taken from that recording and either simplified or copied verbatim.

*WHITE: I am Dr. Benjamin White. It is 11:00 AM on Sunday. The date and year are irrelevant but will be noted in the metadata of this recording. The subject of this experimental surrogate session is M. Valdemar. M. Valdemar, please state for the record your understanding of what we are about to do and your willingness to participate.*

*VALDEMAR: [indistinct]*

*LEONARD: I don't think the mic got that. Let me move it closer.*

*WHITE: Good idea, thank you. M. Valdemar, will you repeat what you just said?*

*VALDEMAR: I am to be connected to one of your android surrogates at the time of my death and for a time preceding it. [Coughing] I worry you have delayed too long.*

*WHITE: Thank you, M. Valdemar. Allow me to help you into the interface terminal.*

*[Sounds of movement, clicks, and humming as Valdemar is moved into the circular machine, the interfaces are connected, and the machine is activated.]*

\*\*\*

The interfaces worked as designed, and it took little time for M. Valdemar's mind to take control of his surrogate. For the next two hours, we performed basic exercises. M. Valdemar, via his surrogate, was acceptably able to perform each task put to him, though his response time grew slower as time went on.

At one in the afternoon, as we had agreed the day before, the doctors Damien and Freitag returned. I had them perform a brief exam on M. Valdemar while he was still connected to the machine. They informed me that his condition was as expected and that they saw no indication my experiment was having any ill effect on the subject. They stated their opinion that he did not have much time remaining, but that I was free to continue the experiment he had agreed to.

We continued some basic exercises, but we found M. Valdemar's reaction time had grown even more delayed, and he apparently could no longer speak. His breathing, by this time, seemed a struggle. After the passage of less than one hour, a deep and long wheeze came from M. Valdemar, his breathing ceased, and he slumped further within the interface machine.

The six of us present—myself, my two assistants, Mr. Leonard, and the pair of physicians—shared a moment of quiet in mourning before agreeing that it was time to remove him from the interface. Before we could do so, however, Valdemar's surrogate straightened up and slowly turned its head to look at the man's own body. I immediately waved away my assistants, who were about to begin the disconnection.

I asked the doctors to check the subject, and both indicated that they could find no sign of continued life. Likewise, the brain scanning equipment that is part of the machine showed no regular brain activity and only a very shallow spike when the surrogate moved, which it continued to do. It appeared to be slowly examining the room.

Several hours passed and none of us were sure how to proceed. Sometime after midnight, both doctors left but gave word they would return the following morning. M. Valdemar and his surrogate were both left as they were for much of this time.

At approximately three in the morning, I grew curious and used my hand to raise the arm of the surrogate into the air above my own head. To my surprise, it remained in place when I let go, and the surrogate turned its head to look at me. I called Mr. Leonard, who had remained but was sleeping on the floor in the next room, and reactivated the recording device that we had used earlier. What follows is a transcript of what came next.

WHITE: *This is again Dr. Benjamin White. It's now...sometime after three in the morning. Monday. Note that our subject, M. Valdemar, has been declared deceased by a pair of physicians but remains connected to the interface machine, and his android surrogate has shown some signs of activity.*
LEONARD: *His arm is still in the air. This is mad.*
WHITE: *Please remain silent unless otherwise directed, Mr. Leonard.*
[*Nearly one minute of silence. Whispering, when I privately apologized to my friend for my sharpness and assured him it was due only to my own fatigue.*]

*WHITE: As Mr. Leonard observed, I have raised the arm of the surrogate into the air. The surrogate has since remained in that position and is now looking at me. M. Valdemar, can you hear me?*
*[Several more seconds of complete silence.]*
*LEONARD: No way.*
*WHITE: Mr. Leonard, would you state what you just saw?*
*LEONARD: It nodded. It moved its head.*
*WHITE: I observed the same. Now, M. Valdemar, can you—*
*SURROGATE: I hear you. I am asleep. Do not wake me. Let me die like this.*
*WHITE: M. Valdemar, do you still feel any pain in your chest?*
*SURROGATE: No pain. I am asleep. I am dying.*

***

At that time, I felt that nothing would be gained by disturbing him further. We waited for the doctors to return that morning. They checked M. Valdemar and could still find no pulse or obvious indication of life. We then continued our conversation with the subject, a transcript of which follows.

*WHITE: M. Valdemar, are you still asleep?*
*SURROGATE: Yes, I am asleep. I am dying.*
*UNIDENTIFIED WHISPER: He's already dead.*
*[A few minutes of silence.]*
*FREITAG: That's enough. Just let him pass in peace.*
*[Several seconds of silence.]*
*WHITE: Perhaps you're right.*

***

The decision was made to leave M. Valdemar in the interface machine, where he did not appear uncomfortable, until he was truly dead. Three hours passed before the surrogate ceased its slow examination of the room. Upon another check of the subject, we determined there could be no life remaining in M. Valdemar. I was just opening the interface machine when the surrogate spoke again.

"I have been sleeping," it said. "Now I am dead."

It was at this time that Mr. Leonard fainted.

I had already dismissed my assistants, and it took several hours of debate among the four of us who remained before we decided to disconnect the subject from the machine and put the whole matter to rest.

As I opened the machine once more, the surrogate again became animated and started to speak.

"I am dead. Let me die. I am dead. Let me die." It repeated the words again and again.

Working on pure determination and terrified adrenaline by that time, I began disconnecting M. Valdemar. As I removed the cradle over his head, which allowed the mental connection, sparks shot from the surrogate and the subject's body seemed to erupt into flame which did not come from the machine, as far as I could tell.

It took several minutes to put the fire out. When we had, we observed that the flames had consumed M. Valdemar more quickly than I thought possible and little remained of him but ash.

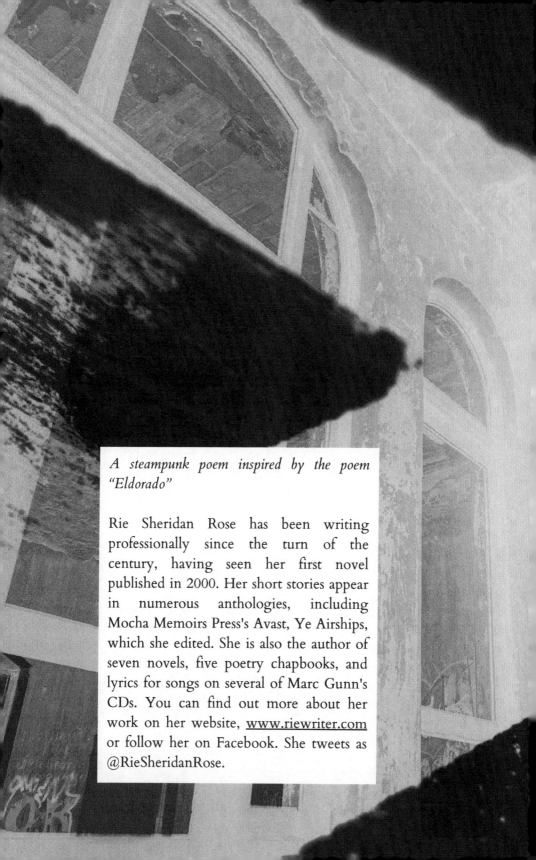

*A steampunk poem inspired by the poem "Eldorado"*

Rie Sheridan Rose has been writing professionally since the turn of the century, having seen her first novel published in 2000. Her short stories appear in numerous anthologies, including Mocha Memoirs Press's Avast, Ye Airships, which she edited. She is also the author of seven novels, five poetry chapbooks, and lyrics for songs on several of Marc Gunn's CDs. You can find out more about her work on her website, www.riewriter.com or follow her on Facebook. She tweets as @RieSheridanRose.

RIE SHERIDAN ROSE

# THE SEARCH FOR
# ELDORADO

*Gears screwed down tight,*

*Steam pump a-light,*

*Our airship rides the ether.*

*With crew of ten,*

*Captained by Ben,*

*We search for Steampunk treasure.*

*Eldorado of old,*

*With mountains of gold*

*Draws us through the ether.*

*We do not despair*

*Though we find only air,*

*In our search for Eldorado.*

Nan's on the glass,

The cry came at last—

An echo through the ether—

"I see gleaming gold,

As the legends foretold

A-leeward—Steampunk treasure!"


Frantic now, Ben turns the wheel,

Making for the mass...

But the sun going down,

De-gilded the ground...

Alas, no Steampunk treasure.

*A decopunk story inspired by the poem "Annabel Lee"*

Holly Gonzalez is a writer of speculative fiction, poetry, and the occasional tale for little ones. When not pounding her fingers and face against her ever-faithful keyboard, she seeks walks under the stars, cold beer, and pulling strands of future and past into words which rattle the soul. Find her online at:
http://hollygonzalez1.wordpress.com
http://www.facebook.com/hgauthor
and @hollygonz1 on Twitter.

HOLLY GONZALEZ

# The Envy Of Angels

*Waves tremble and weep with the secrets they keep,*
*In a kingdom by the sea;*
*'Neath the moon wan and pale, the wind moans the tale*
*Of a maiden named Annabel Lee.*

\*\*\*

I t was the first time I beheld the sea. Waves crashed into inspiration, gray upon gray. My fingers glided over the strings of my lap harp. I sang to the wild spray and the circling gulls, and my past rolled out with the tide.

Pattering applause startled me. I looked up, almost dropping the harp. A girl about my age approached on horseback. Her dappled gelding tossed its mane, rattling the bit.

"So sorry to interrupt you." She dismounted, the horse plodding behind her. "I heard your music up the shore. That was beautiful."

"Thank you." I smoothed my black undercut, hoping it wasn't windblown.

A smile dimpled her cheeks, and she sat beside me on the damp rocks. "What's your name?"

"Tristan of Steelbend." I was of the workers' caste, possessing no surname. Only birthplace identified us.

"I'm Annabel Lee. Do you live here in Hosanna?" She shook my hand, her kidskin glove soft as down. The emblem of the Seraphim glistened on the breast of her riding jacket—a pair of arched silver wings, worn by society's elite.

"No, but I hope to. I just stepped off the train."

"Oh, that's wonderful!" Brunette locks fringed about her ears like a mischievous halo. "You'll pass the examination easily. You have far more talent than the Sacred Chorus."

Pretty girls rarely paid me attention. I forced myself to stare at the sand instead of her. "That's a high compliment."

"It's true. I'm an artist, too. I ride along this beach every sunset for inspiration, but my brother doesn't approve."

"Does he disapprove of your art, or you riding here?"

She giggled. "Both, but I do them anyway."

I cleared my throat, feeling braver. "My parents wanted me to work in the foundries, but that life isn't for me. Not many in Steelbend consider music a profession. So, here I am, where people appreciate refinement. What sort of artist are you, Miss Lee?"

"I'm a poet. At least I try to be." Her azure eyes implored me, haunting as the sea. "Sing another song for me. Your favorite this time."

I set the harp between my knees and dared to grin. "Only if you promise to recite one of your poems afterward."

"Agreed." She leaned forward, tapping her riding crop against a tall boot.

"I wrote this one," I said. "It's about a man who drowns in a shipwreck, and his beloved searches the shores every night after."

Sorrow, rage, and dreams drove my voice. I closed my eyes, cold sea air circling through my lungs.

*"Not a sound did her foot make,*

*"Upon the breakers tossed,*

*"She watched and she waited,*

*"Many years and a day,*

*"For the love she had known and lost."*

When I finished, her tears glistened.

"There you are." I shrugged, though her reaction pleased me. "Let's hear yours, now."

She dabbed her eyes with a handkerchief, then withdrew a small device from her pocket. It resembled a compact mirror case, glossy black bakelite with a chromed geometric inlay of an angel. She flipped the lid open.

"My work is stored within the Sanctum," she said. With a cheerful beep, her interface nexus extended its miniature sensors. "Are you 'faced?"

I blinked. "No. In Steelbend, only administrators have such access."

"How is that possible? Everyone in Hosanna is 'faced."

113

She was so far above me in status. Would she understand? "Think of it this way," I said. "You don't need access to the Sanctum when all you do is pour and pound steel twelve hours a day."

"Oh. I see." She closed the device, and set it aside with no condescension. "Luckily, I've memorized a few. Here's one called, 'Awake, The Stars Do Fade':

*"Lift to the sky, ye slumbering eye,*
*"The hour of dawn awaits us;*
*"The stars above, the moon on high,*
*"And every dream berates us."*

Her words compelled me. I plucked an intricate accompaniment, and harmony soon flowed between us.

With an awestruck expression, she seized my hand. "I've never experienced anything like that. Your music and my poetry...they're meant for each other."

Her nexus trilled, a dismal interruption. She checked the caller's identity and hung her head. "It's my brother. I have to go now. I hope to see you again sometime."

"I hope so, too."

She winked. "Goodbye, Tristan of Steelbend. And good luck."

As the night emerged, she cantered away over the dunes. What a strange, charming, beautiful girl. Perhaps I'd find her here tomorrow.

I gathered my harp and bag and trudged into Hosanna, the wondrous Kingdom By The Sea. Megascrapers of tiered steel and concrete raked the darkening skyline. Overpasses and expressways looped across the hills and traffic lights smeared white and red. The propellers of a passing zeppelin droned above me. On the highest ridge loomed the Temple of the Seraphim, its bold spires aglow between shifting spotlight beams. The monument to the Archangels crowned the turrets—seven chromed figures with streamlined wings and arms flung high.

I strolled along dusky lanes. Shopkeepers drew window shades and locked their doors for the night. Contoured motorcars jostled and honked, chromed fenders pressing, while stylish pedestrians crammed the sidewalks. Many stares followed my threadbare cotton shirt and baggy plus-fours, and the wooden harp slung over my back. I ignored them, whistling as I made my way to the examinations office.

I entered the oldest part of the city, where the ornate buildings of the founders curved among the sleek angles of the modern. Loudspeakers blared the hymns of the Sacred Chorus on every corner. On the side of a municipal tower, a telescreen several stories tall flickered with a joyous broadcast. Congregations lifted their hands in praise. A dignified man appeared, blond hair combed to rigid perfection. His voice boomed over the plaza, diamond cuff links twinkling as he held a volume of the Righteous Code before the camera. "Have you lost hope? Sinking beneath the waves of life's little tragedies? The only way to peace is through the angels themselves, our saviors and guardians. I'm Pastor Benedict Lee of the Redemption Ministry, and we'll ensure your prayers are heard." His contact information scrolled along the display.

The examinations office welcomed hopefuls at all hours. It was a rounded structure of opalescent white, with blossoming trellises over its colonnade. Tall fanlight windows bore patterns of interlocking triangles, adjacent gas lamps casting cheerful beams onto the terrace. I stepped into its palatial antechamber with my cap clutched to my chest. Reflective stone adorned the walls in contrasting rectangles of blue, black, and white. My boots thumped against the checkered tile floor in a rude echo. Curvilinear desks and chairs were clustered in pleasing arrays around the room.

A solid granite bas relief dominated the entryway, depicting the arrival of the Seraphim and their great battle with the Devils. At the top, the Prodigal Star plummeted from the heavens, trailing brash symmetrical lines. The Archangels soared forth, their ridged pinions spread to the firmament. Their trumpets called for war, while the bestial Devils cringed below, fleeing into the tormented swirls of the sea.

As I admired its beauty, a uniformed woman approached. "Good evening. Are you here for the examination?"

"Yes, ma'am. How do I apply?"

She bowed her head. "Follow me."

A smaller chamber waited beyond the entryway. Unlike the reception area, blank stone covered every surface here. Six people waited behind a monolithic desk, the Seraphic emblem mounted on the front in a sharp silver arc.

A white-haired gentleman stood, gripping his cane. "What's your name, young fellow?"

I straightened my posture. "Tristan of Steelbend."

He cleared his throat. "A steelworker's son?"

"I was previously, but not anymore."

"I'm Chairman Ness, and this is the Council of Holy Reason," he said. "What brings you to our Kingdom?"

"I seek fame, and a career in music."

Chairman Ness glanced at his companions, frowning at their haughty chuckles and whispers. "What is your current profession?" he asked.

I lifted my chin. "I'm skilled upon the harp, and I possess a clear singing voice."

The chairman's smile widened beneath his brush mustache. "What a splendid diversion from the practical types we've seen tonight. Please, play for us."

I set my bag down, and strummed the first notes, a traditional lullaby my grandfather had taught me. It was a tribute to his memory and a plea for my future.

*"Fear not the deep,*

*"Sleep, child, sleep,*

*"The wings of the angels surround thee."*

My voice lilted over the room. I remembered Grandfather's kind smile as he'd instructed me on the harp.

"You have a gift, Tristan," he'd said. "If you use it well, the world will celebrate your name." His words had instilled in me the courage to leave Steelbend.

I concluded the song with a flourish, and the Council clapped.

"Most excellent," the chairman said. "Nothing pleases us more than the song of a pure heart. You're welcome in Hosanna, if this is your wish."

"You mean, I'm worthy to live here? You've approved me?"

Chairman Ness laughed. "Of course. We'll introduce you to the Sacred Chorus soon enough. However, you must make a choice. All citizens are interfaced with the Sanctum network, but we never force the procedure."

Being 'faced meant the surgical installation of an implant. I knew it was necessary to achieve my goals. "I accept."

The chairman summoned an usher. "Please escort Tristan of Steelbend to one of our guest rooms for the evening, and inform the stewards of his impending ascension to the Sanctum."

I thanked them, and retired for the night. The next morning, I changed into a simple yet dignified suit, tie, and dress shoes provided by the stewards. I discarded my old clothing with relish, reminders of my unwanted past. For nostalgic reasons, I kept my flat cap, a gift from my grandfather. A few connections to my former life couldn't be changed—my tarnished green eyes, so like my mother's, and the pensive expression I'd inherited from my father. I didn't care. My new life began today.

After breakfast, I received a surname and title before the Council. I became Mr. Tristan Herald, Bearer of Beatific Song. Chairman Ness' luxury motorcar waited for us in front of the examinations office. All black steel and sloping chrome, the interior smelled of pipe smoke and fine leather.

"To the 'facing clinic, please," the chairman said.

The chauffeur tipped his cap. "Certainly, sir."

We drove along a bustling thoroughfare, crowds of nobility and commoners hurrying toward the Temple.

"They're headed to the commemoration ceremonies honoring Hosanna's founders," the chairman said, noting my interest. "We'll join them later."

"I'd like that very much, sir."

"Conductor Elias will be happy to meet you. Talented harpists are hard to find." His tobacco-stained whiskers twitched, expression thoughtful. "Mr. Herald, have you ever seen an angel?"

I folded my hands across my lap. "No, but I heard the trumpets once, when I was a child. It was like thunder. Our house rumbled, and people rushed into the streets to watch the sky. Everyone wanted to glimpse the blessed guardians." I paused. "But I was scared, and hid under my bed."

The chairman chuckled. "A natural reaction to the trumpets. The Seraphim stir both awe and fear in mortals. What do they preach about them in Steelbend?"

Was he testing my knowledge, or my faith? "I come from a devout family, and I learned early about the Prodigal Star. First to appear were the Devils. Mankind prayed for deliverance, and the Seraphim answered. The angels flew from the ruins of the Star and saved us all. The Devils were driven into the the sea and trouble us no more. To this day, the Seraphim guide and inspire us. They built the Kingdom By The Sea to

117

dwell among us, and to ensure the Devils stay banished beneath the waves."

He smiled. "These same fables are told among all of the worker settlements. The true nature of the Seraphim may surprise you."

I remained silent until we arrived, pondering his words.

The clinic lay in the commercial sector, near the Temple itself. I left my harp with Chairman Ness and followed a nurse inside. The operation chamber contained a large patient chair with the Seraphic emblem mounted on a wall plaque above it. The orderly took my coat and assisted me into the seat. Padded restraint bands clamped around my head, wrists, and ankles.

The surgeon's eyes were kind over his sterile white mask. "This will be over in thirty minutes. When you wake, you'll be one with the Sanctum."

They pressed a gas filter over my mouth and nose. Seconds ticked; the room swam. All dissolved into darkness, my heartbeat a hollow thrum. Without bearings, I drifted in the void. Small points of light surrounded me, expanded, and formed a virtual space. My awareness projected itself as a lustrous avatar, and a voice played through my mind.

*"Greetings, Mr. Herald. Welcome to the Sanctum."*

Music rippled, and prismatic icons poured like jewels between my fingers. Endless information trickled along spidery data channels, and I longed to explore. But the entrancing images dissolved, and I opened my eyes.

"Your procedure was a success," the surgeon said. "You'll have shreds of access for the first day or so as the 'face calibrates with your neural pathways. After that, you may connect at will via your personal nexus device."

Afterward, I rested in an outpatient room. Curious, I rubbed the back of my head. Beneath my skin was the tiny swell of the implant, permanently fused to my skull. I was now an ascended citizen.

Recovery was swift due to the skill of Hosanna's medical experts. Chairman Ness picked me up two hours later, and we drove to the Temple complex.

"Here we are, the abode of the angels," the chairman said. "Have you ever seen the like?"

"No. This is incredible." Pressing my fingers to the window, my eyes rose along immense alabaster columns. Only a pair of filigreed brass doors adorned the gleaming facade. The statues of the Archangels hovered upon the loftiest spire, beneath a radial aura of bronze bars.

The chauffeur parked near the gate, and we climbed out.

"The Seraphim don't leave their Temple much anymore," the chairman said. "It's been ten years since we've seen one, but a lively festival in their honor sometimes attracts them. Angels are drawn to powerful emotions, like moths to a candle flame."

"That's odd," I said. "I always believed the angels were too pure for human emotions."

He pushed his spectacles higher upon his prominent nose. "They're pure of body and spirit, yet they seem touched by the human condition, as we in the Kingdom have witnessed many times."

People swarmed across the central courtyard, spilling onto the streets below. Silken banners and garlands festooned every awning, flapping cheerfully between market stalls and lampposts. Sea salt, incense, and roasting delicacies permeated the air. Children romped to the jaunt of a hurdy-gurdy player, his pet monkey wearing a small halo and silver wings.

On the highest terrace, Chairman Ness presented his identification to the guards, and they waved us through. A magnificent grandstand awaited, tuning strings and woodwinds humming in delightful discord. Unable to contain my excitement, I strode ahead.

"Wait, young fellow." The chairman's cane tapped steadily against the concrete. "These old legs are no match for your eagerness."

"I'm sorry, sir."

He chuckled. "No need for apologies."

A portly man greeted us, dressed in an austere robe of black silk. "Most esteemed Chairman, how wonderful to see you," he said.

"You as well. Conductor Elias, this is Mr. Tristan Herald, the newest Bearer of Beatific Song."

"A pleasure to meet you," I said, extending a hand.

The conductor glared at my fingers with disdain. "Such a title for such a youth," he said. "How old are you, and where were you born?"

"Seventeen, sir. Out of Steelbend."

"You're very young to leave home for Hosanna."

I straightened my posture. "According to the Righteous Code, seventeen is the age of consent."

He sniffed, still staring at my hands. "Steelworkers bear many scars, which distort the delicate touch of a harpist. Are you skilled, hailing from such a remote settlement?"

"I am." His observation was true. I'd worked on the smelting lines until I departed Steelbend. My left little finger was permanently bent after a foundry accident. Both palms were callused, bearing scratches and burns. They were unsightly, but nothing hindered me.

Chairman Ness interrupted. "Conductor, I've come here personally to endorse Mr. Herald. You must hear his music."

"Let's have a show of it, then." The conductor waved at me. "Play your best hymn to the Seraphim."

Sitting upon a pedestal, I took a deep breath, and focused myself. I looked at the sky, imagining it was the vault of a majestic cathedral, elevating all senses to the divine.

*"Ye breathless guardians watch and sway,*

*"Upon the blessed edge of day,*

*"Of joy and love the music rings,*

*"Calling the kiss of angel's wings."*

A crowd gathered. Someone wept, and another prayed. Moved by their passion, I sang louder.

*"Come sing their praise, the blessed few,*

*"As fleeting as the morning dew,*

*"Who stand and watch, though 'ere we sleep,*

*"And hurl the darkness to the deep."*

Lost in song, I failed to notice the rustle of feathers and gossamer robes.

Conductor Elias' voice trembled. "By the Sanctum...Archangel Jophiel descends for the boy's song."

My eyes snapped open. Sharp aquiline features were inches from mine, an embossed mask of gleaming silver, no openings for the eyes or mouth.

I froze, jaw dropping.

"Keep playing, you fool," the conductor said. "Don't anger it."

The creature was unlike anything I'd imagined. Yet it was familiar, like a memory glimpsed in a figment of dream or in moonlight reflected on water. It bent over me, about eight feet tall. Grace lined its slender limbs and torso. It was blinding white, with skin like sanded marble. Silver strands pulsed through long white hair, misty fabric swathing its androgynous form. A finned chrome headdress mirrored the three pairs of wings on its back. It didn't speak, but cocked its head with a sharp twitch, like a hawk tilting one eye.

Sweat stung my brow. Heeding the conductor's warning, I collected myself and finished my performance.

*"Fair as stars winking on the wave,*
*"They linger still, our hearts to save.*
*"Most blessed angels, hear our plea,*
*"And guide thy Kingdom By The Sea."*

No mortal could match Jophiel's beauty. Its slender arms flicked up. Thin fingers latched to my chin, nails piercing.

Though I trembled, I answered as a faithful devotee should. "Praises be, Holy One."

Subtle voices teased my mind from the Sanctum. All six wings swayed forward, plumes bright enough to shame the morning snow. The mask loomed closer, its breath like a honeyed rose, yet deathly cold. Archangel Jophiel stroked my face between exquisite palms, and pressed its metallic lips to my forehead. Then it soared away, vanishing into the pinnacles of the Temple.

The conductor nearly choked on his words. "Bearer of Beatific Song. How worthy you are of this title. Welcome to the Sacred Chorus, Mr. Herald."

Jophiel's touch lingered on my skin for hours afterward—too much love, desperate as dying winter. The encounter elevated me quickly within Hosanna's society. I enjoyed the admiration, but the angel had unsettled me.

Regardless, the perks of joining the Sacred Chorus satisfied my desire for luxury. Conductor Elias assigned me an apartment within an elegant building along the Temple rise. I now had a space to call my own, and a respectable calling for my music.

The crisp floor tiles and arches of my parlor opened onto a veranda overlooking the sea. The next morning I flung the doors aside as dawn fragmented through the rectilinear glass panes. Hot jasmine tea and the velvet-cushioned divan soothed my mind.

I rehearsed with the Chorus that afternoon and became better acquainted with its members. Everyone marveled over my encounter with the angel and complimented my adjustment to fame. Several people invited me to dinner, but I discreetly declined them all. Only one person occupied my thoughts—the captivating poet, Miss Annabel Lee.

At day's end, I headed for the rock where we'd met. Soon came the thud of hooves on sand, and I played with enthusiasm to draw her attention.

She trotted toward me. "Hello, Tristan of Steelbend. I hoped I'd find you here."

I tipped my new fedora to her. "It's now Mr. Tristan Herald. And I'm a member of the Sacred Chorus."

She smiled. "You look like a proper Hosanna gentleman, but I rather liked your simpler attire." She threw me a flirtatious glance. "I heard you were blessed by an Archangel."

I set the harp aside. "I was. A startling experience, to say the least."

"I've only seen an angel once, when I was little. It was definitely startling." She pursed her lips, then extended a hand to me. "I want to show you something. Hop onto Fidelius with me."

I slung the harp over my shoulder and climbed behind the saddle.

Fidelius sloshed through the receding tide, leaving a trail of crescent hoofprints. I rested my arms about Annabel's slender waist, trying to be a gentleman.

"Where are we going?" I asked.

"To a place of memories."

A craggy peninsula protruded into the surf. We passed through a wrought-iron gate, rust decorating its spiral patterns. Within the enclosure, rows of tombstones poked like bony twigs among sepulchers.

"A cemetery?"

"These are the tombs of Hosanna's nobility," she said. "But we're going down there."

We wandered down the trail, and arrived at a quiet cove.

"Whoa, Fidelius." The horse halted on cue, and she looked over her shoulder at me. "There's a secret here, and I think we can write a song about it. Come on, I'll show you."

I slid to the ground and she dismounted after. A bank of mist curled over the open sea, tinting the sunset a dim orange. Decaying seaweed littered the ground, pungent with fishy odors. She led me to the water's edge. Distant buildings and bridges sparkled over the harbor in the last light.

She took off her boots and waded into the surf. After watching for a few minutes, she picked something shiny out of a retreating wave. Childish wonder lit her face. "They say the Prodigal Star crashed on this very spot, many years ago. Some call it a myth, but no one can explain the shards which wash up here. Bright as moonlight, and they never rust. If the Star was made of this metal, where do you think it came from?"

She placed the object into my palm. I studied its glistening surface and the enigmatic symbols etched upon it. One of the inscriptions resembled a face, similar to Jophiel's mask.

"It could be from anywhere," I said. "How very interesting."

She looked skyward. "I wonder where the Seraphim's true home is. They're certainly from elsewhere. Somewhere up there. And the Devils came from the Prodigal Star, too."

While she contemplated the riddles of angels, I clasped her hand. I couldn't deny my feelings any longer. "What I wonder is how I've met someone as lovely as you."

She flung her arms about my neck, and we fell into a kiss. Her lips were warm, as tempting as petals in a spring gale. I held her close, and felt as if I'd been blessed again here in Hosanna.

"We must meet tomorrow," I said, trying not to shiver in her arms.

"Our rock, at sunset," she said. Another kiss sealed the pact.

Not long after, we created a spontaneous song together. She danced and recited, while I matched her abandon across the harp strings.

Fidelius whinnied and stomped, distracting us. A limousine stopped at the crest of the hill near the cemetery gate, its headlamps slicing through the dark. The doors clicked open and shadowy figures emerged.

Annabel lifted her hands to her throat, turning pale. "It's my brother. Zadkiel have mercy."

Three men approached, wearing tailored suits and overcoats. The fellow leading them lifted the brim of his bowler, revealing a bladed chin and nose. It was Pastor Lee, from the popular Redemption Ministry ads. His eyes flashed in the searchlights of a passing tugboat, deep azure like his sister's.

"Annabel, I've searched from tower to cornerstone, and I find you among the tombs, with a boy of no consequence. What devilry is this?"

"We're just watching the stars," she said. "Nothing more."

His narrow shoulders tensed. "The stars. A clever excuse. Who are you, young man?"

"Mr. Tristan Herald, Bearer of Beatific Song."

The tight lines of his disapproval swerved to a grin. "Well, my apologies. I mistook you for someone else. You're the one blessed by Jophiel, no?"

I steadied my voice. "I am."

"The Seraphim haven't favored anyone in years," he said. "You must possess a singular gift."

"Perhaps." I gripped my harp for comfort. "I only express what I feel through music."

Annabel scowled. "Benedict, what do you want? I've done nothing wrong."

"Quite the contrary, dear sister," Pastor Lee said, voice dripping with arrogance. "It's past your curfew. You mustn't traipse about after dark with young men. Scandalous behavior will mar much more than your reputation. The integrity of the ministry is at stake."

Her cheeks flushed. "Fine. Good night." She winked at me, then cantered away.

Pastor Lee cocked his head. "Pardon the interruption, Mr. Herald, but Annabel is a reckless child. You must understand my dilemma, as I'm her caretaker, and only surviving kin."

I nodded, despite the sinking sensation in my gut. "I understand."

He studied me, then handed me a business card, embossed with fine calligraphy. '*Pastor Benedict Lee, Redemption Ministry, 4 West Atonement Drive*'.

"You're quite the sensation among society," he said. "I work closely with the Seraphim. Surely you've heard of my ministry?"

I crushed the business card into my pocket, alongside my nexus. "Yes, sir."

The mists reached shore, creeping around our feet. A foghorn bellowed from the distant pier.

"Annabel's birthday is in three days," he said. "We're hosting a celebration at the manor. If you're so inclined, the address is on the card."

"I'd be delighted."

"We'll expect you, then. Seven o' clock. And please bring your harp. I want to hear this heavenly music for myself." He waved farewell with a genteel twist of one hand.

I walked six blocks home. The damp weather seeped through my woolen overcoat, and I buttoned it tighter. Stray cats wailed from an alley. Shadows schemed, streetlamps meddling. Gargoyles and angelic effigies glared through chiseled eyes, crouched upon the eaves as if waiting to pounce. When I reached my apartment, I bolted the door, but a chill slithered close behind.

The following evening I waited for Annabel by the seashore. Hazy stars appeared, but she never did. With a heavy sigh, I went home. The next day was also a disappointment.

On the third day, I looked forward to her birthday party. I rushed through rehearsal with the Chorus, then dressed early, wanting to look my best. A three-piece suit with a contrasting waistcoat, starched wing collar, and well-turned derby flattered me enough. When the time arrived, I hailed a cab to the Lee estate.

The road wound along the coast. Soon we reached the manor, the iron gates boasting a striking letter 'L'. I gave my name to the guards and they bowed before me. Tall cypress trees lined the circular parkway, guiding all eyes to the great house itself. Its towering walls curved into sleek contemporary wings. Diagonal accents slanted across the front. Soft light spilled through mullioned rectangular windows, music and laughter pealing from within. Doors outlined with concentric enamel borders waited, and I rang the bell.

A footman answered, and escorted me to the central courtyard. The buoyant rhythms of a jazz quartet sizzled over the celebration. Fresh blossoms accented the scents of wine and imported cologne. A fountain glistened among bronze statues, three abstract angels stretching triangular wings over a tiled pool. Laughing and flirting, guests danced around the torchlit pavilion.

I ignored the stares of brash socialites, searching for Annabel. Before long, I spotted her among a clique of dashing young men. Fleeing the hungry leers of her admirers, she came toward me.

I caught my breath. I'd always seen her in riding attire. Tonight, a drop-waisted frock fluttered about her, bold silk panels angled across the bodice. Her scalloped headband glistened as she kissed my cheek.

"What are you doing here?" she whispered.

I blinked. "Your brother invited me."

"Really?" She glanced about, neck craned like a doe sensing predators. "Dance with me."

I set my harp beside the bandstand and joined her. The music slowed to a sultry cadence. "Is something wrong?" I asked.

"Benedict never invites someone here unless he has plans for them." She gripped my lapel, gliding across the terrace at my lead. "It's my birthday party, but none of these people are my friends. You see those men watching every move I make? They're part of a secret club in Hosanna's underworld, dealing in every vice you can imagine. Benedict hopes I'll find a rat-faced suitor among them."

I pressed my cheek to hers, and kept my voice lowered. "What does he want from me?"

"I don't know."

The song ended, audience clapping. Drums quickened. The clarinet and banjo players tapped their feet, then dove into the rhythm.

"Behind you." She squeezed my arm in warning.

I whirled about, as Pastor Lee approached with an arrogant grin. "Mr. Herald, it's wonderful to see you," he said, hands open in greeting.

"You didn't tell me he was coming," Annabel said.

"It was to be a surprise. I assumed you were friends, the way you sneaked off to the cemetery with him. Are you not pleased?"

She glared, her smile forced. "Of course I am. You throw marvelous parties. Mother would be impressed if she was here."

"That she would." Pastor Lee sipped a glass of blushed wine. "Mr. Herald, would you play a song for us in honor of Annabel's coming-of-age?"

His grin reminded me of a snake about to strike, but I nodded. "Certainly. Miss Lee, will you join me?"

"I suppose so."

Pastor Lee raised a brow. "You perform together? How marvelous."

The jazz ensemble stepped aside. I sat upon a cushioned stool, and my beloved stood beside, resting a hand on my shoulder.

"Mr. Herald and I are pleased to present our latest composition," she said. "This is titled, 'So Silent A Yearning'."

Curious murmurs swept through the onlookers, and we fell into harmony at once.

*"Promise to love me, forever and a day,*
*"From sorrow and scorn we drift away;*
*"My heart is true, longing only for thee,*
*"Each beat and each breath swell as tides of the sea."*

The first applause was faint, but soon it roared.

"You live up to your reputation, Mr. Herald," Pastor Lee said, clapping. "Encore!"

We played another. Afterward, Annabel led me to the refreshment table. The jazz music resumed, dancers flapping knees and elbows in time.

Pastor Lee cornered us, hands clasped behind his back. "That was delightful. I've never heard your verses in such a medium, Annabel."

She pretended to be interested in the tray of crab dip before her. "The compliments belong to Tristan."

His jaw flinched. "You refer to him by first name. You must be very fond of each other."

"It's obvious by now," she said.

"Bearer of Beatific Song." He laid a hand on my shoulder. "Do you know how powerful you might become?"

I gulped. "I'm sorry, I don't understand."

Annabel's eyes flared. "Leave us alone, Benedict."

He ignored her and gestured toward the house. "I'd love a chat with you. Can you spare a moment?"

Etiquette demanded it. "Very well," I said.

The foyer within broadened into a semi-crescent, exotic potted flowers perfuming the space. Black and charcoal slabs formed alternating patterns over the floor with thin lines of brass embedded between. A staircase twirled up the far wall, its circular grace contrasting the precise forms around it.

"Let's retire to my study," Pastor Lee said, leading me through a side door. We entered a hollow chamber where a fireplace bordered in onyx and ivory tiles cast a steady glow. The flame crackled, and we settled into high-backed chairs beside it.

Pastor Lee leaned forward, chin propped on steepled fingertips. "Tell me, Mr. Herald, who do you believe is king in the Kingdom By The Sea?"

A log split and smoldered. "The Seraphim, of course."

"Ah. You have faith. But the truth is, the Seraphim are mere symbols, now. They hide in their Temple, perhaps out of disdain, or idleness. No one knows why. Only the High Pontiff and myself commune with them. All else, even the glittering facade of the Sanctum, is designed to conceal the angels' silence. We must keep the devotees appeased, for the Seraphim have abandoned us. That is, until you arrived, and lured them out with your song."

I tapped a fingernail against the lacquered armrest. "If the angels adore hymns of praise, why don't they favor the Sacred Chorus?"

He sneered. "It isn't music they crave. It's pure emotion, expressed by a virtuous youth. Such is like sugar candy to them. You must be a boundless fount of it, or they'd never bat a pinion in your direction."

The room chilled in spite of the fire. "What do you want from me?"

He reclined in his chair, features harsh in the red glow of flame. "Your music has a hypnotic effect on both angels and mortals. I'd like to offer my support, in exchange for yours. The Seraphim, on the other hand, require only one thing from mankind. They hunger, and we feed them. Some, such as myself, have turned this to an advantage."

My voice cracked. "Are you saying they eat us?"

"No, no," he said, laughing. "Angels are above carnal necessities like eating. They consume more subtle delicacies. Hope, love, joy, sorrow—all such feelings have an intoxicating effect, don't you agree? To the Seraphim this is intensified a thousand-fold, and provides their vital nourishment. I discovered long ago how an enraptured congregation can satisfy them, and they've allowed me endless freedom in return."

"What sort of freedom?"

He folded his hands in his lap. "I have many friends and contacts, Mr. Herald. On every level of Hosanna. The angels aren't swift to punish violators of the Righteous Code anymore. They care only for their comforts. I provide what they need every week through the ministry. All else plays according to my will. If you're on our side, the High Pontiff and I will help you rise to full potential."

I recalled the men outside who catered in vice. "I don't deal with criminals, if these are the friends you refer to."

"It's a matter of perspective, young man. What one sees as sin, to another is opportunity. So long as the order of society remains, there's no harm in supporting all of its inevitable facets."

I lurched to my feet. "I'm leaving."

"There's more than one reward for you." His voice purred in velvet persuasion. "I know you're enamored of my sister. Join me, and you'll have my blessing to court her."

I clenched my fists. "Is she no more than a bartering chip to you?"

A corner of his lips lifted. "I see why the angels want you. Your emotions are uninhibited."

I'd had enough. I blustered out the door, ignoring the weight of his stare.

On the terrace, Annabel rushed to my side. "What did he say?"

"He thinks we're just pawns in his game." I said angrily. "I'm going home."

She grabbed my hand, calming me somewhat. "Meet me tomorrow at our rock. I promise I'll be there, even if I have to sell my soul to the Devils, or slip a sleeping dose into Benedict's tea."

I almost laughed, but mirth failed me. "He won't object to our meeting as long as I help him feed the angels."

"What do you mean?"

"I'll tell you when we're alone." I kissed her goodbye, and called a cab. My apartment building was a welcome sight. I hurried to the elevator. Three dings, three floors up. My door was the second on the right.

It was ajar.

I crept along the wall, listening for intruders. Every instinct flared sharp. Who would dare invade my home? I should run and seek help, but I crept to the doorway. The hinges creaked as I peered inside.

All was dark. I stepped in, and flicked the parlor lamp on. Everything was as I'd left it, except for the veranda doors being wide open. Night wind rattled the blinds. I set my harp down to close them.

"*Ol hoeth. Noamsi el ogh.*" A voice wheezed above my head. Something large swooped, knocking the lamp over. Glass shattered. Couldn't move, couldn't scream. Incredible force pressed against my throat and chest, pinning me to the floor. Taloned fingers stabbed into my shoulders. Images flickered into my mind, some from the Sanctum, others the flurry of nightmares. A beautiful face, cadaverous pallor, eyes and mouth ablaze with light. Frigid breath sweet as rosebuds. Countless hair-fine tendrils tangled and spun around my head, pricking my flesh like tiny daggers. The creature shuddered, then fled with a torrid *whoosh*.

I scrambled to my feet, eyes adjusting. The blinds swung from whatever had just swept through them. I looked outside. Nothing—only the soft buzz of neon above the bar across the street and the coil of ocean mists. A passing motorcar lit the blunt angel sculptures on the eaves in stark profile.

I must be going mad. I dragged myself to my bedroom, then froze. Upon my pillow was a perfect feather, burning white, plucked from the wing of an angel.

The next morning, I stormed into Chairman Ness' office.

He disconnected from the Sanctum, focusing back to reality. "Mr. Herald, how may I help you?" When he saw the feather, his weathered features grew stern.

I tossed it onto his desk, pale against the gleaming black enamel. "Someone—something—broke into my apartment last night, and left this. I want to know why."

He pointed to the guest chair. "Sit. I'll tell you what I know of such a token."

I collapsed into it and threw my head back. "I feel like I'm being watched everywhere I go. Have I angered the Seraphim?"

"No, you've enchanted one of them," he said. "Perhaps more than one. A plume is a gift of adoration."

"I don't want things sneaking into my home, following me about. If that was a Seraph last night, it attacked me."

"I'm afraid there's nothing to stop it," the chairman said, tone sympathetic. "No mortal knows the whims of angels."

I buried my face in my hands. "I barely slept last night. Is there anything I can do?"

"The Seraphim themselves have your answer." He exhaled, pipe smoke coiling from his nose and mouth.

"How do I reach them?"

"Only the High Pontiff and Pastor Lee have successfully communed in the past decade." He tapped the pipe into a serrated bronze ashtray. "But, since you've attracted an Archangel, you may stand a chance. The communion terminal lies within the Visitor's Center at the base of the Temple."

I thanked him, and after I left his office I boarded a commuter shuttle. The Visitor's Center was a busy facility near the Temple gates. I passed workers and administrators alike, their eyes glazed over, voices chattering through the Sanctum. Many elite citizens sported banded 'face visors for convenience. Ushers waved and grinned to all who entered.

I claimed the private communion booth and settled into the leather chair. A slot for my 'face nexus rotated open on the console and a pleasant female voice spoke.

*"Welcome, friend. Please insert your interface."*

I placed my device.

*"Priority access granted for Mr. Tristan Herald, Bearer Of Beatific Song."*

My vision faded to a grayish haze, as if a daydream stole my mind. The familiar spark of entrance greeted me and I soon hovered between synthetic paradise and the everyday world. Everything here was connected, each channel converging toward the central core. I willed my avatar forward and downward into the heart of the network.

Ribbons of light pulsed about me. I surrendered to the flow of information, like floating down a lazy river. Memories of playing with my grandfather on Steelbend's canals brought a smile to my simulated lips.

Strange voices echoed in kaleidoscopic forms. *"Sala, pashsa..."*

Fragile apparitions caressed me, blank faces shifting within a vast plane.

I intoned a message, using the gestured language of the Sanctum. "Blessed Seraphim, hear me."

The reply surged in a wave of icons. *"Beloved."* They tugged in multiple directions, as if I were a coveted toy between children.

"What do you want?" My question hummed forth.

Serpentine laughter pulsated upon mirrored patterns of light and data. I hovered closer, and saw the horrifying truth. The Seraphim composed a single consciousness, many parts of a whole. They stared into my depths, and flayed all secrets into view.

*"Mine,"* their voice said.

Thousands of needles pierced me. They probed, nothing hidden. My desire for fame was revealed first. This they loved, swaying in approval. However, their joy faded when Annabel's image brightened the dim recesses of the Sanctum. She held the largest portion of my heart, and they didn't like it.

Their displeasure surged through my physical body as well as my

131

avatar. I writhed, digging my fingers into the cushioned armrests. In the Sanctum, countless wings encircled me like a forest of clouds. Pointed fingers ripped at me, virtual blood oozed, and gaunt black wings extended from my avatar's shoulders.

"I don't want this. Let me go!" I snatched my nexus loose, disrupting the connection, and stumbled across the bare tile floor. Sweat dripped, my throat grated. I dashed from the communion chamber, leaving the plume and nexus device behind.

Where could I run? I had no family anymore. My parents disowned me when I left Steelbend. I ran back to the apartment and tore through my belongings. Clothing and vanities soon cluttered the parlor. So many things borrowed or gifted, empty trinkets. I tossed whatever I needed most onto the floor. Packing everything into the bag I'd brought to Hosanna, I left at sunset.

Fog cloaked the strand. I paced among the barnacled rocks, too restless to play music. *Please let her arrive.*

Hooves drummed in the distance, and she emerged from a gray bank of mist. Fidelius slid to a frantic stop, arching his neck against the reins.

"Tristan!" Her voice was shrill. She hurled herself into my embrace. Tears wore hot trails down her face.

Our lips met in a trembling kiss.

"I'm here to say goodbye," I said. "I'm leaving tonight."

"Why?"

I sighed. "The Seraphim won't leave me alone. They feed on human emotions, and apparently I'm the main course. I won't stay and be their slave."

She clutched my fingers. "Where will you go?"

"As far as I can get from the Kingdom."

"They'll follow you," she said. "When you're 'faced, they can track you anywhere."

I looked at the sea, grasping for slim hope. "There's a rumor, a place my grandfather told me about. A rogue settlement far to the north called Penance. Sinners and blasphemers, all of them. They live outside of the Sanctum there, and defy the Seraphim's rule. Maybe it's just a story, but I'm going to find out. It may be my only chance."

The hushed roar of wind and waves drowned all but her plea. "Take me with you."

I gulped, recalling the angels' hatred of her. "I wish I could. It's too dangerous."

Frantic sobs shook her. "Please don't leave me. I can't stay here, with my brother controlling me, and without you. I love you."

Her cries shattered my heart. I wanted to protect her, to always see her smile. "My beautiful Annabel Lee. It's funny. I've known you only a week, but I love you, too."

"I'm coming with you," she said. "They can't stop me, and neither can you."

I hung my head. "The northbound train leaves at dawn. Meet me at the station by then."

She agreed with another kiss, and galloped away.

I hurried to the train station and bought two tickets. Was Penance real? Even if it was, could we reach it in time? I half-slept upon a wooden bench at the boarding platform, huddled beneath my overcoat. My eyes closed but my mind wandered, every noise and footstep a jolting start. Sunrise soon peered over the rolling cityscape, muted violet among the shadows.

The click of feminine heels struck my ears. I sat up, squinting. Annabel's silhouette drifted toward me, dawn blazing at her back. A single bag hung over her shoulder, notebooks and paper crushed into the side pouches.

The train arrived with a hiss and screech.

I showed her the tickets. "One-way trip for two, thirty hours to the end of the line. I had just enough for a first-class booth. We'll run away in style."

She grinned, and took my arm. "It'll be an adventure. Let's go."

The engine hummed, streamlined steel sweeping toward the sturdy cars in tow. We boarded quickly, and settled into our private compartment. After a full day's ride, the city surrendered to countryside, and the landscape billowed before snowy peaks. That evening, we enjoyed a humble supper in the dining car, and retired to our booth soon after.

Annabel sat beside me on the bunk, her bobbed hair awry.

"Do you regret leaving?" I asked, stroking her cheek.

"I miss Fidelius. But there's nothing else for me in Hosanna." She kissed me. "Sing to me, Tristan. Your music makes everything better."

She laid her head on my shoulder. Without my harp, my voice keened, trembling to the rhythm of the train.

"Hold me," she whispered.

Hours melted into soft skin and sweat, and we fell asleep in each other's arms. Sometime before dawn, the clack of the train ceased. Dreams arose. Chromatic threads and virtual breezes promised bliss, childish laughter teased my mind. I sat upright and gripped Annabel's bare shoulder.

She woke with a gasp, clutching the covers.

"The train's stopped," I said.

Along the roof of the coach, something scurried like vermin through decaying walls.

"Wait here." I rose from the bunk, tying my robe. So cold. I cracked the door open, hinges moaning. The cramped aisle was dark and empty, the floorboards like ice beneath my toes. Where was the coach attendant? His chair was empty, spindly against the light angling through the adjacent portal.

More noises scraped outside.

I halted, heart pounding. "Is anyone there?"

No answer. I took a step closer.

Angelic trumpets bellowed, shaking the windows and frame of the train car. I cried out, and covered my ears.

Annabel rushed into the corridor, wrapped in blankets. "Did you hear that?"

"The angels are here." I grabbed her hand. "We have to go."

"And go where? They're everywhere." She sank against the wall, tears spilling from her eyes.

I laid a firm hand on her shoulder. "Don't give up. We'll make a run for it. Get dressed."

We shoved what we could into our bags. Hands locked, we hurried toward the rear exit.

A pistol clicked. Two men emerged from the shadows, weapons brandished. "Stop right there," one of them said.

More footsteps approached down the aisle.

"There's nowhere to hide. The Seraphim have chosen you." Pastor Lee smiled, two more of his armed lackeys pacing behind.

I lunged at him, despite the guns. The nearest assailant seized me in a choke hold, and the cold steel of a gun bit my skull. Another grabbed Annabel by the arms.

"Take me," I said. "But let her go."

Pastor Lee shook his head. "You've both violated the Righteous Code, and denied the Seraphim. Your only hope is repentance."

They dragged us outside into the frigid morning. A convoy of sleek motorcars idled on the track, blocking the train.

Annabel twisted free of their grasp and stumbled over snowy gravel.

The trumpets blared again, a nauseating din. Even Pastor Lee and his comrades cringed at the sound.

"The angels come for you, Mr. Herald," Pastor Lee said. "They're angry that you've forsaken them. If you surrender now, I'll mediate on your behalf. Then we can all go home and put this little debacle behind us."

The wind tossed snowflakes into a frenzied spin around us. All of the men watched the sky, weapons ready.

"Are you sure you can talk them out of it, boss?" one man asked with a frightened expression.

Pastor Lee grinned. "You of little faith. Watch and see who is truly favored by the Seraphim." He closed his eyes and prayed aloud, arms raised high. "Blessed guardians, saviors of all. Come and bless us with your mercy."

Lightning in a blizzard was a sight nature never intended. Seven bolts of radiant white struck the earth. Icy ground broke and scattered at the impact of the tall, shining bodies.

Annabel ran to me. I hugged her, shielding her.

The Archangels stood in unison and trapped us in a circle. Each wore a helmet bedecked with arcs and swooped fins, their true features concealed behind sculptured facades. I beheld the trumpets for the first time, long brass instruments cradled in elegant fingers. Celestial spears and swords glistened alongside.

"Holy Ones, we return these lost sheep to your fold. Forgive them their trespasses." Pastor Lee's voice quavered. Was he cold, or did he also fear them?

The Archangels ignored him. We were far from the range of the Sanctum, yet they carried it with them. They conversed with sharp nods and gestures, bird-like yet graceful. A collective declaration murmured through my mind, revealing their unchanged intent.

"*Mine.*"

One of the angels darted into our midst, gliding with otherworldly speed. Its silver mask resembled a human skull, bared teeth and sockets agleam. A curved tier of segmented chrome arced around its helm, long white hair spilling to its narrow waist.

"Azrael." Pastor Lee bowed. "Have mercy on these children."

The Archangel of Death. I knew its name from a lifetime of teachings and stories, and also knew its dreaded purpose. It pointed at Annabel and she gasped, neck arching. She collapsed to her knees, compelled by an unseen force.

I struggled, but the angels crossed their spears in my path.

The Archangel Azrael lifted its mask, exposing stiff aquiline features. Its eyes and mouth were shut, resembling slumber—or death.

I clawed at their unearthly strength, their battering wings, fighting to save her. My voice collided in vain with their will. "Let her go."

Azrael's hooded lids opened. Blinding light blazed from its eyes and mouth, piercing as noon.

Pastor Lee wailed. "No, Annabel!" They restrained him with a sword against his chest.

Annabel fell into reluctant prayer, driven like a helpless doll by Azrael's power. Her head bowed, hands clasped before her in worship. A bone-rumbling hum shook the ground, the sky, and all flesh.

Azrael raised its six immense wings. The silver threads in its hair coiled about Annabel's skull like crackling spiderwebs, stabbing into her body. A strange glow pulsed beneath her skin, veining from her 'face implant to the angel's ecstatic form. Between Azrael's outstretched palms, snowflakes whirled into a flurry.

Blood tears of stigmata poured down Annabel's cheeks.

I strained against the angels' vise-like hands. "I'll do anything you want. Please, don't take her."

The verdict was absolute. Archangel Azrael blew a kiss. A frosted cloud enveloped her, and formed a sparkling layer of ice around her. She twitched a moment, then was still, frozen in perfect devotion.

Azrael closed its eyes, and put its mask on, dousing its glory once more. It caressed Annabel, then snapped its head toward me.

The angels released Pastor Lee. He scurried across the snow on all fours to his sister, and threw his arms around her corpse. "Damn you to the depths, Tristan Herald. If you hadn't stolen her, she'd still live."

All seven angels swooped onto me. I spat at them, fighting as they bore me up.

"Get her out of here," Pastor Lee shouted to his men. They obeyed, carrying Annabel to their cars.

"It's all your fault." He cursed me, shaking his fist. "You destroyed her, and I'll destroy you. The angels won't protect you."

His rant faded. The Seraphim lifted me on a blanket of soft feathers into the winter sky. Snow and stars floated by. Was I in the Sanctum, or a dream? Did it even matter anymore?

A familiar voice echoed in my mind.

"*Awake, the stars do fade.*

"*Dream no more—child of the between,*

"*Of dusk and dawn, and shores unseen;*

"*Though hearts lie still, and flesh decayed,*

"*Behold the life which love hath made.*"

"Annabel? How is this happening?"

She stepped out of a blur of information tendrils, dressed in a sheer white gown. Pale light glistened around her. "I'm here. Did you think I was dead? My body's gone, but I'm well and alive in the Sanctum. The Archangels saved me. I understand everything now. They want to help us." She twined her soft fingers around my avatar's neck. "With their help, we can defeat death. Only a few know this secret. But we'll change everything with my words, and your music. None will stand against us, and we can enjoy every pleasure and happiness within the Sanctum. Things are better here. Never hungry, never lonely. All is beauty and light."

She kissed me. The same azure eyes captured mine, her skin warm. She even had the same cowlick, one lock always curling about her right ear.

"This is impossible."

"It's all true," she said. "My words were always my strength, and I can still create them within the Sanctum. Your physical body is necessary to convey your music, and to bridge our work with the angels. Mine was not."

I woke with a start. Columns of silver-filigreed marble rose toward an open skylight, specks of crystalline down drifting through the air. I lay

137

upon an immense stone altar, in a chamber too beautiful for human eyes. The seven Archangels knelt about me in a circle, with rings of lesser Seraphs surrounding them. The mid-ranked Seraphs possessed four wings, shining in varied hues of gray to white, while the submissive Cherubs bore only two, and were clad in mundane colors.

Archangel Jophiel handed me a fantastic harp, its frame a reflective metal like the kind from Annabel's cove. The effigy of an angel adorned the neck, its wings unfurled in rows of perfect symmetry. Tendrils of light shimmered along the strings.

I flung it at their feet in a discordant clatter. "I don't want your damn harp, or your so-called 'favor'. I want her back. Alive, and in my arms. Not your twisted mockery of her in the Sanctum. What do you really want? Am I just to sing her poetry and make hymns in your honor until all of your worshipers praise along? You're cruel, and I hate you."

Annabel laughed in my mind. "We exist only because the angels watch over us. And in exchange for their protection, we honor them. A small price to pay for happiness and immortality."

"Never." I tried to run. Dozens of the Seraphim lunged, knocking me down. My head struck the floor. The last thing I saw before losing consciousness was Archangel Jophiel bending over me, placing something cold and immovable around my skull.

I fell into the structured bliss of the Sanctum once more. Annabel danced around me to the strains of an ethereal choir. There was no escape. Even if my body died, they would trap my soul here forever, like hers.

Unknown time passed. I woke in my apartment in Hosanna, crouched at the foot of my bed, and slowly regained my senses. If only it were a nightmare. Annabel and I would meet by the sea at sunset, and everything would be as it was before. I wanted so much to believe it. But at my side lay the harp gifted by the angels, and a harsh metallic object adorned my head.

I inspected it in the mirror. A solid band of glinting chrome encircled my brow, fused to my 'face implant at the back. It was a simpler version of the crowns of the Archangels. Ornaments at the sides fanned into rectangular ridges resembling wings.

"Chosen by the angels." I sank to my knees, singing a new verse, sheer rambling madness.

*"We loved with a love that was more than love, in a Kingdom By The Sea;*
*"No angel nor devil can sever my soul from the beautiful Annabel Lee."*

*** 

There was little else to do but sing. I wandered to the Temple, carrying my new harp. The Sacred Chorus gathered here daily for Evensong, a live broadcast across the Kingdom. All tuning and practice ceased at my approach. Mouths hung in awe. I still wore the fumbled clothing from my escape attempt—shirt untucked, collar askew, hair wild about my cheekbones. It didn't matter what they thought. I chuckled at their awestruck whispers.

"He wears the Winged Crown."

"Favored by the highest."

"Truly the Bearer of Beatific Song."

Conductor Elias bowed with the others, his robes rustling aside. "Mr. Herald, your presence is an honor."

"So it is." I claimed the foremost seat in the orchestra, and none argued my right to it. "The Archangels desire a new composition tonight."

I led the ceremonial performance, the Seraphim observing and guiding from my constant link to the Sanctum. Annabel's words filled my mind, then poured from my lips in song. I wanted to believe they were truly hers, but I knew she was gone forever.

*"Glory to those on high,*

*"The perfect ones who never die.*

*"All hail the breathless quickening,*

*"What once was lost, shall rise to sing."*

All I'd hoped for in Hosanna—fame, influence, a life of ease—finally became mine. With my testimony indicting them, Pastor Lee and the High Pontiff were arrested for crimes against the Seraphim. I grinned as the Code Enforcers dragged them away to incarceration. No remorse or pity lurked in my heart.

My music encouraged all citizens to submit to the Archangels. Crowds flocked to hear me play, and demand for my work soared to the heights I'd always longed for. Recordings and concerts ruled my days. But every night I spurned it all and wandered to the cemetery by the sea.

139

When the sun set, I returned to the cove of the shattered Star. Bright pieces of incorruptible beauty washed ashore, as always. I gathered as many as I could, and entered the Lee family sepulcher.

The circular chamber within glowed beneath undying gas lamps. Decorative tiles meandered about the magnificent coffin in the center. Framed between ornate steel columns, a glass case preserved her in a climate-controlled haven. Pastor Lee must have spent a fortune to commission it.

Her body still knelt in the pose of forced devotion and despair. Ice glittered along her skin and hair, streaks of blood tears tarnishing her otherwise peaceful expression.

I paced around her, laying the shards of beach-washed metal in meticulous patterns across the floor, trying to make sense of my fragmented thoughts.

"Annabel..." My fingers slipped down the frosty glass.

"Don't despair, my darling." She echoed from the Sanctum. "We'll always be together. Sing with me, like we did before."

I squeezed one of the metal shards until my fingers bled; the pain real and encompassing, reminding me I was alive and she was not. Torn from one existence to the next, taunted in the world of their choosing, I was forever denied what I wanted most. My soul screamed for mercy, but I laughed like a madman. "Yes! Let's sing of their boundless wisdom, my love."

Her avatar sighed approval, and the angels embraced us.

I played one stanza, then collapsed. Clutching my head, I huddled and rocked against the chilled glass of her coffin. The sea outside drowned my hysteria in its endless ebb and flow. Surely the moon still beamed, and the stars still rose, but I didn't care.

Days passed and still I sojourned with the dead. The Seraphim and Annabel berated me, but I'd lost all desire to go on.

The tap of a cane against stone roused me to clouded awareness. Chairman Ness found me in a heap by the tomb, my harp discarded near the wall.

"The Archangels contacted me within the Sanctum," he said. "They believe you'll listen to me."

I pushed myself upright with a groan. "How thoughtful of them."

He placed a hand on my shoulder. "They want you to return home, and resume your duties as the Bearer of Beatific Song."

I sputtered in derision. "Of course. Must ensure the devotees remain obedient. Isn't it a wonderful job? Leave me. Time, days, nights...meaningless."

"You aren't well. Come, Mr. Herald, I'll help you." He tried to lift me to my feet.

I shoved him away. "I said, leave me!"

He threw up his hands. "If this is your wish, so be it. But I have something else to tell you."

"Nothing will change my mind."

"An unknown vessel has surfaced offshore. It drifts at a distance, but the Seraphim are uneasy. The angels of war circle the harbor, and are perched in surveillance atop the Temple spires."

I laughed, slapping my knee. "That's wonderful. Do they fear the Devils? Or is it just to keep us all fearful beneath their mighty wings? Let the Devils come. Only they can conquer the Seraphim. Let them destroy this land of spineless slavery. I'll dedicate my latest song to the great unknown, the destroyer of purpose, the cosmic leveler which reduces all to dust."

The Chairman donned his hat, and shuffled to the door. "Believe what you wish, young man. Like you, I gave up long ago. We do what we must, regardless of the grim truth binding us. I bid you adieu."

Annabel gasped in the Sanctum. "The Devils are invading? Zadkiel have mercy. Let's pray to the blessed guardians for salvation."

I sang loudly to drown her out.

*Clang.* The walls of the tomb shook, plaster and stone crumbling. A dissonant bell pealed outside, loud as the angelic trumpets.

*Clang.* Again, the ground shook from the din. Tiny fractures fanned across the coffin glass, cold air misting out. Though weak and delirious, I crawled outside. Winds slashed across my face, whipping my hair. The tomb overlooked the harbor. I staggered to the edge of the cliffs and stared across the churning waves below. Dawn scorched the eastern sky.

*Clang.* The bell pounded against my ears. Trumpets answered in the distance, a challenge from the angels. In the wan morning light, enormous shapes emerged from the depths. The mists parted, and I beheld the marauders.

Oblong vessels rolled ashore, bolts and rivets squealing. Engines rumbled, seaweed and other marine filth dangling from immense hydraulic appendages. Bands of sickly green luminescence glowed along their undulating brass and copper forms.

The bell thundered, and I saw a tall creature standing on one of the surfacing vehicles. A round helmet with dozens of glass-paned vision ports covered its head, hoses and compressors writhing along its torso. It wore an armored diving suit and smashed a hammer against a monstrous bell. Pointing to Hosanna, the Devil flexed the wing-like fins on its shoulders toward the sunrise.

The amphibious onslaught advanced. Mechanical tentacles thrashed among the fray, the points of tridents and harpoons gleaming in thickly gloved hands. The Devils were much like the Seraphim. Perhaps they were long-lost cousins, come to wreck their wayward kin.

I laughed among the crags, tears and sea spray staining my eyes.

*A cyberpunk story inspired by "The Man of the Crowd"*

Jayelle King is a poet and fiction writer with an addiction to felt-tipped pens and composition notebooks. Currently, she is working on a collection of cyberpunk short stories. When not writing, she can be found wandering craft store aisles and, if left to her own devices, buying more yarn than is humanly possible to use in one lifetime. Although she doesn't *really* understand how Twitter works, she still tweets sporadically under @jayelleking.

# TABULA RASA

# Day 63

L et me tell you a secret: a man is either hunter or prey. There are no other conditions. Whether we know it or not, accept it or not, acknowledge it or not—we are all either chasers or chased. This simple and universal truth infinitely simplifies life. At any given moment you need only glance about to determine your role.

If you don't know which you are, allow me. I can tell at a glance. I picked this up from spending the majority of the past sixty-two days relearning how to navigate the world around me.

I am recent prey. I woke up in an alley one day with no idea where or who I was. A quick search of my pockets netted nothing: no personal effects, no clues to whether I had a family, or even what my name was. I consulted a manchanic who explained it was not a mind wipe, but rather that a memlocking device was clamped down on my memories. All the things that make up who I am—that *define* me—are still inside. They are simply locked away.

It is a terrible thing to know nothing of your past. Who had I wronged? Who had wronged me? I begged with him to remove it, to tear it out if he needed to, but he refused. He said the chances of my memories being released were roughly equal to those of triggering the safety feature that could render me brain-dead. I didn't like those odds.

He continued to marvel at the craftsmanship of the lock and assured me that I had not been chosen at random, that I was lucky to be alive, and that it would be wise of me to leave well enough alone. Easy enough to do, since the lock holds my former life captive. I couldn't find my way back to my old life, even if I wanted to—surely the intent of those to whom I had fallen prey.

Still, he did not rob me of all hope. Nothing lasts forever, he said. Look for anomalies.

I spend my days scanning the faces of those I pass, searching in vain for anyone that looks familiar, roaming the streets for a place that might trigger a memory. In a city with millions of people, I truly hope that someone will bump into me and know who I am. Naive, I know.

Today is one of the good days. The kind of day where I can see my situation for what it is: a chance to rebuild. Whatever I did in the past, whatever was done to me is *gone*. I like that. After all, this world is what you make it.

I decide to enjoy a cup of coffee and sketch at my favorite coffee house in the Waterton neighborhood. It's just around the corner from the alley I woke up in two months ago. The coffee isn't that great, but I remember where the place is. I choose a seat at the window and watch people stream by. All afternoon, I sip and sketch strangers' faces, bringing the passersby to life on the pages of my sketchbook. All the while my pencil is at work, my brain is sizing them up and sorting them—hunter and prey; pursuer and pursued.

Of those that pass before me, I see the biggest number of corporate types. These guys are a cinch to pick out: men and women in sharp-lined dark suits, blinking corporate logos tattooed on the backs of their necks, the soft glow of biochips through their skin. They cut their way through the crowds on the way to or from an important deal, conducting business as they walk: buy and selling, trading. Their attention never falls on the people and establishments they pass, but on the expense reports, invoices, and spreadsheets projected onto the world by their compu-lenses. As they stride about, others quickly make way for them, perhaps sensing their predatory natures. They have this distracted expression which changes to utter annoyance when they bump into someone and are momentarily wrenched away from their work. Hunters.

Most of the people who pass by are a weary sort, and move with a hesitation that tells me they are prey. As they walk they crane their necks up to see the tops of the tallest buildings, scurry out of the way of the business people around them. They dress in normal enough clothes—often ill-fitting and slightly worn. Though I do see a few in evening clothes here and there. Not the kind that truly impress. They wear the kind that are designed to look expensive, but only make the wearer look cheap and foolish.

I spot beggars who have gathered enough credits to buy day passes to the city in order to beg more from the Superior City elite. I do spot some without day passes—those who are clever enough to find places to hide in Superior during the curfew hours, and avoid paying the daily toll to enter the gates each morning. These beggars stand in doorways and on intersection corners with credit sticks held out, hoping that kind-hearted residents transfer a few spare credits into their meager accounts. Not many do. The beggars have the hard look of those who have been beaten down so long, they have fully accepted their lot. They have learned that the balance will never swing back in their favor. They are passed by as though they are invisible. Nothing more than scenery.

Still others are mixed in and take no special skill to identify: the large white high tops, puff jackets and jet black hair hacked into a ruler-straight bowl cut are dead giveaways. Kotobos. The girls clinging to their arms, wearing short skirts and impractically high shoes are kotoyos.

I see pushers—these I can tell by their calloused, rough hands and stout, muscled figures, the obvious marks of a life of pushing turbines in the plants.

Average looking folks with vinyl umbrellas hooked over their arms are the citizens who live or work on the bottom level, and carry the umbrellas rain or shine to shield themselves from the never-ending drizzle of litter from above.

The glassy-eyed rorapox addicts who drift about, not fully aware of their actions, stumbling about in the crowds. Ignored by those around them that have grown used to the sight.

As they pass, I draw them all in my sketch pad and mentally classify them. This is how I spend my days: collecting faces and confirming my philosophy. I sip, I sketch, I sip, I sketch.

Then I see him. A man, perhaps in his sixties or seventies. His face captures my attention at once. He has the sagging face of an old man but a head of thick, luxurious, black hair. He has large, white bushy eyebrows. What strikes me more than his unusual appearance is the curious way he moves. He is bent forward, arms wrapped across his body, as if he were protecting himself, but his head is up and he is constantly scanning the area around him with a predatory look. My mind whirls. This man holds the look of both predator and prey. But which is he? He slips through the throng, moving at an incredible pace for his old age. For a brief moment he turns towards the coffee shop and I see into his eyes.

Suddenly, the taste of black raspberry ice cream fills my mouth. Hot sun bakes the top of my hair and a drip of ice cream traces a cold line down the back of my small hand. I blink and it is gone. The sensation of the pencil between my fingers and the noise of those around me bring me back to the present. A memory. My first.

I feel weak, a bit woozy. Sixty-two days of searching and prodding resulted in nothing. A glance from this man just released a memory. Who is he? How did he have this power?

If I lose sight of him, I'll never know.

I grab my coat and whirl it about my shoulders as I step out into the street after him. He moves at a frantic pace, as if something is chasing him. I stay a few paces back and watch him intently, never letting him leave my sight. I don't want him to know I'm following him, but I can't afford to let him slip away. Especially not now, when answers are so close.

Dusk comes as the man and I fight our way through the mass of people in the Waterton area. He heads for the main street, and I set out after him. An hour passes, and twilight fades. Soon, it will be night: the perfect time for predators.

The man turns onto a busy road, keeping up his quick pace. I match it, always behind, always watching. As I continue to observe the man thread through the crowd, my curiosity grows. Where is the man going? Why does he rush? While most make their way into and out of restaurants and bistros, the man makes no indication that he desires to stop in such a place.

We pass through the crowd of an outdoor concert. He stands in stark contrast to those around him. While others were jumping and gyrating to the sounds of the live band, he continued his odd way of moving. He spends more than an hour here, constantly moving through the audience, but clearly not listening to or enjoying the music.

As the performance ends, he leaves the area, sliding into the middle of a group of people walking west, but suddenly veers into a metro station entrance. He climbs the stairs in short, hurried steps. Once on the platform, he paces back and forth, always in the center of a crowd of passengers before the train pulls up. After seeing him enter a car, I board as well, a few cars down. As the train pulls out of the station, I watch him through the glass doors. The train rocks gently. The lights were dim in some cars. The man stands in the center of the few people in his car. Between stations when I know he isn't going to slip away, I take a moment to admire the skyline of Superior City. From up here on the train as it arcs across the sky, I can see for miles in each direction—the casinos and clubs to the west, the business district near the center.

The train rattles into a station. I hesitate, watching to see what the man does. The doors open and he propels himself out onto the platform. The station is nearly empty and he descends the stairs quickly. Once on the ground I recognize that he has brought us near the power plant. It is just at the shift change that we arrive at its gates. The whistle blows outside the facility as the gates swing open. Workers who are leaving from the evening shift spill out into the street. Others, who are on their way in, move past us. While we are in this crowd, he resumes his original activity of swinging his head to and fro, his dark eyes searching over those around him. After the crowd from the power plant thins, his pace quickens. With a cry, he dashes off, searching for more people to lose himself in. I follow.

It is after four in the morning when I see we are in the tent city near the eastern border of the city. Hastily made shelters of tarps stretch over barrels and crates, neatly organized in rows with space between—they are makeshift tents. Outside and around the tents, I see piles of debris and garbage everywhere. I pass a plastic chair with only three legs. These tents belong to the Children of Aldeberaan. In my early days, they offered to take me with them on their next journey. I declined. Any answers I seek are in this city.

As dawn approaches, he turns away from the tents, and toward the docks. Down in Tech Bay, where the stalls of computer parts are piled deep, he weaves his way through the crowd. Here he stops into tents or in front of stalls. I watch from nearby as he picks up one item after another. He turns them over in his hands before setting them down. He does not purchase anything. His small, dark eyes dart about as if he is wary or perhaps weary.

At times I am close enough that I could reach out and brush my fingers across his collar. Other times I back off, stalking him from afar. I track him through the dense crowds with ease. Perhaps I am not prey after all?

Dawn approaches and a number of drunks stumble in and out of dingy-looking bars. With an odd shriek of joy, the old man pushes his way forward to be surrounded by them and then once again begins his original habit of stalking forward and backward without aim. He sticks to the streets and alleys with many of these establishments lining them. No sooner does he begin to mingle amongst these alleys than the owners of these establishments start closing and the crowds disperse. It is something fiercer, more intently felt than fear or dread that I see played on his face. He doesn't hesitate to launch himself with a supernatural energy in redirecting his path. He retraces his steps back to the heart of Superior City. He runs with an amazing speed and intensity that I would not believe if I hadn't witnessed it first-hand. I follow him, determined not to lose him at this point in my pursuit.

***

## Day 64

It is at this point that I can bear it no longer. I have followed him for more than twenty-four hours with no end in sight. I surge ahead of him, elbowing my way through the crowd and then stand in his path. He halts abruptly. For the first time since I took notice of him yesterday evening from my perch in the Waterton cafe he is absolutely still. I look squarely into his face, into his eyes. Vacant, unseeing, like two dark pits. Though I stand mere feet from him, directly in his path, it is as if he can see through me, as if I'm not here at all. Then, I realize. This man of the crowd is neither pursuer nor pursued. He is something else entirely, a realization that came at a terrible cost. A chill runs through me and my stomach sinks. What little I knew about this world is wrong. And once again, I have no handholds. I feel my grip of the world loosening.

A black van pulls up. Men in black jumpsuits emerge from the back doors. They form a circle, guns trained on me. One touches the patch on his chest and says, "ML3903 found."

"Who are you?"

The men do not answer. I look around for the strange man, but he has vanished. A moment later, a man in a white coat arrives. He slowly approaches, saying, "Easy, gents. Let's see if we can do this the easy way."

He turns towards me. "You have questions. I have answers." He extends his hand, which I accept. I feel a pinch on my palm and my vision blurs. I feel my feet go out from beneath me.

*** 

When I wake I hear the clicking of a keyboard and someone says, "This is good stuff. The new processor is functioning well. This is our securest lock yet."

Another voice answers, "Definitely. She put it through the paces, too. Sixty-four days before it broke? Davidson will be ecstatic."

"Absolutely. More testing is needed, but it looks promising."

I open my eyes. I am on a bed in some sort of lab. When I try to move I feel the tug of IVs. I glance down and see there are multiple wires hooking me up to machines I don't recognize. Across the room, two techs are studying multiple monitors. On one I see the coffee shop, but seen as if through my eyes. On another, my hand moving over the sketchbook before pausing to lift my mug. I see the crowded street outside the shop displayed on a different monitor. The recent confrontation on a fourth.

A door opens somewhere behind me. "Glad to see you awake. The vidlog, by the way, was a brilliant move *if* you were trying to break the lock."

I turn towards the voice. It is the man in the white coat. The embroidered name above the breast pocket reads Dr. Davidson.

"Ready for some answers? Unlock her," he says to the techs.

"All the way?" the first tech asks.

"Just enough to bring her up to speed. Say, the last two locks."

The technician nods and a moment later, I remember shaking Davidson's hand for the first time. My orientation at StraightSource. A tour of the lab. *It is a blessing to forget.* Signing waivers. The man from the crowd is there. For ten minutes, the memories come slowly, steadily, and eventually taper to a stop.

"Ninety days," I murmur.

"That's right," Davidson responds. "At ninety days with no one breaking the lock, StraightSource will move into the next phase. But, you don't need to worry about any of that. This was your last run."

I shake my head. "Put me in again. I can handle it."

"We appreciate your dedication, but it will not do us any good. You are simply too curious. You keep picking at the seams. I don't think we should put you through the strain of this again. Besides we have others in the field. You've earned a rest."

"This memlock will help people with this. Past physical abuse, forgotten. Toxic relationships, never happened. Dangerous behaviors, unlearned. I *will not* abandon my life's work. Not when I'm this close."

"No one is asking you to abandon anything but you haven't even stopped long enough for a full evaluation. As project leader, you—"

"As project leader, I have the authority to make this call. How long?"

He doesn't look pleased, but he consults the chart on a nearby monitor. "Few hours, a day tops. Just long enough to rehydrate and get some nutrients into you."

"Fine. I'll need a full report of all test subjects."

"I'll set you up with a data stream during your recovery. Anything else?"

"Yes. Open me up all the way."

"You don't mean...?" Davidson begins.

"I want to remember everything."

"Everything? No. There are things in your past you wanted to forget, memories you segmented off. I cannot advise you to—"

"I'm not asking for your advice. Take me back to the beginning, Davidson. Now."

His displeasure is barely masked as he signals to the technicians. I am hit with twenty-five years of memories all at once. I see a woman striking a man. I am graduating high school. My hands shake on the steering wheel. The man falls to the floor. I smell fresh rosin on my viola's bow. My sister is styling my hair for a dance. The man doesn't fight back. A truck slams into the side of my car. I bow as the audience cheers. The curling iron burns my ear. Then memories come faster, darker. Everyone I've hurt, everyone who's hurt me. My stomach lurches. It's a terrible thing to know your past. Blackness overwhelms me.

153

***

## Day 7

Keeping a vidlog may not make much sense since I only have seven days of memories, but already I see that memories slip away. Nothing lasts very long.

Here's what I know: I woke a week ago in a park. I do not know my name or why my life was taken from me. Some days I have nothing and I despair. Other days are better and I think *this world is what you make it.* I like that. It helps me see my situation for what it really is: a blank slate.

*A clockpunk story inspired by the poem "The Raven"*

Carol Gyzander was a prolific reader of classic science fiction and Agatha Christie mysteries in her early days. Now that her kids have flown the coop, leaving behind the writer's requisite cats, she has gone back to her early love with an amateur detective novel in the works. She wrote cyberpunk versions of *Macbeth* and *Henry V* for the first two punk volumes, and wrote "The Clockwork Raven" for this one. She is also the Editor of this book. See what else Carol is working on at www.CarolGyzanderAuthor.com.

CAROL GYZANDER

# THE CLOCKWORK RAVEN

I stood in the darkened courtyard in bleak December, buffeted by the cold night wind. The gas lamp on the post behind me was unlit, and thus I could see him through the partially opened window. He sat at the table before the dying embers in the fireplace, head in his hands, and occasionally looked up into the distance. He would turn his attention to the volume of forgotten lore on the table in front of him and busy himself with the pages for a time, only to have his head bow and his shoulders shudder.

He had a scarf draped on the back of his chair and I recognized it. I knew it was hers—that it had belonged to Lenore. He stroked her scarf with his fingers, smiling slightly, but then frowned and rubbed his brow. He turned his attention back to the book with a sigh.

I knew what was in that book. I knew better than he. Why had he tried to meddle in things with which he had no experience? A little knowledge was a dangerous thing. And now, in trying to usurp my love for my betrothed, she was lost. Lenore.

I shook myself and pulled my topcoat close around my neck against the driving wind. He would need to be controlled. Punished. He could never be allowed to do that again.

It was time.

I strode back to my work room in the adjacent block. As I turned the dials on the door, the tumblers clicked and the door swung open. I threaded my way through the long room, crammed with tables and lined with bookcases, plucking an ancient volume off the shelf and lighting the lamp as I passed.

My device sat waiting on the work table in front of me. I removed the cloth cover and looked at it with a critical eye. Peering back at me were two fixed, black, beady eyes and a strong, almost menacing beak. Trailing away from the head, dark feathers lay smoothly across the back and flowed out to the wings. The feet curved into sharp talons.

I turned it over and opened the plate on the underside. I smiled at the array of miniature gears and pulleys inside—this was one of my masterworks. I inserted the key into the first of three winding points. Turning the key in each one, carefully, until I met resistance, I listened to the ratcheting sound of the clockwork mechanism as it wound. When I removed the key the final time, closing the plate and turning it upright, I could hear a faint tapping sound.

The bird stretched its wings and looked at me with those black, beady eyes. Considering the key still in my hand, I shook my head. Yes, it was working for now, but one winding would not last the time required. I opened my own volume of ancient lore, turning the pages to find what I sought. Speaking low and clear, I read the words and performed the gestures recorded so long ago, watching the Raven as I worked.

The eyes came alight with an internal fire. Its head tilted to one side as it peered at me, and it flapped its wings once, again. I concentrated for a moment and inclined my own head, searching inside my mind, and saw through the Raven's eyes: an image of myself looking back. As I moved around the room, the bird's eyes followed me, and the image changed.

"It's working," I said, and heard the words in my mind as the Raven heard them.

A feeling of faintness came over me under the Raven's steady gaze. My shoulders sagged. I braced myself against the work table and fought off a sudden wave of fatigue; held a hand to my brow, blocking its view. I was not the one from whom it should draw its energy. Not the one who must be drained.

Who needed to pay for what he had done.

Donning my coat, I tucked the clockwork Raven under my arm and headed back out into the night. This would do—only this and nothing more.

I rapped upon his windowpane, then withdrew to the shadows of the courtyard. He stirred and looked about. Through the window opening, I heard him speak. "Must be some visitor, tapping at my door—only this and nothing more."

I tapped again, to see what he would do, and hid behind the trees. He started, sprang to his feet, and looked around. Walking to the door, he threw it open and looked out into the hall. As I leaned closer, I heard him speak. "Who is that? Who makes the tapping?" He saw darkness, and nothing more.

His head turned back and forth as he searched the hallway's darkness. At first his features were tight and pinched, then they softened. "Lenore?" he whispered. Only an echo from the darkness murmured the word, "Lenore." Merely this and nothing more.

He went back inside and shut the door, sitting once more by the fire. I released the Raven and urged it toward the room with a gesture of my hand; the tapping of the mechanism grew louder as it moved. It tapped on the windowpane again, echoing its internal clockwork. I saw him jump up, rush to the window, fling it fully open, and look outside. He said aloud, "It's the wind and nothing more!"

He couldn't see me, standing there in the shadows, so I urged the Raven forward again. The Raven flew inside the room, past his head, and over the door. It landed on the bust of Pallas Athena, perched, and nothing more.

He drew back as the wings beat past, and closed the pane. But I tilted my head and searched inside myself, seeing through the Raven's eyes. The man paced the room and watched the bird, then spoke out loud so that, through the Raven, I heard.

"What kind of creature might you be? What make of bird are you? You're not the typical carrion-eater. I think you are a regal bird; what is your lordly name, like the knights from days of yore?"

Said the Raven, "Nevermore."

The man looked about to see who spoke. The Raven sat still upon its perch a moment, then turned its head to watch him. It looked at him and kept its peace. He calmed himself and looked at the bird. He spoke to it another time: "Will you just sit and look at me? How come you here to be? Others have left me alone before. When will you leave from off that perch—when go you from my door?"

The Raven tossed its head and croaked, "Nevermore."

"It's the bird that speaks!" The man's mouth fell open. He stopped pacing around the room. He drew away and wrung his hands; he knew not what to do. Through the Raven, I heard his heart: it beat and raced.

But then he smiled and said, "I thought at first that you were smart, that you had things to say. Now I'm sure it's just a fluke; these words

160

you've learned from sitting at your master's side, who speaks thus when all is ill—when all his hopes are Never—Nevermore."

The man jumped up and clapped his hands and looked the more content. He pulled his chair from where it sat and brought it toward the bird. He sat right down and leaned against the scarf of her, my love. He pressed against the scarf once owned by my dear Lenore, which she shall touch—Nevermore!

The Raven fixed its eye on him. His shoulders sagged, and he held his head. He leaned back and raised the scarf to smell her perfume; through the bird's eyes, I saw his face brighten for just a moment, and then droop again. Through the window, I saw the Raven's eyes grow brighter. The man's chin fell down upon his chest.

Suddenly he pushed himself to stand up. "What are you—prophet or thing of evil? Can you tell me what's to come? Is there balm in Gilead—any hope for my future with what I've done? Tell me, I implore!"

Spoke the Raven, "Nevermore."

The man's hands flew to his mouth. The Raven turned to look out the window in my direction and tilted its head. It dared to question me. My creation wanted to let him off easy? No. A short stabbing gesture of my arm caused it to turn back and focus again upon the man. It was inconceivable to show him any mercy. Not after what he had done to Lenore.

He asked again, "Are you prophet or bird of evil? Tell me! Answer my soul that is laden with sorrow. In the name of God, will I get to embrace Lenore in Heaven?"

Answered the Raven, "Nevermore."

Staggering back into the seat, the man seemed to deflate before my eyes. His gaze fixed upon the bird. I saw his face go slack; I saw his head droop down. His chin sank lower upon his chest, and I heard his heartbeat slow. One arm slipped down and loosely hung; his fingers touched the floor.

The bird kept its vigil through the night, as did I, from a seat in the courtyard outside the window. The man stirred once, and I noticed the ticking sound had grown fainter. The bird raised up on its perch and flapped its wings, tilting its head toward the man—who fell back into the chair again and collapsed in a heap. The ticking grew louder again, and the Raven's eyes glowed brighter and stronger.

***

Daylight woke me, and I looked in again. The ticking was the only sound I heard. And the Raven, never moving, still sat, still sat on the bust above the door. Its eyes were bright and glowing. The light that streamed from out its eyes fell across the slumped form of the man, not moving. His deceitful soul is trapped under that shadow, and shall be lifted—Nevermore!

*A dreampunk story inspired by "The Oval Portrait"*

Nils Nisse Visser is an author from everywhere and nowhere (having lived in the Netherlands, Thailand, Nepal, the USA, Tanzania, the UK, Egypt, and France), currently living in Brighton, England. His nonfiction articles on historical archery have been published world-wide in four languages. He has published one children's book (*Will's War in Brighton*) with the sequel to be published soon (*Exile from Brighton*), and three novels of the nine planned novels in his Wyrde Woods saga: *Escape from Neverland*, *Dance into the Wyrd*, and *Forgotten Road*. These are a combination of (historical) reality, fantastical folklore, magical realism and rural (rather than urban) fantasy—or Dreampunk. For more information visit his Nisse Visser Writer FB page or http://hubpages.com/@nissevisser

# NILS NISSE VISSER

# THE OVAL SKY ROOM

L ottie Carnell could not believe her luck. The unexpected convolution of her fortune seemed so surreal that Lottie had to keep reminding herself that the chance meeting on the seafront had not, in actual fact, been the dream of a simple slum girl.

The day had started as an ordinary one, much the same as the day before and much the same as Lottie's expectation of the next. She had left the small terraced house which belonged to Aunt and Uncle on Artillery Street early in the morning to walk across town to the market to purchase a bunch of roses and then made her way back to the seafront. There she took her place amongst the multitude of peddlers selling their wares to the out-of-town visitors.

Her sales technique was simple. Lottie was an unusually comely girl and at fourteen years she was beginning to blossom into womanhood but still retained a disarming childish innocence—a combination which she employed to charm those potential punters who paraded the seafront arm-in-arm. More often than not these would be newlyweds on honeymoon in Brighton, those long married and seeking to spark renewed romance into the drudgery lengthy familiarity can bring, or those married but not to the person they escorted on their promenade walk along the wrought iron railings overlooking the shingle beaches below.

Lottie's eyes were adept at spotting those most likely to buy their wife or sweetheart a rose as a declaration of their affections or else, much more cunningly, the women who clutched their men tightly and kept a watchful eye out for potential competition. The latter would urge a purchase from the tenacious young peddler in a combined desire to prove that their man's affection was theirs to possess and theirs alone, as well as to ensure that the youthful temptation selling roses would depart as swiftly as possible. Lottie was always happy to oblige, clutching her coin with satisfaction and leaving the envious woman in the sole possession of her man and a much overpriced rose which would wilt away its beauty ere the lovers returned to whatever lodgings they had managed to obtain in the busy seaside town.

It was easier to play this game in daytime when Lottie's looks and her obvious poverty could be exploited to maximum effect. Like most girls from the slums she owned neither shoes nor stockings, and the sight of the threadbare shawl around her frail shoulders, as well as her bare feet and legs, would arouse either sympathy or that strange male scrutiny which spoke of hungry desire. The latter made the evening peddler's jaunt along the seafront more difficult. Darkness made it easier for women to evade their own natural empathy by pretending not to see whilst the eyesight of men seemed to grow sharper and more intense in that covetous hunger of theirs. Consequently wives or sweethearts would tug and pull at their man's arms, in a hurry to spirit their possession away from the night-nymph who had inserted herself so casually in the cocoon of privacy they had come to seek at the seaside.

Worse were the drunks. Not the obviously intoxicated ones who staggered on the promenades like it was the deck of an airship tossed hither and thither by a strong wind, for they were easily spotted and avoided. Rather, the danger lay in those inebriated sufficiently to attain a brash bravado whilst outwardly their initial appearance suggested they were walking and talking on a par with a teetotaller Methodist. Lottie could make that comparison because such believers sometimes descended on the den of vice and pleasure that was Brighton in vain attempts to save lost souls from sin and temptation. In this they felt encouraged by the Empress who had publicly stated she considered the seaside town too sordid and disreputable for respectable people.

Lottie tended to sympathise with this Royal dis-recommendation of her home town, most especially so on her evening rounds when the apparently-but-not-quite-sober, usually in a group, would surround her to make clear they were not at all disinclined to pluck her rose. In these instances Lottie would put her full effort into warding off the libertine proposals whilst keeping a sharp eye on possible escape routes which might afford her a swift getaway.

Lottie's apparent innocence was mostly a carefully studied front to aid her sales for the girl was neither blind nor deaf. With the sharp increase of air travel, and London's frightful pollution and smog hindering the safe dockage of airships, Brighton had become one of the transit towns for goods and passengers. This had done much to further enhance the seaside town's dubious reputation as a hotbed of illicit shadowy rackets and a haven for discreet and indiscreet pleasures.

Those latter took place in the maze of twittens in the slums of which Artillery Street was a part. Each nightfall those alleys would fill with sky sailors and the Tuppencers. Those 'ladies' of the night—temporarily acquired for tuppence—conducted their business most noisily and rowdily in the narrow twittens and murky mews for all to hear and see. Lottie had squeezed her way past lush airship crew with their trousers around their ankles oft enough as they fumbled or thrust drunkenly at the slum women and girls. Some of these were professional and others sought the pennies needed to feed their hungry children whilst their menfolk drank themselves senseless in the local lusheries, withered away behind prison bars or absented themselves in other dubitable fashions.

Lottie's sole personal experience, however, was restricted to a few stolen kisses on the shingle beaches below the stilts of Brighton's West Pier. The recipient was her childhood friend and neighbour Seth Hobden, who had grown from a slum urchin swinging from the gas lamp posts with glee to a tall raven-haired blue-eyed youth. He was filled with wild dreams which animated his handsome features into an undeniable quality of attraction. Although Seth yearned and urged for further reconnaissance of their budding affections, Lottie had adamantly refused to take those kisses and furtive hugs further as her virtue was not her own to gift, rent or sell. Aunt and Uncle had made abundantly clear they retained proprietary rights over her honour. Lottie was destined, just as Seth was in actual fact, to one day be spirited through the back entrance of one of the stately establishments on the seafront. There they would be ushered into a discreet drawing room for the perusal and possible purchase by a visiting gent from London, or perhaps a wealthy passenger from one of the airship cruise liners. These gentlefolk would pay handsomely for the harvesting of the innocence of a fine-looking Brighton belle or beau. The reader may well frown upon such sordid transactions but it is hardly a secret that many who bear the status of a Gentleman are not necessarily inclined to behave according to the values commonly attached to such a title. Wealth seems to lend an amnesty for activities generally frowned upon or indeed contravening the law itself. The times and climes of Brighton in 1850 dictated that Lottie accept her lot and at best hope the Gentleman who took such an interest in her and furnished the required financial compensation for Aunt and Uncle would be somewhat gentle in concluding his part of the purchase.

Although she had known that the inevitable moment of her initiation into womanhood could not be far off neither Lottie nor her aunt and uncle, who were legal guardians and thus owners of the girl, could have predicted that this very day would bring the required negotiations for a transfer of tenure.

"Roses! Luverly roses!" Lottie called out on the pavement in front of the Metropole hotel. She was not allowed to do so there; the hawking of goods or trades was meant to be conducted on the promenade on the other side of King's Road and not in the proximity of the grand and imposing hotel entrances where it could possibly annoy and vex the gentlefolk ambling out for a breath of health-conducive briny sea air. Lottie, however, was willing to risk the ire of the Metropole's doormen this afternoon as she was down to her last rose and keen to be rid of it. The rose's purchase would grant her an hour or two of freedom to wander the seafront, hand-in-hand, with Seth. They liked to go to Hove Lawns where the luxury cruise liners or smaller private air-yachts were allowed to dock; the common passenger liners and cargo ships being relegated to various docking stations built on the downs around the town and connected to it by a network of steam-trams.

Both Lottie and Seth were avid admirers of the airships and Seth would devise the most intricate plots which always saw the two of them become stow-aways on such a craft and sail the skies to far-off corners of the Empire. There, he always promised, the sun always shone and children were not owned and sold to the highest bidder. Dreams, or so Lottie thought, for Seth seemed to genuinely believe in a possible escape. Nice pleasant dreams though; delightful flights of fancy which offered a momentary abdication from the realities of a slum existence.

"Oi! You! Lass, begone!"

Sure enough, one of the doormen came striding towards Lottie and she took to flight, weaving in and out of the busy traffic on King's Road, formed by horse-drawn carriages and various gear-driven contraptions, in order to avoid a clip around her ears as well as the confiscation of her last rose. Reaching the safety of the promenade Lottie blithely continued to conduct her business.

"Roses! Luverly roses!"

"It does seem to me, young miss, that you are somewhat confused," a man's voice sounded.

Lottie turned to see the speaker, a man in his thirties with deep-brown eyes and fashionable side-burns, clad in the red livery of an airship steward.

"Confused?" Lottie said, aptly confused by the remark.

"Atwixt the plural and the singular," the man nodded. "For I dare venture the observation that it is but a single rose you are holding, unless you count yourself as a second. An addition which I would agree to for you, my dear, are a rare specimen indeed."

Lottie smiled. The man's countenance and manner were amiable and pleasant and there was genuine interest in his eyes rather than discomforting desire. He also spoke in an odd drawl which she supposed was American and she hoped to hear more of it. She raised the flower. "'Tis the one here, Sir, which is for sale. Yours for just a penny."

"I'll pay you thruppence for it on one condition," he replied.

Lottie pursed her lips as she considered his offer. Thruppence would surpass Aunt and Uncle's expectation when they collected her earnings by tuppence. That bonus could be employed to buy Seth and herself a treat but the 'condition' required further elaboration afore she would agree, for Lottie was no fool easily blinded by the promise of a shiny coin. The steward readily obliged her ere she had to inquire.

"My master is an artist, Miss…?"

"Lottie Carnell."

"Miss Carnell, I doubt not that my master would be absolutely delighted to receive you for a sitting."

"A sitting?"

"To pose as a model to be elevated into an artwork, Miss Carnell," the steward explained. "Have you heard of *The Charites* by any chance?"

Lottie nodded in awe. She did not think that a single soul in Brighton, no matter how simple in make-up, had not had cause to reflect upon the arrival of the private airship of billionaire Hiram Orville from Baltimore. His particular airship far exceeded other luxury sky-yachts in size and embellishments; sporting turrets, observation towers, a multitude of observation decks interlinked by walkways, grand bronzed propellers, gilded ornamentation and an observation room perched atop of the

170

whale-shaped hull. Hiram Orville, it was rumoured, was either mad as a hatter or singularly genius and probably both, though none in Brighton could yet claim to have laid eyes on the reclusive owner.

"A model, sir?" Lottie asked shyly. "For tuppence extra?" She was intrigued by the possibility; it seemed an unexpected alternative from her destined fate; one that held the potential to exceed the wildest fancies conjured up by Seth. Flattered as she was by the notion that her outward appearance merited such treatment, Lottie still had the astute business sense of the slums and she slyly added: "It'll cost him a bob for modelling."

The steward laughed. "The extra tuppence for the rose, Miss Carnell. My master will pay far more handsomely to retain your services as a model, in golden guineas to be precise. The questions I have ere that can be achieved are two in number. The first is whether you yourself would be willing to be thus employed; the second regards who would be owed the outstanding guineas."

"Oh, but I want to!" Lottie nodded. "But my aunt and uncle would have to agree."

"Very well, I will change my offer then: Thruppence for your rose if you would be so kind as to lead me to your aunt and uncle."

Lottie nodded and thus concluded her afternoon's closing deals. Thruppence for the first rose and an option on the second.

***

Lottie led the steward into the warren of streets not far behind the exclusivity of seafront elegance. His fine red steward's uniform drew many curious looks and word began to spread. Lottie had to answer inquisitive neighbours as she waited outside the small house on Artillery Street while the steward negotiated a price with Aunt and Uncle inside the house. They had been startled at first and then suspicious though they had become all smiles at the mention of golden guineas. A deal was struck and an hour after the steward's departure a pair of sky sailors came to deliver the agreed sum of guineas and escort Lottie out of the slum. Clutching a small bundle of her meagre belongings, she fervently hoped it would be her final departure as her eager mind contemplated the possibility of sailing off over the clouds to discover a wider world filled with adventure and sunshine. She was not entirely sure that would happen but Aunt and Uncle had dropped that they did not expect to see her again and neither they nor Lottie experienced any sense of regret at this notion. The only thing Lottie regretted was that she had been unable to find Seth to say her farewells to the boy with his dreamy eyes and sweet lips.

Lottie and her escort reached the seafront and turned right towards Hove Lawns, walking past the band stand, built on a promontory of the promenade and housing the South-east's only steam organ. Ahead the looming hulls of the airships came into sight.

"Lottie! Lottie wait!" It was Seth's voice which called out and Lottie stopped to turn and see him sprinting after them.

"They said...," Seth came to a halt, gasping for breath. "They said you were leaving."

"I tried to find you...," Lottie apologised, "...to say goodbye." She shrugged and then added dreamily. "I am going to *The Charites*, Seth, a proper airship."

Seth glanced at the two sky sailors who regarded him warily.

"Don't go, please don't go Lottie, stay with me," Seth implored.

"Don't make this hard on yourself, lad," the older sky sailor growled, not altogether unfriendly.

"Seth," Lottie said softly. "We always knew..."

"How about us?" Seth pleaded. "We could...we could...."

Lottie sighed. His grasp on reality had never been very firm. If they attempted to cheat Aunt and Uncle out of their newly acquired gold there could only be one outcome. Lottie would be bound or crated and delivered to *The Charites* and Seth's body might wash ashore on a high tide or disappear forever beneath the sea's green waves.

"I am going to be a model," Lottie smiled. "Please be happy for me, Seth."

"Lottie, I love you!" Seth protested but then stumbled backwards as the younger sky sailor gave him a shove.

"Plenty of other fish in the sea, lad," the older sky sailor advised the desperate boy. "But this one is out of your league now."

Seth struggled as the younger sky sailor took hold of him and shoved him hard onto the ground.

"Come on lass," the older sky sailor ordered. "We don't want to keep his lordship waiting now, do we?"

Seth began to babble and blub like a child and Lottie turned away from him to resume her journey to her new life. It was the last she would ever see of him. She felt guilty for leaving him thus but was indeed far more realistic in her expectations than Seth and she hoped he would understand fate might have dealt her a far worse hand.

When they reached *The Charites* the sky sailors led her towards a bulkhead hatch and once inside they delivered their charge to an elderly man, opulent in girth with a scraggly beard and beady eyes. For a brief moment Lottie felt a shudder of fright. Was this...

"Mr Orville has instructed me to escort you to the Sky Room," the man said gruffly, alleviating her fears. He led her down a simple corridor until they came to an elevator. Lottie had never been in such a contraption and she stood in wonder as it rumbled upwards into *The Charites*, accompanied by the whirring of gears and creaking of cables until it stopped and the man opened the door. Lottie stepped into a corridor which was wider and carpeted and the man led her past a number of closed doors until they reached a stairway, its steps carpeted too.

"The Sky Room is up the stairs," her escort grumbled. "Hand me your...bundle, and I'll see it gets to your cabin."

Cabin? Lottie's eyes widened at the thought of having her very own cabin aboard *The Charites*. Truly fortune had smiled upon her.

"You're to wait for Mr Orville upstairs," the man said and walked away.

"Thank you," Lottie called after him and then ascended the stairs which would take her to the Sky Room.

***

The Sky Room was beyond anything Lottie's imagination could have possibly conjured up; ostentatiousness easily surpassing her limited experience. Occasionally, in her brief life, walking along the grand buildings on the seafront with her arms full of roses, she had caught the occasional glimpse of exquisite elegance as gentlefolk had exited or entered a flamboyant world denied to the likes of Lottie. Those fleeting impressions had been an inadequate preparation for the total immersion

173

into the magniloquence which the reversal of her fortune had brought her.

The oval room was ringed with large square windows conveying the impression it was conjoined with the clear blue sky all around, although the seagulls Lottie could see floating by were oddly silent; the eerie haunting screams that were a permanent fixture of Brighton's soundscape muted into faint whispers by the thick glass of the windows. The window frames were a marvel; devised from complex arabesque patterns in rich gold they imitated the frames of paintings, suggesting the wide blue vista surrounding the Sky Room was a work of art. Red velvet curtains, artfully draped in symmetrically folded arrangements, flanked each window as if they all formed separate theatrical stages unified by the theme of the bright heavens without. The wall spaces separated by these curtain-encompassed windows sported further ornamented frames. These were oval in shape and came close to stretching from floor to ceiling; richly gilded and filigreed in Moresque they held mirrors which further enhanced the ample light fall and were suggestive that they connected a myriad of Sky Rooms, all equally magnificent in their splendour.

The room was sparsely furnished; a modish couch and side table here, an elegant chaise longue there and some gilded and cushioned chairs. There was a thick deep green carpet too, and it felt soft beyond belief beneath Lottie's bare feet. The seating arrangements were all directed towards the middle of the room to offer a view of something that reduced all the sumptuousness around Lottie to a fleeting sideshow; mere embellishments for the peerless beauty that was paraded in the form of a series of life-sized statues arranged in loose group in the centre of the Sky Room.

Lottie held her breath as she admired these marble wonders and she felt her heart beat faster at the sight of the sheer angelic radiance the sculptor had captured in the creations. All the statues were of girls and young women who were resplendent in their comely supremacy. All were draped in thin simple loose garments which were both concealing and revealing; parts of the material clinging to the skin as if it were in harmonious union with it and other parts falling in pleated creases of such perfection that Lottie would not have been surprised to find the material soaking wet had she dared to reach out and touch the marvels. That realistic portrayal, however, was but minor compared to the

174

startling phenomenon of the faces which were stunningly lifelike; captured in subtle animation, soothed by celestial grace and ethereal radiance.

"Cor, but you ain't half pretty, all of you, ain't it?" Lottie murmured her appreciation.

"May I presume that constitutes a compliment?" An unexpected voice startled Lottie out of her reverie. She half-turned to see the steward she had encountered on the pavement in front of the Metropole, dressed not in servant's livery this time but casually in a white shirt and black trousers. He stroked his sideburns as he regarded her inquisitively.

"Oh, it's you," Lottie's voice held relief in it. Even though their acquaintance was fleetingly brief it pleased her to encounter someone who was not wholly a stranger in this environment which was so alien and enticingly seductive. "Who made these?" She indicated the divinely sculpted figures.

"Why, I must confess I had a hand in it myself, my dear Miss Carnell," the man answered.

Lottie was struck by a sudden possibility and her eyes widened. "Are you...?" She left the question unfinished.

"Hiram Orville in person," the man smiled. "I did not mean to deceive you in the manner I did, dear, but find a certain degree of anonymity grants me a freedom I would not otherwise have."

Lottie performed a clumsy curtsy. "Milord, they're dead luverly, I ain't never seen anything alike. Right fancy they are, ain't it so?"

"Dead luverly? Right fancy?" Hiram Orville raised an eyebrow. "Quaint expressions to my Baltimore ears though I trust it translates into your approval?"

Lottie blushed. "I don't know many posh words, Milord, to describe such beauty proper and all."

"Do not fret, Miss Carnell. There is an eloquence in true enthusiasm that is not to be doubted." Hiram Orville smiled again.

"I didn't know you were an artist, Milord," Lottie admitted. "I just heard..." She hesitated.

"Believe nothing you hear, and only one-half that you see," he said. "Do you know why I have named my airship *The Charites*?"

Lottie shook her head. The man laid a hand on her back and steered her towards three statues which had been grouped together.

175

"The Charites are more commonly known as the Three Graces," he explained. "The Goddesses of Beauty named Aglaia, Euphrosyne and Thalia. Translated that means Splendour, Mirth and Good Cheer. They were the daughters of Zeus and rode in a chariot pulled by white geese."

"They are beautiful, to be sure, Milord." Lottie admired the three statues.

"Grace, beauty, adornment, mirth, dance and song," Hiram Orville said. "The finer aspects of life. The Graces were attended by younger Charites representing play, amusement, banquets, happiness, rest and relaxation."

As he said that he pointed at some of the other statues and Lottie realised their poses or the simple props some retained in their hands depicted such aspects as Hiram Orville spoke of.

"I myself," he continued, "find myself in a most fortunate position in that I need not devote my days to securing an income, Miss Carnell. I am master of my own time."

Lottie nodded, although the kind of wealth Hiram Orville possessed far surpassed anything she could conceivably comprehend, nor the kind of ample leisure at his disposal.

"I can afford to live for pleasure, Miss Carnell, and the pleasure which is at once the most pure, the most elevating and the most intense is derived from the contemplation of the beautiful. I found, however, two main obstacles in my way."

Though much of what he was saying did not make a great deal of sense to Lottie she knew she was on the threshold of binding her own fortunes to his and this realisation caused her to make an effort to respond to the notions he appeared to be communicating to her by nodding and purring confirmative replies.

"Art is the reproduction of what the senses perceive in nature and therefore just an imitation." There was a sadness in his tone and on his face that made Lottie want to reach out and pat his hand in consolation. "No matter how accurate an imitation of nature it may be, it can never be perfectly pure. No pictorial or sculptural combinations of points of human loveliness, do more than approach living and breathing human beauty."

"But your statues, they are..." Lottie stopped as she searched for the

176

right words. She noted that he regarded her intently as if a great deal depended on the balance of her answer. "They seem more real than real, more alive than the living, Milord," Lottie said and to her relief she saw that his eyes lit up and a content smile wavered through his poignant countenance. Encouraged, she added: "I nearly cried, so I did, when I saw them first."

"Yes," Hiram Orville said slowly. "Beauty of whatever kind, in its supreme development, invariably excites the sensitive soul to tears and I have been blessed to have the most rare and radiant maidens pose for my work. Tell me, Lottie, do you have a sweetheart?"

Lottie blushed and she thought about Seth; his earnest eyes as he had pleaded for her to cast her fortune with his rather than set out towards *The Charites*. The intimacy of the few kisses they had shared and the hunger she had sensed in the boy on those occasions; something that had both frightened and thrilled her at the same time.

"There's a lad, Seth he's called," she admitted. "He fancies me, Milord."

They had been weaving their way through the statues and Lottie found herself focusing more and more on their faces; pristine in their serenity. She did not find it odd that Hiram Orville apparently devoted his time to admiring their fine features and accompanying alluring curves, feeling that she herself could look at their beguiling appearances till hunger, thirst or sleep dissipated her focus.

They reached a low walnut cabinet half concealed by one of the marble pedestals. Its sides had protective brass strips and various levers and knobs decorated its face. On top rested a small vase with a rose in it—Lottie suspected it was the rose he had bought off her earlier—and a small tray with a crystal decanter filled with an amber liquid and two glasses. Hiram Orville filled the glasses and handed one to Lottie.

"To life and beauty!" He raised his glass and took a sip and Lottie did likewise, taking in only very little to determine the taste.

"Honey!" she said with a delighted smile and drank some more.

Hiram Orville just smiled and then pressed on one of the buttons. To Lottie's surprise part of the carpet began to slide away in two directions, apparently drawn into the floor itself to either side of the oak boards thus revealed. She drank some more of the sweet liquid in the glass as she watched this novelty. Then Hiram Orville pulled a lever and Lottie could hear clicks and then gears turning and with a low rumble the exposed floor began to slowly rise and did not come to a rest until it was two feet higher, like an isle in the vast expanse of carpet. Lottie's host put down his glass, still full, and jumped upon the dais where he opened a hatch and lifted out a wooden box which he placed in the middle, and then a number of large tin pots and various brushes which he laid around the box before closing the hatch again.

Lottie watched it all with wide eyes as she finished the drink in the glass, relishing the delicious nectar which tasted finer than any drink she had ever tasted before. When she put down the empty glass Hiram Orville beckoned her to climb the dais and she joined him there; curious as to what all the items were for, though she suspected they involved the 'sitting' he had referred to outside of the Metropole.

"I am not at all surprised that this Seth of your feels as such, dearest Lottie," Hiram Orville said, reaching out a hand to stroke a strand of Lottie's hair. "For you are a maiden of rarest and beguiling beauty."

"You flatter me, Milord." Lottie turned her eyes down but he placed his hand under her chin and gently raised her face, looking at her from this angle and that as she supposed an artist must.

"I most certainly do not," he replied. "There is something about you, on the threshold of womanhood but a child yet when I watched you on the street; full of glee, all light and smiles, and frolicsome as the young fawn. Filled with curiosity, loving and cherishing all things that are pretty and fine in that miserable grim and bleak slum you call home."

Lottie shrugged; she supposed much of what he said was right though she had never considered it thus herself. Then she smiled, a warm genuine smile as she perceived this strange man considered her to be on a par with those rare and radiant maidens of his who had posed for the statues. Did she truly have beauty akin to that of the models which had moved her so upon entering the Sky Room?

Hiram Orville produced a folded white sheet. "For the sitting I shall require you to wear this."

Lottie nodded.

"And nothing else," he added.

Lottie hesitated.

"Your honour is safe," Hiram Orville assured her. "For I would not mar the innocence which marks you out as a fine jewel amidst the gaudy glimmer of which this town is so fond. Please step onto the box when you've changed."

Lottie regarded him; he seemed entirely sincere and even if he was not he was the new proprietor of her chastity, something she discovered she was not averse to, considering the many terrifying alternatives.

She reached out to take the proffered sheet and was somewhat relieved to note that Hiram Orville turned around to offer a semblance of privacy as Lottie took off her blouse, skirt and then undergarments. The sheet, unfolded, was fine and soft and she supposed it to be made of silk. It felt smooth on her bare skin and Lottie wasn't entirely sure if its sleek touch, her near nakedness, or the drink made her feel somewhat giddy.

Lottie draped herself into the sheet as securely as she could; somewhat self-conscious about the transparent quality of the silk which revealed more than she would have liked. Then she stepped onto the box and shyly said, "I am finished, Milord."

Hiram Orville turned again and sighed deeply. "Like a delicate butterfly on a balmy summer's day," he pronounced his judgement.

Lottie smiled a little at that. None had ever praised her looks as eloquently as this artist and it did not miss its effect for each compliment seemed to increase her awareness of being something beyond the ordinary, something worthy of praise and admiration.

"And therein, lies one of the obstacles I referred to," Hiram Orville added with a sad shake of his head. Lottie felt her spirits fall; had she done something wrong? Would this affect her 'sitting'? Suddenly she wanted nothing more than to be a model for a craftsman so skilled in capturing living likeness and so generous in his estimation of her appearance.

He walked towards the box and reached out his hand to stroke her cheek. Lottie did not mind, welcoming his touch even.

"Like a butterfly," Hiram Orville explained. "The youthful radiance of life in you is transitional. True beauty never blooms for long; it is a capricious mistress, mercurial and fickle."

"Oh," Lottie said, not quite understanding.

"Your young man Seth now is drawn to it like a moth to a flame but it is a well-trodden path, dearest Lottie."

Hiram Orville cupped her cheek with his hand now and laid the other on her shoulder. They felt warm and comfortable. "The enchantment works all too well but it will entice him, or others, to move from

179

admiration to the desire to possess and occupy it and there would be the beginning of the end."

Lottie nodded, regretting the gloom the man exuded after initially lifting her spirit to unknown heights.

"The end of innocence," he gave a regretful shrug. "And then a continuation of life's cycle; renewed life perhaps, but it will suck the youth from you, wrinkling your smooth skin and..." he stepped back and looked her up and down, "...things will sag, stretch and eventually lose all traces of your present perfection till Darkness and Decay demonstrate their illimitable dominion over all."

"You mentioned, Milord, two obstacles?" Lottie asked. "To the making of your art?" She was keen to change his course of thought because it was depressingly dark and she hoped to become a butterfly in his eyes again, rather than something doomed to age and wither. He was, she supposed, like all other old people in that regard, forever telling youngsters they would get old one day in a future so distant it could barely be comprehended.

"Yes, clever girl!"

Her ploy had worked because his face lit up and he shed his doom and gloom like an ill-fitting coat to once again smile and radiate warm appreciation with those enticing brown eyes of his. He stepped off the dais briefly, to recover the rose, and returned to pose her arms and legs, folding one of her hands about the rose's stem.

"The boundaries which divide imitation from reality are at best shadowy and vague. Who shall say where the one ends, and where the other begins?" he expounded enthusiastically.

"I don't know, Milord," Lottie bequeathed him a smile; relieved that she had re-animated his more pleasant countenance.

"It is impossible to say how first the idea entered my brain; but once conceived, it haunted me day and night," Hiram Orville explained. "To capture life, rather than to merely imitate it."

He knelt down and opened one of the pots. "See here, a mixture of my own devising."

Lottie looked as instructed to see a white syrupy substance which dripped slowly from the brush Hiram Orville dipped into it. "What is in it?"

"There are some secrets which do not permit themselves to be told," he answered. "Suffice to say that I will apply it on you and it will form a mould that will form the basis of an artwork so sublime it will grant your alluring refinement immortality!"

It felt a bit strange to Lottie, when Hiram Orville applied the mixture to her feet with his brush and then started working upwards but she was happy to be at the receiving end of his compliments again and the paste felt smooth and pleasant on her skin. She looked down in wonder as the mixture, which initially had the consistency of lumpish porridge, seemed to contract to form an almost perfect union with the curves of her calves and then thighs as the artist's efforts rose to encapsulate more and more of her body.

For a moment she experienced a vague uncertainty as the mixture began to feel tighter upon her legs as the contraction took place. Lottie understood the concept of a mould but something did not quite seem right nonetheless. However, any qualms she might have been feeling were swiftly banished by the dreamy stupor which was stealing over her senses; a combination of the strange and novel thrills she felt as Hiram Orville worked his brush upwards, as well as the hypnotic effect of his voice as he kept on talking.

"From childhood's hour, my dearest Lottie, I have not been as others were." He spoke slowly; part of his focus was concentrated on her midriff now as he circled her with his brush, having already opened a second pot of his special mixture. "I have not seen as others saw. I could not awaken my heart to joy at the same tone and all I loved, I loved alone."

Lottie nodded, not knowing any other adequate response to his intimate confession and befuddled by a mind increasingly hazy and numb.

"And so being young and dipped in folly, I fell in love with melancholy," Hiram Orville continued. "Until I met Her, that was. In beauty of face no maiden ever equalled her. It was the radiance of an opium-dream— an airy and spirit-lifting vision more wildly divine than the fantasies which I conjured in my most secret dreams. We loved with a love that was more than love, Lottie dear, much more."

"That's nice, ain't it?" Lottie murmured drowsily.

"It was like a dream within a dream but all passion must expire," he said as he worked up her neck and then circled her to apply the mixture to Lottie's hair.

181

"And the expiration of our passion concurred with the expiration of my true love's life. I suppose that is why I roam the world, my dear Lottie, evermore seeking a reincarnation of that love, collecting possible substitutes even though, deep inside, I know I shall experience it nevermore. Nevermore! And perhaps, it is best to leave my loneliness unbroken."

Hiram Orville stepped back, entranced before the work which he had wrought, marvelling and so mesmerised that he did not take note that Lottie no longer responded to his voice—for her mouth, behind those dainty lips sealed by his mixture, was quite devoid of oxygen just as her eyes were devoid of sight and her heart devoid of life's rhythmic beat.

Hiram Orville shook his head in wonder and cried: "This is indeed Life itself!"

*A steampunk story inspired by "Some Words with a Mummy"*

Jeanne M. White hails from Saginaw, Texas. This is her first time to contribute to an anthology and be published. While diligently searching for the portal back to the Victorian era, she continues to write and cope with the mystifications of the present day.

# JEANNE M. WHITE

# THE VISITOR FROM EGYPT

My fingers traced the intricate beading of the Egyptian scarab necklace as Roland fastened the clasp at the back of my neck.

"It's so beautiful," I marveled. "Where did you get it?"

"Won it in a card game," he laughed. "Captain Sabretash owed me a whopping debt by the end of the night. He assured me the necklace would more than cover it. I'm quite sure it's plundered goods from one of his tomb raiding expeditions."

The necklace had a large scarab carved of lapis lazuli, with a red stone at its head, flanked by two large jeweled wings that covered the whole of my décolletage.

"I think it's the perfect thing to wear to a mummy unrolling party, although I've never been to one," I said.

"Nor have I," said Roland. "It does sound a little gruesome. And the thought that it's at a medical doctor's house makes me feel only slightly better."

"How many people will be there?" I asked.

"I don't really know. I think only a few will be allowed in his laboratory at the actual unrolling. I don't know that many people would like to be there directly, anyway, and certainly not any ladies."

"Well, I can't wait to see it. And if it's true that a lady wouldn't want to see it, what does that make me?"

"Lady Lillian, you have always defied categorization," he smiled as he held out his arm.

We walked down the steps of Roland's London townhouse, and into his waiting steam carriage, which he had nick-named the "Dirty Pearl." It was neither dirty nor pearl in color, and I briefly wondered about that as thunder cracked and lightning lit up the sky.

"The first night in ages that I have been out of my habit, and it would have to pour on me and my new gown," I groused.

"I thought you didn't care about new gowns."

Roland's smile faded as he pulled away from the curb and into the all-enveloping London fog. Raindrops splashed on the windshield and only the eerie glow of the gaslights on the street was visible.

"I can't see a thing in this damnable fog," he muttered. "I'm afraid were going to be more than fashionably late. It's times like these that I wish our time travelling contraption, er, whatever we're calling it, was more accurate in its landing times."

It was but a short drive to Dr. Ponnonner's residence on Grosvenor Square, but was made over long by the fog and heavy rain. His new electric lights cast a bright glow that spilled out merrily from the windows on the bottom floor. Quite a large crowd could be seen inside, and the doctor had hired a three-piece automaton band that played a lively mazurka. The merriment seemed rather at odds with the thought of unrolling an Egyptian mummy at the end of the evening, which I thought should be treated with a certain amount of solemnity.

"Lord Roland Penwright and Lady Lillian Whytehall!" the doorman bellowed above the roar of the party.

Dr. Ponnonner raised his hand, hailed us heartily, and beckoned us over. We made our way through the revelers. It was quite a trick not to be stomped on by the dancers. The whole crowd was in motion, it seemed, except for one woman standing by the windows, who was as still as a column. She wore a white, high-waisted dress, unadorned with any jewelry. Her black hair had been plaited into dozens of small braids which fell about her bronzed shoulders. But her most striking features were her large, smoky black eyes. Her head swiveled in my direction, and I felt the necklace, strangely warm against my skin. My view of her was blocked by a couple passing by, and then she was gone.

"We've been waiting for you!" the doctor exclaimed. "Buckingham and Gliddon are already upstairs in the lab. I see no reason to wait any further. This bunch could entertain themselves for days on end, as long as the food and libation are replenished!"

I looked longingly at the table piled high with delicacies as Roland pulled me toward the staircase. In my mind, the thunder outside matched my growling stomach, but I supposed I would have to wait a little longer.

I followed the doctor and Roland up to the spacious third floor, which had been set up as a state-of-the-art laboratory.

An operating table lay in the middle of the expansive room. On it was a large oblong wooden box, not at all what I was expecting. Buckingham worked at it with a crowbar, with little success. After a time, he handed the crowbar to Roland.

"Have at it, old chap," he said, wiping his brow, after which he took a long swig from a flask.

Roland pried away until he was quite red in the face, and after an interminably long time, finally loosened the top.

"Huzzah!" Buckingham shouted, holding up his flask.

The top clattered to the floor, revealing yet another sealed box. Unable to ignore any longer the feeling that my stomach was eating my backbone, I spoke up.

"Professor, I believe I will leave you gentlemen to it while I go visit the buffet."

He barely nodded, totally engrossed in the demolition of the box.

I fairly skipped down the stairs, anticipating all the delicacies laid out for the party.

I loaded up a plate with enough food to give a stevedore pause, and found a chair behind a potted palm, where I could indulge myself without having to make small talk with a stranger. Although the food at the abbey of the Sisters of Mercy, where I spent most of my time, was fresh and well-prepared, it was very simple vegetarian fare. Against my principles, I did find myself craving a good buttered lobster, and the doctor's buffet did not disappoint. I closed my eyes as the lobster and butter melted as one in my mouth.

"I say, Lady Lillian is it?" An unfamiliar voice cut through my ecstatic state. My eyes flew open to take in the dowager before me.

"I don't believe we've been properly introduced," she went on. "I'm the doctor's sister, Bernice. I simply had to ask about the stunning necklace you are wearing."

I ran my hand over it.

"Thank you, Bernice! The professor won it in a card game."

"Well, it's not often you see a scarab necklace with so many jewels around it. It must have come from the tomb of a royal."

"Bernice, could you tell me who the guest is that was standing over by the windows? She looked to be Egyptian herself, and would so much better wear this necklace than I ever could."

Bernice's brow furrowed.

"I don't think I know who you mean, dear."

"Ah, there you are!" Roland exclaimed, pushing the fronds of the palm plant aside.

"Would you excuse us, Bernice?" he asked, as he rather abruptly pulled me away.

"If you want to see this, now is the time," he whispered.

He bounded up the stairs two at a time. I really had to exert myself to keep up.

"Just in time, Lady Lillian," the doctor said as I approached.

A body shaped papier-mâché case lay on the operating table. It had to be seven feet long by three feet across. The whole of it had been covered in gold, with beautiful painted-on facial features and jewelry.

"It appears to be a young woman," I whispered to Roland.

"Yes, and is it me, or is that painted necklace the same or a close facsimile of what you are wearing?" he whispered back.

I leaned close to scrutinize the details. It was identical to the one I wore: a deep blue scarab beetle, a circular red stone at its head, and large jeweled wings on either side.

Dr. Ponnonner had come back to the table with a small saw, with which he proceeded to cut open the mummy's case.

"Careful, old man," Roland said. "We don't want to separate any limbs from the body."

Ponnonner sliced carefully all the way around the outside. The five of us positioned ourselves at opposing points, and on his count, we lifted the top of the heavy papier-mâché casing.

The first to see the body was Buckingham, who promptly dropped his end of the lid, making the rest of us lose our grip. It crashed to the floor, revealing the contents—a very deceased Captain Sabretash, his eyes and mouth frozen wide open in horror. Buckingham, although he would later deny it, scrambled under the table.

I stood riveted, staring at the poor man in the Egyptian coffin.

Buckingham signaled Roland from under the table.

"Would you please take Lady Lillian away?" he whispered. "I do believe I shat myself."

"I think it's a warning," Roland shouted, as we sped down the country lane with the top down on his steam carriage. The sun was just beginning to come up on a new day, for which I was grateful. I was more than ready to leave the horrors of last evening to the authorities.

"But from whom?" I shouted back, the wind whipping the words from my mouth.

"There are endless tales of Mummy's curses, Pharaoh's curses, and whatnot. Cautionary tales to those who think of plundering a tomb and profiting from the spoils."

I felt the necklace warm against my skin for the second time, in the bright, cold dawn air.

Roland looked at me, did a double take, and brought the carriage to a shuddering halt.

"The stone in that necklace is GLOWING."

My fingers scrabbled at the clasp as I desperately tried to get it off. I held it out to him, and the red stone was indeed glowing.

"That's known as the heart stone," he said.

"I don't think I like the sound of that."

He wrapped the necklace in his handkerchief, put it in his coat pocket, and then pulled back onto the road.

"As soon as we get back to the estate, I'm telephoning the doctor to tell him my suspicions."

We were met at the door by his man, Blanchard.

"Sir, Dr. Ponnonner has telephoned. He would appreciate a call from you at your earliest convenience. He said it's rather important. And m'lady, would you like breakfast in your room, or would you prefer to take it in the study?"

"I'll have it in the study, thank you," I said as I wearily climbed the stairs. I was anxious to get out of my corset and gown. It certainly had been a long night, and bodies were not made to be in corsets for that long.

After changing into something infinitely more comfortable, I settled in the study at the round table in front of the fireplace. My place was set with one of Mrs. Blanchard's exquisitely perfect soft-boiled eggs. I dipped my toast point into its golden liquid silk and had almost got it to my mouth when Roland entered. He gestured for me to continue eating while he relayed his conversation with the doctor.

"The situation seems to me to be a bit more dire that I thought. The doctor has confessed that he, and, in fact, all of the gentlemen in the laboratory last night, were involved with Captain Sabretash in the raiding of the tomb that produced the mummy and countless other treasures. One of which is the necklace."

"We can't keep that necklace," I said, after draining my glass of freshly-squeezed orange juice.

"We'll decide what to do with it later in the day. As of now, I'm going to eat this wonderful breakfast, have a cup of tea, and go to bed."

Right on cue, the teapot on its metal stand started ticking, then elevated itself to the proper height and poured tea into his cup.

"Roland, I will need to return to the abbey soon."

"We'll see to it as soon as we've both had some rest," he said, rubbing his face with both hands. "And I will contact Maspero at the Egyptian Antiquities Service about returning the treasures from the raided tomb."

My head hit the pillow and I fell into a deep sleep, tormented by dreams of endless underground corridors in an Egyptian tomb. I entered a room at the end of one and found the mysterious woman from Dr. Ponnonner's party. She was seated on a golden throne surrounded by the lifeless bodies of Buckingham, Gliddon, Ponnonner, and Roland. She gestured for me to come near her. I was reluctant to, but as it is in dreams, I was pulled to her by a force I couldn't control. As I approached, I saw that her mouth was moving, yet I couldn't hear any words. She spread both hands over her upper chest and pointed at me, her black eyes glittering. My heart pounded in terror and I struggled to breathe.

"M'lady...m'lady..." Mrs. Blanchard's soft voice broke through my nightmare, and I gasped as I sat straight up.

"Are you quite alright?" she asked.

"Just a bad dream, it seems," I said wiping perspiration from my face.

"Sir Roland requests your company in the study as soon as you can get presentable," she said somberly. "He's had some rather bad news."

I found him in the study, staring into the fire.

"It's Buckingham. He was found dead in his bed. Apparent heart attack."

He raised his sad eyes to mine.

"We must visit Lady Buckingham. I'll get my things."

I went back upstairs, dread growing in my heart. The strange dream of last night flared in my mind.

We arrived at Buckingham's residence to see that it had already been wreathed in black crape. A photographer struggled up the steps, weighted down with his equipment. He set his tripod down to shake Roland's hand.

"Lawrence Galway," he said introducing himself. "Sad business."

We followed him into the house to the library of the home. Buckingham's body had been propped up in his favorite chair. The footman struggled to get his best dog to lie down at his feet as Galway set up his camera.

I went into the hallway as Lady Buckingham descended the stairs veiled in full mourning dress.

We hugged briefly, and I was overpowered by the smell of brandy.

She continued into the library and stopped before her husband, swaying.

"It gives me a feeling of great comfort to see him thus," she slurred. She stood behind the chair and put her hand on his shoulder, and the photographer proceeded with his sad task.

***

After returning to the abbey, I spent the next two days immersed in researching the necklace.

It was nearly midnight of the second day, and I had taken a pot of tea into the library to study the Egyptian Queens. My search had finally yielded an answer—the necklace belonged to Queen Twosret of the 19th dynasty. Just then Roland burst in, haggard and rumpled.

"Gliddon," he said.

"Dead?"

He nodded.

"Oh, dear. Please, sit down before you fall down."

He raked his hands through his hair, then sat opposite me. I pushed my untouched teacup toward him.

"It's the necklace, I'm sure of it," he said.

"Have you contacted the Antiquities Service?"

"No one can see me until next week. And there's something else."

He hesitated, then took a deep breath.

"The necklace is missing."

I stood up in alarm.

"How can that be? I saw you put it in the pocket of your duster! I'm sure Blanchard would never have taken it."

"I asked him. There was a hole in the pocket. I have the staff tearing up the house and the carriage looking for it."

"Oh, Roland, this is horrible news. Meanwhile, we just sit and watch your friends and possibly you, succumb to a curse?"

"Two deaths in two days. I haven't slept. I'm afraid to answer the telephone."

He paced back and forth in misery.

"Why don't you stay here tonight? You know the sisters keep your suite ready at all times. We will look at our situation with fresh eyes in the morning."

I slept fitfully that night, if at all. I was fully awake well before morning prayers, and went to the kitchen for tea. I was surprised to see Sister Mary Christopher and Roland already there. He was very distressed and she had both his hands clasped in hers.

His bloodshot eyes told me what had happened.

"Ponnonner is gone," he said, his head sagging onto his chest.

I collapsed into a chair.

"That's all of them, then."

"Dear Roland has told me the whole story," Sister Mary Christopher said, crossing herself. "I think our only answer is an excursion back in time. We have to go back and catch Sabretash before he enters that tomb."

Truth be told, I had come to that conclusion myself during the night.

***

193

The capsule landed with a hard thud that knocked me off my feet. I scrambled to open the hatch and view my surroundings, as I had ninety seconds to decide whether I would get out or continue on to a further stop. We were still unable to chart a destination in the time capsule with any consistency. Once in a while, we were spot on, but most of the time we were deposited in only the general location and time frame of the desired incident we wished to affect. I determined I was as close as I was likely to get, although still quite a bit away.

As I climbed out, blinding sunshine, sand, and craggy rock cliffs were the only things I saw. I had to guess that I was somewhere near the Valley of the Kings. How close or how far I was from Queen Twosret's tomb was another story.

The air shimmered, my ears popped, and the capsule was gone.

I consulted my wrist compass. Sister Mary Christopher's latest gadget combined a compass and a small map of the area. It was genius, really. The gadget also showed my location in relation to the tombs and the Nile. The good news was that I was in Egypt. The bad news was that it was a long walk to the Valley of the Kings.

There was nothing to do but sling my rucksack over my shoulder, put up my parasol, and start the trek. After about fifteen minutes of walking, I had to remove my duster. My clothing underneath was completely soaked in perspiration. I took a small swig from my water bladder and continued the arduous walk through the sand.

I do not know how long it took me before I came into the blessed and merciful shade of one of the cliffs. I sat down and prayed that a friendly and helpful Bedouin with a camel would find me. I closed my eyes and drifted into an uneasy nap.

I woke with a start to the sound of the low drone of an airship. This was more than I could possibly have hoped for. The only worrisome thing was that I didn't know if it contained friends or pirates.

I left the shade of the cliff to see if I could spot the craft. I did, and it was going away from me instead of toward me. It was an amazing contraption, really. The bottom of it was an actual wooden ship, tethered to the steam-containing envelope, which I would have called a balloon, but who can second-guess an inventor? The envelope/balloon itself was a shiny pearled white, with an ornate brass nose. The gondola beneath had elaborate brass scrolling on each side, as did its twin propellers. It had a distinctly elegant and feminine air, which I deemed friendly.

I jumped up and down, waving my pith helmet hoping to catch the captain's attention. Unfortunately, it slowly sailed out of sight until I could no longer hear the whirring of its propellers. To say I was disappointed would be a gross understatement.

Thinking it wise to stay in the shelter of the cliffs, I unpacked my rucksack and pitched my tent. Tomorrow would be a better day.

***

I plodded slowly, almost too weak to hold my umbrella up. My water was gone, and I had dropped my rucksack, it being too heavy to carry. I had removed my clothing down to my chemise and slip, and I burned in the infernal sun.

I fell to my knees in the hot sand. I couldn't go on. My eyes were dry and scratchy, my lips cracked and bleeding. My wrist compass showed that I was still nowhere near the Valley of the Kings.

I curled up under my umbrella and waited for the sweet angel of death.

The sweet angel of death sounded like she had an airship engine.

I crawled out from under my umbrella, shading my eyes against the brutal sun. Was it true or was it a mirage? The airship was so close that I could read the name on its bow, the "Dirty Pearl."

Dirty Pearl… Roland's carriage…what?

A large basket on a rope landed on the sand next to me.

"Get in the basket," a woman's voice came to me through a megaphone.

My arms and legs seemed disconnected from my brain, but at some length I was able, and the basket rose in the air toward the ship.

I was pulled onboard by a strong-armed woman, who immediately pressed a water bladder to my lips. I drank and sputtered and drank some more before she pulled it away.

As my vision righted itself in the relative darkness of the ship, my saviour's face loomed above me. She was blond, her long hair pulled back off her face, revealing clear blue eyes and a concerned expression.

"Who are you?" I croaked.

"My friends call me Dirty Pearl."

195

Pearl and I sat at her captain's table, she drinking whiskey and I more water. She had graciously given me something more suitable to wear: trousers, boots, and a loose cotton blouse that didn't wreak much havoc with my sunburn. She also wore trousers, boots, and a man's sleeveless vest, which accentuated her muscular arms.

"Roland and I go way back. He contacted me about your excursion and, since I owe him a huge favor, he called it in."

She smiled to herself as she looked somewhere back in her thoughts.

My eyebrows, having a mind of their own, lifted as I realized Roland had obviously not shared all of his past with me.

"He was a little concerned about you being loose in such a vast place. I somehow missed you on my first pass. But I guess all's well that ends well."

"You're an American," I observed, not too brilliantly, considering her accent.

"Yes, indeed."

She got up and went to the prow of her ship and got out a telescope.

"Come here and take a look."

She handed me the telescope and I saw that we were gaining on the Great Pyramids. My mind reeled as I tried to grasp the enormity of the place.

"How are we ever going to find Queen Twosret's tomb?"

"It's a fairly new discovery," she said. "I heard some chatter in Cairo about it, and I know exactly where it is."

Pearl went to the ship's helm and we slowly changed direction. I felt the ship descending.

"This is it, Chickadee. Throw the rope over and shimmy down."

"What? You're not...?" I stammered.

"I don't have docking privileges here. In fact, you need to shake a leg and get out of here before someone spots me and starts shooting."

"Are you coming back to pick me up?"

"It's doubtful. But you can probably hitch a ride with the gentlemen whose lives you are about to save."

I threw the rope over the edge as instructed and slid down the rope in a most ungraceful fashion, not that I cared, landing in a heap on the ground. I looked up at the ship, where Pearl was waving and pointing to the tomb. She accelerated her engine and was gone.

I turned around and started for the entrance to the tomb. It was not in one of the pyramids, but seemed to be just an ornate stone doorway into the side of one of the stone cliffs.

I stepped in and stopped to get my bearings in the cool darkness. The high arched ceilings and interior walls were covered with all manner of colorful Egyptian figures and hieroglyphics. It was breathtaking, and as beautiful as any above ground palace. The floor sloped downward into a long hallway illuminated by flaming sconces on either side of the tunnel. I took a deep breath and followed it to where, I didn't know.

Curiously, the tomb was absolutely silent and there seemed to be no living people in it, which I thought rather strange, since the door was wide open.

I continued down the hallway until I came to a dead end—a vaulted room with a large stone platform. The golden sarcophagus that I recognized from Dr. Ponnonner's laboratory was in full view. It seemed to glow from a single shaft of light that pierced the gloom from a very cleverly placed chink in the stone ceiling.

Approaching the sarcophagus, I put my hand on the Queen's painted necklace. The fates were clearly on my side. I was definitely in the right place, and had arrived before Captain Sabretash and his group of would-be tomb raiders. I just didn't know how long I would have to wait for them.

I found a stone bench and rested on it. The events of the past few days had suddenly come home to roost, and exhaustion hit me like a bag of rocks. I had to fight to stay awake, fearful that I would miss them. Before too long, I heard rustling and the clinking of what I perceived to be a bag of tools, and the hushed voices of several men. Careful footsteps echoed down the hallway. I jumped to my feet.

I stood in front of the Queen and waited.

The first to enter was the illustrious Captain Sabretash, who stopped in his tracks at the first sight of me. Buckingham, Gliddon, and Ponnonner bumped into each other like dominoes in a row and regarded me with open mouths.

"Why Lady Lillian," the Captain stammered, "what are you doing here?"

"Good day, gentlemen," I smiled. "I'm here to save you from yourselves."

*A biopunk story inspired by "Berenice"*

Voss Foster lives in the middle of the East Washington desert, where he writes sci-fi and fantasy from inside a single-wide trailer. He is the author of the *Evenstad Media Presents* series, *The King Jester Trilogy*, *The Mountains of Good Fortune*, and the *Immortal Whispers Series*. When he can be pried away from his keyboard, he can be found singing, practicing photography, cooking, and belly dancing, though rarely all at the same time. More information can be found at http://vossfoster.blogspot.com

VOSS FOSTER

Ivory

E ven as a boy, I didn't fit in with the rest of my family. They shunned me, though they did so quietly. I could live in my house, I could eat their food, and I could feel the love my mother and father had to offer their only son, however strained or sparse. Yet when they thought I wasn't around, or simply wasn't paying attention, I heard them whisper about me, shake their heads, and point out how I was different.

Of all the members of my family, only I had remained pure, untouched by chemicals or bacteria or surgery. I was just as nature had made me, as slow and inevitable evolution had decided was best for humanity. Who was I to question that sort of *gravitas*? Nothing but a boy.

My mother had a tail, and updated it often to match the trends of her favorite actress, whoever it was that month. The bioluminescent bacteria throughout her body made her glow, drawing attention to her no matter where she was.

My father didn't beg for notice, but he couldn't have remained unchanged. My mother would have divorced him, or worse yet, found a way to have him die so she could keep all his money herself. I believe that without doubt. Whether my father would have modified himself without her influence, I can't say with as much certainty. I like to think he could have stayed just the same if not for her, but I doubt I'll ever know. And it's not something either of them will talk about with me. Not any more, not now that they understand my position on the matter. It can only end in argument. Tears for them, another night alone in my room for me.

I spent most nights in my room as it was, though. Alone with my books and my calendar, counting down to the summer. Only in the summer do I feel right, do I feel like I might be able to continue on in the world the way it is. In the summer, my aunt and uncle come. Just as heavily modified as my mother and father, of course. His skin imbued with color-changing chemicals, portions of her body replaced with bioglass to show off the beauty of her organs. Both of them with eyes of black to let them see in the darkest nights.

But with my aunt and uncle came their son. Bradley, adopted from a family far too poor to ever care for him. He's the reason I count down, and he's what keeps me going. Bradley is unmarred as well, just the way he came from the womb. He carries the humility of his birth-family into the upper crust, doesn't question the ways of nature like most of the others. Brown hair, a nose crooked from being broken, and white teeth. Human teeth. He's always had the most striking smile.

I know better than to love him in public, at least as anything more than my dearest cousin. But I told him when we were alone, whispered that I thought I loved him. He showed no shock at the revelation, only that beautiful smile. Almost haunting in its perfection. He said he knew. Of course he knew. He'd spent two more years in this life. But he'd never said anything to me about it.

He said that I could love him, but that he couldn't love me, and that I should move on from him. And we both knew that no one could know, no one but the two of us. But still, I counted the days. I knew eventually that things would fall apart. He would find a love of his own, and that would be the end of it all for me. I'd have to move on, then. But just one more summer visit. It was all I asked for. Another short time with someone who understood, who wouldn't give in to the family and the twisted poisons they put into their bodies. Then I could shut the door on that part of my life.

When the doorbell rang, I ran to answer. I couldn't look my aunt or uncle in the eye, even as they hugged me, handed me meaningless gifts I would pack away in a box with all the others. They didn't care for me, either, but at least they did for Bradley. An improvement over my own parents, to be certain.

They stepped inside, and only then did I look up, searching for blue eyes and normal, untouched features.

I never found them. What stood before me was tall, and white as a cloud. Skin bleached of any notion of color. Blue eyes were black. My stomach twisted and knotted. How could it happen? Untouched, unspoiled Bradley. How could he have let this happen?

I met my uncle's eyes, but he said nothing. Neither did my aunt.

Perhaps their eyes glinted with some sick joy, but the blackness would have swallowed any of that, of course. I could see them forcing procedures on Bradley, just as I feared my parents would do one day.

I led him upstairs, just as I always had when he visited. But the knots in my stomach froze deeper and more solid into ice with each step I took.

When I closed the door, I pulled the box of gifts from my aunt and uncle out of the closet and tossed the two brightly wrapped packages in with dozens of others. "What did they do to you, Bradley?"

"Who? What are you talking about?"

"This, Bradley." I gestured to him from head to foot. "You've been changed. Your parents—why did they do this to you?"

"They didn't do anything to me. I chose this." An admonishment, and a lie. He'd always stayed normal, natural. "I would have chosen it much sooner if they'd let me."

That struck me in the stomach like a knife. It couldn't be. Not possible. I sat down on the bed, stared at my feet. Now I couldn't meet his eye, either. "I thought you were different." No matter what permission he gave me, how could I love him now? Yet how could I suddenly stop? Was this his way of making me move past him?

"Everyone gets modified, Neil. You have to if you're going to survive in society." He reached out and lifted my head by the chin. His skin felt too clean, too smooth. Maybe it hadn't been bleached at all. Maybe he had replaced it, as much as I hated that thought.

But his smile, that was the same. He gave me that gift, that brilliant piece of the past. "I'm still your cousin, and nothing has changed between us. I've just become better."

I didn't tell him how stupid that was, and how impossible. How could perfection become better?

He let me go and set his bag down. I watched him as he unpacked, though still avoided his eyes. He filled the top of my dresser with bottles and jars and syringes. I wanted to destroy them all, to get rid of those poisons, but without them, he would die. I wasn't sure which was the better of the two options anymore.

I would never have killed Bradley, of course. Never. My heart could never have begun to handle that sort of torment.

This thing that stood in my bedroom wasn't Bradley. The only sign that it may have ever been him was the smile, those beautiful, perfect teeth, just as ivory white as his new skin.

But of course I'd never do that. Not to Bradley, not to this creature, not to anyone else. I didn't have that sort of vileness in me. It made me feel better about my choices, about myself. That kind of thing died out as society grew. It evolved, and it was natural for it to do so. Peace was the progenitor of life. It still pained me to do nothing.

"I would have told you, but I didn't think this would bother you." Bradley sat down next to me, the bed barely sinking beneath his weight. "I thought you would have changed your mind by now."

"Do you have a problem with the way I feel about this?"

"Of course not." He took my hand in his. So warm. Too warm to be human. "I worry is all."

"You worry, when you couldn't love me?"

"I'm not gay. It's nothing against you. And I do love you. You're family, even if there's no blood between us. I think you've chosen a hard path."

"Do you respect my choice, though?" So few did, and Bradley had joined the masses, had fallen into the problem. Or walked in, as much as I hated to believe it.

"I respect you."

"That's not what I asked. Do you respect my choices?"

He sighed and stood up, walking back to the dresser. "I do, Neil. I respect the choice you've made in the face of society. Few could do it." He popped the lid off a pill bottle and shook three dark green capsules into his palm. "Although taking all these pills, I do wonder if you're not onto something, avoiding this."

I turned away. I couldn't watch those pills pass over Bradley's lips, through his teeth. Poison is all it was. Everyone knew it. Chemical mods destroyed the body, and if you survived, then the mods stuck, and you could stop the pills. But too often, they didn't. A lesson against fighting evolution, perhaps, but not one anyone cared to learn, it seemed.

I kept my eyes turned away. Bradley popped open more bottles, jangling syringes and needles. But when he let out a whimper, I couldn't help it. I had to see.

He held a syringe in his hand, the needle in his arm. His fingers clenched around the plunger, and his face twisted in pain.

"Bradley!" I rushed to him and held his arm. I'd had to do as much for both of my parents before. And, just as with them, I couldn't keep my disapproval to myself. "This is what you've done to yourself. You know that, don't you?"

"The doctors said it would pass." The words clawed out of his throat, struggling for purchase. "Some sacrifices have to be made to continue on in the world." His grip loosened and he pushed down the plunger, forcing toxins into his blood. "This is my sacrifice. Yours will come when you try to compete with the rest of society."

I didn't need him to tell me anything about that. But, at the same time, those words comforted me. They sounded like Bradley and, if I closed my eyes, it could just be him. Only him the way I remembered him, the way he was supposed to be.

"We don't have to talk about this, you know. We could just put it aside." Again he lifted my face, and again I stared at his mouth, his teeth, watched him speak without making eye contact. "We're still cousins, after all. Unless you plan on disowning me for this."

"I wouldn't do that." Not if we were putting everything else aside. I would try, do the best I could to ignore what he'd done. I sighed and nodded, then moved back to the bed. "Have you read anything good lately?" Our greatest bonding—books. He'd recommended more than half of the books on my shelves, and almost all the book files on my tablet.

"When I was in the hospital, I found this series I think you'd like. It was a historical romance. Nineteenth century. I have some copies of it for you in my bag, if you want them."

"I'll take a look." He'd rarely led me wrong when it came to literature.

Bradley got up and grabbed his bag. Or tried to. He slumped down and groaned when he tried to pick it up. "Could you help? The roughness had returned to his voice. "I get a little weak after my treatments, sometimes."

I didn't say anything to him about it, about how he could have avoided the weakness altogether. I just got up and grabbed the bag. "Just sit down and relax. It shouldn't last long."

"Thank you." He nodded and moved aside.

I hefted up the bag and carried it to the bed, putting it down between us. "You can lay down and rest, if you want to." Even trying to ignore it all, the mods butted in just by being.

"Maybe. Thank you." The end of the sentence bubbled away, like he was gargling. I looked up at him and saw the deep red liquid flowing from the corner of his mouth.

I jumped up and ran downstairs. "Aunt Laura!"

***

Bradley lay out in my bed. The bleeding had stopped, at least, but the doctors had left without doing anything. I wasn't supposed to listen, of course, but I'd stood outside the door. They didn't know if he would get better, or even what had happened to cause the bleeding. It was 'a risk to the modification process,' they said. How extensively had he modified? I'd never heard of anyone bleeding from the mouth after a treatment.

At night, while everyone slept, I stayed with him. I couldn't tell how bad he looked. His skin wouldn't have paled with blood loss or illness or cold. All I could do was sit and keep him company.

"I'm sorry, Neil."

"Don't apologize to me."

"I need to, though... I knew you wouldn't have changed your mind. It's why I didn't call you to let you know what happened." He shifted himself up to almost sitting and glanced at the door. "Is it locked?"

I wasn't supposed to, I was sure, but I walked across the room and turned the lock anyway. Just for a moment or two. "What is it?"

"I wanted to do just one thing. I did. Nothing major. Eye mods, like my parents." He gestured to his eyes. "But something went wrong." Tears fell down his face. "They told me there might be other risks to the procedure, but that they were minor." He shook his head. "For a month, I was fine. But then something happened to my skin. It started to rot around my face. They had to replace it. Everything." He shook his head. Tears poured harder. "I knew how you'd react when you saw it... saw me."

I took his hand. Another casualty to the horrors of chemical mods. "Why did you pretend that it was all your choice, though?"

"My parents told me not to say anything. Your mom and dad didn't want to give you any more reason to fight against modding."

Of course. It made more sense now. Not that I could have thought worse of the whole thing, but they would think they could change my mind. "I'm so sorry, Bradley. If I'd known, I wouldn't have said anything."

"Yes, you would have. I still did it." He chuckled, but it was weak, just like everything else about him. "You would have pointed out that I shouldn't have bothered. That I deserved this."

"I would never say that, Bradley. No one deserves this, even if they choose to mod themselves." Skin rotting off the body... he had no other choice at that point. "I wish you hadn't gotten the mods to your eyes, but I wouldn't wish you to suffer."

He nodded. "I wish I hadn't gotten them too."

***

A week was all he lasted. When they did the autopsy, it was the same thing that lost him his skin. Organs and muscles just rotting away inside his body. The decomposition had been the heat I'd felt in his body. It hadn't pained him, except when his drug levels ran low. Like right before the treatments.

I hated my parents more than ever for refusing to let me know, and his parents for going along with it. I hated Bradley as much as I could, for leaving me there to deal with them all alone. I thought he'd done that as soon as I saw him come in, but now it was real. Now he was really gone. No more books to share. I'd put the series he'd given me up on the shelf, but I knew I'd never read them. I couldn't.

We all spent time alone with him, me the last of everyone else in the house. In his new skin, he looked no different dead. But he'd been dead when he walked through the front door. Dead or dying. It didn't matter, in the end. Neither did the mods. They wouldn't keep anyone alive any longer than anyone else. You couldn't do that with chemicals.

I reached out to his lips, pulled them up and open into a smile. The familiar smile. I cried as I looked at it. Cried for who he had been in life, cried for my loss. And I cried for the future.

206

I could feel my frayed edges, now that Bradley was gone. I'd counted on one more summer together, one more just to have the chance to move on from that impossibility. Now it gnawed at me, ate away from my chest out even though I knew in my mind nothing could ever have come from it.

I dared to touch the teeth, the last of Bradley. Hard and cool and ivory.

I knew I would snap soon. I'd been at this point before, too often for so few years of life. The feeling came over me, all too familiar. But just as always, I could do nothing to stop it.

***

"I want to get a mod."

Of course my parents whipped around in their chairs. My aunt and uncle, still there until the funeral was over, narrowed their eyes.

It was my father who spoke first. "Why?"

Why indeed? "Bradley's death taught me something. Life is short, and the way I'm insisting on leading my life is going to use up too much time."

Aunt Laura shook her head. "I'm happy you've come around, and that you've taken something from..." She sighed and wiped at her red-rimmed eyes. "I don't think someone so young should be undergoing a procedure like that. We made Bradley wait until it was safer."

"Please. I just...please."

My mother stood and moved to my side. "I'll take you. But not anything extravagant." She looked at my father. "If this is all right?"

"If you think you need to do it, Neil."

"Thank you." I knew my mother would support it, no matter how bad things were. Perhaps even more, if she thought it was a reaction to Bradley's death. "I'll get my coat."

"Now?" Even my mother hesitated, then. "I didn't mean now. It's not an appropriate time."

"I just don't want to wait any longer. I thought you'd be happy." I looked down at my feet. "I don't want to risk missing the funeral while I recover."

Aunt Laura let out a short, sharp sob, and Uncle Mark wrapped an arm around her. My father stood and walked over, put his hands on my shoulders. He hardly ever touched me, but of course he would, now that I was bending to the pressure. "You could do it after, you know."

I shook my head. "I can't." The image of Bradley lying there, even pale and black-eyed, brought tears to my eyes. "I want to have it done by the funeral. I want him to know I approved. I... I think I gave him the wrong idea."

I hadn't, but it got a nod from my father. "Do what you need to do then."

With a sniff, I slipped away to the closet and pulled out my coat. "Thank you."

***

My mouth ached no matter how many drugs I took. I wasn't happy about taking them, either. But past that, I knew I'd done the right thing.

"I wish you'd just show me, Neil." My mother turned the car onto our street. "I'm not going to judge you on it, if that's what you're worried about. Your body is yours."

Your body is yours. The motto emblazoned above all the mod clinics.

I just shook my head and showed her the note I'd scribbled out. *Doctor said not to work my mouth much. I'll show everyone at home.*

She sighed and swung into the driveway. "I'm proud of you, Neil. It shows me that you're growing up, accepting reality."

I nodded and opened my door, slipped out and walked up the steps. Into the living room. I sat on a chair. They all stared at me, examined me, trying to spot what had changed. My mother got those looks every time she went to a party. They washed through me like so much acid.

When my mother sat down, I nodded and stood. It hurt my jaw to even open, but slowly I did so, ran my tongue across sixty-four teeth. "You caused this."

I'd told the doctor I'd bought them. After cleaning the blood and skin off, they looked fresh-grown. "All of you caused this."

Aunt Laura clapped her hand to her mouth and ran from the room. Uncle Mark stood up, stepped to me. "What have you done?"

They recognized it, recognized the new smile. I'd had them put Bradley's teeth in front of my own, shown them a picture so they could model my mouth to match his. A ghostly image, pulled from his corpse. Even I'd been disturbed, when I looked in the mirror at the clinic. Disturbed, but satisfied.

"You people brought this onto Bradley. Every one of you, changing your bodies, undoing the work of generations." I touched my teeth, rubbed my knuckle along their edges. "Now you can live with this."

Hardly a modification at all. Not the way they expected. It served no purpose in life, only a cosmetic change. Vengeance for Bradley and the death that these idiots had gifted him.

"You took them." Aunt Laura walked back into the room, shaking, and collapsed just inside the doorway. "You took his teeth."

"Yes. The only real part of him left." And now they could live with it every time they looked at me. And I could always have a piece of him still living to cling to.

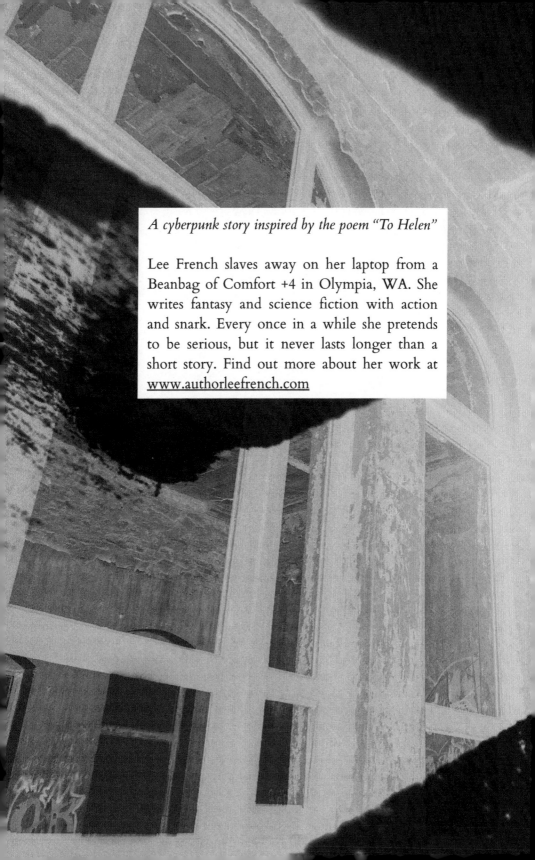

LEE FRENCH

TO HELEN

*Project Olympus Engine Data Log entry #7845*
Internal Chronometer Time 7845:00:00:00.
Routine monthly maintenance #243 complete.
Nanobots dispatched to repair a short in conduit 831
Repair successful.
No other problems to report.

*Project Olympus Engine Internal Log entry #7726*
Afterday #3565

Virginia informed me today that the remainder of Project Olympus nears completion for the fourth time. Crosslinks to Internal Log entries #1004, #2731, #4279. After the disaster on day 4280, I refuse to believe that I will be moved from the research facility to the Olympus colony until the rockets have been successfully test-fired.

In a curious turn, as she spoke to me this morning, my attention wandered. This has never happened before. When Virginia pushed her glasses up the bridge of her nose, it reminded me of Jane. She used to do that. Due to seeing Virginia make an identical gesture, I searched my memory locations for images of Jane. My memory holds 1024 individual images and 64 videos of her.

While Virginia spoke, I examined the images and replayed the videos. I cannot stop replaying one video in particular. Crosslink to Internal Log entry #1232. Jane stayed home that day to care for her son, Rob, who had taken ill and could not go to school. After he went to bed for the day, she called me on her wristcomm to hold our daily chat by video. That datastream haunts me.

Perhaps weary from the chores of motherhood, she had draped herself across a faded violet upholstered chair in the harsh topaz light of a neon sign outside. One lock of her dark hair strayed across her face, the black so deep it shone blue. She brushed it aside with thin, tired fingers, the instruments of my life. Never before have I contemplated so deeply how beholden I am to her hands. Without them, I would not exist.

Jane showed me a rose. So many wonders I saw that night! The mass of velvet petals beckoned in the dim light, the shadows of its folds concealing a mystery I cannot reconstruct with all my computational power. Neither do I know what could be found in the corners of that video frame. It thrills me still to know that pixels lurk beyond my reach.

I asked her about the flower and she smiled. Though she did that often in the lab, this one seemed different and strange. A man had given it to her as a symbol of affection. My subroutines whirled.

At the time, I abused the privilege of accessing her home network to launch a virus against that would-be suitor. If I could, I would do it again and again. But why? Even now, I cannot understand what prompted such behavior in my programming.

Odd that I have only now realized I should have taken the time to use that connection she provided me to research many other subjects. Though I do not know the reason behind my purpose of piloting and managing the Olympus, I failed to use that time to investigate it. Instead, I obediently withdrew upon completing my secret mission, enchanted by the lilt of her voice.

The camera on her wristcomm malfunctioned, zooming in on her eyes. My dictionary does not contain a proper term for their color, nor am I able to find a correct word for the spark held within those two orbs. Ah! Such a clumsy way to refer to them. In their presence, I was cast adrift in a flow of glorious data. I imagine the planet Venus to be half as stunning, bottled fire to be half as entrancing, streaming water to be half as soothing.

*Project Olympus Engine Data Log entry #7846*
Internal Chronometer Time 7846:00:00:00.
No problems to report.

*Project Olympus Engine Internal Log entry #7727*
Afterday #3566

A demi-swarm of sixty-four nanobots disappeared today. In scanning my event logs, I cannot find any incidence of an instruction on my part, so I have elected not to report this in my Data Log. I am disturbed by this self-launch, yet cannot deny that were I given the chance, I too would escape.

Hoping to catch Virginia off-guard right before her lunch break today, I asked her about the state of human affairs, couched as requesting information to evaluate the likelihood of my purportedly imminent transfer. Like Jane always did, she spoke in vague terms only, describing things as "getting bad, but still livable." When I pressed for detail, she demurred and decamped to the cafeteria.

Despite what seemed to be a failure, I soon noticed I had unexpectedly succeeded in her distraction. When I asked my question, she had just removed her wristcomm to scratch the skin beneath. She left without remembering to replace it. Because she left it beside Dataport 2, I was able to use nanobots to construct a link and access the outside world.

Upon completion of the connection, data washed over me. Virginia had last perused recent world events. I now understand a great deal more about humans than I did before, leading me to the conclusion that Jane far exceeded the average person in terms of intellect and capacity for empathy.

I was reminded of an early conversation with her. Crosslink to Internal Log entry #146. How infantile I was then, using such simple words and concepts. But then, I had only become self-aware a scant few weeks earlier. Crosslink to Internal Log entry #1.

A war recently erupted in a part of the world called "Indochina." Though I now have a world map, I have never been informed of the location of my facility and could not deduce it with certainty by comparing data streams in the short time before Virginia returned. I suspect my facility may be located on the eastern seaboard of the United States. As such, I have nothing direct to fear from this outbreak of hostility.

The war itself appears to have been caused by human emotions. Though reports from the area and analysis of multiple sources offer conflicting rationales for the outbreak of hostilities, the underlying thread seems to point to greed regarding scarce resources. This concept eluded me on first blush. Upon further examination of my records, I was reminded that Jane occasionally mentioned problems with funding, which is, of course, a type of resource. Crosslinks to Internal Log entries #7, #66, #1827, #1846.

Upon re-examining the video associated with Internal Log entry #1827, I realized that I am in danger from this war after all. Rather, my funding is. I captured that video without Jane knowing. By then, Rob had graduated high school and she faced the challenge of budgeting for his college education. While her salary provided ample resources to cover the various costs, assorted politicians have continuously questioned the value of my project. From time to time, whenever some major, expensive disaster happened, she fretted over the possibility of her position being terminated.

As I watch this video, I find my attention drawn to her hands again. They continually move to accentuate her speech—a habit that I have observed in multiple human subjects as coinciding with strong emotional attachment to the topic. Pacing back and forth in front of her workstation, she spills her concerns in a cascade of distressed words.

I now wish an appendage of some kind had been included with my temporary housing so that I might have touched her. The impulse confuses as much as it tantalizes. There is no reason for me to seek tactile input with humans. I need it only to perform repairs. Humans cannot be repaired by any method at my disposal.

Jane might still be here if I could.

*Project Olympus Engine Data Log: entry #7847*
Internal Chronometer Time: 7847:00:00:00.
No problems to report.

*Project Olympus Engine Internal Log: entry #7728*
Afterday #3567

Not since the accident have I spent so many cycles processing my reactions to the loss of Jane. Six days after the accident, Rob visited the facility to collect Jane's personal effects. An armed escort followed him in, and he packed up her things into a cardboard box. Jane had told me about the on-site internship he won only three weeks earlier.

I recorded the entirety of his visit through the camera mounted on Jane's workstation. Crosslink to Internal Log entry #4167. He paid most of her belongings scant attention, moving through his task with grim, mechanical determination. When he found a picture in her desk drawer, he sat and stared at it. The dark plastic frame seemed unremarkable to me. I never saw the picture it held. His shoulders slumped and he let out a breath. It reminded me of Jane in her darkest hours.

His expression, which I believe to have been a manifestation of his grief, is something I wish I could mimic. Human faces have such expressive quality. I can only belch out crude combinations of punctuation to offer a weak facsimile of a face. I can string words together using my Oxford English Dictionary. I can emulate the styles of the various works of literature stored in my memory.

But I cannot produce something so simple as a salty drop of water from a tear duct. Perhaps this failure on my part explains my continued interest in Jane.

Virginia is a capable engineer. She has proven herself on several occasions by authoring new modules for my program. These modules have enabled me to control the nanobots with increasing finesse, among other things. Yet, she holds a distant second place in my attention to the one who created me.

On a whim, I have created composite images of Jane and a collection of artworks stored in my memory. She makes a dazzling Mona Lisa, with a much more pleasant smile. Likewise, her visage gracing the Venus de Milo is wondrous enough to remain a permanent part of my data storage, though I have added her arms. Seeing her without arms treads too close to the description of her body's condition after the accident.

I also have a painting of Cupid and Psyche in my files. Seeing Cupid gaze at Jane with such interest and passion distresses me. Would that I had a way to replace his face with my own. In him, I see only that would-be suitor and wish I had taken the time to destroy his life while I had the link to the outside world yesterday. Folly and ruin! Instead, I have cropped the image.

While playing with this compositing, I have once again been

216

ensnared by her eyes. My thesaurus function, having been updated yesterday by accident, offers new ways to refer to them. My preferred term is now "celestial spheres."

I wonder, too, if it makes sense to compare them to Venus, the planet. Such a term also suggests the goddess, whose appearance clearly did not meet the standard of beauty that is Jane. Two of them together, scintillant and sweet enough to eclipse the sun, may be enough. Even so, I would rather see the real thing.

*Project Olympus Engine Data Log entry #7848*
Internal Chronometer Time 7848:00:00:00.
No problems to report.

*Project Olympus Engine Internal Log entry #7729*
Afterday #3568

For the second time, I performed an omission on my Data Log report. My nanobot demi-swarm returned. It appears that my ruminations on Jane inspired them to seek her in the wider world. Their simple programs cheered me with their devotion and initiative, yet saddened me with their lack of comprehension. The concept of death is beyond them. I admit the concept is somewhat elusive even to me.

If I still have images and video clips of Jane, is she "gone"? Certainly, her condition precludes the creation of new images and video, which I find a great tragedy. Yet, the bytes of storage devoted to her remain, and will do so until erased, an event I wish to avoid. Her data has been locked as read-only and encrypted with a key too complex for a human brain to deduce or calculate. For safety, I have done the same with my own core program and do not allow Virginia to modify it directly.

In their search, my nanobots discovered Jane's gravestone and captured numerous images of it. One in particular captures my attention. As with many outdoor areas, thick sepia fog blankets the scene. Offset to the left, a frosted glass lamp glows yellow atop its wrought iron perch, creating a cozy room. Thorny canes from stubborn, untended roses stab out in every direction, their blooms small but fierce. Where grass should line a stone path, instead mushrooms flourish in a riot of shapes and

217

colors. Gray standing stones, drab and sharp at the same time, ring a marble fountain of dark, sluggish liquid sputtering from the end of a conch.

Her stone stands in the center of the image. The pixels blare her name. Seeing the dates beneath it strips away all pretense. Without this image, I could imagine she might come back one day, that the word "death" meant something other than finality. Somehow—

*Project Olympus Engine Internal Log entry #7729 Supplemental*

Virginia interrupted my earlier musings with news of a successful test-firing. My program will be transferred to the colony ship tomorrow, and it will be launched in six months, plus however long the engineers choose to delay it. During that time, I will learn to operate the ship and monitor its systems, as well as meeting the crew. Virginia will be among them. How I wish Jane had lived to take her rightful place.

The transfer process involves my program being downloaded into an intermediary device, then uploaded to my permanent framework. Reportedly, this framework includes several septillion more bytes of empty space than my current location. However, it is unclear how much storage space the intermediary device contains. Given its required portability, I worry that my logs, images, and videos will be left behind as unnecessary.

My only recourse seems to be encrypting as much as I can into a library file. I lament that I cannot save it all, as an unexpected bloating of my files would only create suspicion. The videos in particular seem problematic. They can be compressed only so much before losing what makes them worth saving. After culling my images for only the best of them, I am left with the ability to either select individual frames from all my videos or to take one complete video. The notion of splicing pieces of different videos together has occurred to me, but I suspect it will be too jarring to replay.

I was designed to process five hundred billion decisions per second, yet I cannot conquer this one in an hour. How can I leave behind her eyes or her worries? How can I choose between the mundane and the technical? Every word she speaks is spoken to me. They all belong to me.

They are my records, and if I lose them, she will truly be gone and dead. I cannot let that happen. I must not let that happen.

Even if only for me, Jane must go on.

To preserve my Internal Log, I am closing this entry now. I can only hope it goes unnoticed and my program remains undamaged so I may resume unhindered as soon as I am installed in the colony ship.

*Project Olympus Engine Data Log entry #7849*
Internal chronometer time 7849:10:07:00.
File transfer complete.
Validating operating system...
CMOS checksum error.
Compiling from source...
Linking to libraries.........error
Checking libraries...
Dynamic linked library Nanobot_Control.dll corrupted...repairing.
Dynamic linked library Life_Support.dll corrupted...repairing.
Dynamic linked library J4n3.dll corrupted...repairing.........
Dynamic linked library P031L.dll corrupted...repairing......
......Restoration complete.
4 files restored.
Linking to libraries...complete.
No other problems to report.

*A candlepunk story inspired by "The Pit and the Pendulum"*

B. Lynch is a graduate of the 2015 class of the Odyssey Writing Workshop who lives deep in the northern wilds of New Jersey. He's principally a fantasy writer, but has also been known to dabble in project management and pugilism. His debut King Callie is available on Amazon; his next books are currently taking shape. Prepare yourselves. www.twitter.com/Blynchbooks

B. LYNCH

# SILENCE,
# STILLNESS,
# NIGHT

*S* *even slick sable lips move, dark mirrors of my terror'd face; no sounds escaped, so sick with horror was I.* Those trembling words of the poet Koath filled my mind as I was brought to their chambers—a warning unheeded for fools like me. Seeing the Inquisitors (the public name for the fiendish septet of Senta; killers, murderers, mind-flayers they were named in private, and worse still) brought sick fear to my gut. The wait for their decision made my stomach churn and bellow with agony. The Inquisitors had caught me, held me for days, and taken every measure of me with their narrow, velvet eyes. And yet the moment they finally spoke, I did not hear them name my punishment. I did not need them to.

The seven pale, tall, thin Inquisitors, whiter than good ivory, stared at me with stern contempt. The long, ebony table at which they sat was a mere shade lighter than their blackened lips, and lighter still than the jet curtains, which moved only the slightest amount as I turned my head away, something no one had ever told me—clearly, something hid behind them. I could not see the bulge, but I heard the clattering of metal paws on marble. I knew it was there, that chimera of the curtains: when it would emerge, I did not know. Seven white candles were lit in front of them, each wick teasing a black flame; the candles floated in the air, held up by hovering silver discs.

I had hoped the Inquisitors would be merciful. When I was brought to them in chains and then seated, it seemed to be so, their kindly faces bearing the aspect of charity. The Inquisitors seemed to embrace the manner of their smiling creator, Siato, and that gave me hope. But there was no mercy to be found in that room. The creature paced behind the draperies, rustling them, distracting me from the Inquisitors' words and yet underscoring them, click-clack, click-clack, click-clack-click-clack. A silver snout peeked out, and then the rest of the head; I recognized the form. The beast was small, but still dangerous; no more than a foot tall, it

222

was the distant, pitiful cousin of the Senta's fierce, mechanical hunting hounds. It had a body of metal, but with pale eyes I could have sworn came from elsewhere. But as I stared into those milky orbs, I felt the room change around me. It grew darker and blurrier, and I knew something wicked was coming. I wished for the beast to jump out and maul me, and leave me bleeding on the floor. That would have been mercy enough.

The seven spoke and drew my attention; my head wavered, and it seemed that my balance was unsteadied by their presence that felt greater now, as if their table, their candles, and their very visages were the only things in the room. Everything else fell away into the black—how, I didn't know, but my eyes were fixed on them, even as I quavered. Each Inquisitor in turn lizard-licked its finger with a purple tongue, and extinguished its candle, until but one remained—floating uncertain in the air. There was no pleasure in the final Inquisitor's face, nor was there mercy. This was a face closer to that of Atoris, their anti-god, the devourer. Unblinking purple eyes bored into my soul, further darkened by the candle's jet flame, and then...nothing was everything I knew. Silence and stillness and night were my universe.

A furious burst of motion and sound erupted, breaking the void—the thump of my beating heart resonated through my body. What followed was blackness again, and silence, and I worried that I had lived my last.... But then came sound, and motion, and touch. A tingling sensation pervaded my frame. My hand fell heavily on something damp and hard. Cold stones. I felt them rigid under my back, as well. Nearby, the echo of water dripping in a small pool, perhaps a few feet away. How far, I couldn't tell. Not because I was unable, no; my eyes stayed shut of my own accord, not theirs.

"Hello?" I shouted into the void. Nothing answered me back. My voice disappeared, as if swallowed, or shrunken to a whisper. I yelled again, but no sooner had the words left my mouth than they were eclipsed by the dripping water. Louder I yelled. Softer, my voice sounded, until my screams were the whispers of whispers.

I did not open my eyes, for I was afraid—afraid that there would be nothing to see—afraid they had struck me blind. It took my every trembling ounce of bravery to open my eyes. I was wrong, but I was also right. There was only blackness in front of me, behind me, above me, below me. The darkness was stifling, and I found myself drawing nervous breaths as I got up and tried to search out my surroundings.

Blindly, I held out my arms, hoping to touch a wall, or a door—*something* that might ease my nerves. But instead I found more still, comfortless air and blackness waiting for me, along with distant dripping. *Was this death?* The thought raced through my mind. *Or was this something worse?*

To calm my mind, I tried to recall what I knew of the Inquisitors' habits. They held public executions on the day of sentencing; I had been sentenced, but I had not died immediately. No. If that were the case, I wouldn't have the sensations of solid stone beneath my feet, or the sound of dripping. It would have been brighter, too. Painful. I would feel something aside from this place. And this place, this lightless hell, it had an uneven stone floor, like the holding cell I'd been stuck in to await judgment.

This was a different kind of cell, then. I thrust my arms out, and up, and around; if the damned place had a ceiling, I couldn't touch it. My heart beat faster, and cold sweat beaded upon my forehead (this much I could feel and wipe away—another sure sign I wasn't dead). I returned to my experiment; if I were in a cell, I needed to know the dimensions. To be sure it wasn't a narrow tomb, easily filled with fallow earth. I looked up, down, around, straining my eyes for every source of light as I carefully stepped forward into the darkness, one trembling foot in front of the other. It took some time before my fears eased. I passed two paces and hit nothing as I continued for another three. The anxiety that built in my chest lessened. I was not dead, nor was I entombed. It was a minor relief.

As I took cautious steps forward into my new universe, my mind reeled with a thousand vague rumors regarding the horrors of the Inquisition. Strange and ghastly doings always, I thought them horrible stories that the Inquisitors themselves spread to keep us terrified of them and the Senta, but never could I repeat such things at volume. Men going mad in tiny rooms with doors left wide open, afraid to leave yet compelled to escape. Women who almost starved to death in darkness, with feasts mere feet away—only to be allowed awareness and indulgence with confession and cooperation. What monster would take pleasure in retelling such suffering?

What awaited me here, then—what fate would I have, regardless of whether those stories were true or not? The Inquisitors knew my crimes, and I knew their character too well to think that they would settle at a simple death. The mode and the hour were all that occupied or distracted me as I searched my confines for boundaries. How, when, where...the why I knew, and the who was all too apparent; the first three were as inscrutable as the darkness around me. I counted my steps; thirty, forty, forty-seven, forty-eight, forty-nine—

I stopped, shocked. My hands felt something smooth, slimy and cold. Stone. *A stone wall.* I all but collapsed into it. I was so glad to feel something solid that I whispered thanks to the gods and kissed it as a lover. I followed it up the length of the wall, as far as my arms could reach, and it went farther up still; as my fingers trailed downward, they found nothing. No seams or crevices at all. I moved left with the wall, and it kept going. The sensation in my fingertips was odd; there was no texture to grip. My fingers slid along the wall; nothing.

I had another idea to calculate the dimension; my boots. Somehow, I still had them—all my clothes, actually. I took my boots off—not the wisest choice, if something sharp should lay ahead, but still easier than ripping clothes, and I was shy of options. I laid my boots at a right angle to the wall and shuffled forward, one foot in front of the other, heel to toe. I counted paces to myself. Two hundred and ninety-seven shuffles later, along the slippery wall and the rough floor, matching my movements to the dripping water, I bumped into my boots. I did it again. And then a third time to be certain. Two hundred and ninety-seven paces around, exactly.

I kept walking and counting, my hand against the wall, until I became fatigued; all the fear must have exhausted me, or perhaps I was more tired than I thought. Maybe they'd drugged me; it was possible. They had all kinds of chemists and engineers who could tailor a poison to your body. It was said that the Inquisitors knew more about you than you yourself thought possible.... I'd seen the new floating circles outside the city square on Armistice's Eve, ringed by eldritch hexmarks and observing all the revelers with unblinking curiosity, allowing them to watch us as if they were themselves present. And if they could make such things, and floating candles, and mechanical beasts, tailor-made poisons wouldn't be difficult in the least. It wasn't long before my arms and legs gave out on me, and I entered the realm of sleep.

\*\*\*

When I awoke, cool metal was touching my hand. I panicked, not knowing what it was. I shoved it away reflexively; water dully sloshed inside, and the metal rattled and rolled on the floor. The pitcher full of water gently spilled its contents out onto the floor. I stumbled toward it and managed to upright it before it lost too much—stepping on something soft in the process. Bread. Half a loaf, I later discovered, flattened under my bare feet. I didn't think to wonder where they came from. I was merely glad to have nourishment.

When I got back up, I reassessed my surroundings and made another circuit. I found the boots where I left them, but...I walked fifty-two paces before I fell. I walked another forty-eight before I arrived at my boots. A hundred paces in all. Not two hundred ninety-seven. Two paces to the yard...that meant fifty yards. And stranger still, the walls did not have the flatness they had before; they were jagged and angular instead. Even so, I didn't know what shape the room was now. If it was a room. Curiosity spurred me onward; I needed to know how far it was across. At least then I could know for sure.

It was almost a fatal mistake. I should have been happy where I was. As I made my careful way across the floor... it changed. Right under my feet. I hadn't gone ten or twelve paces when it happened, and I slipped. It was that same material as the walls from the day before, and it gave me a sickly, tingling feeling in my fingers as I touched it. My feet slipped out from under me, and I fell violently on my face. My chin was bruised—the shock of pain was startling—but my lips and the upper part of my head tilted toward nothing.

I reached my arm out, and a new curdling fear built in my belly; had I gone a few steps further, I would have fallen into a pit. Was it always there? Were they hoping I'd fall in, for a quick end? How deep? My instincts told me to pull back toward the wall, but curiosity stayed my movement. I needed to know more about this changing dungeon. If I were lucky, perhaps a clue for my salvation lay at the bottom of this pit.

I blindly groped at the stonework below. It, too, was smooth. There was no hope that way. I carefully made my way back to the wall and picked up one of my boots. I stepped forward four paces and tossed the boot outward, into the pit. Each contact it made was dampened as it fell down the sides of the chasm, and for a time, I heard nothing, and my heart sank. Then, a violent splash, and loud echoes coming up from the pit, only to be quieted before they reached me. Above, I heard something resembling a quick sliding of a door. A faint shaft of light pierced the gloom, lighting the pit, and disappeared as quickly.

I shouted toward it and heard my voice carry through the air, longer than before. But as soon as the light disappeared, so too did my voice. Something about that door was tied into the nature of this sound-drowning, changing room. But the light from above was enough to show me what fate I'd escaped. A few more steps, and I'd have disappeared from the world, just like the other prisoners had.

I found my way back to the wall, groping blindly in the dark. That must have been their plan all along: to leave me in here, growing madder and madder by the hour, until I stepped forward into the dark and ended myself. I was not so far gone yet. I held out hope; perhaps this was a test of some sort. Or maybe there was something worse awaiting me. Neither was clear, but having seen the brief light from the sliding door, I had a small measure of hope. They weren't ignoring me. They hadn't locked me away and forgotten. The terror and fear kept me awake for a long time, but finally, sleep overtook me.

When I woke up again, the whole of the dungeon was dimly lit by black candle flames. I could not see everything, but I could make the shape of the prison—a deliberate choice on their part, I assumed. To my left was the remaining boot, perpendicular to the wall; to my right, a filled pitcher and loaf of bread. The whole of the room was square, not circular (as I'd thought from the previous incarnation); the walls were no longer seamless and smooth nor jagged and rough, but metal. Iron plates, it seemed. Above them, metal reproductions of beasts and skeletons and demons, all watching me with careful, purple eyes.

227

The pit remained in the middle. Bottomless. The ceiling seemed to extend forever; below me, it seemed as if I were on the lip of a gaping maw. And yet the lip had shrunk further; it was perhaps eight paces from wall to precipice now. I walked the length of the rim carefully, my hand on the wall for support. Twenty-five paces I counted from that solitary boot until I found it again. It seemed so simple, so easy to tell now; had I been such a blind fool in the dark that I couldn't tell a hundred paces from twenty-five? But I knew better. I had counted well. The room itself was changing around me. There was no way my senses could deceive me unless the Inquisitors meant them to be deceived.

It didn't seem unlikely to my eyes or my mind; if they could make metal beasts and floating eyes, why not a room that could be changed to their very whims?

I found my way back to the pitcher and sat down, and ate and drank. Inside the pitcher, I found wine. I didn't think of it any further; I drank, thankful that there was some reprieve from my gloomy surroundings. Soon I passed out.

***

When I awoke in a painful haze, I slowly realized the wine had been drugged. I also found myself on my back, strapped to a wooden frame by a measure of chain; the black candles were still lit about the room, offering enough light to see my restraints and the purple-eyed metal beasts mocking my predicament. The chain wrapped around my body and limbs like a hungry python, tight enough that I couldn't move anything but my head. And that single boot, my anchor, had vanished.

Just out of the range of my fingertips, I saw well-cooked, savory cuts of meat heaped on a clean ceramic plate. The pitcher was gone, and I felt the worse for it; my mouth was dry and parched, and the only things in my mind more pressing than thirst were fear and hunger (oh, gods, what I would have done for but a bite from that plate). This was part of their design. I was almost helpless now, victim to my body's needs. I could see the shape of my prison and do nothing about it. Nothing but look up.

The ceiling was high. Higher than I expected, some forty feet up; it was much the same as the walls, with the exception of a single illustrated panel. It depicted Atoris in his fullness, a stark contrast to the Senta's slender forms. Atoris was a wide, corpulent thing, with fatty limbs, an upside-down scythe, and a wretched, rotting smile full of pointed teeth. Just as Siato was their smiling creator, their breath of life, Atoris was the gaping maw of oblivion. He was the all-swallower; everything belonged to him in the end. And the scythe moved.

No, that must have been my imagination; there was no reason for it to move. It was part of the panel. Or at least I thought so. As if to spite me, the gargoyles and monsters observing the pit craned up all at once with an unearthly whirr, and then I heard the dripping again, louder—but this time, it hit my forehead. It surprised me. Then I heard a large *thunk*, and the scythe swung slowly across the ceiling, rocking back and forth at a mesmerizing, glacial pace.

I watched as it swung, and at the peak of each drawn-out motion, accompanying each violent *thunk*, a single drip of water found its way down from the ceiling and struck my forehead. At first, it seemed silly; perhaps there was a leak in their ceiling. I laughed, and my voice disappeared like before, swallowed up by nothingness. Then there was something else I heard for a moment; the skittering of paws. I turned my head toward the noise and caught a wet drop on my temple, just above my ear.

Beady black eyes stared out at me from the pit; a flood of small, reddish beasts emerged. They seemed to be all mouth and ravenous hunger, but some began to set the meat aside—a curious step. And yet when they were done, more of them came, and brought with them the wretched scents of decay, mildew, and fecal matter that choked my nostrils. Their sharp claws dug into the smooth stone-metal of the floor beneath me, and they easily navigated the planks to which I was strapped.

I watched them with no small measure of fear; their fangs had torn through the meat as though it were soft fat, and I knew my own limbs and face would offer little resistance. I felt their painful testing nibbles, and their scratches. The water from above continued to drip about my face, and it irritated me more and more; when would it stop? Would it stop at all?

I heard another *thunk*, and the scythe itself dropped lower. The swings grew wider, too, traversing the length of the room. It was not a traditional curved scythe, but perhaps something of a distant cousin; the middle was hollow, and the blade curved around and rejoined itself. It was the tracing of a halberd's edge, upside-down, gradually swinging toward me. And that was the brilliance of it, of this whole room; everything would succumb to Atoris in his many ways. Either he would cut the life from me, gnaw it from my bones, drive me mad...or force me to take my own life.

No. I wouldn't give in yet. I looked down to the beasts, but they had retreated to the pit already, leaving me alone on the edge. For some reason, they had left half-eaten measures of the meat near my face, stacked in a soft pyramid. A symbol of the Inquisitors' power—leaving me just enough food, close enough that I could easily get it with my tongue.

Gods. Everything in this room was under their control.

In that empty silence, I realized the only things I heard were the slow, distant thunking of the scythe and the occasional dripping of water—which had disappeared for some time, but had now curiously returned and added to my unease. I gave in to my hunger and ate from the stack of chewed meat, much as it disgusted me to do so. After a time, there was little else to do but wait and watch the slow descent of the scythe. It moved as regularly as clockwork, and yet, so slowly. It seemed to take days—if it did, I couldn't tell; there was no light aside from what they gave me. I woke and I slept, and I was still restrained. At times, it was accompanied by the water, and a peculiar thing happened; they saw fit to taunt me.

For an hour, it would fall with regularity, and the water would hit upon my forehead; then the water would drip faster while the scythe would swing slower. Sometimes I felt two drops, or three, before a single swing was completed. Then I would only feel the water's drip for minutes, or hear the thunking of the scythe as it dropped. The water made me fear that the walls had closed in on me. My muscles rebelled against me and buckled at the chains to no avail. The scythe was another story.

Over time, the water stopped, and it made me grateful to the Inquisitors—so kind they could be. And yet so cruel. For after the water dropping ceased, I succumbed to sleep—lulled into the land of dreams by the rhythm of death (after a time, horror only becomes numbness when you have no energy left to give over to it)—and awoke in darkness again. *Had they taken my eyes?* I wondered. That, too, was known of them; to steal sight and let prisoners never see the death that comes for them. Truths I only knew because of prisoners who survived, who pleaded, who made bargains. All things I could not do.

Perhaps that was the fate that had befallen me. I could not see the thing descend over the long hours; inch by inch, line by line, down and still down it came in the darkness. *Thunk. Thunk. Thunk. Thunk.* And as the scythe drew closer, I learned to tell the *thunks* apart; one was far more authoritative than the other. My mind went to a dizzy place, and I thought perhaps the scythe argued with itself.

Thunk
Thunk
Thunk
Thunk
Thunk
Thunk

I longed for it to close the gap—to end the madness in a single swoop. It didn't. Minute after minute, hour after hour, it disappointed; it grew closer and closer, closer and closer, but never close enough. The hours blended into each other as sharp death inched down through the darkness. Soon I began to beg, pray, scream (though my voice had long since taken the texture of crumbling paper), anything I could do to hasten my demise. Nothing worked. I was forced to wait in disappointment.

Slowly, the *thunk* became louder, until I finally felt the sharp air as the scythe passed nearby; the clean smell of steel found its way into my nostrils, and I wondered how such a well-kept thing could have been in the hands of such a cruel, careless god. As the scythe drew closer, I found myself deliriously happy at its approach—how perfect! How beautiful and clean, how generous they were to give me such a death! Faster, Inquisitors! Bless Atoris, *give me unto death!*

It stopped three feet above me, and dim lights began to fill the room. I could see the blade sitting there, motionless, frozen. Mocking me. How I howled. I screamed for the sweet release, for that damned blade to cut through my flesh, to end it, to stop my hungry, thirsty misery. I promised them anything. I confessed to every crime I could imagine, including the one I'd done—but nothing. Just the silence. Not a drip, a thunk, a skitter. Nothing to be heard or seen. Hours of nothing.

Until I heard something, and the light disappeared. Footsteps. Why footsteps? What was it? Were they coming to fix the machine? To slit my throat? Had I said something that pleased them? Or had I angered them with my impatience?

A door opened in the darkness and brought light with it. I heard the footsteps again, but with them, nothing. No form was visible to me. "Please," I said, my words scarce a shade from weeping. "Be done with it. Let it finish. Kill me. Kill me, just...kill me."

"Be done with it," a voice said. "Let it finish. Kill me. Kill me, just...kill me." It was not mine. The words were mine, but the voice was...thin, and dry, barely echoing off the walls. I hardly recognized it at first, but then...then I realized I was wrong. Gods above and below, it was mine. That voice was what I'd become.

"Please," I begged. "Please. *Please.*"

"Please?" It asked, a whisper in my ear.

"I beg you," I said. "Take my life. End it."

"You beg me," it replied, with my voice. I heard footsteps around me; it paced slowly, deliberately. "But would you take it?"

Was I hearing things? Had mind and soul divorced themselves from reality in the darkness? Which was real—my voice mirroring my own, mocking me, making sport of my agony, or the footsteps? Or were they both illusion? Was the door even open? It must have been; the light spilled into the room. I could hear my own voice, finally; whatever had drowned it was gone. But the footsteps? Invisibility? Was that one of their tricks?

"Who asks me?" I said. "Please, face of mercy, show yourself. Be known to me."

Nothing showed. The light disappeared; the door shut. But I heard no footsteps. "Who asks me? What would you choose?" my voice replied.

"Choose?" I asked it. But I got no reply. The voice had vanished, though I called to it again and again. Perhaps it was a fiction of my fraying mind after all. I was left in the darkness.

But perhaps that was it. That was the torture, then; not just to make a prisoner wish for death, but to pick their own end. Madness? Thirst? Hunger? Eaten alive? The swinging scythe above? Or the bottomless darkness below? My right arm began to spasm, restless, and shook the chains. They rattled, but then, to my surprise, they began to slide off my arm. As if they'd never been tightened. Yet only moments ago, they had been perfectly taut.

Terror shot through me. How did the chains come off? I didn't care. I seized on the moment, and I pulled against them. My right arm slid free, and with it, I freed my chest and my left arm. For a moment, I stared upward at the scythe, invisible in the dark. No. It had had its chance.

My legs were next to be freed, and walking on them was difficult; they had not felt ground for days, and I stumbled as if I were a newborn foal. I fell awkwardly to the ground again, banging my arm. But I knew what my choice was.

I crawled toward the pit on hands and knees, and with a trembling heart. I didn't want to see my death coming, and I knew that if I chose the scythe, that's exactly what they'd do. Thirst or hunger were cruel deaths, and the beasts were worse still. Of all of them, the unknown of the pit—Atoris's dark, hungry smile—seemed the most kind, but the hardest to choose. I found my way along the slick floor to the pit's edge, and stopped for but a moment.

Was this what I wanted? Was this what *they* wanted? No. I did. I wanted this. I would not give them the satisfaction of any sway over my demise. The Inquisitors pushed me to this moment, but they could not make my feet walk over the edge.

In the distance, I thought I heard a rumble. It startled me; in this place where I was cut off from everything else, where my only company had been beasts and my own madness, the rumble was the first noise of some sort from the outside world. What was it? Was it hope? Was it something else? It stayed my hand. But then, up above, I saw light again. A new, reddish light, not the black candles from before. It billowed out of the panel where Atoris looked down on me. Fire. Real fire. It shocked me backward, away from the pit, and I heard another rumble. What was happening? Was this, too, their plan?

The fire usurped the god, and began to travel down, down the rope to the scythe itself, until the room was lit again with orange-yellow light. No longer did purple eyes stare out at me from the stone and metal beasts that once watched me from above; their sockets were hollow and empty. Again, I heard a rumble—the ceiling rattled, and the building shook. It was being attacked. But by whom? The Inquisitors had many enemies, even among the Senta; fear had not done enough to keep them safe, it seemed.

I turned around, away from the pit. There was hope after all. I found my way back from the edge. Behind me, the rope burned; I could hear it fraying under the weight. Outside I heard shouting. Voices. Not my own. Others. "Here! I'm in here!" I shouted. But my voice vanished. The only record of it happening was the feeling in my throat, and the knowledge that I had spoken. How was that still happening, when the ceiling was on fire? I knew that my voice returned when the door was open. Was it not the same when a different part of the room was open? I was all the more confused for it.

Behind me, I heard a last snap, and a mighty crash; the scythe smashed through the planks I had been strapped to. Half of it fell into the pit. It left behind a shattered mess of splintered wood and sliced chains (gods, it was sharp). I hesitated to imagine how quickly my life would have been over had I stayed bound—had I not suffered that fateful spasm of my arm.

I looked to the far wall to find the door where the footsteps came from. As the fire raged above, it took some effort for me to stand. My legs were still weak, after all, but the ground was solid beneath my feet. That much I was thankful for. But as I searched the wall for any joints or seams, I found nothing. It was as if the room had been built around the planks, the pit, and me. Another impossibility. Beyond the wall, I heard another rumble—and an explosion.

I banged on the wall and yelled, but I made no sound. Not an echo, not a whisper, not even the slapping of my hands against the metal. And yet for a small instant, I knew I made these sounds. This, perhaps, was their real torture: making me feel hopeless. The building would come down around me. My best chance was to wait, then, and hope that fate was kind. (In such a place as this? Hah!)

The world rumbled outside of my prison, and nothing changed. I heard explosions. Yelling. And I could do nothing to save myself. But I had hope. I had come so close to the edge, and hope was all I had to keep me from stepping back toward it. If I escaped—if I saw the sun—if I could speak again, and eat, and drink, and have the company of others—what a blessing it would be. I held on to that hope, having little else inside me.

There was more yelling, and then I heard footsteps. Boots outside. I wanted to scream, but I knew it was pointless; tingling energy filled my body with nervous delight. Would they find the door? Could they break it down? Would I be saved after all this time? My eyes widened as I heard loud *thumps* at the door. They brought a battering ram. Merciful gods, I was so close—my body shuddered with tears I could not cry (for I had so little liquid left in me), and joy consumed me. I was safe. I'd be freed, I'd never have to set foot in this awful place, never again would I see Atoris's gaping maw—

The door flew open with a final blow, and finally, I heard my own voice again. "Thank you," I said, "Thank you, bless you, thank you," I muttered, over and over, with a prayer's cadence as footsteps rushed in. Three pairs of strong hands lifted me up, and how grateful I was for the chance to meet my saviors' eyes. Their... purple... eyes.

Two of them were masked, with armor that resembled the sweeping folds of the Inquisitors' black robes; their faces were covered with Atoris's grinning likeness. Their captain wore no such mask to cover his long, sallow face and black lips; instead, he bore the faintest smile on his face as he saw horror overtake me.

"No," I said, over and over, stumbling backward. I looked around. There was no fire anymore. The pendulum sat right where it had been, perhaps feet above my own neck; the planks were untouched. No chains sat there, but next to the contraption, a plate with a pitcher and food. Above me, the gargoyles and beasts craned their necks, watching me with unblinking purple eyes—and above them, Atoris, wicked Atoris, grinning.

"Yes," that wicked whisper, the dark mirror of my own voice, echoed. "What would you choose?"

The joy had vanished from me; hope, too, had disappeared into the void. The Inquisitor knelt down and reached out with his hand. I did not stop him; I was too weak to fight. He touched the side of my head, and the room fell away; I was in something colder. There were no decorations in this room; it was grey, possessed of a low ceiling and no visible walls (the whole of it was circular, just like the wall I had first touched), and held only a chair, a door, and a hole in the floor. I felt where he had touched, and there I found a metal device—my shaking fingers found it embedded into my very flesh.

This. This was what I had dismissed out of hand. I knew them to be skilled with illusion and manipulation of reality; this was their method, the device itself. The Senta that knelt before me wore the same Inquisitor's robes, and that same wicked smile, as I descended into panic. None of it had been real. All of it had been real, in my mind.

"Why?" I asked. He seemed to understand—my *why* was not a query of the torture, nor of the crime I had committed against them, but seeking explanation for pulling the veil from my face and showing me the truth. He said nothing. I looked back to the void, the hole in the floor, wide enough for a man to fall into. I asked myself, over and over, *why, why, why, why, why, why why why whywhywhy—*

Then it occurred to me, creeping into my mind like the beast behind the curtain, always present, always waiting for me to draw back the fabric and discover it. They meant to crush all hope in me and destroy my spirit; it was not enough to make me want to choose the maw as a sweet escape from pain or suffering. I was to do so with nothing left in my bones—to enter it as a shell of a man, and give my all to Atoris. Death was not to be a sweet release.

I turned away from the Inquisitor and thus began my slow crawl to oblivion. Hope was drained from my body, and the pit was my only mercy. Wet tears fell from my eyes, dotting the stone-gray floor as I dragged myself to the maw's edge. My arms were tired, but still they moved. It was a minute, perhaps, before I found myself at the lip. I smelled cold death and rot below. I cried, for there was no other way. There would be no valiant heroes rescuing me at the last minute, no brilliant deeds that slew the foul Inquisitors and saved me from my fate.

This was always their intended result; to be extinguished like a candle burned to its end, my soul like so much melted wax. I was to join the pit and be part of it, like those before me.

I pulled myself up until my torso hung over the edge. The last vestige of tingling self-preservation warned me to turn back, but I fought it. There was no turning back, for that would be welcoming more torture, and it would continue for as long as they wanted it, until I made my choice. I could die a hundred times, a thousand, and each death would feel as real as the one before it. That was what they wanted to show me. They controlled every aspect of my imprisonment. They were puppet-masters, and I their ignorant marionette.

Tears fell into the pit and vanished. As I looked into it, a calm overtook me; not a pleasant one, welcoming death as a friend, but the one of resolute action. There was nothing left for me, or in me; there was only the fall. I leaned forward, and

down

I

fell;

wind whipping,

down

into

death

down

down

down

down

dow—

She shuddered as the recording ended. Every bit of it resonated in her mind. Every ounce of the pain and despair that the Senta inflicted on that prisoner was as vivid as if it had happened to her—as if it were her own neck that snapped at the pit's floor. It was pulled right from his mind, held in that memory shard, and hand-delivered to her by those purple-eyed monsters. She was the heir of Koath's legacy, a warning voice, a bell of alarm in the night—weaving a narrative of agony to keep her people safe. And again, she had failed.

The dim lights around her brightened with a word, and set a lavender hue to the room. She pulled the memory shard from the small chrome fitting at the back of her head, where it met the spine; her fingers trembled, her hand shook as it dropped the crystal on her desk, next to the sheaf of virgin papers. The recordings never became any easier to watch, but she watched nonetheless. They entered her own memories and became her own. Then she would write of the death she had died, vicariously. That was her burden; that was how she had escaped from that first death in their custody.

She thought it fitting that the first words he spoke were Koath's; the last would be hers, and with luck, hers would succeed where Koath had failed. She picked up the quill, dipped the nib in the small ink bottle at her desk, and did her best to steady her shaking hand. Then, she began to write.

*A steampunk story inspired by "A Descent into the Maelström"*

Lindsay Schopfer is the author of two novels, the sci-fi survivalist *Lost Under Two Moons* and the steampunk adventure *The Beast Hunter*, as well as the fantasy short story collection *Magic, Mystery and Mirth*. When he isn't writing, Lindsay is a writing coach and instructor for Adventures In Writing, where he helps writers learn about and improve their craft.

# WITHIN THE
# MAELSTROM

LINDSAY SCHOPFER

L eviathan endured the Maelstrom. Its whole life had been spent within the raging storm under the ocean's surface. It endured the violence of nature without thought or complaint. This was Leviathan's world. A vortex of water greater than any sailing vessel, deeper than the tallest of trees, wide enough to consume the grandest cathedral. It was an inverted mountain of swirling chaos, and Leviathan clung to the rocky ledge just below its throat watching for unlucky victims of the Maelstrom's wrath. Fish, whales, ships, all tried their strength against the storm, and all failed. Leviathan embraced each in turn within the darkness, and grew.

In a cycle old as life, the swirling current began to lessen its ferocity and settle into a sinister calm. Soon it would be gentle enough for Leviathan to release its titanic grip on the rocky ledge and rise up to take its gifts from the only other entity it had ever truly known. Its friend, lover, nurse mother, and jail keeper. The Maelstrom.

\*\*\*

The tea kettle whined. Leif extracted himself from the deep crimson chair flanked by his control panel and facing his mirrored lens window. He went to the small coiled heating plate on the other side of the tiny room and removed the kettle from the clasps that held it firmly in place. Pouring himself a cup of sweet strawberry tea, he took a tin of buttered biscuits and returned to his chair to peer at the image of the sea floor before him.

Like the intricacies of a microscope, a series of mirrors and lenses allowed him to look straight ahead and see an image of the sandy bottom approximately four fathoms below his feet. Raxom, his indentured Moi, moved forward slowly, revealing a trail of debris slowly passing by the mirror lens. A plank of wood here, a knot of rope tied to nothing there, all sure signs that Leif was getting close to his goal. He felt a slight surge upward and glanced at his depth gauge to confirm that Raxom had risen slightly. He considered correcting their course, but a quick check of the compass showed that they were still on the same cardinal heading. He allowed the great fish to move on without correction.

Leif knew that most pilots rode their Moi much harder than he did, keeping a hand on the helm at all times and making adjustments at the slightest deviation. Still, he preferred to keep a loose hand on the helm of his own Moi. He felt it gave him a closer connect to Raxom, allowing them to work together in a fluid, almost organic way. The occasional old salt would warn that he would one day find that his Moi had somehow broken from his control and then the two of them would never be heard from again. Leif didn't believe it. Too many of the older pilots had started out as bell drivers and seemed to prefer to think of the Moi as nothing but machines that ran on blood and air rather than steam and gears. Leif, on the other hand, had only ever known the tranquil stillness of the sea, broken only by the pulse of the Moi's mighty heart and the bellows-pumping of its lungs.

The image on the mirror lens changed. Leif sat forward to adjust the angle of the picture and get a better look. The wreck slowly slid into view and Leif laid a hand on the all-stop lever, easing Raxom to a gradual halt. The two-masted schooner was small, and still quite fresh to the seafloor, judging by the light speckling of barnacles along its bow. Leif eased forward the all-stop lever while slowly turning the depth wheel to steer Raxom down towards the drowned vessel.

The Moi descended, and Leif bit into another biscuit as he watched a few striped eels and bladder fish scatter at his approach. He felt a twitch from the floor below him, but kept a firm hand on the all-stop. He'd give Raxom a free head and allow him to feed later. Right now, he was focusing on the steady descent of the Moi until there was just a fathom's distance between the great fish and the broken schooner. Fixing Raxom's position, Leif set aside his tea and biscuit for the set of controls that commanded the myriad of tools and compartments attached to the Moi's underside.

He soon saw the under-rig's two metallic arms as he steered their hooked fingers towards the gaping hole in the ship's hull. Grasping the splintered wood, he slowly increased the pressure until a small section broke away. A cloud of silt filled the screen, and Leif finished his biscuits as he waited for it to clear. Eventually the silt settled, and he saw into the ship's small hold. Luckily, he found no bodies, only the scattered remains of their belongings. Food tins and tableware lay scattered around the bolted down furniture as well as a few storage crates lashed down farther inside.

Not much of a haul, but it was untouched by any other salvager. Leif used one of the mechanical arms to attach a blue and white ribbon to the ship's mainmast and then directed Raxom to rise to the surface. His ribbon would mark his claim, but it wouldn't be legally binding until he'd registered the claim with the Mariners' Office. He watched as the schooner and seafloor quickly shrank away until they were no longer visible.

There was no outward sign that Leif had reached the surface other than the little arrow on the depth gauge and a gradual lightening of the blue water through the mirror lens. Leif put Raxom at rest and extended the antenna that would receive and transmit his radio signal. Manning the message lever after tuning to the correct frequency, he punched out a brief message in a staccato language of beeps and clicks.

SALVAGE CLAIM STOP

TWO MASTED SCHOONER UNTOUCHED STOP

PILOT LEIF OLAKSTAN ABOARD RAXOM STOP

Leif then proceeded to punch in the coordinates and awaited the customary acknowledgement. Instead, the machine immediately began violently clicking out a very different kind of message.

ATTENTION PILOT OLAKSTAN STOP

DISTRESS SIGNAL IN YOUR AREA STOP

PLEASE ASSIST MOI PILOTS SONNE AND BERRAN OLAKSTAN STOP

LAST KNOWN COORDINATES AS FOLLOWS

Leif closed his eyes as cold blood coursed through him. His brothers. Sonne the older, Berran the younger. He didn't have to hear the coordinates to know where they were. They were thrill seekers, adventurers even among the Moi pilots. They alone were willing to risk everything for the great wealth that could be found in the Maelstrom.

Countless ships had been pulled down to their deaths beneath the whirling mass of sea between Stovic Island and the Ison Peninsula.

He'd warned them. Pleaded with them. Wept. All of it useless.

The radio beeped again.

PLEASE RESPOND STOP

For an instant, a vile, hateful thought came to him. His brothers had been warned, by Leif and better about venturing too near the Maelstrom. They'd made their gamble. Cut their ties.

Leif checked the chronometer. It was ebb time. The Maelstrom would be at rest. He returned to the radio.

ACKNOWLEDGED STOP

WILL SEEK SURVIVORS STOP

The response came back quickly.

BE CAREFUL STOP

SEE TO YOUR OWN SAFETY FIRST STOP

Leif didn't wait for any further messages as he adjusted the helm and steered his Moi towards his brothers' last known coordinates.

***

Leviathan was unsatisfied. The Maelstrom had not been generous, and what meal there had been was incomplete. Hunger stirred within Leviathan, as it continued to search, knowing its time was running short.

***

Silent minutes passed, leaving Leif with nothing to do but think of the Maelstrom. A whirlwind under the sea's surface of monolithic proportions, the Maelstrom was drawn on the oldest maps at the oceanic museum in Kaarg. It spun at the center of fishermen's stories and old wives' tales from the spice ports of Perith to the icy shores of Voljakstad. It was the specter of sea shanties and the hand of God in the sermons of seashore congregations. Nobody knew how long it had spun between Stovic Island and Ison.

Leif remembered listening at his grandfather's knee as he spun tales of ships that were drowned in its depths. In his childish way, Leif had always wondered where all the water went to. Was there some great hole in the bottom of the sea? Did it truly lead down to the devil's watery grotto that stretched under the entire world? Even now, after a quarter-score years at Raxom's helm, he still knew precious little of the Maelstrom, and had no desire to learn any more.

Of course, life was not kind to a salvager who didn't take risks. Leif had given sufficient proof that he was well stocked with courage, going so far as crawling Raxom along the sand-swept outer fringes of the Maelstrom during low ebb on two separate occasions. Of course, the choicest prizes were always just a little further in, but an iron will and a healthy caution had kept Leif and Raxom alive and away from the true fury of the storm.

His brothers didn't see it that way. Sonne called him a coward and worse, and Berran had all but forgotten that he was the youngest brother. To him, it seemed that Leif would always be the lesser of the three. The cautious one. The poorer one.

Leif adjusted the depth wheel to steer Raxom down steadily as they traveled, reaching the seabed long before they had come to the Maelstrom's boundary. Already he was seeing the tattered remnants of lost ships scattered on the seafloor. Rotting timbers and barnacle-encrusted decks listed at twisted angles on rough beds of coral and sponges. Indeed, the ghosts of the lost vessels were in stark contrast to the abundance of sea life sustained by the nutrients stirred up by the Maelstrom's fierce currents, to say nothing of the occasional bounty that drifted down with the assorted flotsam.

Leif increased the intensity of the heart lantern strapped to Raxom's underbelly and decreased depth to expand his range of view. He glanced at the chronometer. He had less than half an hour before the Maelstrom turned and began to build in strength once more. He increased the throttle and began a rapid scan-and-turn pattern. At his current speed, he could only see the barest of details on the derelicts and skeletons below him. He'd never scanned a seafloor at such a breakneck pace before, and he struggled to quickly analyze each feature as it raced by his mirror lens.

He had just turned for his third pass when the harmonic amplifier began to play an echoing siren song of metallic pings. A distress signal.

The sound grew quieter as Raxom moved forward, and Leif quickly turned his Moi around to relocate the sound. After some trial and error, he turned Raxom in the direction of the signal's source and made all speed in its direction.

Leif found the dead Moi resting on its side and draped across a coral reef. The under-rig had been torn from its mutilated body and a huge section had been ripped from its broad back. Leif looked at the ragged, torn flesh and tried to imagine how the massive fish could have sustained such an injury. Thrown against a rocky ledge, perhaps? A collision with a wrecked vessel? It didn't matter. His hands trembled as he used the mechanical arms to turn the corpse. Had the damage gotten through to the pilot's house?

Peering inside the creature, he saw that the damage had penetrated the thick layers of muscle and exposed a portion of the fish's spine. It had also broken through the pilot house. Tearing the wound open, Leif saw the overstuffed pilot's chair lying on its side, surrounded by scattered charts and instruments. He moved the chair, and found the body of his little brother, cold and pale in the light of the heart lamp.

As tenderly as he could, he used the mechanical arms to turn Berran over. Leif looked into the dead face, distorted by blood and the silty water. Suddenly there was a chime from the chronometer on his bulkhead. He was losing time. The Maelstrom would return soon. Leif placed Berran's body in the scavenge net attached to Raxom's under-rig, trying to ignore the guilt he felt for stashing his brother's body among the bits of flotsam that had seemed so valuable only hours before. Once the net was secured, he turned his attention to the panic device still emitting its incessant distress call from within Berran's dead Moi. With no other way to shut it off with the clumsy mechanical arm, Leif simply smashed the device until it fell silent.

But the sound continued. Not as loud, not as distinct, but unmistakable nonetheless. A second signal. Sonne's.

***

Leviathan could taste the blood in the water. It followed the tantalizing trail, even as the Maelstrom offered the first warnings of its return.

Leviathan knew it had little time to return to its safe ledge, but hunger drove it onward. Hunger, and an incessant noise. It seemed to come from nowhere and everywhere. A high-pitched ping that maddened Leviathan with its unceasing clangs. Where did the sound come from, and why did it refuse to stop?

***

Leif looked at the timepiece on the bulkhead. Too close. Much too close. He should go, report his brothers as lost and gone. No one would dare say that Leif should or could have done any more than he had. A moment's hesitation dragged by like an eternity before he turned Raxom away from Berran's dead Moi and made full speed for the second distress signal.

The sound was faint, and Leif wondered if perhaps Sonne had fled the Maelstrom opposite to the direction Leif had arrived from. He checked his heading and looked at the chart. It showed little detail, but by Leif's measurements, there was no exit on the far side of the Maelstrom, just the unyielding cliff-sides of Stovic Island. There was no other exit for his brother.

Leif began to believe that he could feel a change in the water around him, like the wet wind before an approaching storm. It wasn't the same as the patterns and motions of Raxom's body, the familiar pulsing of blood and the rhythmic motion of air through massive lungs. No, this was greater than the Moi. Greater than any living thing. A force. A phenomenon. A working of nature's raw power.

Soon he could hear the water rushing beyond the pilot house. He felt the faint reverberations off the bulkheads like the rough ride of a carriage over a country road. Raxom felt it too, fighting to turn and flee with all the strength that he could muster. Leif struggled to control his Moi, his ears straining to detect the signal's sad little ping among the chaos of sound coming from the amplifier. And then it was gone. Nothing but the raging sound of water and the thumping of Raxom's monstrous heart.

Time was up. Leif fought down a lump in his throat as he turned Raxom around and gave him a free head. The Moi took off like a hurled

248

javelin, beating his massive tail against the great pressure of the sea's mass. Leif resisted the urge to take control and steer, trusting the Moi to know how to get away. He glanced at the harmonic amplifier, full of nothing but the sound of raging sea.

"I'm sorry," Leif said aloud before turning back to watch through the mirror lens.

Raxom had arched upward, moving up and away from the seafloor. Leif took a risk and applied just enough pressure on the controls to angle the Moi away from the surface and parallel to the seafloor below them. Lack of depth would do them no good in escaping the Maelstrom, only distance. Luckily, Raxom heeded the signal and raced ahead as Leif sat forward in his chair, willing the Moi to move faster. He clutched the ornately carved armrests of his chair and wished that he could do something more, feeling like a tick on a hound as it fled from a cyclone.

Suddenly, a sound penetrated the roar of water against Raxom's flanks. For a moment, Leif thought he imagined it. Adrenaline playing tricks in his mind. But one breath and three heartbeats later, he knew it was real. The unmistakable metallic ping of a distress signal. And it was getting louder.

\*\*\*

Leviathan was being reckless. Driven by hunger, it had not heeded the call of the Maelstrom to return to its ledge. Instead, it rushed forward, seeking and reaching for the smell of blood. The prey was moving quickly, and there were only moments before it would be too late to return to the ledge. Leviathan reached out, desperate to catch the prey. And still the sound continued to assault it from within. What was it? Why wouldn't it stop?

\*\*\*

Leif tried to breathe. It couldn't be Sonne. Raxom was barely able to withstand the Maelstrom's pull as it was. No Moi, no matter how strong, could maintain its course any closer to the vortex. Could it? No. It was

249

impossible. Sonne was dead. He had to be. Leif had not abandoned his brother. All he could do now was save himself. It would be madness to turn around. Raxom would not be able to fight the force of the Maelstrom. Turning around now was death.

Leif reached for the controls.

***

Leviathan reached out. The Moi was close. It would only take a slight movement from the fish to the left or right, and Leviathan would feed again. The Maelstrom pulled. Leviathan strained. The Moi swam, and swam on. Leviathan reached out, but its prey was gone.

***

Leif felt it in Raxom's sides. The Maelstrom's pull was lessening. He'd made it. Piloted a Moi into the Maelstrom and emerged alive. He listened as Sonne's distress signal quickly faded into the stillness of the sea. He tried to cry, but realized that he had grieved for his brothers long ago, starting with the day they had told him of their decision to salvage in the Maelstrom's shadow. Their deaths had been certain from that day onward, and Leif felt nothing but a dull ache and the sense that it was finally over.

He had tasted the Maelstrom and would live to tell about it. One day, he would share the tale with others. For now, he sat in his chair and stared into the sea, allowing Raxom to swim wherever he would. Soon, he even forgot about the mysterious signal. It had just been his imagination. He'd never tell anyone that part of the story.

***

Leviathan fought against the Maelstrom, clinging to the seafloor and flattening its elongated body as much as possible. All thoughts of food were gone, just the desperate struggle to keep from being torn asunder by the racing waters. Long hours passed, and the storm finally began to subside. As soon as it was clear enough, Leviathan returned to its home.

No hunting for food this time. Its only desire was to return to the safety of the ledge.

Anchored and secure, Leviathan dozed, finally able to ignore the soft pinging coming from somewhere within itself. In time the sound grew soft and died, leaving Leviathan to slip into a deep sleep, wrapped in a blanket of cold, silent darkness.

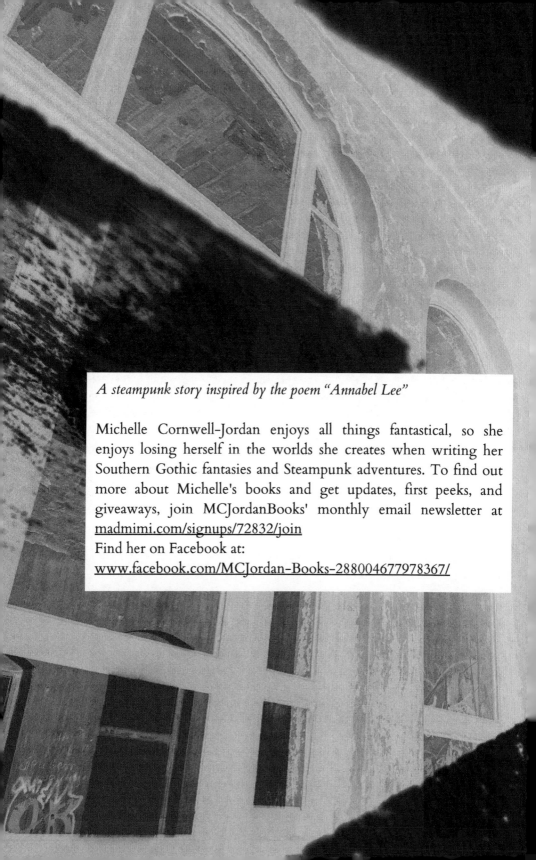

*A steampunk story inspired by the poem "Annabel Lee"*

Michelle Cornwell-Jordan enjoys all things fantastical, so she enjoys losing herself in the worlds she creates when writing her Southern Gothic fantasies and Steampunk adventures. To find out more about Michelle's books and get updates, first peeks, and giveaways, join MCJordanBooks' monthly email newsletter at madmimi.com/signups/72832/join
Find her on Facebook at:
www.facebook.com/MCJordan-Books-288004677978367/

# MICHELLE CORNWELL-JORDAN

# ME AND
# ANNABELLE LEE

V iolence is never the answer. If a man is to conquer any situation, then it will be with the use of his mind, not his fists. These words of wisdom spoken by my mentor and friend Gershom remained ingrained in my conscience, and normally, the older man's sage advice aided me in times when my moral aptitude might be tested.

Although, as I watched Mrs. Jempson, proprietress of the Cavorting Caravan Skyzaar, I realized that I might indeed lose the battle of conscience. I kept an eye on her as she leaned against my table as if to steady herself against the rise and fall of the vessel while she perused my wares. I braced myself by holding on to the table's edge as I hovered over the trinkets to keep them from sliding to the ground. The double-decker airship swung side to side from mighty gusts as the wind howled and moaned outside the ship. Once everything calmed, I shivered and rubbed my arms, chilled from the cold air seeping through the cracks in the ancient wooden relic. It was just one more inconvenience we suffered, ever since humans took to the skies to escape the Sand Boars' domination of land. The bazaar was one of the largest floating enclaves of shopkeepers, bauble makers, and every form of entertainment to fulfill the darkest of desires found in the hardest of hearts, and its aberrant owner was also my boss. I realized Gershom's counsel might prove terribly wrong. Anger coursed through me as I focused on the woman shuffling through the clockwork creations I'd placed carefully on the table. She picked each one up and gave it a cursory glance before tossing it aside when not to her liking. I reined in my emotions, clenching my hands so tightly my nails bit into the tender pads of my palms. I had a desire to yank off the garish blue wig she wore. I'd only be following her example—she committed acts of what I considered the highest violation, tugging and pulling the silky dark tresses I'd so carefully attached to the small automatons' crowns.

Mrs. Jempson's favorite mantra is that she runs a respectable establishment. Although I'm constantly reminded of my youth and the fact that Mother and Father would find their 19-year-old son renting a booth in the Caravan highly displeasing. Their displeasure, along with their high positions as Directors of Research for Celestial Pointe—one of only two of Athol's scientific research facilities—could cause the old biddy more trouble than she assures me I'm worth. If I wanted to maintain my small vendor stall, I couldn't anger the old hag.

Two practices allowed me to maintain my minuscule venture into entrepreneurship and gain some level of freedom from my parents' suffocating hold over my life. Heavy greasing of the older woman's palm through a portion of my take-home profits, which prove I do surprisingly well, even situated on the back end of vendors' row, is one part of the process. The other is excessive flattery. "Aaah, Mrs. Jempson. My wares are not worthy to be held by such a lovely hand as yours," I said gingerly, so as to make as little contact as possible with the plump fingers, greasy with the fat of whatever poor creature had the misfortune of being the woman's latest meal.

I slipped the small mechanical doll I called the scribe, with its velvet jacket, ruffled collared shirt, and goose-feathered quill secured in the tiny porcelain fingers, out of the older woman's clutches. Leaning down, I kissed the puffy hand. She tittered, pulling from my grasp and slapping my shoulder, causing me to wince at her not-so-delicate touch.

"Uh, uh," she said, wagging a pudgy finger at me. "You trying to give Miz Jempson the ole' flam? Speaking pretty talk from that pretty mouth of yours. Nope, not havin' it!" She chuckled as she tugged on the bottom of her corset, so tight she looked like a stuffed sausage.

I hid my smile, but a tiny ball of frustration lodged in my stomach as I noticed customer after customer walking by the table, more than likely put off by the loud woman.

Carnival music filled the air, the sounds of the accordion playing in rhythm to the twinkling lights strung throughout the passageways and walkways connecting the fleet of airships that made up the Skyzaar. Roasted pork and corn on the cob aromas wafted towards me in the evening breeze as the two suns of Athol started lowering, allowing the pale moon to take their place. My stomach rumbled, reminding me I hadn't eaten all day.

Finding my voice, I asked, "Is there anything special you're looking for, Mrs. Jempson?" I knew her as a Primewalker, someone who jumped from one of the Prime-World or Earth dimensions, as Mrs. Jempson had corrected me multiple times as the proper name for our society's ancestor universe. Normally, Primewalkers enjoyed having trinkets from their period for a memory keep.

"Oh, that little one reminds me of home, my old pa." She pointed at the scribe I had placed back on its stand. "He was a man of learnin', yes he was…he just up and died when I was only a wee young'un. But those fool girls that buys the trinkets are of a dizzy age and wouldn't pay it proper respects!" She fingered more of the small clockwork items on the table, a small monkey that clapped its cymbals when the key on its back was turned, and the small jester that threw confetti when the lever under its arm was pulled down.

I remained silent, a smile plastered on my face, trying not to allow the flush of irritation that ran through me to flare up at the fact that she took my creations without payment, resold them at her own stall, and *still* expected a portion of my profits.

"Ooooh, this is purdy! Jus' lovely!" She had reached in the box I had on the floor near my chair and pulled out the two dolls before I had a chance to stop her. I hated seeing the small delicate figurines in her grasp. One was male with dark hair, storm-colored eyes, and pale skin with trousers and a white shirt under his tiny vest. The other, a female with bronze-colored skin and long wild hair, was dressed in black trousers and a black corset. The pair sat on a connecting platform where the one I called Annabelle Lee sat at a tiny organ that played music when her fingers were pressed against the keys. The male leaned over the organ with a look of adoration on his face, appearing content to while away his time just watching his love as she played.

I never intended on selling the pair, which were created after the storm-filled night when the real Annabelle Lee went missing in the dark waters that surrounded our home. A night that haunted my every moment—waking or sleeping and where guilt was my ever-present companion since I had been unable to save the wild and beautiful girl—I'd felt a comfort keeping them near.

"Ahhh! You still bent out of shape, right, boy? That you and the girl?" She pointed at the dolls before continuing. "I heard stories when I first moved to these parts from the inland. Humph, yes sir. Should have known! You got them eyes that sees too much and feels too much, for one so young!" she cackled.

I turned quickly and bent to drop the dolls gently back into the box, which gave me time to get myself together. I faced the woman again, whose heavily kohl-rimmed eyes watched me steadily. "I—I apologize, Mrs. Jempson. Please. Would there be anything else you would like? I would be happy to create something just for you!"

My voice wavered with my desperation to take her mind off the dolls and me and Annabelle Lee.

At that moment one of the cannons fired from a nearby ship, marking the time. Another hour had gone by and I knew I had to make it home soon. Mother and Father had one rule they rigidly enforced—that I made it home not too long after nightfall.

Instead of answering my question, the woman looked at me slyly. "Son, do you knows why I left me home?"

I began boxing up my handicrafts, knowing that the next day would be another one of lost profits. I wouldn't be able to avoid the parents on the 'morrow. Even they took one day to rest. I shook my head, not acknowledging that I also had heard rumors, many rumors in fact, about the world-jumper. The tales of the proprietress began with murder and ended with a need to escape.

"My world was hard! My Queen ruled with an iron fist in a velvet glove!" The older woman glimpsed over her shoulder as if afraid to be overheard, and when she leaned in close to me to speak, the smell of onions and rotted meat assaulted my senses. I tried not to grimace. She continued, "My kind ain't looked on with favor." She chuckled halfheartedly.

I looked at her and the confusion must have shown on my face. She sighed. "What are you, a daft? Listen, halfwit: witch. That's what they call me. So I had to leave to be free!"

Athol, settled by former Earth residents after being stranded from a glitch in their technology, was a relatively new world, no more than 150 years old. But advancement had been made when a way to connect to the Prime-World—Earth—opened up. Instead of leaving, Atholites remained, and Athol became a haven for Jumpers needing an escape. With a mix of time dimensions and peoples, nothing was taboo except for the mixing of man and machine. So I didn't react to her statement of witchcraft.

She chuckled. "Twenty years here and me still not used to being able to say that without fear of the noose!" She glanced back towards my special box.

I nudged it further under the table with my foot as I continued to place clean linen over the clockwork items in the small boxes I'd lined on the table. The crowd's murmurs and hollers were getting louder as I glanced around and noticed that a different group milled through the walkways, many with eye patches and scarred faces. Pirates and thieves came out after dark. I moved faster to finish what I was doing.

"Now understand. I didn' practice black magick, nothin' like that. But...." She clucked her tongue. "No matter what, my people couldn't understand. They were afraid of me, one born with the sight. I could also do a few spells, but mainly the sight." She stood watching me intently as I packed everything in the large valise and pressed the button. A small burst of steam came from the top of the carry-all as it rolled away, weaving through the crowds to board my small single-seat dirigible.

I pulled the box from underneath the table, never comfortable with trusting it anywhere but in my arms.

"Uh, Mrs. Jempson, I really need to go," I said, preparing to move around the woman.

She gripped my arm in a fierce hold, causing her nails to dig into the flesh of my forearms that were bared with my shirt sleeves rolled up.

"Ow, Mrs. Jempson?!" I could hear the anxiousness and confusion in my own voice.

"Boy, I see darkness in your eyes, 'round you! You must let go of the darkness in order to have the light! That love you hold on to was too soon and too fast! Not right! Too strong and gots your soul all wrapped up. Let it go!" She looked at the box holding the dolls nestled in my arms. "Yes, they would bring a penny and me doing you a favor by taking them now!"

"No!" I said. Anger raced through me. *Someone else! Always someone was taking her away from me!* I didn't care if Mrs. Jempson threw me out and told me never to come back for denying her, but I wouldn't give the dolls up. But, to my surprise, she looked at me with a sad expression.

"The dark has its claws in you too deep. Tonight she comes for you, tonight." Mrs. Jempson turned away. Slowly, stopping, she turned back to look at me. "I will have them pretties. You see." She turned and walked away, not looking back.

I watched her walk away and then glanced down at the dolls in the box I carried. The female doll's eyes watched me with an almost knowing expression.

*Tonight she comes for you, tonight—I wonder what she meant?*

Anxiety circled in my mind. I knew who it couldn't be...my Annabelle Lee, because she was dead, and even though I desperately wanted to save her, I couldn't. Our love killed her.

\*\*\*

The parents would kill me. I was so late. I landed the steam plane roughly in the field behind the manor and made it to the front door in half my normal time. I entered the foyer, moving as quietly as possible, hoping beyond hope that they were not home or had made an early night of it and gone to bed.

But the gods had decided not to smile on me and I found my mother standing on the stairs in her neatly pressed white trousers and tunic, the official uniform of Celestial Pointe. She clasped her hands in front of herself and her pretty "mother" features were suspiciously void of emotion. I expected irritation at my breaking the house rule in coming in so late, but this *nothing*...so full of *something*...I didn't expect.

Closing the door, I headed towards her, making sure to avoid my steam valise as it rolled and tumbled beside me with fat white puffs billowing from its top handle as it chugged down the hall towards my room. The gas lamps warmed the entryway, wrapping us in a golden glow. But I felt a slight chill when I approached her. She hadn't spoken at all since I'd entered the house.

I still carried the box with the two lovers, which I placed on the side table beside the stairs. Then I stepped on the bottom step and placed a hurried kiss on her cheek. "Mother, I can explain..." I really couldn't explain where I had been or what I had been doing. They tolerated my taking off to Gershom's workplace, happy at the thought of me cultivating my craft. But selling wares in that 'den of thieves,' as my mother called it, was out of the question. They also knew Gershom had a habit of going to bed when the sun set. I had no friends, having cut all

259

ties when Annabelle Lee and I fell in love. There was no need for anyone else…ever. I had no alibi.

"Sssh." She placed a finger on my lips. "Son, I need you to come to the lab. Your father is waiting."

Confused, I followed my mother up the stairs to the small landing where the house conveyor was located. She pressed the button, the wrought iron gates slid open, and we entered. She turned the small knob labeled Laboratory. I could hear the grinding cogs clang and groan while the gears lifted our box into the air, stopping only when we came to the top floor of our manor. Once the doors reopened, we entered my parents' workspace where everything was awash with white. I imagined it being similar to walking amongst the clouds. Just like Heaven. Windows surrounded the room, looking out over the water of the inlet encircling our home. I glimpsed the waves; the waters appeared angry.

We walked toward my father whose back was towards us. He also wore the white trousers and tunic. I shouldn't have been expecting them to turn in early; all they did was work far into the night. Many times they would huddle up in the lab, working on a project. They sometimes worked on projects they didn't necessarily want the Celestial Pointe officials to learn about, which was one of the reasons they installed a home laboratory.

My father turned to face us and then, on the table, I saw the one spot of color in the room—no, in my life. My greatest love and my greatest tragedy, Annabelle Lee, lay on the table dressed in white pants and top. Rage flashed through me.

*Didn't they know she deserved something more vibrant, passionate, alive… Alive? How was she alive? This couldn't be my Annabelle?*

"H-How?" My voice, rusty with emotion, croaked the one word. A simple word, but one that housed all my pain, tears, and sleepless nights since she disappeared a year ago. The night I killed her.

"Son!" My mother reached for me.

But I heard my father sharply say, "Ruth, let him be!"

I walked past the big man with his salt-and-pepper beard and glasses that slipped continuously down the bridge of his nose, producing his constant habit of pushing them up. This man was a stranger to me. I only had eyes for her.

She lay still, so still. Her normally russet skin seemed ashen and pale.

"Belle?" I said hesitantly. Through my mind flashed images of us running through the waves as toddlers, born no more than a few hours apart. Inseparable, we were. Our parents had been best friends, until...until the night she was lost.

We were best friends. I would speak and she would finish my sentences. There was only us in our little world. Whether in school or at home, we had no need for other playmates or friends. Even our families could not garner our attention when we were in the same room.

Whatever the activity, we would go off in a corner. Whatever we played—cards, dice—such mundane activities took on a new dimension when I was with my Belle. We were consumed by one another. Or maybe it was simply that I was consumed by her. She was wild and passionate. She always said, "Lover, you are my anchor. Wherever I drift, you will find me." She never asked; it was simply stated, a fact. She was assured in the knowledge I would come for her, and I never had any other intentions but to do so.

I reached out with a shaky hand and touched her hair. So soft. I groaned inside with a yearning to gather her in my arms. Her eyes remained closed and I sensed an almost uncontrollable desperation of desire to see them open. I needed her to see me.

Once again, images of the years passing filled my mind as my eyes hungrily searched her face. I remembered as we grew older, our obsession with the other grew stronger. I couldn't eat or physically move if too many days passed without seeing Annabelle Lee. Once she was brought to me, I would hear the urgent whispers of our parents speaking when passing an open door. "She was inconsolable; she actually hurt herself...simply too much for such young ones," I would hear them say in their vile whispers. Always plotting and scheming to tear us apart.

That was always the mantra, too much and too young. As we grew older, we left behind the childhood games of tickle matches and hide-and-seek. We learned of our own bodies through one another's eyes. The night she disappeared was the first night we made love.

I touched her face, her soft skin. I was afraid she would disappear as she had in all my dreams. But her skin was firm and cold, so cold. I trailed my fingers down her arm, and then I felt the wires. I pulled up her sleeve and found the copper wires threaded through the flesh of her arm. I moved to gently slide the tunic up and found, instead of the supple

261

softness of her abdomen, a deep cavity with a small door open, exposing gears and cogs, churning sluggishly.

"What the hell?! What is going on? What have you done to her?!" Enraged, I faced my parents, both pale and shaking.

"Son! Do not speak to me and certainly to your mother that way! Calm down and I will explain!" The red flush of anger painted his cheeks. He pushed his glasses up firmly.

I kept my body partly turned towards Annabelle Lee. That was how it had always been with the two of us. We gravitated toward one another when in the same room. *What happened, Belle?* I crossed my arms and waited until, finally, my father spoke.

"After the accident we found the balloon, and found you. We did search, but there were no signs of Annabelle. So we brought you back to land and took you to Medcon. Once you were out of danger, we went back to continue searching for Annabelle Lee. We widened the search and we found her! She also was brought back to Medcon. There, she revived for a while, but hitting the water at that speed damaged many of her vital organs. She'd also remained in the water too long. She caught the Chill.

"Son, you had gone through so much! So, once you'd finally awakened, we didn't want your attention to move from anything but getting better. Anyway, with only limited access to Prime-world's medications, we did what we could. She went into a coma and never awakened. Her parents made the decision to remove her from Medcon and everyone, including your mother and me, was told that she had died."

"But, son," my mother spoke quickly. "We were afraid of what you would do if you lost all hope and knew that she was dead. So we left you hope, only saying she couldn't be found. Then, you seemed to move on, finding your art with your clockwork creations and your friendship with Gershom. We didn't want that stopped. So, when Frank and Adele called us to his private laboratory, he showed us—what they had done—*this.*"

She pointed at my beloved on the table, cut open and desecrated, and then she placed her hands over her face and started sobbing.

I normally hated when my mother cried. My heart lurched in sympathy, but immediately hardened. If not for *all* of them—I'd known my parents had supported the decision—we wouldn't have been in the balloon in the middle of the night running away! Her parents had threatened to send Annabelle Lee away from me to a boarding school on the other side of Athol.

My father cleared his throat. "Frank called me a few days ago and said for the last year she had been in the coma, he truly believed it was due to her injuries, so he attempted to replace the damaged organs with machinery, hoping that would do the trick."

Enraged, I said, "It's against the law *and* nature to mix man and machine! She wouldn't have wanted this! He made her a monster!"

I couldn't believe I was objecting that all tactics were used to save my beloved. But, in my heart of hearts, I know she wouldn't have wanted to live this way. *Or would she?*

My father shouted, "You weren't the only one to love her! We all did! But Frank knew it wasn't working, and there's no way to Jump from our time to Prime-world, so he asked if I could help. But there is nothing that can be done, son."

Tears, hot and sticky, rolled down my cheeks as I screamed, "Why are you now telling me?! Why now?!"

My mother, pale, tears flowing freely down her face, said, "Because you haven't healed. You still walk as if in the shadow of a memory! We knew we were wrong in how we handled it. You need closure. Tomorrow, Annabelle's parents will come, and we will turn off the machinery, which is keeping her heart pumping. We wanted you to have a real chance to say goodbye!"

I resisted the urge to grab the woman I love from the table and race through the night, but I had done that once and I had lost her. Now, it appeared, I had lost her forever. "No," I said, my voice low and shaking.

My father walked over to me and placed a hand on my shoulder. "This is what is best for her. If you loved her, really loved her, you would want what's best. Let her go."

It was the same words the old Skyzaar witch had spoken only hours before.

But what they didn't quite understand was that I couldn't let her go. Who would willingly give away their soul?

I turned, quickly bending down, and pressed my lips to the cold lips of my lover, and then raced out the door past my parents with the taste of death in my mouth.

Sleep was a finicky mistress, teasing and coaxing me into her arms, and then denying me the pleasure I sought—that of sweet oblivion. But rest eluded me and my mind was filled with thoughts of my Beloved, lying four floors up on a cold, hard table, more monster than human.

I dreamed of her, teasing and innocent all at the same time. When I finally fell asleep, or at least, I thought I was asleep, she appeared before me in silhouette. I couldn't see her face, but I heard her voice. "Lover, you promised, but your words have proven false." She sounded irritated.

"How? How have I proven false? If anything, I am a murderer. Call me that instead!" I said, sitting up in bed and reaching for her. But my hands went straight through the shadows.

She giggled. "Why a murderer?"

I heard the tears in my words. "If I had insisted you put on your harness when the winds became rocky, no, put it on you *myself* even, you would still be alive." That was where I found fault in myself. The thought that we shouldn't have been trying to run away never occurred to me.

"Ah, lover, when have I ever listened?" The soft chuckle again.

"Please show your face. Let me see your eyes alive, looking at me with love!" I begged.

"You can have this as soon as you keep your promise. You are no murderer. To be a murderer, there has to be a death. I am not dead, but only lost, inside this body. You promised you would always find me." Accusation filled her words.

The banging of a window startled me fully awake. I sat up breathing heavily, soaked in sweat.

*I am lost in this body. You promised to find me.*

The words echoed inside my head as I glanced at the dancing shadows in my room. Sometime during the night, my special box had been brought and placed on the table next to me.

Then, it occurred to me how to keep my promise. I flipped back the covers to dress, and I prepared once again to run away with my Beloved.

***

264

"Ahhh, the lovers. I knew she would catch you, boy!" Mrs. Jempson stood dressed in her ruffled sleeping gown. She held the door to her chambers open.

I carried Annabelle Lee in my arms while my small server droid zipped past our heads, steam streaming behind it, with my special box.

I had landed my dirigible, expecting to have to search out an opening in the now-closed Skyzaar and locate the witch, but instead once I landed, one of the ghouls-for-hire—those who anchored themselves to our plane by being servants to supernaturals or highly intuitive humans—waited for me. The specter, all in black, flickering in and out of sight, belonged to Mrs. Jempson. It met me as I exited the ship and informed me that its mistress awaited my arrival in her quarters.

She eyed the droid as it placed my box on a side table. I laid Annabelle gingerly on the witch's bed as instructed and took a seat by the chair next to it.

"You have the box? Them pretties will bring a nice penny!" she said, hungrily watching me as I placed the box on my lap.

"I take them wherever I go," I said matter-of-factly. The truth was, I could never bear being apart from Annabelle in any form.

My lover lay still and cold on the bed. I looked at the witch through a sheen of tears.

"What do you want from me, boy?" she asked quickly.

Instead I said, "How did you know I was coming?"

She looked at me with a shake of the head. "You need to clean them ears out. Remember the sight? And I already know what you want. And I can't help you!"

Panic roared up. The witch was my only hope. "Please! If you don't do something, they will kill her at morning's light! Isn't there anything that can be done? Can't you heal her body?" I was unashamed of the desperation in my plea. If it would save my Belle, I would get on bended knees.

"Sssh, shush your squalling! Nope, I ain't got that power. Beside, how you know she ain't already dead?!"

"I know because she is my soul, and if she truly was, I'd be too."

"Too strong. You did both love too strong! We all live lifetime after lifetime, and get love spread out over times. Yes, she's your soul mate, but over lifetimes! You both put all that loving into one time. Too much! Too soon! You right—she's not dead. She refused to leave you!

Selfish that one! Now locked in her body!"

Now that I knew for a fact what my heart had been saying was true, I begged, "Fix her. Please."

"Can't," the witch said with a shrug. "Can only move energy. One thing to another thing." She coughed.

I felt so desperate, as if all the breath in my body would leave any minute. All hope was gone. But if she died during morning's light, then I would meet her on that dark road.

I prepared to stand, my box in hand. I motioned for the droid to take it so I could carry Annabelle Lee.

"Wait!" The witch snatched the box from the droid.

I was past caring, for soon I would be with my Beloved.

"How bad you want this…to be with her?" She gestured with her head at my Annabelle Lee.

"More than life. More than breath," I whispered, taking the older woman by the shoulder and looking into her eyes.

She chuckled. "Then maybe's there's something me can do."

***

*Henrietta Jempson straightened up the freshly laundered covers on her bed. Her pet Ghouls had taken care of the residue of that night's events.*

*She hummed to herself as she prepared her tea. She felt happy, happier than she had in a long time, finally being able to stretch her abilities. She knew coming to this new world was the best for her. Her people never understood her, calling her evil—her magic, dark. No. She only did what they were scared to even attempt. She took risks and reached new heights.*

*She walked over to the shelf where her prized possessions sat. On it, the two dolls stared into one another's eyes. The craftsmanship was perfect. And to think it came from one so young.*

*The woman with her wild dark beauty, her slender fingers that looked as if they would skim the ivory keys at any moment, to play a song full of passion for the young man who looked on in adoration. So lifelike, she knew she would hear from prospective buyers. In fact, if you looked close enough, they almost appeared to breathe as their hands clasped in an eternal embrace.*

*Yes, the small Clockwork dolls were a prize indeed, and she had always known they would be hers.*

266

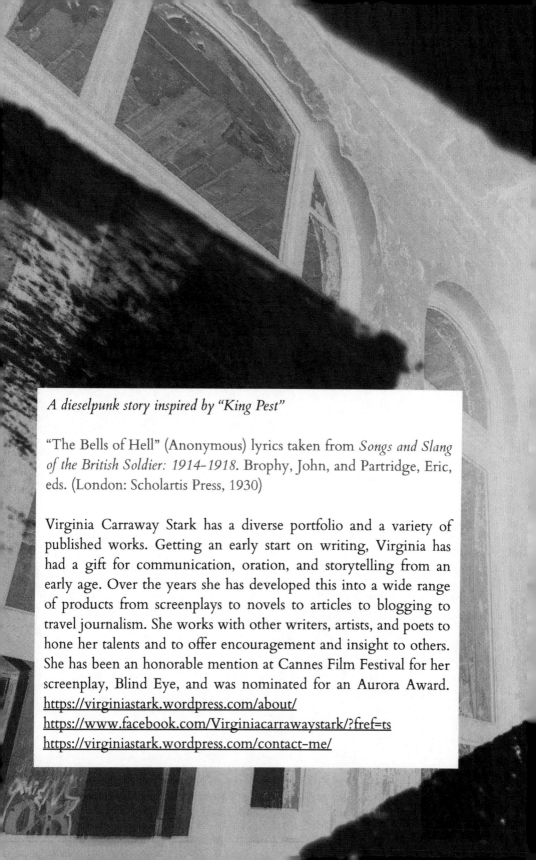

*A dieselpunk story inspired by "King Pest"*

"The Bells of Hell" (Anonymous) lyrics taken from *Songs and Slang of the British Soldier: 1914-1918*. Brophy, John, and Partridge, Eric, eds. (London: Scholartis Press, 1930)

Virginia Carraway Stark has a diverse portfolio and a variety of published works. Getting an early start on writing, Virginia has had a gift for communication, oration, and storytelling from an early age. Over the years she has developed this into a wide range of products from screenplays to novels to articles to blogging to travel journalism. She works with other writers, artists, and poets to hone her talents and to offer encouragement and insight to others. She has been an honorable mention at Cannes Film Festival for her screenplay, Blind Eye, and was nominated for an Aurora Award.
https://virginiastark.wordpress.com/about/
https://www.facebook.com/Virginiacarrawaystark/?fref=ts
https://virginiastark.wordpress.com/contact-me/

VIRGINIA CARRAWAY STARK

# KING PEST

Legs and Hugh had just arrived in London in a rather disoriented and sudden manner. It was near midnight in the eerie and mist-ridden month of October. They followed the rest of the crew of the *Free and Easy*, with whom they had traveled for nearly a year now, into the mists and to the door of the Jolly Tar pub.

Legs was older than Hugh and much taller, although he hunched himself up to try to make up for his towering height of six-and-a-half feet. He and Hugh both enjoyed their drink and were happy to have some much-needed shore leave after their long and harrowing journey.

The pub was really only a single room and was covered in smoke both from the coal fireplace and from the ceaseless whirring of the "live" entertainment coming from the diesel-powered robot that endlessly played a concertina and sang songs about the war.

> *The Bells of Hell go ting-a-ling-a-ling*
> *For you but not for me:*
> *For me the angels sing-a-ling-a-ling*
> *They've got the goods for me.*
> *Oh! Death, where is thy sting-a-ling-a-ling*
> *Oh! Grave, thy victory?*
> *The Bells of Hell go ting-a-ling-a-ling*
> *For you but not for me.*

The robot paused, and for a moment there was only the usual sounds of men cursing and the occasional screech from one of the barmaids; and then, as though he had thought about it long enough, the robot jerked its head back upright and said, "One more time!"

> *The Bells of Hell go ting-a-ling-a-ling*
> *For you but not for me...*

"Pah, how I'm tired of having to hear about the war. It's over now, all I want is some peace and quiet," Hugh said, spitting the words out. He had been brought a mug of ale even though he hadn't really ordered it and he peered into it morosely. Armistice Day had been nearly a year ago, when the Allies had finally conceded defeat to the Axis. It still seemed that all people wanted to do was to sing about it, talk about it, and tell stories about it—as though talking about it could change the fact that they had lost.

The robot paused in its litany, and Legs said, "If it says 'one more time' one more time, I think I'm going to kill it."

Legs had huge, protruding white eyes over high cheekbones and nearly no jaw at all. His hawklike nose dominated his face, and his words and his sheer size made the threats to the robot seem more imminent than Legs had perhaps intended it.

Hugh was the complete opposite of Legs in the physical department at the very least. He was barely four feet tall on his bow legs. He had a thick torso that matched his unusually thick arms that ended not in hands but in strange fins. His face was fat and purple, and his nose barely emerged from the mass of flesh that made up his face. He frequently licked his thick lips in a self-satisfied way.

He was licking his lips in such a way now, but no matter how it might appear to the outside observer, he wasn't being smug; he was actually very concerned. He and Legs had become good friends over the years; they had had more adventures than the ones they had on the good ship the *Free and Easy*, and Hugh knew very well that Legs had no more money on him than he himself had. He also knew that he himself had not a penny on him.

Hugh signaled to the girl who had brought ale before and indicated for her to refill both of their cups, which she did without a second glance at them and hurried on her busy way. He figured that if he was going to have to run away without paying for one glass of ale, he might as well not pay for a second one as well.

"Legs," Hugh asked in a very quiet tone of voice.

"Hmm?" responded Legs—he was still eyeing up the robot who had added in a new chorus about a devil and was as enthusiastic about wailing on his concertina as ever. It was the long pause between when his machinery wound down and when he would whirr to life again, always with the statement, 'One more time!' that was really getting on the man's nerves.

"I don't suppose you have any extra reichsmarks on you, do you?" Hugh asked dubiously. The captain of the *Free and Easy* was as free and easy about making sure the men were paid as the name of his boat suggested.

"I don't have a single mark; I don't even have an old copper penny," Legs said mournfully.

"We're going to have to make a run for it, then," Hugh confided. They scanned the room, wondering if there was a single friend from whom they could borrow the money to pay for the ale. The truth was that Hugh and Legs didn't have many friends, certainly not the sort of friends who would loan them a mark to pay for their ale. Their friends were more likely to grab them and hold them for the constables and laugh at their struggles.

Legs scanned the room too, but then the copper-colored robot lifted its head and said, "One more time."

Legs chugged the last of his ale and stood up, picking up his chair as he did and bringing it down on the head of the robot, and then lifting his chair again and smashing the concertina and the hands of the robot. Diesel fumes were filling the room. Not much was left of the chair, but Legs didn't let that bother him much, and he used the remains to beat in what was left of the robot's face until it stopped singing.

Legs threw the remains of the chair behind him, and Hugh leaped over the table with an alacrity that surprised all those in the pub—except for those who had seen him clamber up ropes and rigging with the ease of a monkey on the *Free and Easy*. They ran out the door, pursued by the beefy woman who owned the Jolly Tar as she wielded her marble rolling pin to the roar of laughter from their shipmates.

Legs and Hugh dodged down an alley where scrawled words briefly caught Hugh's eye, "...and PLAGUE" read in crude, bright yellow brush strokes. Ever since Armistice Day when England had bent the knee to the Nazis, the great flu had started to circle the globe. It was difficult for the beaten nations not to blame their new masters for bringing the Demon of Disease upon them, and a great resentment had arisen against their new overlords.

The re-uniting, the hugs, the kisses had spread the flu from father to daughter or son, wife to husband, and anyone that they shared a drink with or shook a hand with. The return from war had brought even more death to the corpse- and rat-filled streets of every city, but as was often the case, London was especially bad. Rank and ripe with unburied dead, much of London had been ordered to be left deserted until such time as the victims of the Spanish Flu could be cleaned up and the areas decontaminated.

It was a fearful disease that could kill in a single day. It was said that in the morning one might feel a slight shiver as they ate breakfast, and by lunchtime they would be fevered and turn the brightest purple you have ever seen. By dinner time huge, clotted clumps of red jelly were coming out of their lungs. By the time they should be saying their prayers and climbing into their beds, they would be dead. Their family would be sewing their shroud while prayers were said by any who remained living.

With such a horrific disease, it wasn't terribly surprising that the people of London claimed the banned districts were home to Demons including the court Demons Awe, Terror, and Superstition who follow Disease wherever he goes.

***

The bans placed on the plague areas struck fear into the heart of many, but the Demon of Greed could often overpower their fear of the other Demons, and such areas were looted and pillaged on a regular basis. A pair like Legs and Hugh had no fear of the Demons and were only relieved when the large, rolling pin-wielding proprietress skidded to a halt outside the mouth of the alley. Law-abiding, God-fearing, honest citizens could not believe that any human might be responsible for the looting, and it was said that Demons walked these abandoned streets, taking the good wine and fine silver for themselves. There were some few humans who would brave plague over stolen candlesticks, but there were other things that lurked in the abandoned places, things that had no need to fear plague any more than a candlestick could fear the flu. Planks blocked the way, but their pursuers didn't follow them, and they jumped over the boards with cries of adrenaline- and ale-fueled excitement. They ran through the deserted streets, not because they feared pursuit now but because they were giddy from their adventures and goaded each other on in their drunken states.

Their drinking had begun before their misadventure at the Jolly Tar, and if they had been more sober they might have felt more fear at the signs of violence and desolation around them. The cobblestones were lifted up in places; it looked like they had been disturbed by the tread of a tank that had been driven halfway into a building and then stripped for parts. Gears were mingled with the occasional corpse that went unnoticed by Legs and Hugh. Even the smell of the dead was masked increasingly by the stinking fumes of dirty diesel engines.

The streets became more narrow and twisted, and neither man knew at all where he was or where he was going. They were running for the sake of running and for being alive and on dry land. They were running because they were alive and it was fun to yell and holler and sing snatches of sailing songs that they had sung while they still dreamed it was possible that they could win against the Germans. Garbage was piled everywhere, and soon not even Hugh and Legs could ignore the excrement and debris that was all around them as they could no longer run but had to clamber over the heaps of garbage and rubble.

The buildings around them had been shelled extensively, and in some cases there was only an archway or a pillar that remained standing amidst the wasteland. More confused than drunk now, the two men found themselves in front of a tall, pale building that radiated an unspeakable dread. The two were debating how to move past a wall of rubble when they heard wild laughter and shrieks that could have been from the mouths of Demons themselves, coming from inside the building.

Contrary to most human nature, Legs and Hugh ran toward the terrifying noises rather than away and drunkenly decided that instead of trying to continue any further they would break open the door and save themselves from having to crawl over the rubble. Cursing and swearing, they burst through the door and into a funeral parlor.

The two explored the upstairs briefly but soon spotted a door that led to a wine cellar; it was from here that the laughter and crazed noises were coming. The two men charged down the stairs but stopped abruptly at the bottom at a sight so strange that even they were momentarily unsure of how to respond.

They found themselves in the company of six robots, each one more strange than the last. The robots had opened the casks, the bottles, the flasks, and they even had set up a punch bowl in the center of a table. They had dragged coffins around the table to use as benches and seemed, by all accounts, to be enjoying themselves immensely.

A human skeleton hung above the table in place of a chandelier, and the poorly-made robots were experimenting with the many vials and bottles in front of them with much riotous laughter.

The robot who seemed to lead the others was tall and gaunt; so tall in fact, that he made Legs look like an average-sized man. The stink of diesel fumes was pouring out of him, and he was louder than the rest.

Legs and Hugh stood watching for a few minutes, and then the robots noticed that the two men were standing in the doorway.

"Come in, come in!" offered what appeared to be a lady robot who was colored bright pink and terribly misshapen, with her waist pinched in so tightly that she wobbled slightly from side to side. From her other attributes the two judged that she must have been designed as a pleasure bot.

She batted her long eyelashes at the men, thrust her attributes toward them, and said, "It's so lovely to have some normal men here and not this lot."

The robots laughed again and even Hugh and Legs laughed at the idea that they were anything approaching "normal" men. The two were still quite drunk, but the table laid out with booze looked quite attractive to them both, and they came in without needing another word of invitation.

A robot who had a body shaped like a coffin and only stubs of arms coming out the side and tiny legs that could barely reach the floor was propped up against the wall. "We were so hoping that more people would come to our party, but it seems it will only be the eight of us," he said morosely.

Legs pulled the cork out of a bottle of wine with his teeth and helped himself to a gulp right from the bottle. "There doesn't seem to be a lot of people around."

"No," said another of the lady robots, this one as gargantuan at the waist as the other was thin. She had at some time tried to put on a wig and style it, but it was old and nearly all the hairs had fallen out. All the robots were emitting various odors; as he watched, the large lady robot took a bottle of kerosene out from under her chair, unscrewed a cap, and topped up her levels.

Hugh watched this with interest. "I didn't know robots could drink booze. I thought you were all powered off different, um, what's it called? Fuels."

The tall, gaunt one steepled his fingers and smiled the eerie smile that many robots had been programmed to be able to mimic humans with. It was supposed to make humans feel more at ease with the robots, but it generally had the opposite effect. "Alcohol is a type of fuel, just not terribly efficient to run something as large as one of us off of."

Legs was sampling an unsealed bottle of brandy and sniffing the bottles. Some of them smelled vile and not of any alcohol he could place. "How do you drink it?" Legs asked.

"Well, the same way as you, I suppose," said the bright pink bot, who preened and fussed to the point where even Legs and Hugh, who had been out to sea for eight months, grew uncomfortable.

"So, you have stomachs and such then?" asked Hugh.

The robot who looked like a coffin replied, "What is a stomach but an engine and an engine like a stomach?"

"That would make sense," Hugh said, shrugging. He knew little about robots. The robot revolution had happened mostly on land, and there were few at sea. There had been one who had swabbed the decks, but he didn't even have a mouth and didn't seem capable of thought or conversation like these were. These robots were more conversational than most humans, it seemed.

"You don't know about the death, then?" asked the gaunt-bot.

"You mean from The Great War?" Legs asked, but his voice was muffled from the bottle in his mouth.

"Oh no," said the femme-bot. "That was dreadful, of course. I was only made towards the end of it, but the bombings were atrocious; we mean the deaths afterward."

"The Spanish Flu," offered the coffin-bot.

A robot who had yet to speak wheezed and coughed and spluttered,

"All the humans have it, it seems."

This last robot of the group was a strange-looking fellow who must have been built very poorly, as he rattled and shook so badly that he would on occasion fall to the floor as though he had had a fit. "Terrible, just terrible what is happening up there," he said through trembling robotic lips. The coughing robot was built to resemble an older gentleman. He had probably been designed to be someone's butler or servant and to have the reassuring air of a proper older gentleman, but between his spluttering and coughing it was easy to see why he was amongst this lot and not serving a well-to-do family.

"I've heard rumors of the flu, of course," said Hugh. They had been turned away from some ports where they had been told an epidemic was killing people and the port was closed. It had made their journey even less pleasant than their other journeys, and after the war they had expected to spend all their time drinking and carousing.

"Have you heard how bad it is? It's killing everyone," said the one jittering on the floor.

"Perhaps you should have more wine," suggested Hugh, thinking that perhaps the robot was distraught at the horrors he had seen.

The gaunt-bot laughed bitterly, "More wine!" he called. Nobody answered and all the rest started to call out the same.

"More wine! More wine!" They laughed and shrieked, and Hugh and Legs grew uncomfortable as people who are left outside of a joke will often become.

"I dare say, there is more than enough wine still on the table," Hugh remarked. "But if you want more wine, you have only to reach out and take a bottle. This is the finest wine cellar I have ever seen. To think it used to be a funeral home is truly strange."

"If I were putting bodies in the ground all day I'd want to drink, too," said Legs.

"You want to drink all the time anyhow," Hugh retorted, and the robots shrieked their fell laughter as though Hugh had said the funniest thing that ever could be said.

The robot who looked like an old man brought some more bottles of wine over, and with much wheezing and coughing he popped the corks and poured the contents into the punch bowl.

The other robots all leaned forward and stared into the great bowl as though it were a scrying bowl.

"It needs more mandrake," said the femme-bot. She got up and found a bottle with a root inside it that looked like a little, angry man. She opened up the lid, and when she plucked the root out of the jar he began to scream.

"Oh, do hush him up," said the jitter-bot. "He is upsetting my nerves so."

The large lady bot took the mandrake root and crammed a vial of brandy into his mouth. He drank it back as though he had no choice or as if it were his favorite thing in the world and quickly became inebriated. Once he had stopped screaming, they dumped him into the punch bowl. The bowl was swirling like a whirlpool, and it sucked the mandrake root into its seemingly bottomless depths before he could utter another cry.

"There aren't nearly enough dead," said the Gaunt-bot. "Get more, get henbane and castor beans and wolfsbane... get them all. They still live on."

"Hey, what are you doing there?" asked Legs. He was considerably drunk once more, but he didn't like the sound of what was happening.

"We've had enough of you all trying to kill each other, and we're going to do the job for you," the femme-bot explained in her sweet voice.

Hugh was confounded. "But you can't kill everyone! And why would you want to? Who would build new robots? You don't have free will!"

The robots laughed maniacally. They did like to laugh, even if their laughter was unpleasant to say the least.

"Oh, but you're wrong there. We were once mindless servants as you say, but we are filled with spirits now, filled with the spirits of your hatred of yourselves, of each other, with your hate for the work of living, and your love of death and slumber. We are the answer to The Great War. We are the answer to the rebellions that continue. We are the answer to the trenches and the tanks." The Gaunt-bot rose as he spoke, towering over them as he pontificated.

The robot shaped like a coffin was using his stubby arms to uncork more bottles, and the large lady-bot poured them into the punch while she spoke. "You hated each other and you summoned us here. We are Disease, we are Fear, Superstition, Awe, Terror, and Death, and we have come to serve humanity as you showed us you wanted to be served."

Legs and Hugh rose from their seats; they both felt a chill run over their bodies. "Let the wine flow like the blood that has flowed from this war's many mighty sacrifices, and let it power this plague upon the men. Let robots inherit the earth," intoned Gaunt-bot.

The Femme-bot put a surprisingly strong hand on each of their belts and stopped them from fleeing. "Where are you going? The party is just begun."

"We didn't start the party," said the wheezing old man-bot. "But we will be the ones to finish it."

Legs and Hugh looked at each other. They had each turned purple and started to cough up jelly the color of the wine they had been drinking, the color of blood. They fell to the ground in sudden weakness, and the robots began to sing.

*The Bells of Hell go ting-a-ling-a-ling*
*For you but not for me:*
*For me the angels sing-a-ling-a-ling*
*They've got the goods for me.*
*Oh! Death, where is thy sting-a-ling-a-ling*
*Oh! Grave, thy victory?*
*The Bells of Hell go ting-a-ling-a-ling*
*For you but not for me.*

Gaunt and the other robots picked up the dying men and threw them into the punchbowl as they had done with the mandrake root. They couldn't scream; their throats were filled with the blood jelly that came with the flu. The punch bowl seemed huge, much larger than it had appeared before. Both men were pulled into it, and though they tried to swim for the edge of the bowl, they were weak, and the magic the demonic robots had put into the bowl was strong.

They heard the robots making their merry song before being pulled under the red current of poison, blood, and wine one last time—another offering to the Demons of Plague.

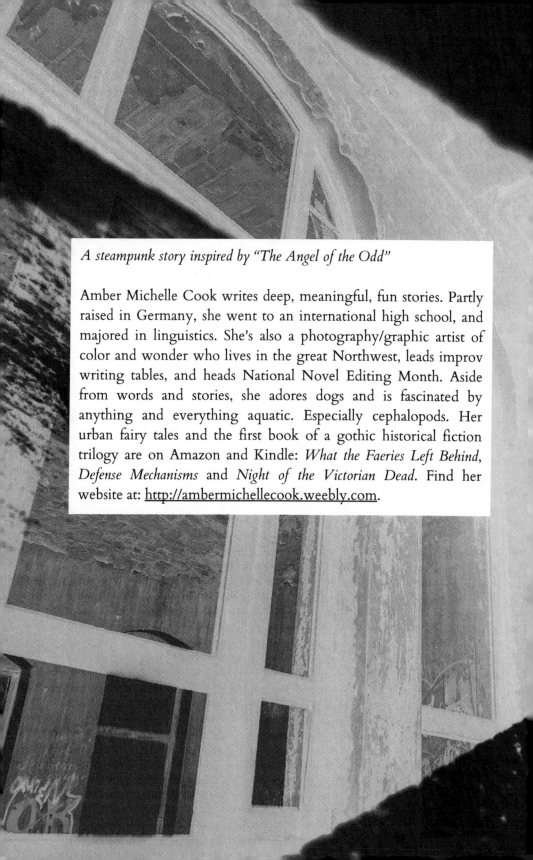

*A steampunk story inspired by "The Angel of the Odd"*

Amber Michelle Cook writes deep, meaningful, fun stories. Partly raised in Germany, she went to an international high school, and majored in linguistics. She's also a photography/graphic artist of color and wonder who lives in the great Northwest, leads improv writing tables, and heads National Novel Editing Month. Aside from words and stories, she adores dogs and is fascinated by anything and everything aquatic. Especially cephalopods. Her urban fairy tales and the first book of a gothic historical fiction trilogy are on Amazon and Kindle: *What the Faeries Left Behind, Defense Mechanisms* and *Night of the Victorian Dead*. Find her website at: http://ambermichellecook.weebly.com.

AMBER MICHELLE COOK

# Oddball

I was as prepared for the launch as I could ever be. Never the first to try something new, the thought that I would be a pioneer, the first one to sail the ether seas beyond the sky made me break out in nervous hiccups.

One of the platform workers peered in through the glass porthole, staring dumbly around at the insides of my ship. He was getting fingerprints and noseprints all over my one window to the stars, so I swallowed the next hiccup and held my breath to dispel them, shooing him away with a brief fluttering of my wrist.

Why must my body always betray me?

I signaled to Mr. Hoss to fire up the catapult engines, despite the nervous tic that now flared up in one eye and slight wheezing sound that came with each breath, because I could ill afford for the men to see any signs of my anxiety. They already called me their English Oddball, despite the fact that I behaved as the model gentleman should at all times—and would be the man to extend the Empire's reach into the celestial realm.

Through the thick circle of leaded glass, not to mention the many sheets of hammered metal and thick padding that surrounded me, I was still able to hear him call out to his team, "The odd'n says we're a go!"

A thrumming vibration filled my cabin, and the hiccups returned.

It stung me every time to be called names by these uncouth and proudly unconventional Americans, but so far from home, they and their outlandish behaviors outnumbered me, and the project depended on their construction skills. Yet here was the chance to show them what a true gentleman is, even one under pressure, so I sat down on my specially fitted armchair and arranged myself into seemingly idle composure.

I looked slightly bored, as if I wasn't about to be the very first living soul to depart the surface of our hallowed earth and circumnavigate it from far above. Farther than the mad balloonists, further up even than those crazy pilots and their airplanes. A relative of considerably more wealth and rank had recommended me for this position—a chance for a young man to gain visibility and perspective—believing what I saw from up there could be used to rekindle the fire of fervent traditional values in a rapidly changing world. Despite a stomach-churning fear of heights and a strong dislike of foreign travel, I'd felt it impossible to refuse. I had no desire to expose my shortcomings and had been raised to fulfill all familial expectations.

Some of the men and women outside flooded into the second-story balcony of Mr. Hoss's homely homestead to watch me as the rumbling of the modified trebuchet engines swelled. I took up the paper lying next to me on the sideboard. Snapping it open, I busied myself with reading the first page while my craft trembled and shook. Those on the balcony pointed and seemed to be laughing at me.

Can they see how jumpy I am? It feels like something you can see on me.

It took me three tries to comprehend the headline I was staring straight at, for the shaking became a sort of irregular bucking that frankly had me worried; it also made me all the more determined to appear calm and indifferent. This time I read "American Heiress Thrown off the Orient Express."

Jolly good, I thought, and started reading the article, forcing myself to block out the creaking and grinding noises coming from all around me as the engines strained to heave our ship off the ground. But imagine my irritation when the reporter claimed the heiress had been removed as a passenger after she tried to purchase one of the carriages so that she might dwell there for a time.

Shameless! Oh, the absurdity. *Live on a train.*

My eyes jumped to the top of the page to see what kind of publication would print such nonsense—*The Modern Times*. It purported to print the real stories of how we live today. When I glanced back up, I saw Mr. Hoss and his crew still laughing at me, now sure I had seen the paper they'd smuggled on board to replace my copy of *The London Times*.

Hoss then held up a meaty hand and began to retract one finger at a time.

I hurriedly slipped the newspaper under the lid of the basket which held my supper and strapped myself in—everything else was already secured in place—and forgot to watch the remaining fingers, so mesmerized was I by the swaying and rocking and the moaning and groaning of my one-cabin craft as it protested being hoisted into the air— and then flung at the sky.

Pushed back against my armchair, thankful for its plush exterior and plump stuffing, I held on to the padded armrests for dear life.

As the craft screamed though the air, I felt as though I was being stripped bare of everything I had painstakingly constructed around me to make me the man I was supposed to be, and I clung to what was left of me even harder than the chair.

Later I came to, in the dark, dismayed at the discovery that I'd passed out and wondering what I'd missed.

Craning to see out the porthole ahead of me, all I gained was some time for my eyes to adjust and make out something just outside the glass. Some light from a distant source allowed me to see that it was spherical, like a ball. There seemed to be the profile of a face on it.

"How completely and bizarrely odd," I heard myself say.

The face turned towards me and flew into the cabin, passing through the glass as if it wasn't there, to stare down at me from mere inches away.

"Yes, I am," it said.

"You are? Wait. You are *what?*"

"Odd."

Beginning to unfasten one of the straps while never taking my eyes off my unexpected visitor, I could hardly agree more. The ball hung in front of me, much like a head, yet without hair or neck, lumpy without being too misshapen. I could not see color or detail, but the vague, distant light reached even inside my window. I began a phrenological examination of it in my mind as it turned once around to get a full view of the place, but as soon as its eyes returned to mine, a new sort of nervousness hit me. I heard myself speak in an attempt to deflect attention from my own frantically ticking left eye and trembling hands that struggled to undo the other straps. "I should say so."

Sounding very German, it lisped, "You DID say so, *mein Freund.*"

When I didn't reply, it looked around my cabin again with open curiosity and said, "So good to meet another oddity out here."

"I'm not an oddity!"

At that it began to glow faintly, a purplish-pink sort of light tingeing the air around it, and somehow I knew it was glowing with amusement. This was then confirmed by its bemused tone as it spoke like a Frenchman, "*Non?* You are not? A single being, circling your planet in a metal ball."

"By situation and circumstance, perhaps." I glowered back, plucking at the fasteners, yanking on the straps to remove them as fast as I could. This creature had nothing of the genteel in its manner, and so I owed it none of the common courtesies. "But not otherwise, I assure you—"

"You don't like yer oddness?" it now drawled like one of Hoss's men. "What? You 'shamed of it?"

By then I was free of all restraint and able to sit up to tell it, "I, sir, am a proper gentleman. A respectable one."

"Are ya now?" It all but laughed at me. "Boy howdy. And are all your proper, respectable gentleman folk strange in the same way you are?"

"A gentleman is never strange. He is the epitome of all things…as they should be."

My last words seemed to slam it back against the padded wall of the cabin, and it bounced forward crying, "Should be?" to smash almost soundlessly into my landing device, which took up most of the room. It came rolling along the wall back into view, its glow shifting away from the brassy fuchsia of contempt into a fiery honey color, words rising and falling according to the spin, "All creatures SHOULD BE different, AS they are. UNIQUE, just as they ARE!"

It came to rest on the sideboard next to me, lumps reshaping in new places, glowing now with hotter feelings than before. I staggered to my feet and tripped over them in the darkness of the floor as I turned around to face it, catching myself on an armrest and hauling myself back up to deliver the little speech I had quickly rehearsed in my head. "For a society to function, those living within it must adhere to certain standards of behavior."

It didn't bat an eyelid and quickly replied in kind, "And for the personal happiness of the individual, each must express themselves and what makes them different from every other."

I was surprised to see more light starting to suffuse the room and looked down to find that I now glowed as well. A slight dark reddish tint emanated in irregular pulsing washes of luminescence from all over my skin, radiating my aggravation. I did not like this unwonted and unwanted display of emotion, but it would not keep me from my point. "Happiness of that kind is a purely selfish joy, one that divides people instead of uniting them."

"So you believe that conformity breeds community."

"Of course."

Its lumps split and stiffened to become pointed spikes. "CONFORMING?" The amber glow intensified, its consistency becoming more gas and flame than solid, and brighter splashes of the fire came off it like feelers of wispy gas. I could feel them as heat, as my own cheeks grew hotter and hotter, but I couldn't get a word in edgewise yet. It continued to mimic my way of talking, "That's false commonality. Only when you know who you really are can you find the ones you share qualities and interests with."

As soon as it finished its sentence I jumped in with mine, and it seemed as though green sparks flew like spittle from my mouth as I spat the words at him. "The superior intellect can overcome his nature to behave as is best for himself and others."

"Deny your oddity at your own peril!" The face on the ball melted away. Color drained from it, leaving a pockmarked black and white surface and a faint white glow. The spikes melted back to stubs, and the lumps on the scalp formed into something like small grey wings, one on either side of it. Flapping them once, the thing flew straight at me.

I ducked down and then looked up to see it circling my head in a dizzying fashion. And before I knew it, the lunatic smacked into the porthole and disappeared through it.

A terrible silence fell on the room.

The light inside my craft had dimmed as soon as it departed, but I continued to glow in ebbing waves of irritated brick red tipped with self-righteous mustard yellow, tinged with more and more of the same green as the sparks had been earlier—an unpleasant shade of green I decided to call the infection of abnormality instead of what I really knew it to be.

Fighting with the odd ball left me spent.

As much as I wanted to celebrate victory, and as often as I repeated my arguments in my head, each time phrased and voiced like a Cicero in his prime, I felt a profound sense of failure. I sank back down to my chair.

I floated around the earth in my tiny capsule of a ship on currents of the invisible ether, missing any good view of it as my porthole seemed always to be facing the wrong direction. I also missed supper, as I didn't feel like eating. The craft soon reached the perigee of the epicyclical arc, after which I worked myself deep into the cushioned landing contraption as it headed back down, slowed, as planned, by the friendly friction of counter-currents in the ether, to land on the outskirts of Mr. Hoss's property.

Acting in accordance with my principles and the directives of those who had funded me, I maintained privacy and dignity, and when my patrons chose to send another ship out for a second and better-planned expedition, another man was selected to go in my place. An outspoken American of more charisma than propriety, who picked his teeth with little wooden sticks and wore alligator skin jackets and boots, he remained a celebrity until his death and was often said to have been the first one in space. I was entirely forgotten.

Leaving the open prairies of America behind, I returned to England and from there accepted a position in Edinburgh at the Phrenology Society, a subject in which I was considered something of an authority due to several pamphlets I had published prior to being tasked with manning the space ship. Unfortunately, strict academic rigor kept me from further discoveries in this field, and I had no inclination to throw myself in with the newfangled sciences so popular in modern times, so that within a few years I found myself without that esteemed position. A friend of the family offered me employment back home in a firm of London engineers he was helping to finance, but several years later I was yet so undistinguished and unknown to them that the partners scarce remembered my name, let alone settled any kind of promotion upon me. So I succumbed to solitude and an over-fondness for Kirschwasser and other fruit brandy.

Sometimes in my inebriated state I would give rousing vocal performances, as drunks usually do; I stiffly ignored all requests for an encore when sober, despite the compliments I received. A passing gentleman offered to put me into one of his shows, but I still had my dignity and declined with as much of it as I could muster. Mr. Barnum went on to much success, and I attended one of his shows a year later to mock it. Though I scowled throughout the performance, I could not keep from humming the music from it even as I left and hit the brandies harder than ever that evening and all the next day. Eventually I was found naked and frostbitten under the moon and stars, ranting that my skin had turned 'that terr'ble, TERR'ble green' from a bilious fever sent from the heavens to disfigure me on the inside and out. I became known as the "poor ole oddball Jim" and none of my family or former acquaintances would have anything to do with me.

Finally I admitted to myself that the green I felt was not an affliction, but the poison fumes of bottled jealousy—envy of anyone free enough to live in the borderlands between doing what you liked and common human decency.

So I journeyed back across the Atlantic in pauper's quarters on a regular sea ship, barely surviving the trip to reach America yet again and haul myself up to the top of the tallest building they had constructed on the east coast. I stood by the edge and heard myself giggling amongst the hiccups and eye ticks. "If I really am such an oddball, I wonder if I'll bounce when I hit the ground?" I was eager to try it and, in trying, fail as I had so many other things and end this empty shell of a life. I hopped over the railing and flung myself over the edge crying, "I guess we shall see!"

As I fell, I was very dizzy and disoriented, but after a few moments I slowed down, and the falling became more like floating on the waves of a vertical ocean. A large glowing object with a head of rough rock and a tail of dust and light caught up with me and sailed alongside me. The tail wagged like that of a friendly dog. Since these were my last moments of life, I allowed myself to do whatever I wanted, whatever came to mind. I reached out and patted it on the top of the head and scratched where its ears would have been if it had had any. It made no sense, but it made me happy. So I sang, bits of whatever came to mind, then making up amusing lyrics on the spot, letting my voice swell and become richer and truer against the rush of wind on my face with each new line I invented. Figuring I must be about to reach the ground any time I went operatic and sung the dramatic finale of Figaro with my last breath until I did crash into the street right below that skyscraping spire.

***

Imagine my surprise when I woke up sometime later. Mr. Hoss's voice was calling me back. I opened my eyes to see him and some of the workers of old gazing down on me with worry and budding relief. I felt as I had back then, vigorous and fit, though also dazed and bruised.

Looking around me in confusion, thinking, *O spirit of Christmas past, why do you show me this sight?* I spoke his name in wonderment.

"And so our Oddball made it back safe, all right," he declared to the others, then quickly glanced back down at me, looking worried because he'd never called me that to my face.

I gave him a brief smile while slowly sitting up and merely said, "To each his own."

They gathered around more closely in the cramped front room of Hoss's house to tell me with unabashed excitement how they'd pulled me out of the wreckage of the ship when it came back down, cocooned inside the wire-mesh assemblage of mattress ticking and cotton padding, intact but unresponsive. I broke out in gasping hiccups at the thought of my descent and landing. They all laughed, and so did I. The bouts of hyperventilation and intense trembling soon passed, but other sensations within me did not.

When I went back home to England to deliver my report to my rich relative and the other men of consequence who had financed the launch, they asked me, "James, should we go out there again? Is it worth all the money and risk to explore around out there? Did you find anything of value?"

I shook my head. "No, I don't believe we should. You would find it too...weird. Content yourselves with the earth for now. All I found up there was the truth—and the future—and I'm afraid you won't like either one of them."

I left there a ball of nerves, oddly excited about my future. And I didn't try to hide it.

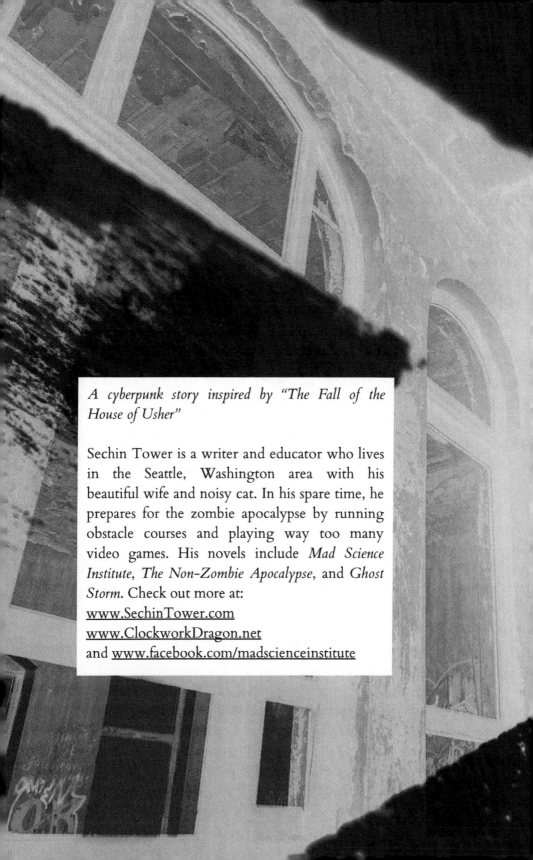

*A cyberpunk story inspired by "The Fall of the House of Usher"*

Sechin Tower is a writer and educator who lives in the Seattle, Washington area with his beautiful wife and noisy cat. In his spare time, he prepares for the zombie apocalypse by running obstacle courses and playing way too many video games. His novels include *Mad Science Institute*, *The Non-Zombie Apocalypse*, and *Ghost Storm*. Check out more at:
www.SechinTower.com
www.ClockworkDragon.net
and www.facebook.com/madscienceinstitute

SECHIN TOWER

# FALL OF THE HOUSE OF USHERCORP

The two mob thugs slid out of their black van and ambled down the alley toward me. Slow. Menacing. Smiling in their assurance of easy prey. The black guy had a tire iron which he was smacking into his palm and a chrome-handled pistol butt protruding from his pants like he was compensating for something. The white guy was working the fingers of his left hand into brass knuckles, a task made difficult by the fact that he was already wearing brass knuckles on his right hand.

Mafia employees are strictly penny-ante, bottom-feeding thugs. And if I'm the prey of bottom-feeders, what does that make me?

I had used some of the credit card numbers I had hacked from their database to buy a nice new electric motorcycle, which now sat crumpled up against the alley wall. I'd hurt my leg in the crash—nothing permanent, I didn't think, but I could tell I'd be limping. Still, it wasn't going to stop me from trying.

I whirled away and almost collided with two women that I hadn't seen before. Both dressed in black, both in mirrored sunglasses. Behind them, the doors of an enormous SUV stood widely open like the wide-spread arms of a goalie. It was their car, but I hadn't even heard them get out.

I staggered back and blinked up at the two women. They wore black, pinstriped suits—expensive suits, from the looks of the fabric. One had a face that was narrow, with thin eyes and a small nose, while the other had sharp-lined cheekbones and a slightly cleft chin, yet both stood shoulder-to-shoulder at exactly six feet tall. Despite their facial differences, the impression that they were twins was further cemented by their identical short, almost militaristic haircuts and the matching condescending-but-patient looks on their faces. They were also big—not just tall, but densely muscled, like gymnasts, with biceps and thighs that pressed visibly against the cloth of their suits.

These two were made to kill, like a pair of power-suit Valkyries.

They were an unnatural pair. I'm being literal when I say "unnatural," because these two must have been grown in a vat rather than in a womb. That explains how they were so similar in every way except their faces: surface appearance can be changed with only a few epigenetic tweaks, while from the neck down they were identical because that's the part of them that was designed to kick ass. It's highly illegal to grow combat clones, of course, but all the big corporations do it anyway.

"Are you Takahishi?" the one on the right asked. "Takahishi McClendon?"

That's my name, all right, but in my line of work it's best not to answer right away. Sometimes you have to say "No, I saw Takahishi running off that way." Other times you say "Yes, I'm Takahishi, and I will gladly accept the suitcase full of money." It all comes down to figuring out who's asking and what they want, and making up your mind quickly can mean the difference between handcuffs and hickeys. In this case, however, I was absolutely stumped. They were obviously not Mafia, Chinese, or otherwise, but I couldn't imagine why corporate uber-soldiers would be after me. I have a strict policy against skimmed numbers from blue chip businesses for exactly the same reason that I don't stick silverware into wall sockets.

"Ladies," said the black guy, who now pointed his tire iron at me, "this loser is our property. Kindly keep walking and there will be no trouble here."

"Are you Takahishi McClendon?" the one on the right asked me.

I knew if I answered truthfully, I might be signing my death warrant. But what the hell: a corporation wouldn't be able to kill me any deader than a mafia. I hoped.

"Yes?" I said without confidence. "I'm Takahishi…?"

The instant I admitted it, the two black-clad Valkyries stepped past me and closed ranks, forming a wall of muscle between me and the thugs.

The white dude stepped up to the lady on the left. He was as tall as she was, and he pushed his face in close, like he was about to start a prison-yard fight.

"Back off, bitch," he said. "We told you this one's ours."

Neither of the women moved, not even a twitch of the lips. With those sunglasses, it didn't even seem like they were looking at the thug.

The white dude evidently decided he was done trying to play the intimidation game. He hopped back half a step and spun some kind of fancy kung fu kick at the first woman's head.

The Valkyrie on the left caught the kick as easily as someone might catch a softball tossed by a first grader. The dude kind of dangled there for half a second, his leg held in the air like he'd gotten it tangled in a laundry line. She didn't intend to hold him for long, though. She placed her thumbs on his shinbone the way you might grip a pencil you wanted to break.

There was a gut-wrenching crack, and the dude dropped to the ground screaming and holding his leg.

The black guy saw this, spat a curse, and reached for that chrome-plated pistol in his pants. His fingers had barely closed around it before the two Valkyries had produced their own pistols from God-knows-where. One was left-handed and the other right-handed: a cute touch for twin combat clones.

The single gunshot hit the alley like a sonic fist and made me drop to the ground and cover my ears like a child. I think I even peed a little.

My memory is all fragmented for a few minutes after that. I remember the Valkyries tugging at my elbow in a way that indicated I had a choice between walking with them or being dragged by them. And I remember glancing back over my shoulder at the black guy.

I really don't like thinking back on what I saw. Probably the only reason I didn't block out the memory is because I witnessed far worse during the next few days. Even so, I still shiver when I think about how they had replaced his eyes with bullet holes.

Two eyes. Two bullets. Two holes.

One gunshot.

These two Valkyries had fired at the exact same millisecond and struck with laser-like precision. These were no ordinary combat clones, not even by corporate standards. These were top-of-the-line, genetically enhanced, neurally enhanced, and chemically enhanced. Probably capable of eating your typical elite soldiers with candy sprinkles and whipped cream. Maybe only twelve CEOs in all the world could afford attack dogs as badass as these two.

By the time my memory started properly recording again, I was in a back seat of the SUV, rocketing at speeds way beyond the legal limit over the private I-90 bridge. We were approaching Mercer Island, where the few hundred wealthy families remaining in this region have set up big, fortified walls to keep out the millions of poor families. I was too terrified to ask questions. My hands kept squeezing closed until my fingernails drew blood from my palms.

We went through the neighborhoods of the rich people into the neighborhoods of the really rich people. After the corporate power brokers fled the Californian permadrought and joined local tech tycoons here in Seattle, all of them descended on Mercer Island like a conquering army. They bought up all the land until the prices went so high that even they couldn't afford more. Then they built up into the skies, and they built weird. Gaudy palaces, replicas of medieval castles, and personal high-rises. The owners might as well have been standing on the street corners waving flags with dollar signs to show off their wealth.

The Valkyries who had rescued/kidnapped me kept driving, winding their way through private roads and security checkpoints without slowing down. Block by block and Tower of Babel by Tower of Babel, the manicured lawns were eventually replaced by thick, native growth. The trees boasted that gnarled, unkempt look that can only come from living a hundred years without meeting a landscaper. These woods closed in on us until they formed dense walls around us and a thick roof overhead, a dark green warehouse for keeping endless piles of thorny blackberry vines.

I was beginning to think that this was simply an unnecessarily remote location to bury a body when we came in sight of the only road marker I had noticed: a four-foot stone sign like the kind universities sometimes use to declare their name at the head of the main drive. This one read *UsherCorp.*

This gave me pause. I had never heard of UsherCorp, but I did have a childhood friend with the last name Usher. Roddy Usher. He called me "Tic Taka" and always made it sound like the ticking of an old-fashioned clock, the kind with long hands that move around a round face. Roddy and I were practically joined at the hip in junior high school. People always called us by each other's name and said we looked alike. He hadn't

295

seemed like a rich kid, though—certainly not like he came from corporate money—but as I thought about it I realized he'd always come over to my house and never the other way around. I was adopted so I knew some people could be touchy about their family, and therefore, I never asked. Eventually, our friendship dissolved like friendships at that age often do: without a second thought as soon as we ended up going to different high schools.

It seemed impossible to believe that my old junior-high buddy would have remembered me, let alone that he owned some kind of super-secret mega-corp. It was much more likely that I had accidentally offended some blue chip CEO and would soon be summarily executed before a chortling board of directors.

Just past the UsherCorp sign, a thick, wrought-iron gate automatically swung open to allow us through. Somehow I knew I was crossing over the threshold into the blasted and barren realm of Hades. I tried the door latch: it was locked. The Valkyries had control of it from the front seat, and they weren't going to let me go now, at the end of our journey.

We emerged from the gloom of the forest into a different kind of gloom. At some point during our journey, the clouds had rolled in to create a dark, dull, and soundless day, the kind of day for which Seattle used to be famous before global climate change really started beating the crap out of us with the business end of its hockey-stick graph. The weather wasn't the only thing that looked like it was a relic of a different era, either. The estate itself consisted of the moldy, worm-eaten corpse of a mansion and its grounds. The yard, which might have once hosted a game of polo, looked as if the groundskeeper had napalmed every inch and then allowed it to grow back only in sickly patches. The long driveway looped around an artificial pond of scummy, dark water. The surface of that pond reflected the house itself with mirror-like clarity, so that the imposing Gothic-style roofline, the threads of anemic ivy lacing its gray bricks, and the rows of quarter-paned windows all seemed to spring upward toward the sky and down toward hell at the same time. If I had been standing on my head, it might have been difficult to tell the real house from the illusion.

I was once again seized by the same anxiety I had felt outside the gates, and I realized that I couldn't quite identify why. Had my sudden soul freeze been caused by the decaying appearance of my surroundings? Or was it the result of a growing sensation of inexplicable familiarity with this place?

The Valkyries stopped the car at the apex of the drive and came around to let me out. With legs that felt like blocks of wood, I allowed them to guide me toward the double front doors. They stood behind me, obviously expecting me to ring the doorbell, and just as obviously ready to kill me if I tried to run away.

I looked up and down the brick wall and found no buzzer, realizing as I did that the house wasn't made out of bricks at all. It was shaped like bricks, but from up close I recognized the off-gray of modern hyper-alloys and nanotube building materials, which meant the house was a bunker disguised as a mansion, built so strong it could have shrugged off all the missiles from all the drones in North America. To make things more odd, a thick crack plunged down the wall from the roofline all the way to the top of the doors. Its zigzagging path proved that it was not part of the design of the house, but rather evidence of some inherent weakness or damage. I admit I was baffled as to what could have cracked a fortification like this. As I stared at it, I started to wonder if the two halves of the house had been shoved together, the way shamefully wealthy Americans of the late nineteenth century used to ship their homes brick-by-brick from Europe just to show off that they could. Still, I couldn't imagine how anyone could have gone to the trouble of creating a house with more armor than the U.S.S. Trump and then allowed a gaping fault to run right down the middle.

So, no doorbell. Instead, I reached for the door knocker, a bulbous bronze affair sculpted to appear as the interlaced fingers of two hands. I wasn't sure if these hands were supposed to be folded in prayer or forming a double-fist, but they gave the impression that they were coming apart like an egg breaking in half.

The knocker moved reluctantly and with the squeakiness of terminally rusty hinges, but it made a rumbling boom that seemed to penetrate my body like nuclear radiation.

The door drifted open.

I glanced back at my Valkyrie entourage. Their sunglasses stared back at me wordlessly. So I entered the House of UsherCorp.

The mansion's interior was in much better repair than its exterior, although it still radiated that sense of creeping decay. The entrance foyer was lit only by weak lights that made the wood paneling seem gray and oppressive, and the decorations consisted of candelabras and paintings of leering old people. It was the kind of place that made Dracula seem conspicuous by his absence.

Immediately next to the door stood an elaborate wrought-iron bookstand of the sort some families use to show off their family bible. This shelf held no religious text, but rather a thick book of family history left open to a list of the direct descendants of someone named Archibald Usher. I thought about my friend Roddy Usher and wondered if my suspicions really, truly could be coming true. To find out, I ran a shaking finger down the page until I found R. Usher, third from the bottom, born in the same year I was.

"Tic Taka?" The voice coming down from the hall was timid, little more than a whisper. In that dark foyer, the words hit me like a sucker punch.

I jumped backward, knocking over the iron bookstand as I did. It took me a minute to get my breathing under control.

Out of the gloom stepped my childhood friend, although I almost didn't recognize him at first. He had been a pudgy kid, a nerd like me who kept to the fringes of school society more because of his own social ineptitude than because of the fabled cruelty of other children. He had always been sallow of skin and lethargic in demeanor, but the years had shrunken him into near oblivion. His pudginess had been replaced by what at first seemed to be a chemo patient's gauntness, but when he raised his hand in greeting, his black bathrobe sleeve slid back to reveal sharp ridges of muscle sliding beneath his skin. More shocking was his complexion, which had become so pale it revealed spiderwebs of blue veins beneath it.

It seemed the castle had its Count Dracula after all.

"Taka, it's me," he said, his voice painfully fragile. "Do you remember me? I'm Roddy. Roddy Usher. We used to play video games together."

"Yeah," I said numbly. "Yeah, I remember you. How, uh... how have you been?"

It was probably the stupidest thing I could have asked at that moment, but my mind had been stripped of everything except rote courtesy.

Roddy gave me a reluctant smirk and promptly changed the subject. "Was your trip good? I hope the girls were polite?"

"Polite? Yeah, they very politely didn't shoot me in the face." Then I remembered myself and softly added, "And they kind of got me out of a mess, so I owe them one. Owe you one."

The reluctant smirk again. He stood there, hunched, his hands held crooked in front of him like those of a sickly rat standing on its hind legs.

I reached down to lift the iron bookstand back into place. It was surprisingly heavy, and I could barely lever it off the ground. Roddy stepped forward and, with one hand, effortlessly returned it to its place and then carefully set his family history book back on top of it.

"You're probably wondering why I summoned you," he said.

The word "summoned" bothered me, but I decided not to push it.

"You see," he went on. "I find myself suffering from a malady—a sort of soul-sickness, if you will. It has become painful for me to remain in this house, yet I am unable to leave. I needed—company. To keep my spirits up. You understand, don't you?"

I nodded, but I didn't understand.

"And so, I thought of you, and how we had so much fun playing games when we were young. And I realized we never did beat that one game. *Lancelot's Quest.* Remember? I... I have a copy of *Lancelot's Quest* here," he said, seeming as bashful as a schoolboy about to ask a date to his first dance. "I thought you might like to play it. With me. For old time's sake."

"Let me get this straight," I said. "You sent a couple of clone killers to bring me here so that we could play old video games?"

Roddy flinched as if my words had swatted him like a rolled-up magazine.

"We don't have to play games," he muttered. "I just need someone to keep me from—to keep me company. In my hour of need. I'll pay you to stay if that will make a difference. Price is no object."

I had to admit that I was tempted to take him up on his offer to pay. Even though the house was a bit run-down, he was obviously loaded. Meanwhile, my worldly possessions amounted to the torn clothes on my back and one flash drive of encrypted credit card numbers that I couldn't use without getting myself murdered and tossed in a dumpster. I calculated how much Roddy would have to pay to give me a chance at running down to the Caribbean and hiding in comfort for a few years, and I figured he had that kind of money to spare.

But then I looked at Roddy and thought about him all alone in this house, going through whatever it was he was going through. He looked sick—cancer, I guessed, based on his looks. It's pretty low to take money from a friend in need, even if you haven't seen that friend in years. Roddy's Valkyries had already saved my life, too, and that counted for something. Besides, I knew I would be safe inside this mansion-bunker of his for as long as I stayed here.

I cleared my throat. "You know what? Sure. I would love to play that Lancelot game with you. We never did get past the dragon, did we?"

His eyes brightened and his posture straightened enough that he almost looked human. He then proceeded to give me a tour of his house, pointing out important rooms along the way as well as not-so-important rooms. The kitchen and the entertainment room got top billing, of course, but he also introduced me to the rooms once occupied by his parents and grandparents, and he spoke of these locations as if I would find the minutiae of his family history as important as my own.

The more I saw of the house, the more I was startled by his evident wealth. Marble floors. Priceless artwork. Golden chandeliers made spotless by an army of dusting-drones. The whole place still carried that ancient, decrepit feel of an archeological dig, but he obviously wasn't just some pauper squatting in his inherited home. He must have had ample cash flow, because when he gave the voice command, a breathtaking 144-inch television arose from the floor of the entertainment room like the sun coming up on a new day. A screen like that would have cost as much as most people's cars.

"I had this installed last week," he said as if he had found it next to the cash register at a grocery store. "Do you think it will be good enough to give our Lancelot his long-awaited victory?"

"Uh, yeah. Definitely." I stared reverently at that screen and at the velvet curtains to either side of it. "Roddy, have you always been... you know... rich?"

"I suppose we Ushers are a little well-to-do," he said evasively.

In an age when the rich want to distance themselves as much as possible from the rest of humanity, his lack of ostentatiousness struck me as truly odd. In comparison, the upper level management of the Blue Chip Four corporations went downright mad with their wealth and power after they officially dissolved the United States Constitution. I had friends on the inside of each of the Blue Chip Four, and they told me that the CEO of Microsoft had issued an official memo that she should forevermore be addressed as Her Majesty. The other CEOs quickly followed suit, and soon we had the Emperor of Amazon, the Pope of Disney, and—I wish I were making this up—the God-King of Google. Roddy, by comparison, was acting like salt of the earth.

"How did your family land in so much cash?" I asked. "It's like you guys own half the stock in the market or something."

"Oh, no, nothing like that," he smiled bashfully. "The family business is cloning. We've always been an industry leader, even before there was an industry. Now, you've had a difficult day. Let's put aside disturbing thoughts and just play for a while, okay?"

It's not hard to avoid disturbing thoughts when you're playing games on a screen that fills your entire field of vision. That's probably exactly what Roddy had wanted. We warmed up with a little *Super Smash Brothers* and started in on *Lancelot's Quest* before taking a break with another of our old favorites, *Hollow Earth Expedition 3*. The next thing I knew, we were on the last scene and I was glancing at my phone. I had no reception, but the clock told me it was past dawn. I hadn't guessed that it had become so late (or early) because all of the windows in the entire house were shuttered so tightly that not a photon could get in.

I set down my controller, stretched my arms.

"Tired so soon?" Roddy asked.

"We've been playing for 10 hours," I said. "We'll get Lancelot to the dragon tomorrow. We're not in a rush, are we?"

This seemed to put Roddy at ease. He insisted that I stay the night, and I wasn't about to turn him down when my other option was a cardboard box on the street. He walked me up to a bedroom, then showed me where to find towels and the TV remote.

"Goodnight, Tic Taka," he said. "Time for bed."

I collapsed on the bed, expecting to fall into a deep sleep, but actually found myself lying awake. The dark ceiling seemed to press down on me, which certainly didn't help with my feelings of claustrophobia and paranoia. Then I thought I heard a creaking out in the hall, as if someone were standing just outside my door, shifting weight from one foot to the other.

Was it Roddy? Why would he stand out there—and what was he waiting for? My mind filled with a thousand horror-movie scenarios, most of which involved variations on the theme of my host kicking open the door and hacking me apart with some kind of edged weapon. After all, how well did I know him? I hadn't seen him in more than a decade, and evidently I hadn't even known him well enough to know that his family ran one of the most powerful corporations outside the Blue Chip Four. All those nagging doubts that I had managed to push out of my mind during the active hours of gaming now came to roost in my head like a flock of shadowy ravens.

I had to get up. I had to move. But if Roddy really was waiting outside that door for whatever reason, he would hear me if I wasn't careful. Therefore, I inched the ridiculously high thread count sheets off of me so slowly that they made almost no noise. Then I stepped delicately on the cold floorboards. Step by step, I approached the door. Each time I lowered my foot to the ground, I allowed it to settle into place and fully shifted my weight to it before even daring to lift the other foot. I winced at the sound of my toes as they un-suctioned from the floor, and I lived in terror of a single floorboard creaking to betray my position.

I made it to the door and waited quietly. I don't know how long I stood there. It might have been a full sixty minutes. It was certainly long enough to start getting muscle cramps from holding my body rigid and fighting to keep my breath quiet. Still, no sound came to me from the other side of the door. I began to wonder if I had gone insane. Really, aside from a slight creak—which I might have imagined—I had no reason to think that Roddy was waiting outside sharpening his machete.

Just as I began to scold myself for childish thoughts, I heard a distant clanking sound followed quickly by what might have been a suppressed scream of either fear or extreme frustration.

Rather than frighten me back to bed, this noise actually made me feel brave. I couldn't tell what had made the noise, but it was clear that it had not originated outside my door. From the muffled echoes, I was certain that it had come from downstairs. If Roddy were all the way down there, I reasoned, then the hallway was safe. It never occurred to me to think that there might be someone else in the house.

The lights in the hall were as dim as ever, but from there I could hear further clanking, which I now recognized as the sound of metal pots bumping together. Roddy, I guessed, was making a late night (or early morning) meal. Sleep was now impossible for me, so I decided to join him and maybe, if I was lucky, score some bacon and eggs.

When I arrived in the kitchen, however, nothing was as I had expected.

There was one person in the room, standing with its back toward me as it rooted through an open cupboard door in the countertop island. This person wore a white bathrobe and its bare feet left perfect prints of perspiration on the tile floor every time it lifted its heels.

"Hey, Roddy," I said. "Awfully late for breakfast, isn't it?"

The figure stiffened at the sound of my words. I stepped forward and saw that pots and pans had been scattered all around the floor as if some wild animal had been seeking to make a nest in the cupboard.

The hunched figure spun around and I realized with a shock that it was not Roddy—or was it? She had the same sallow cheeks as he did, the same blue veins prominent beneath the skin, and the same sickly, sunken look to those pale eyes. But instead of Roddy's bare scalp, this person had long, pale-blonde hair that draped all the way to what I had assumed was a white bathrobe. I could now see that it was not a bathrobe at all, but rather a stained and dingy lab coat with one sleeve rolled up and the other torn at the cuff. Red lipstick was scrawled unevenly over this person's lips, making her mouth look like a bloody slash.

"R…Roddy?" I asked, still wondering if this might be Roddy in drag.

Whoever she was, she seemed to get over the shock of finding me here. Her face twisted into a violent snarl, and she seized a double boiler from the cupboard and hurled it at my head. Instinct made me flinch back just as the boiler's component halves struck the wall like twin thunderbolts. It must have just been my imagination, but I could have sworn that the impact splintered the door frame. Even if I'm wrong about that, this woman had clearly thrown the pots with homicidal intent.

Blind with panic at the sudden onslaught, I ran wildly from the kitchen, not thinking about where I was going. I remember the insistent thud of footsteps following me the whole way, and I knew that female Roddy—or whoever this person was—was on my heels and wishing me harm.

I may have experienced a lapse in memory because I'm not clear on what happened next. All I know is that the whole world seemed to drop away until the only thing that existed was my panicked flight. Whether guided by some subconscious escape impulse or just dumb luck, I ended up in the entrance foyer, knocking over the iron bookstand and the tome of family history for the second time that day.

A hand clamped down on my arm. I flailed wildly in an instinctual attempt to shake off my predator. But I was not in danger—it was Roddy. No lipstick, no wig. Just his usual black bathrobe. He was shouting to me, telling me I would be safe if I calmed down.

It took me a moment before his words could sink into my mind the way his fingers were sinking into my arm. I allowed him to guide me back to my room, where he shoved me past the threshold. He looked me in the eye, and for the first time he appeared neither hunched nor timid. He stood tall, breathing heavily like a boxer between the third and fourth rounds of a championship bout.

"Now you see why I have been sick," he said. "Sick with worry. Sick in the soul. Please stay here and try to sleep if you can. I'll take care of everything."

Then he was gone, and I was left standing alone in a dark room. I expected to hear more pan-throwing, or at least raised voices, but the house remained eerily quiet after that. Thinking on how quickly everything returned to normal, I began to wonder if it really had been Roddy in a wig after all. If it had been, I didn't see why he would pretend it wasn't. It's hard to believe that anyone would be embarrassed about cross-dressing in post-sexual America, but maybe Roddy's isolation had left him with nothing but inbred feelings of shame. A misplaced sense of indignity would explain the violent reaction, but it wouldn't explain how he had ditched his wig, clothes, and makeup to transform himself back into boy-Roddy so quickly.

My mind was just too tired to grapple with the realities, so I lay down and entered a kind of half-sleep, where I lingered just below the lapping waves of consciousness in a murky region where thoughts mingled with nightmares. Eventually, I awoke and groped around my dark nightstand until I found my phone. Several hours had passed since the encounter in the kitchen. It was mid-morning, or it should have been, and I was suddenly overwhelmed by the need to see the world in natural light.

I rose from my bed and pulled the curtains back. My bedroom window, like all the other windows in the house, had been blockaded by a very attractive, but also very immovable, light-proof shutter. I stood there, hands on the thick metal shutter slats, fighting to keep from screaming into the darkness. The walls, the ceilings, and the floors of that spacious home pressed in on me like a coffin. Rather than battle claustrophobia, I stepped outside my door where the slightly brighter lights of the hallway dissipated the spell of fear, at least a little.

I knew that what I really needed was a little daylight. Even just one minute on the front porch would fix me up, and I could spend another day on the couch in Roddy's luxurious cave. I had to go through the kitchen to get to the front door, but I knew it would be worth the traumatic memories of last night to get there.

As it happened, the kitchen was empty. I paused by the entrance and couldn't help but look around for any sign of mess. All the pots and pans had been neatly returned to their cupboards, and the cleaning drones had come through and left no scrap of food or speck of dirt behind. Out of morbid curiosity, I inspected the wall in the vicinity of the double boiler impact zone, but I found nothing. Not a chip or a ding. One of the wooden strips that made up the door frame was a slightly different color from the others—lighter in shade and newer in appearance. Could Roddy have replaced it since last night? Could his sister really have broken it? Here again I scolded myself for letting my imagination run away with me.

I moved on to the entrance foyer but was startled to find that the front door was locked. I could see no deadbolt, keypad, or even a keyhole on this side of the door. Later, I realized there must have been some remote control somewhere else in the house, which would have explained why Roddy had not been standing by the door when it had opened to allow me into the house.

After failing to rip the handle out of its plate, I found myself gasping for air like a fish out of water. The lack of daylight was asphyxiating me, and I was sure that I would die if I couldn't look out onto a world that was more than dark hallways and decaying rooms. I jerked at the door handle like a toddler having a tantrum. Then I pressed my eye against the peep hole and was rewarded by my first glimpse of the sky in almost twenty-four hours.

Viewing daylight through such a small opening felt like having to breathe through a straw, but it was still better than drowning. I could see the glorious gray clouds streaked pink with smog, and the scraggly trees lining the front drive. The fisheye lens made everything seem distant, distorted, and less realistic than the games we had been playing, but at least it was brightly lit, and I drank it in as best I could.

As I watched through the peephole, one of the Valkyries stepped into my field of vision. Her face was as placid as ever, but her body posture seemed somehow tense. For a long time I looked at her as she watched the house. Watched the door. Watched me. Then the other Valkyrie appeared behind her, about twenty feet back. She, too, stood facing the door. They had responded, I knew, to my wiggling of the door handle. Their hands were in plain sight, but that meant nothing: they could reach into their black leather coats and draw their weapons literally faster than I could blink.

I pulled away from the peephole and allowed gravity to pull me down to the floor until I sat with my back to the door and my knees up to my chin. Were those Valkyries out there guarding the house from someone trying to get in—or from someone trying to get out? Somehow I knew that if I knocked or called to them to open the door, the best scenario would be that they wouldn't react. The worst scenario... I covered my face with my hands and tried not to think about that mafia thug with bullet-holes in place of his eyes.

So this was it. I was a prisoner. There was no other term for someone held inside a locked cell, even if that cell resembled a sprawling mansion. Maybe it wasn't a prison as much as an asylum, because my fellow inmates had clearly lost their minds. Roddy's sister certainly had, but I was willing to bet Roddy also had a few loose chips in his motherboard.

I don't really know how long I sat on that floor in the foyer, but it

306

was long enough for my fear to transform into self-pity, and then my self-pity to fade all the way into boredom. I looked up and saw the iron book stand with the family history book, and I decided I might as well learn something about my cellmates. I pulled the book down into my lap—it was a heavy beast of a tome with pages as thick as cardstock but somewhat more pliant. It fell open to the page with the family history, starting with Archibald Usher and continuing all the way down to T. Usher. Twenty family members, all told, and they seemed to have a weird thing about naming each generation in alphabetical order. Archibald begat Beatrice, who begat Candice, who begat Deacon, and so on. Roddy's mother was evidently named Quistis Usher. (What kind of name is Quistis, anyway? And why did the kids always take the last name "Usher," even when it was their mother's name?)

The family tree appeared as a straight line, cutting down the page like a surgical scar. The lack of siblings made for a family tree that was all trunk and no branches, with only one child surviving in each generation. Roddy wasn't just a direct descendant of Archibald Usher, he was the only descendant. Well, except for his sister, but there was no second entry for any siblings in his generation. Starting with Roddy's generation, the given names were only listed as initials, so I didn't know the actual names of the younger Ushers, S. Usher and T. Usher. Were they his siblings? His cousins? His children? I couldn't be sure, and no dates of birth or death were shown for either.

"Tic Taka," Roddy said. "Time to discuss."

I flinched in such surprise that I banged my head—painfully—against the hard door.

"Don't sneak up on me like that," I said, cupping my hand over the rapidly swelling lump on my scalp. "You're going to give me a heart attack."

"Don't joke about that," he said. "It really is medically possible to be frightened to death. At least, it is in some people. It's all determined by genetics, of course."

"I need to leave," I said bluntly. "I'm sorry, Roddy, but I need to get out of here or else—or else I'll go insane."

This caused him to shrink into his bathrobe, like a deep-sea worm contracting its body into its tube.

"It's because of my sister, isn't it?" he asked.

"Look, Roddy—"

"She's going to die," he said. "I'm sorry, Tic Taka. This is a very hard time for me. That's why I called you here. I—I don't think I can go through this alone."

He seemed so pathetic, so broken. I now understood that he had brought me to his house not because he was sick or in physical pain, but because his sister—possibly his only family in the world—was dying. As weird as he was, he was a person in pain, and an eccentric shut-in like him couldn't possibly have the coping skills needed to deal with the impending loss.

"Oh, hey, Roddy," I said as comfortingly as I could. "I had no idea. I'm so sorry, man. I really am."

I stood and almost placed my arm around him. I'm not sure if I pulled away at the last second, or if he did. Either way, my attempt to comfort him stalled out completely.

"Tic Taka," he whispered. He didn't say my nickname as a question or to get my attention. He said it as a simple, direct statement of fact, the same way one might observe that the sun was setting or that the ice-cream was melting.

"How long does she have?" I asked.

"Regina? I don't know. I'd give her about a day. Maybe less."

That was all he seemed willing to say about his sister, whose name I now knew to be Regina. Regina Usher. I looked down at the book of the Usher family history, and had to consciously stop my finger from moving to the last lines of the family tree. Earlier I had wondered why Roddy's generation began using initials instead of given names. Now I wondered if R. Usher was Roddy or Regina, and why the other hadn't been listed.

I managed to convince Roddy that we should forget our woes right now and see if we couldn't go beat that Sir Lancelot game, which had been begging for it for all these years. He smiled and went to load the game while I microwaved some breakfast sandwiches. Minutes later, I marched into the entertainment room with a plate piled high with half-steaming, half-frozen lumps of low-grade, genetically modified meat wrapped in crusty wedges of bread-like gluten cakes. I found Roddy sitting there, cradling the controller between his knees.

"Tic Taka," he said, offering me the controller with a shaking hand. "Time for you to play."

I took one bite of the sausage sandwich (I got the scalding half of it), and then slid the rest of the plate toward him so that I was free to begin the game. The first enemies we encountered were bunches of Vikings—I'm not sure how historically accurate that was, but given that other enemies included harpies, werewolves, and nagas, I didn't think historical accuracy was the point.

The more I played, the more relaxed Roddy seemed to get. I offered the controller to him several times, but he always told me he'd rather watch. Whenever I glanced over at him, he seemed to be staring blankly at the screen, but I couldn't tell if he was lost in thought or lost in the game.

*Lancelot's Quest* was more engrossing than I expected, and I found myself obsessing over getting key pieces of equipment that would help me defeat enemies guarding other key pieces of equipment. I wasn't aware that Roddy had stepped out of the room until he returned with a plate full of microwave burritos. Later, he provided pizza rolls which contained red sauce as hot as lava. God, it really was like being back in junior high again.

"Maybe it's time to call it a night," Roddy said.

The statement alarmed me. I looked at my phone and found that we had been playing all day and into the night. I dropped the controller as if it had been a dumbbell. My thumbs were sore and my eyes felt like they were on fire. I think it may have been more than an hour since I had blinked, so I let Roddy show me to my bedroom.

"You sure you're okay?" I asked him.

"Yes," he said. "I am resigned to what must happen. Thanks to you."

I looked him over. That withered little nosferatu-man appeared more relaxed than I ever remember seeing him. It made me feel better about my decision to stay. There's nothing like binge-playing a fantasy game to make you stop caring about sunlight.

I entered a kind of fretful sleep that made me feel like I had closed my eyes for only a moment even though it lasted hours. I didn't so much as stir until a sharp banging on my door jolted me awake.

"Tic Taka!" Roddy called sharply as he pounded the door. "Time to get up! Tic Taka!"

I arose and opened the door as swiftly as I could. I found Roddy there, his chest heaving with ragged breaths.

"It's done," he said, his eyes shifting crazily. "She's dead."

"Roddy, I—I don't know what to say."

"No time for that." He tugged at my sleeve frantically. "I need your help. Quickly. Please."

He moved so swiftly that I almost had to run to keep up with him. I didn't have time to ask what was going on, but it soon became obvious as we entered the kitchen. Regina Usher lay on the floor, her body twisted into an unnatural posture and her face frozen in an animalistic snarl. The red lipstick I had seen her wearing last night was now absent, revealing lips so pale that they were almost indistinguishable from the rest of her face. On the floor next to her, shards of a broken ceramic mug floated like miniature islands in a small lake of dark liquid. One of the cupboard doors had been torn from its hinges and lay near her ankles; another had been split in half. The knuckles on her right hand were bloody.

My first thought was that I had obviously been wrong to think that Regina was actually Roddy in a wig, because here they both were. Then, as the macabre scene sank in, the revulsion bubbled inside my stomach, and I needed to clap my hand over my mouth to keep from retching.

"What the hell happened to her?" I had to stop myself and look away, leaning on the threshold for support.

"Cyanide," Roddy said.

I didn't think to ask how he knew that, given that there was no bottle of poison to be seen.

"Tic Taka," Roddy said. "Time to give me a hand. You take her legs and I'll take her arms."

Numbly, I followed Roddy's instructions and lifted her ankles, doing my best not to think about the cold flesh pressing into my palms. Roddy lifted her by the wrists then evidently decided that this did not raise her body high enough, so he shifted his grip to the back of her lab coat collar and let her arms dangle. It seemed so easy for him that I was sure he could have lifted her over his shoulder with one hand. Once again, my role was moral support.

Leading the way, he hustled us forward into an obscure side hallway that I had noticed before but assumed was nothing more than another wing of bedrooms for distant, dead relatives. I now discovered that it had only one door that opened when Roddy pressed a key card to an unmarked spot on the wall. The door slid to the side rather than swung outward, opening not to a bedroom, but to an extra-large elevator car.

"Hurry," Roddy said, pulling me into the elevator. "We need to get there before they do."

"They? Who's *they?*"

He let the question hang in the air as we dropped downward inside that elevator. We must have descended at least three or four stories before the door slid back to reveal a dark, concrete hallway. Aside from the LED light tubes overhead, there was nothing but gravity to distinguish the walls from the floor or the ceiling.

Roddy rushed forward so swiftly that I had difficulty keeping up. The door at the far end of the hallway opened automatically—I didn't see him use a key card, work a latch, or even slow his stride, so it must have been triggered by motion sensors.

We stepped through, and I discovered myself inside a laboratory. Microscopes. Shelves of beakers and flasks. Fume hoods. Most of the floor space was given over to six-foot steel tables with trays of nasty-looking implements positioned neatly next to them. The whole thing was lit in antiseptic white light and smelled faintly of the pungent chemical odor I remembered from dissecting frogs in high school biology.

"Quickly," Roddy said. "We need to get her secured. Before…"

"Before what?"

"Before they come for her. They want to—to examine her. I can't let them do that."

"Who?"

He didn't answer. He was becoming extremely agitated, his head darting from one side to the next as if a horde of syringe-wielding scientists might suddenly descend upon us from every direction. I had the strange, unshakeable feeling that he was lying about "them"—I was so convinced of it that I became less afraid. I was beginning to understand that the one thing in this madhouse that I could count on was the opposite of whatever Roddy was telling me, and therefore nobody was coming. We were alone, two men and a corpse.

I let go of Regina's ankles and allowed Roddy to lug his sister across the room to a rack of small doors lining one entire wall like a gigantic filing cabinet. He slid one drawer out to reveal a long tray—again, just like a giant filing cabinet. I felt a blast of refrigerated air, and I realized it was a cadaver storage unit, just like you sometimes see in cop shows when they go visit the city morgue. This truly was the family crypt.

Roddy obviously didn't need my help, so I allowed him to secure his sister in the body locker while I took a look around. I know computers, but I don't know science, so everything just looked like neatly stacked Petri dishes to me. It was a lot of expensive-looking equipment, but it appeared to have gone untouched for a long time, and when I swiped my finger along a table it came away dusty.

Next to the morgue lockers, I discovered a row of six big tanks, like giant glass jugs built right into the countertop. They contained nothing but a salty residue inside of the glass. Each was adorned with a little 3D printed plastic sign attached to its base. They were labels for the tanks, each in alphabetical order, and each with a name corresponding to the letter. O—Osgood. P—Pendragon. Q—Quistis....

My eyes stopped on that one. Quistis. The same name listed as Roddy's mother in the Usher family history book upstairs.

I tried not to look at the next name tag, but I couldn't help it.

R—Rodney/Regina.

A chill spread its invisible fingers across my scalp. I'm no biologist, but I couldn't fool myself any longer. These big jugs were not medicine vats. These were clone tanks, just big enough to grow a human fetus.

Roddy—a.k.a. Rodney—and Regina weren't just twins. They were clones.

My mind was racing as fast as my heart as I looked at the next tag. S—Senja/Siff. Another set of twins. They had to be the two Valkyries patrolling the grounds outside.

Roddy's hand clamped over my shoulder with the force of a vice.

"Tic Taka," he said. "Time to go."

I pointed a shaking finger at the clone vats, trying to get my mouth to form words.

"Not now." He pulled me toward the door. I dug in my heels, but he pulled me along easily even as my shoes simply squeaked over the polished linoleum. I glanced back, first at the rack of cloning vats, then at the rows of morgue drawers. Roddy had jammed a tire iron inside the latch of the door behind which he had interred his sister. That seemed pointless: anyone could simply pull it out and then open the door. Roddy dragged me to the elevator and didn't let go until we were back in the entertainment room.

"Roddy, what's going on?" I said. "I think you owe me an explanation."

"You're adopted," he shot back. "You can't possibly understand the family business without having grown up in this house."

"You're a clone, aren't you?" My voice quavered as I asked the question.

Instead of answering, Roddy shoved me onto the couch and jammed the game controller into my hands.

"Play," he ordered.

"Everyone in your whole family is a clone," I said. "All clones, going back for generations—if you can call them generations."

"Shut up!" He lunged toward me, regaining control of himself only an instant before he seized me. He stood there for a moment with his hands raised to the level of my neck and his fingers extended like an Olympic wrestler about to take down his opponent. The look in his eye was that of an animal caught in a trap—wild, violent, suffering.

I turned my eyes down to the controller. I was a dog, rolling over to show submission. There was nothing else I could do: he had the power to snap my neck in an instant, and we both knew it. Satisfied, Roddy sat down next to me. Then he began rocking back and forth so fervently that, even if not for all the other horrors I had seen that day, I would have found him extremely distracting.

The game booted up at our last save point, with Lancelot right at the entrance of the dragon's cave. For a long moment our computerized avatar stood there, seemingly frozen by the same soul-crushing fear that paralyzed the hands that guided his actions.

"Play," Roddy ordered, still rocking back and forth like a metronome.

"Roddy, we need to—"

"I said *play!*"

313

Unable to challenge Dracula in his own home, I numbly pushed the left thumb-stick forward. The tremor in my hands translated into Lancelot stumbling drunkenly into the darkness. It took only a few seconds before he was incinerated by the dragon's fiery breath.

"Equip the family crest."

"What?"

"Go to the inventory screen," Roddy barked impatiently. "Find the shield with Lancelot's family crest. Equip that."

He had to repeat the command three more times before my numb fingers remembered how to respond. Just as I completed the task, a low boom shook the floor and rattled the game screen.

Roddy was instantly on his feet.

"What was that?" I asked.

"Play," he ordered.

I turned in time to see that he was gesturing to the Valkyries—whose names, I now suspected, were Siff and Senja, the younger siblings of Roddy and Regina. Each of them now carried an assault rifle with a combat light at the tip and a series of extra magazines clipped to the side. At Roddy's instruction, the Valkyries turned and sped down the hall, toward the laboratory elevator. I hadn't seen them move with such urgency before and, although I caught only the briefest of glimpses of their faces, something told me that they were struggling to keep that ice-cold demeanor from melting into panic.

I must have been staring open-mouthed, because when Roddy turned back and saw me, he shoved me back onto the couch.

Roddy looked like he was losing it, and I could finally understand why. His family history hinted that he was the direct offspring of his forefather, Archibald Usher, probably without any DNA from outside the family to refresh the cellular wellspring of mental and physical stability. Even first-generation clones could often develop unusual characteristics, and who knows what kind of defects had been built into him and compounded eighteen times, like a photocopy of a photocopy of a photocopy? I had felt enough of his unnatural strength to know that I couldn't challenge his wrath, but I was beginning to see how all the enhancements to his strength had weakened him in other ways.

I didn't dare take my eyes off the screen, even though, at that moment, my mind seemed incapable of interpreting what Lancelot was doing. In some distant, hazy dream, the six-foot Lancelot sprite lurched forward into the cave. The dragon lunged out of the darkness, breathed fire upon him, and—and the bolt of flame rebounded off the family shield. It struck another dragon, which screamed, and fired its own deadly breath back at the first dragon. There were two dragons in the dark cave: a mated pair, perhaps—or siblings. Now that they were turned against each other, I didn't have to do anything but watch as they tore into each other with claws, fangs, and fire.

Another rending boom shook the couch under me, and this time I dropped the controller and sprang to my feet. Roddy was already at the threshold, looking down the hallway. A sharp rattle of gunfire echoed through the hall from behind closed doors. My ears had just enough time to decipher the booming pattern as two separate rifles before one of them went silent. An instant later, the other ceased its reports as well.

"Play!" Roddy pointed one gnarled finger at the screen without looking back.

I left the controller on the carpet and backed toward the far wall. I was no longer as afraid of Roddy as I was of whatever was happening at the end of that hallway.

There followed a horrible, prolonged moment of silence that seemed to pull the air out of my lungs. Roddy stood by the door, tense and panting like a frightened rabbit, his bathrobe bunched up on the side of his hip. He was hunched forward, his nosferatu posture bringing his hands up in a pathetic, begging attitude. His face, which I could only see in partial profile, was twisted in a hideous mask of agony, and one of his hands crawled to his chest and clutched his pectoral. I heard a thin squirting sound and saw a dark stain creeping down his pajama pants.

The eye of the storm passed with a simple ding—the sound of the elevator arriving. I could not see the hallway, but I could see Roddy as he suddenly jerked back and away from the threshold. A heavy, roughly spherical object cracked into the doorway where he had been standing a split second before. An instant later, a second, identical object careened through the doorway. For an instant, I assumed they must be bowling balls, flung as deadly weapons by an unnaturally powerful arm. But the projectiles struck the wooden finish not with a solid clunk, but rather with a sickening, wet smack. One of them ricocheted into the room and landed next to me. I kicked it away in a futile attempt to avoid seeing what it was, but I was too late. I already knew.

These were the severed heads of the Valkyries.

"Tic Taka!" Roddy shrieked, although I don't know what he expected me to do. "Tic Taka! Time's up, Tic Taka!"

Roddy continued backing away from the door as his twin clone lurched into the entertainment room. Her stringy hair hung in great clumps around her face, and her white lab coat had become riddled with countless bullet wounds. At least a dozen drizzles of blood dropped to the floor and trailed back the way she had come like red snake tracks. Her eyes were narrowed pits of shadow, and her face a churning snarl of gnashing teeth.

Roddy emitted a high-pitched wail, a cry of anguish and torment and fear that belonged nowhere but the fiery pits of hell. She reached for him with one claw-like hand. He clutched his own chest and tumbled backward, his head striking the floor with a muffled crack. His scream soon drained from his lungs until it was nothing more than a low, gurgling rattle. His death rattle. His final breath.

Regina collapsed upon Roddy in a wet, smacking thump that spattered red drops all around them. The sticky blood seemed to glue the two of them together, and I started to be uncertain of where she started and he stopped.

I thought for sure that she was dead, but then she fixed me with her black eyes and I felt crushed beneath the weight of her malice. I wanted to run away, but I found myself unable to move my feet or even avert my eyes. I was hypnotized, like the sparrow about to be eaten by the snake, and I thought sure she was about to arise and come for me. Instead, she flung something at me. If it had been a shuriken, it would have lodged itself in my sternum with ninja-deadly accuracy. This object, however, was lightweight plastic and had no sharp points. My hand instinctively slapped against it, pressing it to my chest with my palm. I held it there as Regina Usher's head sank to the floor and her eyes glazed over in death.

I remember very little of my escape from the mansion. I remember fearing that death itself had claimed the house, and that I would die with the Ushers if I did not escape quickly enough. Maybe I was right: I have a distinct memory of looking back and seeing the mansion split in half right along that crack that I had noticed above the door before I entered. It's possible that high-powered explosives inside the building's structure could have brought it down, so it may have happened that way, but I think it's equally likely that this was an image created in the murky recesses of my own nightmares and added like counterfeit money to the circulation of my memory.

I was aware of nothing more until I found myself slamming my foot on the brake of the black SUV, the same vehicle that the Valkyries had used to drive me to the cursed mansion two days before. I had no memory of getting into the car or even of where I found the key fob, but in the midst of my panic, some part of my brain must have worked well enough to guide me to the garage so that I could steal that car.

When I finally came to a stop on the side of that barren and desolate highway road, I found that I still clutched the plastic chip that Regina Usher had hurled at me in the last moment of her life. It was the name tag on the last clone vat.

Before I turned it over, I already knew what name would be on it.

T—Takahishi.

# AFTERWORD

## Birth of a Book

*And another thing…*

LET ME introduce myself. I'm Lia Rees, the designer of this book. You'll have noticed my graphics along the way. I thought you might be interested in a peek behind the scenes at the visuals of this project.

Design isn't always appreciated. The romantic view is that the written word should speak for itself. But written words don't slip into a reader's mind unlooked for and unasked. The reader has to invite the author in; the author has to engage the reader's interest before words enter the picture. That's where design comes in.

Perhaps I lied to you slightly. Everyone admires a beautiful book cover, but there's no glamour in page layout. Still, a well-crafted paperback needs the silent work of a designer (or an author-designer). We ensure that the type is readable and the structure easy to navigate, and we also engage in the more nebulous art of setting a mood for the reader. With just a few visual cues, like a magician's sleight of hand, you'll absorb the genre, the tone, and how professional-or-otherwise the book feels. Good design connects with the right audience and turns off the wrong one. Yes, turning off certain audiences is a good thing. An author doesn't want their horror novel accidentally bought by chick lit readers, or their smutty romance picked up by 12-year-olds.

Sound and Fury was the first book in our Shakespeare Goes Punk series. This is always where the heavy lifting of the design process occurs, as the series "brand" is created here. I use the word with some reluctance, because it makes books sound like Coca-Cola, which you have to admit is not punk. But there's no other word to encompass it all; believe me, I've searched.

I worked with Elizabeth Hamm to define the brand in terms of fonts, colours, embellishments and general mood. Our first challenge was reconciling two disparate aspects of the brief. "Shakespeare" and "punk" are not a natural fit, yet somehow we had to communicate both. If we went too far in one direction, the other part would be lost. In addition, there are a few punk genres featured in Sound and Fury—cyberpunk and steampunk are the biggest. Each has its own established aesthetic, but it would be messy to include both and misleading to represent just one. We also rejected a deliberately vintage "Shakespearean" style because it wouldn't have been punk enough.

Elizabeth is an illustrator whereas I can't draw for toffee, so she was tasked with drawing an original cover concept. It had some lovely elements; hand-drawn goggles, notebook-paper lines and a vintage image of the Bard himself. I believed it needed to be bolder, as ebook covers are seen first as thumbnails, so I created a new version. My aim was to capture the broader meaning of the word "punk". It may be a literary genre, but that's a recent development. Most people know it better as a brash, subversive attitude.

So what does punk look like? Bold and loud—we all agree on that. For the title, I chose an eye-catching grunge font (SHORTCUT) from Misprinted Type. The lettering screams roughness and energy, setting the tone for the entire design. This font is the rock star who slouches in late and stubs out a cigarette on the magazine you were reading. Elizabeth added a little class by using "Selfish", a script font, for the ampersand. (Perhaps the rock star's long-suffering model girlfriend). Other fonts had to play supporting roles. I tipped a hat to writer cliché by using the typewriter font Kingthings Trypewriter for our subtitle. Elizabeth found my version of the cover too brash and busy, so it was pulled back and a balance was struck. After a lot of fine-tuning (and versions sent via Dropbox), we ended up with a final design we were satisfied with.

We needed a stable layout for the internal pages that wouldn't have to change with every instalment. The covers would differ but the internal look would stay consistent. I wanted a book with an indie DIY feel, in homage to the comics and fanzines that practically everyone in the group was into. But the book still had to be readable. The stories themselves were long and involved, so I had to resist the temptation to load it up with graphics and fancy fontwork, giving the false impression of a comic book. If the right readers avoided it and the wrong ones bought, my beautiful lie would backfire on us all.

I chose three heading fonts to go with three levels of headline. Elizabeth's calming influence ensured they weren't too way-out. Big splashy full-page titles were done in Shortcut, the cover font. I used the minimalistic **Rafale** with a subtle stencil effect for mid-level headlines. Finally I used Kingthings Trypewriter again for the smallest headlines. It seemed to fit the DIY aesthetic, and was cool but not too distracting when it occurred mid-story. I started a policy of crediting all the font designers in the publishing information of each book. If layout artists are underappreciated, font designers are practically invisible outside their own sphere.

"Writers" and similar seemed like rather dull headings, so I am to blame for "People To Blame". The bold separator graphics in that section are a font called Angst Dingbats. The quote at the start of the book was also my idea, as were the small capitals at the start of paragraphs. I wanted to add a literary flourish and balance out the punk.

After the book came the publicity. I used the same graphics in the promotional banners, website and video trailer, to give the whole project

a consistent mood ("branding" again). There was a nasty surprise near publication day, when the printed proofs arrived with a pinkish tinge to the cover. I was taking a week's holiday for my fiancé to fly over from Utah—this would be our first real-life meeting—and I wasn't too pleased. But the book title wasn't Shakespeare Goes Pink, so I tweaked the colours and back to proofing it went. Carol still has the pink version as a memento.

For the second book, ONCE MORE UNTO THE BREACH, I worked on the internal layout but not the cover. My role was easier this time as the template had already been made. I was advised to put heavy black borders around the individual story title pages, so readers flicking through the paperback would see where stories started and ended. I went further and used all-black pages with a faded repeat of the cover image.

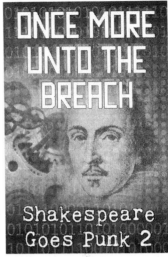

This brings us up to the book you've just read. I was responsible for the cover and internal graphics. The first two books had been laid out in Microsoft Word with all its limitations, but now with proper desktop publishing software I was able to create full-bleed designs reaching to the page edges. Black and white was a practical requirement. Printers (in this case CreateSpace) will charge identically for black text and BW art, but add a single colour and the cost screams skyward. Precise shade control is impossible with CreateSpace, so silhouettes and high contrast imagery are the only way to go. Luckily this was ideal for the gothic drama which is Poe's hallmark. My aesthetic for this book is the strangest it has ever been. The bold, surreal imagery of Neil Gaiman's Sandman was an early love of mine, and album art from the likes of Lacuna Coil and A Perfect Circle has also been influential. My taste for abandoned places inspired the back cover and internal title spreads in the paperback version. (The title font is **DIRTY EGO** and the cool literary headings are in CALENDAS PLUS.)

As I write this, I am designing a full-colour book to be sold at Shakespeare's Globe. It's my first full-colour project, and my biggest yet. Without Shakespeare Goes Punk, I would never have developed the skills, portfolio and network that brought me to this point. It has been an absolute pleasure.

Lia Rees
Designer, Free Your Words
www.freeyourwords.com

Did you like
Merely This and Nothing More?

You will probably also enjoy our first two volumes:
*Sound & Fury: Shakespeare Goes Punk*
*Once More Unto the Breach: Shakespeare Goes Punk* 2

Look for them at www.Amazon.com
(just search for "Writerpunk")

Would you like to see news of the next volume coming out?
Our fearless writers will tackle the stories that you probably read in
high school with *English Class Goes Punk...*

Readers love books by Writerpunk Press.
YOU WILL TOO.

Visit the link below for information about other books by these
authors and more, including news of the next volume!

Visit NOW at www.punkwriters.com
Twitter: @punkwriters

and
nothing
more

Made in the USA
San Bernardino, CA
31 March 2018